LIBERTAS

Alistair Forrest

SAPERE
BOOKS

LIBERTAS

Published by Sapere Books.

24 Trafalgar Road, Ilkley, LS29 8HH

saperebooks.com

ISBN: 978-0-85495-427-8

For Lord Cormack (1939-2024) who, long before he became Baron Cormack or even the esteemed historian, author and politician Sir Patrick Cormack, taught me how to accept criticism as my English teacher at school.

CHARACTERS

In Munda
Melqart, known to family and friends as Pito; son of Hann, the
baker and grandson of Ciro, Munda's warrior-priest
Pidray, Tallay and Elvir, Melqart's sisters and brother
Lizard, Melqart's best friend
Leandra, another friend
Dagan and Zebul, sons of Neran, would-be warrior-priest

Romans
Gnaeus and Sextus, sons of Pompey the Great
Lucius Marcellus, procurator of Munda
Dracus, veteran soldier responsible for army training
Titus Labienus, army general
Marcus Vipsanius Agrippa, *duovir navalis* (navy commander)

Others
Drenan and Turon, Kemeletoi mountain men
Ziri, Ayyur and Izem, warriors from across the sea
Sekis (Pipsqueak), orphaned child of the plains
Nahalia and Bashira, slaves rescued from Egypt

HISPANIA

■Corduba

Munda■
Gades ■   ■Apollacta

MAURETANIA

■Rome

ITALIA

Messana
           ■
Utica ■ SICILIA ■Syracuse
Carthage

WESTERN MEDITERRANEAN 1ˢᵗC BCE
Modern names: Gades/Cadiz, Munda/Monda,
Apollacta/Marbella, Corduba/Cordoba, Messana/Messina

PART ONE: THE NOBLE KEMELETOI

ONE

Munda, Hispania Ulterior, 51 BC

I knew from the look in his eyes that he wanted to kill me. He advanced deliberately, his weight perfectly balanced, his wooden shield held to chin height. He made short stabbing gestures with his rusting sword and hissed like a snake about to strike. But it was the coldness in his dark eyes that made me step back.

Around me the sounds of training ground sword drill clattered and crashed, with grunts and curses, even laughter. But these all faded to the edge of my senses now as my opponent, Zebul, advanced. Teenagers both of us, with dislike bordering on hatred in our eyes.

I barely managed to adjust the cumbersome shield to take the first blow as his sword swept downwards, the force of it juddering through my forearm and wrenching my shoulder, throwing me off balance. Another step back. Zebul grimaced as he freed his sword, which had bitten into the soft wood of my shield.

'A man is most vulnerable at the moment when his blade strikes your shield,' Dracus had repeatedly told us, 'so you must strike immediately. No matter how hard the blow, throw your weight forward and thrust to groin, rib or neck.' Dracus, our trainer — a squat, muscular and scarred Roman veteran — had shown us the wounding places beneath and around the breastplate, and we had given a collective gasp when his armourer had handed out real swords, the points blunted and the edges filed and softened. 'It's time to get used to the weight and feel of real weapons,' Dracus had announced, his voice a soldier's growl. 'We have men younger than some of you in our legions. Now show me what you have learned.'

But I didn't throw my weight forward. The lesson had fled from my mind. Zebul's next blow was to the side, but my shield arm was leaden, sharp pains shooting through my shoulder, and I could not move the heavy shield nor think of anything but retreat. The blunted sword hammered into the padded leather protecting my ribs, and I doubled up with a grunt. The pain brought tears to my eyes. Stupidly, I turned my head to where I had last heard Dracus give the command to engage, a forlorn appeal forming on my lips, presenting Zebul with the easiest of targets. He smashed his shield into the side of my face. There was a flash, like white sheet lightning, followed by a strange whistling noise in my head as I toppled backwards to sit on the hard earth.

Slowly, the world came back into focus. First, I saw Zebul's sandaled feet, streaked with the training ground's dust, then the form of my opponent as he stood over me, a triumphant expression on his face. He was still hissing like a madman, twitching his head repeatedly to flick black hair from his eyes, his lips taut in a smile of victory. The whistling noise stopped abruptly, the sounds of battle returning. I felt the weight of my unused sword in my hand, tightening my grip on the hilt as anger surged dizzyingly behind my eyes.

The anger gave me strength and speed. I swung the heavy blade without thinking, twisting my body to give the sweeping blow more force as the blunt edge found Zebul's ankle with a satisfying crunch. He let out a high-pitched yelp and collapsed in front of me, dropping his sword and shield as he clutched his ankle. I stood, overcoming the dull ache that throbbed in my head, kicked his sword aside and looked down at him. His eyes were watering and for a moment I thought he might cry, but Zebul's reputation among the youth of our town, and that of his elder brother Dagan, was built on the kind of brutish prowess that masks their callow ignorance. He spat curses at me through clenched teeth.

I looked over to Dracus, uncertain what to do next. With an amused expression, the trainer was slowly shaking his head. The other boys continued their swordplay, and I realised that none of them was putting much effort into the drill. Lizard was living up to his nickname by darting to and fro, bobbing his head in mock challenge, more like a dancer than a soldier.

'Enough!' called Dracus, his small black eyes still watching me as I stood over Zebul. Instantly, the drill ceased, all heads turning expectantly to the trainer who now circled us with the stiff strides intended to emphasise his authority but which we all found comical and often mimicked behind his back. Zebul was struggling to his feet, unable to put any weight on his injured ankle. I offered a hand, but he swatted it away angrily, still cursing.

'You fight like girls,' Dracus snarled, striding to the centre of the training ground, picking up Zebul's sword as he passed us. 'Except for these two —' he turned and looked from Zebul to me — 'who seem to forget that they are on the same side, or would be if I could enlist any of you in a Roman legion.'

For a moment he studied me, then snorted. I think he attempted a smile, but his cruel lips were hidden by thick, black stubble and his expression looked more like a scowl. I tried to smile back but winced at the sharp pain spreading through my cheek and neck. I could taste blood inside my mouth where Zebul's blow had crushed the soft flesh against my teeth.

'Melqart here would be dead, of course, if his fight had been with sharpened swords. Why? Because he took a step back even before Zebul struck, and then he hesitated when his first opportunity came. The rest of you seemed intent on tickling each other, not practising the moves I taught you…'

Zebul took no comfort in that. He had not taken his eyes off me while Dracus spoke; there was hatred there, like a surging, destructive force that I could almost touch. It was a darkness that had been growing for some years, subtly at first, then swelling like the grumbling thunderstorms that prowl among our mountains. I returned his gaze, uncertain how to meet the evil in him. Lizard had been right when he warned me to keep my distance from Zebul and his brother.

'Take your weapons to the cart for return to the armoury,' Dracus was saying, 'and young Zebul, you can ride too, as it looks like your ankle will need some attention.' Zebul looked as if he was about to object, but Dracus had turned on his heels, his command final.

'What happened to your face?' Lizard asked as we walked home through the olive groves to Munda's main gate. 'Quite an improvement, I reckon.'

I gave him a playful push, the muscles in my injured shoulder protesting. 'Zebul was in a bad mood.' I wanted to say more, but my jaw felt like it had been kicked by the mule that was drawing the weapons cart behind us.

'But you had him down in the end.'

'I was just lucky. Got him right on the point of his ankle.'

'Good. Might bring him down a peg or two.'

I looked back to where Zebul sat on the old cart, a loose wheel giving it an ignominious lurch with each revolution. He was watching me with undisguised venom, so I turned back to Lizard, trying to put the image out of my mind.

'I don't know which is worse, Dracus's bark or Zebul's bite,' I said.

'Give me Dracus every time,' Lizard laughed. 'At least you know where you are with him.' A cleft palate gave Lizard a perpetual grimace, the cause of remorseless teasing throughout his childhood, but I admired the way he had never taken other boys' cruel words to heart. We had enjoyed an easy friendship as we had grown into teenage years — I the more studious and serious, Lizard ever the joker with boundless energy. He was comfortable with his nickname, which nobody questioned as it was so apt. Only Lizard's parents knew what his real name was.

We walked in silence toward the old wooden gate, always open because the rusted hinges no longer worked. The wood was bleached and twisted by the summer sun, held up only by the forlorn remains of palisades clinging desperately to each other. They served no defensive purpose for a town that welcomed travellers and foreigners, even Romans. With defences that had been breached by goats, dogs and children, nobody in Munda had a mind to fight off strangers, most of whom were traders seeking olive oil, herbs, spices and smoked hams, or Romans who kept their weapons sheathed and enjoyed the town's surprisingly civilised hospitality.

Including Julius Caesar himself.

The man lauded by my Latin tutor as the conqueror of Gaul and the most famous man in the world had once visited Munda. Nine years earlier, when I was a child of five, he had ridden into Munda's wide valley at the head of a century and decided that our insignificant, peace-loving little town was the perfect strategic place for his new procurator to live. He had given us Lucius Marcellus — or had he given Munda to Lucius Marcellus? Either way, the townsfolk didn't mind one bit, because the procurator was a genial war veteran who had served under Pompey the Great — as famous as Caesar, my tutor had said — and as soon as he had built a lavish villa for his family, he had ordered the construction of drains, sewers and open baths fed by the perpetual springs that give Munda its soul. There was now also the start of a new road north to Lacibis and south to the sea. Yes, there were taxes to pay, but there was work for idle hands, and with a few exceptions everyone appreciated the procurator for making Munda's paradise look and smell more like paradise. Julius Caesar had come to impose a procurator and had made his interference seem like a generous gift. The people liked Lucius Marcellus. Perhaps next he would have us build a new wall and new gates.

My thoughts were interrupted by the sound of my name being shouted in desperation.

'Pito! Pito!'

This was my nickname, a shortened version of Agapito, which means "little loved one" in the old tongue. In truth, I preferred it to Melqart, the ancient god after whom I was named.

It was my sister Pidray, running through a gap in the dilapidated palisade and raising a dust storm, her long black hair careening from side to side.

'Looks like your pretty little sister,' observed Lizard. Three years my junior, Pidray was not yet a woman, but neither was she a little girl. I ignored the reference to her undoubted beauty as a feeling of unease came over me. I ran towards her. I could see she was crying.

Pidray put her hands on her knees as much to steady her shaking legs as to bend and draw breath. She was unable to speak as she sucked in the hot, dusty air. Her long hair fell across her face, so I gently took her shoulders and coaxed her upright, looking into her large brown eyes.

'What is it, Piddy? What's the matter?'

She buried her tear-streaked face in my chest, managing to mumble something incoherent between deep sobs, so I again took her shoulders and looked into her eyes.

'It's Baku,' she managed.

'What about Baku?' I couldn't help but fear the worst. 'Is he…'

Pidray nodded, biting her lower lip hard. She sniffed and took a deep breath. 'Yes, Pito. Baku's dead.'

For the second time that day, my head swam and the whistling noise returned like a tormenting demon.

Pidray looked at me through tearful eyes. 'Papa needs you,' she said thickly. 'Come quickly.'

My grandfather was the last of Munda's warrior-priests, but he was neither warrior nor priest. Baku was our affectionate nickname — his real name was Ciro, and he was not a warrior because he did not even own a sword. Under his long years of paternal care, Munda never needed anyone to wield one in defence or attack.

He was a priest only in the sense that he could resolve disputes and heal troubled souls with gentle words. He did not believe in the gods, or at least was never heard to speak of them, or blame them for the hard times as most people do. His wife, Delphi, my grandmother, was a woman who could nag and gossip with the best of them, but even she had never been able to penetrate the old man's aura of composure or deflate his generous spirit.

Baku was the last of the warrior-priests because Caesar, then governor of all Hispania, had imposed a new, higher level of authority on our humble community. His procurator had sole authority to turn Munda into a model Roman town. This did not worry my unhurried grandfather in the slightest, or my father Hann, even though he showed all the qualities necessary to be the most likely successor as warrior-priest, senior elder, or whatever Procurator Lucius Marcellus might want in a community spokesman. Neither Baku nor my father was the least bit interested in titles or self-importance; in fact, my father had let it be known that he did not want any high office, whether nominal or active, and would prefer to continue to be Munda's best and only baker. Nothing more, nothing less. The only person who had bridled at Caesar's conceit had been Zebul's father Neran, who, perceiving that his opportunity would come with my grandfather's inevitable passing, had set his heart on becoming the next warrior-priest. He had even attempted to garner support among the more gullible townsfolk. It was a long and fruitless campaign.

Neran had shifty eyes and his head was strangely shaped, like a wolf's. He was small, with a midriff bulge fed by the unpredictable ales that emerged from the evil-smelling barns of Tanasus the brewer on the edge of town. Quite how he produced two tall, skilled brawlers like Zebul and his brother Dagan was beyond the understanding of Munda's gossiping womenfolk, but then they could see plenty of Neran's cruelty and greed in both boys. Fortunately, Neran's campaigning fell on deaf ears — there could not be a greater contrast between Baku's gentle intelligence and wit, and Neran's boorish egotism.

But in any case, the wolf-man never got his chance, because Caesar came to Munda and changed the rules. The grand title of warrior-priest was no longer necessary in a town that was being steadily Romanised. Neither was there need for a council of elders, the grey and toothless ancients venerated by everyone except their women. Rome's new order gave them no option but to retire to the shade of a huge fig tree in Munda's square, where the mountain spring played its hypnotic music, there to discuss the merits of Tanasus's ales and complain about the heat.

Baku, though, was not one for idling away the day. He was my hero, warrior-priest or not. He gave me the benefit of his wisdom in tracking wild boar, studying the eagles when they hunted rabbits and snakes, and making contraptions in his ramshackle tool shed — wheels and axles, levers that could lift impossible weights, and even models of great war machines that could hurl a bread roll clean through the kitchen window, causing the old maid to shout and curse and my mother to chuckle uncontrollably.

Baku adored my mother, Adela, and adored every child she bore. Each new life she brought into the world gave him more strength, more love. And my mother adored him back, the more so with each new baby — there was me, Pidray, my other sister Tallay, then little Elvir, who arrived with clenched fists and a wail that announced that he wanted to be the warrior Baku never was.

But now Baku was gone.

He had been mending a wheel. Eshmun the cheesemaker had mentioned to my grandfather that his cart had a broken wheel, and Baku had insisted on taking the broken pieces to his workshop, knowing that if Eshmun was pleased a fine cheese would be on the table that night, the perfect accompaniment for my father's fresh bread and a flagon of wine from the cellar. Baku was hammering the last rivet through the iron band, completing everything he had promised, when he left. My mother brought him a cup of pomegranate juice, and he nodded to her to place it on the workbench, expressed his thanks with a chuckle, and died. He just slumped over the mended wheel, a life that had gone full circle. At first, my mother thought he was just resting his chin on the wheel, which for some reason didn't fall over. Then, worried that he wasn't moving, she touched him on the shoulder. He slid to the ground and lay still. My mother felt for a heartbeat and listened for a breath.

But Baku wasn't there anymore.

TWO

I woke early and watched tiny specks of elusive dust dance in the dawn light. Even the small birds that normally frolicked at dawn seemed subdued. I threw off the light cover and scratched at several mosquito bites.

Even in his pain, my father had noticed the bruising on my face, where I had taken the full force of Zebul's shield. 'Brains versus brawn' had been his dry observation after I had recounted the fight. 'Brains win again, eh?' But there was no sparkle in his eyes, no smile of conspiracy.

I pulled a simple tunic over a pair of woollen breeches hemmed at the knee and crept past the room where my sisters and little Elvir slept, careful not to wake them to the day's sorrows. I found my parents consoling each other in the kitchens. The great ovens were cold, there were no aromas to savour, and the long-handled paddle was idle for the first dawn in many years. In the courtyard beyond, Baku's body lay on a pallet, awaiting his journey to the sacred spring where he would be mourned for a day by the people. Later he would be carried shoulder-high outside the palisades to where his funeral pyre awaited him, built from pruned olive branches and the gnarled black trunks of old almond trees, all discarded so that new life could bloom.

I helped myself to yesterday's crumbling barley loaf. My parents were locked in a still embrace, eyes closed. I went into the courtyard to say farewell to Baku before the elders came to take him away, crouching beside him to touch his shoulder. I closed my eyes to hold back the tears. *Wake up, whisper our next adventure*, I willed. *Let's explore the woods together and lift stones to startle curled snakes and the leathery toads that live near the brook. Mama will shout after us her list of things not to do and tell us to be home before the sun touches the mountain peak.* But when I opened my eyes I was no longer a child, and Baku's spirit had not returned.

'You can fly like an eagle,' I whispered, 'and one day I'll fly with you.'

A grieving lament thickened the still air, punctuated by the shrill keening of old women. My father stood before the sleeping warrior-priest, and next to him Delphi's shoulders jerked with each desolate sob. My sisters wailed as young girls do when they don't know what else to do. Elvir, beside me, was silent, confused. I reached down and ruffled his curly hair, noting how much he had grown while I had been distracted with my studies and Dracus's harsh sword drill. Elvir looked up, all wide-eyed innocence and tenderness. He loved Baku too, but not as much as I who had been the apple of his eye. I crouched and smeared away his tears with my thumb as my father knelt at the edge of the shimmering pool, cupping his hands to collect the eternal gift. He carefully carried the water to Baku, letting the living jewels fall on his unmoving lips.

Lucius Marcellus came forward from the mourning crowd and took the place of one the elders who did not look as though he had the strength to be a pallbearer, and helped carry Baku outside the town. There we gave him to the stars, carried there by a riotous multitude of flames and sparks that shot high into the night sky, bearing his spirit away. This was how a good man was carried to Adon's city, my mother said, where his lover Astarte guards the departed souls, but to me it was just a story. Like Baku, she had never believed in the old gods, but we were all happy to listen to her stories of love and war in the heavens.

Elvir yawned as Baku was consumed. He was shielded from the fierce heat by my mother's skirts, watching the fire's livid dance on the tear-streaked faces around us. The people had loved their Warrior-Priest; it had been easy for me to share my grandfather with them because he exuded such compassion and generosity. Everyone belonged to his family, even the cruel Neran, who chose that solemn moment to approach my father with shifty eyes and honeyed words, seeking his support to put his name forward as Baku's replacement. His sons at his side were bristling with raw, distasteful arrogance. My father frowned and replied that nothing was so important that it could not wait. With a look of disgust on her face, my mother swept little Elvir into her arms and whispered that it was time for bed. I heard her sigh as she looked upwards where a thousand stars shone in the night sky.

'Which one is Baku's star?' Elvir asked, following her gaze.

'The brightest,' she replied without hesitation, 'the one that shines with Astarte's joy.'

Zebul heard her and scoffed, then spat on the ground as he walked away. My mother pretended not to notice, but I think she saw my anger reflected in the fire's glow and restrained me.

'Pito, carry Elvir for me. He's getting so heavy,' she said. When I looked again at the retreating Zebul, she added firmly, 'Now is not the time. Let it go. Think what Baku would have done.'

I knew in that moment that Baku would have taken Zebul aside and talked calmly to him with an arm around his shoulders, gently chiding and at the same time reassuring.

But youth has a different passion. I was fourteen years of age and had not known hate or jealousy. Petulance, of course, but never spite. There was too much love in our family to allow the darkness in.

But there was a darkness in Zebul that seemed to want to insinuate itself wherever he went. A serpent in the shadows. It wasn't just that he had snarled and scoffed at my mother, or that he spat before her, it was the look on his face when the evil in him expressed itself. Now that darkness was strangely illuminated by the flames of Baku's pyre.

By next dawn I was as grouchy as an old bullfrog. That was why I devalued Baku's memory by brawling with Zebul like dogs in the dust. I could not help myself.

My father had given me a woven hemp bag containing a dozen flat loaves to deliver to the tavern, and I was hoping to find Lizard to brighten my day. But when I saw Zebul, my mood became blacker still. He was with several other boys, including his brother Dagan, all preening themselves before some of the town's older girls who often gathered at the spring. I tried to ignore him, but he sauntered towards me with a contemptuous sneer, positioning himself so that I had no option but to face him.

'Well, baker-boy,' he said loudly enough for his admirers to hear, 'I see you've brought my breakfast.' He held out a hand but I deliberately thrust the bag behind my back. Laughing, he reached behind me, playing his game. I think he expected me to turn and run, but when I stood firm he grasped at the bag, the loaves spilling to the ground. Angered, I put a hand on his chest and leaned towards him, my sudden boldness a shock to both of us.

'You dishonour my family and this town,' I said, and pushed harder so that he actually staggered. For the briefest moment a look of confusion crossed his face, and in that instant I gave voice to my indignation. I told him he was a disgrace to a community that put nobility and peace above the heartless campaigning of his wolfish father, and he had been disrespectful to my mother. I knew when I said it that his reply would be with fists, but I was filled with rage at his twitching and strutting.

A more familiar Zebul recovered his composure, no doubt aware that his audience needed to be impressed. He thrust his nose right in my face, his fists curled at his sides. This time I did not step back. I would fight and probably lose.

But he didn't strike. Instead he snarled.

'*Cunnus*!' Spittle formed at the corner of his mouth, and his breath smelled of sour wine. 'You think you're so special, don't you?' One of the girls shouted encouragement, whether to me or Zebul I couldn't be sure. The boys urged us to fight.

I was so determined not to give ground that I felt the weight of his muscular chest thrust against mine. But I had said my piece, and now I didn't know what to say next. I couldn't think of an insult to hurl back at him, so I just glared at him. He took my silence as a sign of weakness, pushing harder and spitting oaths and curses.

That was when I hit him. Or tried to. What else could I do? Fall over backwards like a clumsy fool? My blow was aimed at his side, just below the ribcage, but it turned out to be no more than a firm shove. Zebul staggered back, a look of surprise on his face. He hadn't expected me to strike the first blow, but then he realised it had given him the right to retaliate. He shoulder-charged me, arrowing his lean frame at my chest, pushing me to the ground. It knocked the wind out of me, but instinct took over and suddenly we were scrapping. Fists, elbows, feet and teeth were our only weapons as we gouged and grunted, each desperate to get on top of the other to win the fight. The boys that stood around yelled encouragement — I still could not determine whether they shouted for the bully or the underdog — but Zebul was stronger. He somehow managed to put his full weight on his elbow as he pinned me by the chest, driving the breath out of my lungs, but I clung on desperately, holding him close so that he could not aim a telling blow. I tried to bring my knee up into his groin, and at the same time use my forehead to stun him, but my efforts were weak and ineffectual. We lay in the dust, chests heaving, locked together like lovers.

That's how the fight ended. A shout from across the square snatched away the attention of the onlookers. Vaguely, I became aware of Lizard's voice and the sound of his sandals slapping on the hard ground. He shouted again, 'They're coming! Romans — lots of them!'

Zebul loosened his grip. He clearly wanted to finish what I had started, but he had now lost his audience.

There were several small children with Lizard, who all stopped and stared at us, astonished at the sight of two older boys grappling on the floor like a pair of delinquents. I was ashamed and pushed Zebul off. He leaped lithely to his feet and aimed a kick at my head, which I dodged, then turned to Lizard, who was staring at me with a mixture of concern and disbelief.

'What do you mean, there's Romans coming?' Zebul snapped.

The other youths crowded round. Lizard offered a hand to pull me to my feet. He ignored Zebul's question.

'You all right?' he asked me.

'Yes, fine,' I replied, brushing dust and grime from my knees and elbows. I looked disconsolately at the loaves where they lay scattered and ruined. 'Never mind me — what's going on?'

'There's a column of soldiers coming from the north. Romans, I think.'

That was enough for Zebul and the other youths. They ran off towards the main gate, which gave an excellent view of the broad valley and the road running north to Lacibis.

'What is it with you and Zebul?' Lizard sounded exasperated. He looked me up and down, and I realised that my tunic was torn at the neck and smeared with dirt. I did not look or feel like the grandson of the warrior-priest we had honoured such a short time ago.

'I know what it must look like,' I said apologetically. 'But I just couldn't help myself. I saw the cocky bastard and tried to wipe the smile off his face.'

Lizard wasn't fooled. 'Somehow, Pito, I think there's more to it than that. You can tell me all about it later. Come on, let's see what's going on in the valley.'

Lucius Marcellus and Dracus rode out to meet the visitors at the head of the procurator's guard, twenty leather-clad Hispanics each with a long-bladed spatha sheathed at his side. They looked ragged and ill-prepared compared with the approaching column, a century of mounted men wearing polished leather jerkins and iron-bossed helmets, riding in twos on the narrow track. Their well-groomed horses were held in check, walking steadily and ignoring the small dogs that ran yapping in wide circles around the foremost riders. At the column's centre, two large carts were drawn by lumbering oxen, dictating the slow pace of the visitors. A dust cloud hung lazily in the air behind them, drifting gently across the valley like a ghostly shroud.

Word had spread quickly throughout the town, and the crowd that gathered at the gates was growing. Munda had not seen more than a handful of Romans travelling together since Caesar had come to give us a procurator. The children who now watched wide-eyed had not been born then, and the memory had faded for many of the older folk who now pointed and stared, speculating wildly about the arrival of so many soldiers. I spotted Zebul and Dagan pushing their way to the front of the onlookers, followed by their faithful supporters, so I nudged Lizard and pointed to a rocky outcrop that would give us a better view, away from Zebul and the chattering crowds.

Lucius and his small troop had ridden carefully down the hillside from his villa, picking their way through the estate's orange orchards and olive groves, and crossed the shallow brook. They now halted beside the track to await the approaching column. Lucius sat easily in the saddle, his stallion's tail casually swatting away flies, both rider and beast seemingly unconcerned at the arrival of armed cavalry. He wore no helmet or armour. Behind him, his men craned their necks, as if sizing up unfamiliar newcomers.

A shouted command and the raised hand of the leading Roman halted the century as one, only the languid oxen continuing for a laboured step or two before realising the horses in front of them had stopped. The officer dismounted, unstrapping his helmet as he walked up to Lucius and saluted. Lucius remained in the saddle, leaning forward to talk to the officer, one arm laid casually across the saddle's pommel. The officer talked for some minutes, as if making a report, then Lucius turned in the saddle and pointed towards a flat area of ground that lay to the north of the brook where it entered a winter swamp, dry now in the heat of the summer. The officer saluted again and returned to his men, shouting new commands as he mounted.

'They're staying,' observed Lizard.

'Looks like it,' I agreed. 'Could be a good day for Tanasus. Those men look thirsty.'

'A good day for some brisk trade all round.' I realised I would be needed at home. My father would be eager to supply bread for a hundred men on top of the town's needs.

The column was moving again, wheeling west towards the spot chosen for their camp. As they passed the gates, I noticed that the girls were no longer devoted to Zebul and Dagan but were giggling and pointing at the passing soldiers, some of whom waved back and laughed.

'Better lock up your sisters,' Lizard chuckled.

Munda was immediately plunged into an unfamiliar whirl of frantic activity. Ours was a small mountain town that preferred to be ignored. Even the merchants and messengers only passed through on their way to more influential places like Corduba in the north and Gades to the west. We were Hispania's forgotten paradise, my father was fond of saying.

Lizard wanted to come with me to help my parents produce enough bread and pastries to feed a small army. We passed old Tanasus and his strapping sons loading barrels of ale and wine onto their dilapidated cart, the mule's head hanging forlornly at the daunting task ahead. Nearer the square, Eshmun's newly mended cart and several others that had seen better days were being loaded with cheeses and hams, and at every street corner piles of fruit and vegetables, the more vibrant craftily hiding the rotten, were being tossed into reed baskets that the women carried proudly on their heads. Children skipped and darted, uncertain of their role in the town's sudden awakening, the wisest seeking a reward to fetch and carry. The first tantalising smells from my father's bread ovens lingered in the still air; he would make a tidy profit from the visit of so many hungry soldiers.

He barely looked up as we burst in, but my mother noticed the state of my torn and grubby tunic.

'Pito, what have you been up to? Look at the state of you!' she chided. Fortunately, she was too busy to wait for an answer, which anyway would have been a lie made up on the spot. Instead she sent me to find a clean tunic and made a fuss of Lizard, who looked embarrassed. Lizard escaped her attentions by teasing my sisters, who were kneading dough, adding ground almonds and spices, and giggling as they experimented with phallic shapes. I returned wearing a clean tunic that instantly dampened in the hot kitchen.

My father, his lank hair hooked behind his ears and rivers of sweat running down his neck, waved towards the courtyard and sent me to find the wooden bread trays and ready the cart. Lizard came with me. The cart and trays were in daily use, so they were always in good repair — they had been made and maintained by Baku. Lizard was particularly impressed with the cart. It was superbly crafted, with two wheels and shaped handles for pushing or pulling. The wood was painted with bright red minium, for which Baku had paid a visiting merchant a small fortune, and although the pigment had worn away in places, the cart was named "The Flying Poppy". It was the envy of every trader in Munda.

Lizard was running his hand along the curved handles in admiration of Baku's craftsmanship when there was a loud thump on the door. A gravelly voice called for my father. I opened the door cautiously. It was Dracus, out of breath, a sweat-stained leather jerkin laced tightly over his barrel chest.

'Ah, young Melqart,' he growled. 'Is your father here?'

'Yes, sir. I'll get him. Come in.'

Dracus strode into the courtyard and nodded to Lizard. I called for my father, who promptly appeared, wiping his hands on his flour-dusted apron.

'Dracus?' He sounded confused as to why the procurator's only Roman officer should be visiting. 'What is it?'

'Lucius Marcellus asks for your company at the camp.'

'Is it urgent?' my father asked. 'I was planning to go there anyway, with supplies for the soldiers, but there is much to do here first.'

Dracus looked confused, as though he was used to everyone obeying his commands without question, but he was talking to one of Munda's most important citizens and I knew that Lucius would have reminded Dracus to watch his manners. 'Just as soon as you can, sir,' he said with an attempted smile. 'The procurator has also asked me to bring Neran.'

So it was something so important that both the son of the departed community leader and the man who most wanted the job had been summoned. My father seemed to have the matter under control.

'In that case, you go and find Neran and I'll meet you at the camp.' It wasn't a suggestion. Dracus knew he had been dismissed. He nodded, looking sheepish, and left. My father turned to me, a quizzical look on his face.

'Wonder what that's all about,' he mused. But before I could say anything, he snapped his fingers and pointed to the cart. 'We'll load up what we've got. You two can come with me to the camp, then one of you hurry back for more supplies. Let's see what's going on in the big wide world of Roman rule.'

THREE

Lizard insisted on pushing the cart. To him, it was like a new toy and several times my father told him to slow down as we could barely keep up, but eventually he let Lizard and The Flying Poppy put distance between us. He wanted to talk.

'Anything you want to tell me?'

I had hoped that he had been too busy to notice my dishevelled state when I had returned to the house, but my father missed nothing. I shrugged my shoulders, not sure what to say, hoping he was thinking of something less embarrassing than his son scrapping with another youth in front of who knows how many revered citizens. But his silence said he wasn't. He waited for me to confess. I decided to broach the subject with a question.

'When is it right to fight, Father?'

That threw him a little. He was thoughtful, then he said, 'When you are forced to defend your family, or when your life is threatened. It's always possible to turn away from anything else. Why do you ask?'

'I needed to defend mother. A youth was disrespectful to her last night.'

'Let me guess,' my father said, turning to me with a smile that said I might escape his anger. 'Not Zebul, by any chance?' I nodded. 'Brains against brawn again. And I'm not surprised. Your mother warned me that you might react in some way. Tell me what happened.'

I told him, leaving nothing out. There wasn't much to tell. If the Romans hadn't come, he might have been mending my broken bones and dressing my wounds. When I had finished, he just smiled again and we lengthened our strides to catch up with The Flying Poppy. I think that, deep down, he was proud that I had not let the slight to my mother pass. He never mentioned it again.

We came up to Lizard at the edge of the camp. He stood open-mouthed, firmly gripping the handles of The Flying Poppy and watching the soldiers corralling their horses, hammering tent stakes and mounting cooking pots onto tripods made from their spears. In the centre of the camp, the two wagons had been stationed side by side with enough space between them to rig a large shade, and a crude table had been erected, upon which was a large cloth. Lucius and the centurion pored over this, giving us the impression that it might be a map.

My father told us to follow him and he set off towards the two men. Lucius looked up as we approached and beckoned us over.

'Welcome, Hanni-Ba'al!' he called, no doubt emphasising my father's full name for the benefit of the officer. They greeted each other in the Roman style, and my father was introduced to the visiting officer, Publius Tullius Celer, a young man with a shock of dark hair and a serious-looking face. The cloth was indeed a map, but I was not near enough to make out the markings.

'I have the first delivery of breads and pastries for your men,' my father said to Celer.

'Take them to my quartermaster over there —' the officer pointed to where the first deliveries of fruit and cheeses were being unloaded nearby — 'and he will pay you.'

'Perhaps your son can do that,' Lucius interrupted, and turned to Celer. 'Hanni-Ba'al will have a lot to contribute to our discussions.'

'Very well,' said Celer, looking from Lizard to me, no doubt trying to decide which of us was my father's son. He waved us both away, and Lizard was off again with The Flying Poppy.

The quartermaster reminded me of Dracus. Nothing we could say or do would make him smile, and nothing made him speed up his meticulous weighing and counting out of coins. It took an age to sell him the first batch of bread, biscuits and pastries, even when we reminded him that we had to return to Munda for more. Eventually he seemed satisfied, as was I when he offered a sum that was more than my father had told me to expect. Once again The Flying Poppy was hurtling across the dry grassland towards the town.

As we passed the makeshift headquarters, we saw that Neran had arrived to join the discussions, thankfully without Zebul or Dagan anywhere in sight.

It was almost dark when my father returned, looking tired and troubled. Lizard had gone home, delighted with the coins my mother had given him for his enthusiastic hard work, and she had prepared a simple meal of smoked ham, cheeses, olives, pickled garlic bulbs and plump figs to go with the last few flat loaves that she had set aside. Elvir had dressed up as a soldier and was prancing around waving a wooden sword and yelling his nonsense war cry at Pidray and Tallay.

My mother poured my father a goblet of wine and sent the children to bed. My father hugged each of them in turn, drained his cup and crunched on a piece of garlic. I studied his face as he chewed. He was tired, unshaven and a little dishevelled, but there was something else, perhaps sadness or an air of resignation.

'What is it, Hann?' my mother asked him.

'I think they're going to have a garrison here,' he said slowly. He paused while we thought about the implications. Soldiers recruited from Munda and the surrounding communities, trained to fight and no doubt sent to war, because the Romans never seemed to be at peace. His second sentence was equally alarming. 'They asked me to take on the responsibility of listing all the young men of Munda who are eligible to join the army.'

My mother looked at me, horrified. I put my hand on her arm to reassure her, but it was a pointless gesture.

'Of course I refused,' my father said quickly, seeing her distress. 'But that doesn't mean it won't happen. Lucius asked Neran to do it instead. He was delighted, naturally.' Right at the top of the list would be Dagan and Zebul, with notes in the margin suggesting that they were definite officer material.

'And where does that leave you?' my mother asked.

'Ah well, that's an interesting point.' There was a hint of a smile. 'There's more to all this than setting up rows of barracks and handing out swords to all our young men. They want a thorough map of the area. They're going to build roads and new fortifications, plant crops and develop farms. They even want to know about the mountain people.'

Almost as many people lived in and around the sweeping upland valleys of Munda and Lacibis as in the towns themselves. There were small homesteads concealed by close-ranked olive trees, wooden shacks nestling near the winter brooks, shepherds' lodges higher up, and even dwellings in the myriad caves formed beneath rocky outcrops. But you could walk all day and not be aware of this, unless the country folk wanted you to see them. Reliant on Munda for summer water and essential supplies, or to sell their produce milked from the rich earth, these stealthy folk were often seen at the markets or on the edge of social groups, forging their network of sales or just gleaning the latest information. They spoke the old tongue mixed with the most common Latin words and wore an aura of the spirit world like a deftly woven cloak; they were held in awe by the townsfolk despite their rugged, wiry appearance and unkempt, unfashionable clothing. Like the spirits that guided them, they knew the art of sorcery and would vanish in the blink of an eye.

And now the Romans were interested in them.

My mother, who had learned her herbcraft from the mountain people, smirked. 'The Romans won't even get near them,' she scoffed. 'What a ridiculous thought.'

'Exactly,' my father smiled. 'But they don't know that. What's more, this time I volunteered.'

That was most unlike my father. My mother was about to protest when he held up both hands to calm her.

'Think about it, Adela. Neran is going to march all our young men, including Pito —' at this point he looked into my eyes — 'straight into a legion where, likely as not, they will be killed or mutilated.' He choked on these last words. 'I don't want that for my son. He's no coward, I know that, but all of us in this family have greater things to achieve than marching to far-off lands to die for the Roman cause.'

I gave a slight nod of agreement, sensing the power of his words.

'So I told them that yes, I would be delighted to help them improve their understanding and relations with the people of Munda and the mountain folk. What's more, I told them I knew exactly the right person to start work on their precious map.'

He was still looking at me when he said this, and my mother's eyes brightened with understanding.

'So,' she said slowly, 'when Neran comes knocking to order Pito into the ranks, he will already have been given a much more important job by you?'

'Precisely. But only if he would prefer that to a short career as a soldier.'

I chuckled. 'Do eagles fly in the sky?'

My father laughed, and my mother tried to smile.

I needed an assistant for my new job, so I found Lizard and we went to see the Roman officer, Celer. He showed us the large cloth map, which had disappointingly few markings on it — just the towns of Lacibis and Munda and a line showing where the new road might go. He rummaged in one of the wagons and emerged with sheets of parchment and ink, which I knew were expensive, as such writing materials were rare in Munda.

He told us he was a cartographer. He was not a Roman by birth, but one of us, Hispanic. He had chosen a military career, taking a Roman name, and had risen swiftly to the rank of centurion. It was not a hard life as the land was at peace, which meant that his century was deployed more and more in a scouting role. They patrolled the wild country around Corduba to create maps showing the best routes for new roads, where the easiest river fords were, and likely sites for new settlements. They also noted the fertility of the land for crops and animal husbandry to feed the growing city of Corduba and the ever-hungry legions based there.

Then, at the March equinox, a delegation had arrived from Rome under the two young sons of Pompey the Great, and suddenly there was a new urgency instilled in the military machine. The Pompeys wanted to create new legions, new roads for them to travel on, new mines and new weapons production sites. Celer's talents were spotted by the younger

Pompey, a quick-witted youth of sixteen named Sextus. Between them, Celer and Sextus identified the key strategic cities and ports, and searched through the governor's library for any information and maps that would help them in their planning.

And that was when the Pompey brothers had rediscovered Munda.

Celer had brought with him some yellowing parchments showing the routes that Caesar had taken during his year as Governor, with untidy notes about each town visited. There was a long entry about the appointment of Lucius Marcellus as procurator at a small mountain town called Munda and a map showing the junction of three trade routes: north to Lacibis, west towards Gades, and south through a mountain pass to the coast. Celer told us how he had immediately been despatched to take new instructions to the procurator that Munda was to be elevated from a trading post to a strategic military base. And the Pompey brothers would follow in due course.

'Tell me, Melqart, how will you go about this task?' Celer's immaculate Latin and formal tone had initially surprised me, but I was used to it now. I wondered if everyone in Corduba was so meticulous.

'We'll climb, Titan,' I said, turning to look in awe at the mountain that towered behind Munda. 'From the summit, we can see what the eagles see.'

'Most enterprising,' said Celer.

'Very clever,' said Lizard cheekily.

The eagle circled, watching us climb through the sparse thorn bushes on the hill nearest Munda, which would give us a good view looking down on the town before tackling the daunting mountain for a wider aspect. We rode ponderous mules, chosen for their sure-footedness and steady pace, a third on a lead rein, carrying supplies, waterskins and writing tools.

At the summit, we studied the tight knot of whitewashed houses at the centre of the town, and a scattering of larger buildings clinging to the streets and roads that led outwards to the three gates, two of which had long been reduced to piles of stones. Above us loomed Titan, where the eagles nested, high enough to be honoured with a snowy crown in the coldest winters.

A flat rock provided rest. Lizard untied a waterskin and a leather satchel and passed them to me. For a while neither of us spoke, admiring the view. The eagle lost interest and drifted south towards the mountain.

Shielding his eyes from the sun's glare, Lizard looked north at the treeless valley, which stretched like a plain towards Lacibis. The track ran past several hillocks where goats and sheep grazed together, watched by sinewy shepherds and their raw-boned dogs.

'We'll get an even better idea when we climb Titan.' I was scanning the side of the mountain, hoping there was a hunter's track to make the task easier. 'We'll be able to see much further in all directions.'

For a few moments we enjoyed a freshening breeze and tossed small stones to make the crickets scatter. Then I unrolled a bleached sheepskin and, taking a charcoal stick from the satchel, began to sketch the scene below.

At first light the next day we began our ascent of Titan. Once past the orderly ranks of pines and the more free-spirited junipers, we saw fewer signs of human habitation, save the occasional shepherd's lodge, stone hovels with turf roofs to provide refuge from the incessant summer sun. We saw only one of the semi-concealed cave houses built by the mysterious mountain people and, recalling the interest that Lucius had expressed, we dismounted and called out. Nobody emerged, nor was there any sign of the family that lived there. But when we continued, I had a strong feeling that we were being watched, even on the open slopes of Titan where only stoic sandwort and thyme competed with threadbare grasses in their struggle for survival.

The journey to the top of Titan took most of the day. We followed the line of a ridge that climbed gently upwards and then flattened, offering the easiest route for the mules. We dismounted near the summit for the last part of the climb, which was too steep even for our reliable mules. It was hard going. Every muscle in my thighs and calves protested as I pushed myself to keep up with Lizard, whose wiry frame was more suited to the demanding ascent. My shirt was soon soaked with sweat and my feet were beginning to blister as we pulled and cajoled the mules ever closer to the peak. But I had never been happier.

A pair of eagles flew close, almost causing me to lose my balance as I clung to a tuft of grass to gaze upwards at their elegant flight. The majestic birds slowed, tiny adjustments in their outstretched wings giving them absolute power in the thin air, and for a moment I could look into the larger bird's eye. I sensed, rather than saw, the dignity and wisdom of the lord of the skies. Then they were gone, dropping swiftly to the lower reaches to hunt, leaving me with an overwhelming feeling that I had encountered a superior being. Munda's protector-god.

The view from the summit of Titan was breathtaking. The air coursed through my tingling body, enlivening my spirit and merging with the lichen-covered rock beneath my feet. I closed my eyes and breathed in its dizzying power. When I opened them again, I noticed that Lizard was for once still. He was looking down on Munda, studying the layout of the town. I looked south. There, behind the huge mass of three more mountains, between which the trading track wound south, I made out the soft line of the sea's horizon. The journey to the coast had been made less perilous by the hard work of the procurator's road builders, a full day's ride on a strong stallion. However, few of the town's youths had been allowed to venture that far. I drank in my first view of the ocean.

Lizard was still studying Munda's valley as I unstrapped the satchel from the pack mule. I took a fresh sheepskin and placed it on a flat piece of ground, weighting it with rocks against the strengthening breeze. Then I began to mark out the peaks I could see in every direction, the valleys between them, and their relation to the sea.

The Romans would have their maps to show Zebul and Dagan where they could march their hapless young soldiers.

FOUR

The storm came upon us without warning.

We had taken a whole day on the breezy summit making our maps, but then warm air from the south came at dusk, forced upwards by the mountains. The clouds cloaked Titan in a clammy grip, stealing all visibility in a few heartbeats. I suddenly realised I could not even see Lizard or the mules, and my panic-stricken shout was cut short by a blinding white flash. The simultaneous sound exploded inside my head and threw me to the ground. Stinging needles of rain lashed my body as I covered my head with my hands, cowering before the god in his mighty anger.

I called again, and thought I heard Lizard's shout. I looked up just as another flash illuminated Lizard's staggering frame. I leapt to my feet and ran for the now darkened place where I had seen Lizard, the rain soaking my clothes and stinging my eyes. I collided with Lizard, and both of us gave in to our fears, clinging to each other in a shivering, watery embrace.

'We have to find the mules!' I yelled in Lizard's ear.

'I think they ran off!' he shouted back. 'We'll have to wait until this passes.'

'It'll be completely dark by then. Maybe they're not far away?'

'All right, but we must stay together.'

Another flash of lightning seemed to be slightly further away, but the responding crash threw us to the ground again, a wave of energy that took my breath away and made my ears ring with its sudden, brutal force.

'That way, I think.'

I couldn't see where Lizard was pointing, so I shouted, 'You lead, but we must stay together!' I grasped a handful of Lizard's sodden tunic.

We stumbled around Titan's summit, knees cut and bruised from frequent falls, calling and whistling between the thunderous crashing, but we neither saw nor heard any sign of the mules. We began a descent on what we thought might be a path, still shouting for the mules but with a growing sense of futility. The thunder seemed to be rolling away, but just as our spirits were lightening a little, another flash surrounded us and the god threw us to the ground again.

The fall was inevitable. Uncertain whether the trembling blackness was the thundercloud or the night, we pressed on, desperate to find the mules with our supplies and equipment. Lizard slipped on a wet rock, landing on his behind. Still clinging to Lizard's tunic, I was pitched forward into nothingness, pulling him with me. Both of us slid downwards on a steep, stony slope that tore at our skin, grazing our faces, elbows and knees. We scrabbled at the loose rock, unable to halt our fall, then suddenly we were airborne again, flailing hopelessly in the wet darkness. Lizard's landing was cushioned by a gorse bush, but I landed on top of him, my elbow breaking his nose and my hip crushing his ribs.

I thought Lizard was dead. I shook him, but there was no sound, so I put my ear close to his mouth to listen for breath. For a long moment none came, then Lizard grunted and sucked in air, a throaty groan giving voice to the searing pain that shot through his chest.

'Can't move,' he managed. 'I think my ribs are broken.'

'Lie still then,' I said, checking the movement in my arms and legs. Though painful, nothing was broken, but my ankle throbbed.

'But the mules…?'

'I think they're lost. We'll wait here for daylight.' I couldn't think what else we could do.

'No food, broken ribs, and probably bleeding all over…'

His complaint was cut short by several streaks of white lightning that stabbed at the mountain above us.

Dawn, when it finally came, was as bright and cheery as the previous night had been black and terrifying. Lizard was sleeping fitfully, so I heaved myself to my feet to look around. Gingerly, I put my weight on my injured ankle and found that I could do no more than hobble, so I stood still to survey the mountainside. It was still in shadow, whereas the next mountain was bathed in sunlight, so I deduced we were on the western slopes, far away from Munda, with no knowledge of the route back home. I was ravenously hungry and shivering uncontrollably.

It was when I looked north, the direction that we must take to get home, that I saw the figure. A child, or a small adult, crouching on a rock just too far away to distinguish any detail. I narrowed my eyes and watched, but the figure didn't move. I tried waving. There was no response.

Lizard groaned and opened his eyes.

'What the… Where…' He winced as he tried to sit upright.

'So the great explorer awakes.' I tried to be cheerful. 'What would you like for breakfast?'

'Just water. Pass me the skin.'

I laughed. 'If we can find the mules we'll find your water and, if I'm not mistaken, there's some half decent cheese and a little wine left. How do you feel?'

'Not my finest.' Lizard managed one of his twisted smiles and gingerly felt his ribs. Deep purple and black bruises ringed his eyes and his nose was bent at an unnatural angle.

'You don't look your finest, either. Where does it hurt?'

'Everywhere.'

I offered a hand. 'Can you walk?'

Lizard eased himself to his feet. 'Reckon so. And you?'

'It'll be slow, but we'll make it. There's someone over there, watching us.'

Lizard looked to where I pointed, but the small figure had gone.

'There was someone perched on that rock over there,' I said, almost apologetically. 'My bet is that it was one of the mountain people.'

Lizard picked an ant off his shoulder. 'Well then, we have the choice of stumbling around looking for mules, or seeing if we can find your mysterious vanishing sprite.'

'My thoughts exactly. Let's go.'

Stiffly supporting each other, we made painfully slow progress to the rock where our observer had been spotted. As we approached, we could see a pair of tiny birds pecking at a bundle, trying to unpick a large folded leaf bound with a leather cord. The birds flew off, chattering angrily, as we approached. Beside the rock was a clay flagon.

'Is that what I think it is?' Lizard quickened his pace, leaving me to hobble after him.

Lizard pulled off the cord and opened the green parcel. I limped up to see a small black loaf, perhaps more a cake, solid and heavy with preserved fruits. Lizard broke it in half and we ate hungrily. I reached for the flagon, pulled out the wooden stopper and sniffed the contents.

'Smells of honey and herbs,' I said, and took a mouthful. It was sweet and warming, and immediately I felt my spirits lighten, and strength returning to my legs. I passed it to Lizard, who took a long draught and handed it back, a satisfied look crossing his bruised face.

'So we've got friends in these parts,' he said, wiping a dribble of the golden liquid from his chin. 'But where are they?'

I scanned the mountainside but could see no sign of life, no track, not even the squabbling small birds or the pair of eagles that had watched our ascent. Our side of the mountain was still in shadow, but opposite us the hills and peaks were now being brought to life by the warm sun, above them a cloudless sky — a promise of respite from the night's despair.

'Look here.' Lizard was examining some marks that had been scratched in the yellow and black lichen covering the rock. 'If I'm not mistaken, that's an arrow that points over there.' We looked, following its direction, but there was nothing to be seen.

'Again, it's a simple choice,' I said confidently. 'Someone took the trouble to bring us breakfast and now someone wants to be our guide, too. Come on.'

We resumed our tortuous trek, following the arrow's direction, which seemed to lead towards the lower part of a rocky escarpment. It took an age to reach it, but when we rounded the craggy outcrop, our hearts sank. We were at the top of a steep incline that dropped alarmingly down into a ravine, scattered with boulders and loose rocks that would give no foothold. It would be impossible to climb down that way, especially with our injuries. Beyond the ravine was the treeline, close ranks of pines covering the gentler slopes of the hills beyond, contrasting sharply with the mountain's desolate terrain.

We sat on a rock, looking around for a route that wasn't going back the way we had come.

'At least it's a great view,' said Lizard.

'That's not helpful,' I grunted.

Movement at the edge of the trees caught my attention. I nudged Lizard and pointed downwards. Three dark shapes were moving out from the shadows, squat and powerful.

'Boar,' I said, recalling the times I had followed the tracks of the ferocious pigs with Baku. The three foragers were following the ravine's edge, no doubt looking for a route to the brook below them. The largest of the three led watchfully, the two slightly smaller animals following with their snouts close to the ground. Even at this distance I could sense their power and wondered what it must be like to spear one for the table.

More movement above drew my gaze. An eagle circled not far above the treetops, behind the rearmost animal. It kept pace with the boar, shortening its drifting sweep in an effortless glide, watching and tracking, its wingtips curled upwards and its regal head looking down. Perhaps it was hunting for small animals disturbed by clumsy boar hoofs, I thought, or even just amusing itself by following the fierce creatures. I watched the unusual display, unable to take my eyes off the eagle. Lizard, speechless, gave a low whistle.

Suddenly, as if wary of hidden danger, the three boars turned and trotted into the undergrowth at the edge of the forest, disappearing from sight. The eagle moved with them, keeping close to the trees.

'What's that about, do you think?' asked Lizard.

'Not sure,' I replied, mystified. 'Eagles don't attack boar. Nothing bigger than a rabbit, usually.'

'Perhaps they're enemies,' he suggested.

'Or just playing games…'

But Lizard had lost interest in both eagle and boar. 'It's back the way we've come then,' he sighed as he heaved himself to his feet, wincing at the pains in his chest and side. His foot slipped and he half turned as I steadied him, and suddenly we were looking at a roughly scratched arrow that had been scraped into the rock where he had been sitting.

'That's great,' I laughed. 'You've been covering up our next clue.'

But Lizard was already staring in the direction the arrow pointed. It was just possible to make out a scar that ran across the top part of the slope, possibly a path. It angled slightly upwards then gently down towards a rocky gash in the side of the mountain. I scanned the route we were being invited to take. It looked perilous, but was certainly leading us in the right direction.

And as I looked at the point where the path disappeared, I thought I saw something move. Narrowing my eyes, I watched. Then, ever so slowly, a head and then a pair of shoulders appeared around the rock face. The distance was too great for us to make out any features, but the child was definitely watching us.

Our guide was gone by the time we had scrambled to the place where we had seen the urchin appear. But there was no more need for surprise parcels and hastily scratched arrows because we were now within sight of home. Peeping between two hills we could see the white houses of Munda, like eggs in a nest. And nearer, tethered to a bush next to a brook, our three mules grazed contentedly. There was nobody in sight.

The mules barely acknowledged us as we approached. We quickly checked the pack mule to find that all of our crude maps and writing tools were still there and were pleased to find that more of the fruit bread had been added to our sparse supplies. There was also a full wineskin looped over the wooden pommel.

'Someone's looking after us,' I said happily, looking around in the hope of seeing one of our benefactors. 'It would be nice to meet them, but I suppose they're too frightened by your ugly face.'

FIVE

The first time the eagle swooped past we were merely startled. Gliding low from the direction of Titan, it flew so close that I felt the air ripple as it passed. We looked at each other, open-mouthed.

The majestic bird rose over the pine trees with two languorous beats of its huge wings and circled near the edge of the forest. I shook my head in disbelief.

'Must be lost,' I ventured.

'Or it's attacking us,' Lizard said with a note of alarm. 'Look.'

The eagle seemed to be turning back towards us. Again it came low and passed us with a shriek, panicking the mules. We struggled to control them, and Lizard clung to the pack mule's rein as it tried to bolt. This time the eagle settled on the larger of two rock outcrops near the treeline, a long stone's throw from us. For a moment it held its wings outstretched as if to balance, then folded them carefully as it seemed to watch us.

'This is going to sound completely ridiculous,' I mumbled loudly enough for Lizard to hear, 'but I get the strangest feeling that eagle is trying to show us something.'

'Yes, you sound completely ridiculous,' said Lizard. 'Let's just go home.' He nudged his mule forward again.

'Wait,' I urged. 'What harm is there in going over there just to see?'

Lizard reined in his mule. 'You go. You'll probably get your eyes pecked out for your trouble. I'll wait here.'

'Your trouble, Lizard, is that you have no sense of adventure,' I said as I dismounted, favouring my good ankle on the hard ground. I hobbled towards the eagle as it twisted its head from side to side. Crossing a shallow brook, reduced to a trickle in the summer's drought, I approached the Lord of the Skies. I reached out a hand to touch the base of the towering rock on which the eagle perched, needing to steady myself as I looked up into an unblinking eye, fearfully aware of the great talons that could shred flesh and the curved beak, hard as iron. The giant bird did not move. Cautiously, I looked around. I could see nothing untoward. Then I looked down.

That was when I found the boar trail. Beneath my feet the ground was stripped bare of grass, hoof prints marking a favoured run where the wild animals came to the brook.

I edged carefully between the rocks and saw that the trail led down from the edge of the firs that clothed the foothills, where their rich loam created a forest of delights for the wild pigs to feast upon. I could even smell the rank odour of the boars' passing, imagining the yellowed tusks of an adult male, its black coarse-haired flanks and the menacing stare in its devil eyes. Though I had tracked boar with Baku, we had never encountered one, except those roasted on great spits on feast days. Neither had my grandfather ever intended to risk my life or his. That was left to the young men of Munda, who proved their physical prowess with spear and knife.

I backed away from the eagle, which spread its wings and lifted effortlessly away. I watched him beat those great wings that bore him towards Titan's peak and decided that the world had gone mad. An eagle had shown me the perfect place to ambush a wild boar.

Lizard and I hobbled the mules near the western gate, unloaded the maps and walked wearily towards my home. It was trading day, and the busy streets of Munda were awash with colour: there were bright fruits from the orchards, hams and shanks of meat where the flies swarmed, pots with garish designs, and the wares of woodworkers and jewellers. Dogs fought beneath the tables until dismissed with an angry boot to sulk in a quieter alley, while cats used their wisdom to find food.

Of course, my father had sold every loaf of bread, every last pastry and all of his sweetmeats — the latter chiefly given away to persistent children.

My mother's table in the market street was, as ever, laden with her herbs. Garrulous customers rubbed aromatic leaves between their fingers, sniffing inquisitively, as if just to be in their vicinity would bring peace and healing. Of course, her secret herbs, those that really did bring healing, were reserved for those in need and remained hidden in our kitchens.

My mother did not see us approach, as she was speaking to a woman whose hair was dyed with henna. Her expensive gown was silky and woven with colours that changed with every movement, her turquoise sandals threaded with silver. I knew her to be the nurse of the procurator's two young children, born to parents of an age when childbearing should have been an impossibility. But as my mother often said, there were no impossibilities in Munda.

'The remedy must be taken four times a day,' I heard my mother say as I approached. 'They will baulk at it, but they will recover by sundown tomorrow.' She was smiling, though the other woman seemed uncertain. 'And then Hann will bring his flat bread that returns iron to the blood, laughter to the eyes and all the noise that children make.'

That was what the nurse needed to hear. 'Thank you, Adela, thank you.'

She tried to press a silver coin into my mother's hand, and though I silently willed her to accept, I knew she would not. The nurse hurried away in the direction of the procurator's villa, and it was only then that my mother reached out a slender arm towards me.

'Pito.' She smiled at me, then at Lizard, a look of concern crossing her face when she saw his bruises. 'What happened to you? You've not been fighting, have you?'

Lizard laughed at the thought. 'I tripped and fell when we were running from the storm.'

My mother put a hand to her mouth in alarm. 'Oh, the storm. We were worried for you both last night. Was it terrifying?'

'Passed right by us,' I said. It was a half-truth. I changed the subject to my discovery of the boar trail but it came out like a stream of nonsense, and anyway she had turned to search for one of her unguents. She smoothed a healing cream on Lizard's face while he squirmed and objected.

She turned to me. 'Find your sisters and tell them to assist me here,' she instructed. 'And don't you dare go chasing dangerous pigs around the countryside, nor bears or wildcats. You leave that to the village hunters.'

I planned to stay at home for several days, working on the new maps for Lucius. It turned out to be a week because I was struck down by fever, no doubt brought on by the ordeal of surviving a mountain storm.

The Roman century had left for Gades while Lizard and I had been on the mountain, and I was so weakened by fever that I didn't notice the sons of Pompey ride past Munda and go straight to the procurator's villa. I left the maps untouched and forgot the boar trail, the eagle, and my scrap with Zebul.

'I'm worried, Hann. His skin is so hot,' I overheard my mother telling my father in hushed tones at my door.

He calmed her, as he always did. 'Hasn't the doctor told us that Pito will recover, that he needs rest? I promise you he will be up to his tricks again in a few days.'

'But I'm worried that he…'

'Hush, Adela, he will be fine. He seems unusually withdrawn, I admit, even delirious at times, but if you keep on with your fine broth he will soon be rushing to and fro, teasing the girls and inventing new games for Elvir. He might even break some more of your pottery…'

'That I would welcome,' said my mother, and she smiled again at last.

Eventually my body was repaired by my mother's broth and my father's bread, and I once again busied myself with my map drawings for Lucius. I also helped my father in his bakery. Though his bread was baked at dawn and mostly sold before the noon hour, he worked ceaselessly in preparation for the next day's supply, charming the merchants for the finest wheat, barley and corn, and preparing the yeast and bowls of herbs and root shavings for the darker loaves that were in such demand. Word had spread to surrounding settlements and my parents had even hosted emissaries from the coastal communities, Roman officials in their fine, embroidered tunics and merchants with their shifty looks and suspicious minds. But my parents' secrets were not for sale, and none of these saw the labelled pots and jars or my father's notes and theories about nature's bounty.

Despite his devotion to his trade, my father always had time to talk with me and encourage my questioning. I learned that our ancestors had been great sailors and explorers, taking their knowledge and fine goods to all parts of the world, then settling in great communities of peace and prosperity like ours. Of course it was not always like this, he told me, because the world was full of greed and war. It seemed that little had changed as news reached even our mountain domain of great battles between civilisations, and even war between the lofty Roman generals themselves.

My father spoke of the noble Hannibal who had fought the Romans, even taking his army across the sea and through our lands to strike at their capital city. He recounted the story of the Numantians, how they withstood the Roman general Scipio and chose to die in the flames of their city. This had proved futile, because now the Romans were sending their generals and politicians to live in Hispania. Men such as Lucius.

'Does that mean we are Romans, Father?' I asked innocently.

'What do you think? If a general from some far-off land walks into our village, shakes his sword at us and tells us we are Romans, does that make us Romans?'

'No.'

'You are right. But how does that make you feel?'

I was uncertain how to reply. I thought of the procurator but did not recall any fighting, only the new order that had come to Munda with paved streets, houses that did not leak during the winter rains, and buildings like the temple, where any villager could go in prosperity and peace.

'Well, I suppose it's a good thing,' I said, hesitantly. 'I mean, we are not slaves...'

'Indeed we are not. Yet others have not been so lucky. I have heard that life is very different in the East and to the North, where the Romans put down rebellions with their slaughter and rule with a rod of iron.'

'Why is it different in this part of Hispania?'

'It hasn't always been so.' He paused, thinking. 'But everything changes in time. We learn from history. We discover that an army, like the Romans have, is not the true soul of its people. It is made up of a lot of angry soldiers who have a lust for killing. We have never seen an army here, and I hope we never do. Oh, there are bandits and robbers just as there are anywhere else, but here we have learned that peace and love are greater than war and death.'

'But now Lucius wants to raise an army right here in Munda.'

My father put his hands on my shoulders and looked into my eyes. I saw gentleness and care in his face. 'I doubt he will succeed. Any soldiers he trains are far more likely to be sent to another land to fight. There's a great big world out there, vast oceans and lands that we have never heard of. There's so much for generals and their armies to go and conquer. You can be certain that none of them are ever going to come to a little, peaceful place like Munda to wage war.'

It was during one of our lengthy discussions that I digressed to the subject of the boar trail. It had not occurred to me that to adorn the village feasting table with a roasted boar you first had to thrust a spear into it, killing it before it savaged you with tusks that could maim for life, and certainly kill a boy of fourteen years.

What I loved about my father was that he never refused me anything without suggesting an alternative. He had an amused twinkle in his eye, and we formed our conspiracy. Rather than going after a boar myself, I agreed to observe and report the movements of the animals so that the seasoned hunters in the village could do what they did best.

And so, with my strength restored, I set off early one morning in the direction of Titan, whose rocky face was bathed in the early sunlight and crowned with wispy cloud like an old man's hairs. In my pouch was a hunk of bread still warm from the ovens, a little of Eshmun's sticky goat's cheese and a clay flask filled from one of the spring pools.

I left the village by way of the secret path that followed the ravine through which Munda's waste tumbles. This was not the foul, stinking slime you would find excreted from towns that do not have the blessing of abundant springs like ours; the ravine was washed clean and it was deep and rocky, with a maze of caverns hidden behind the tumbling streams. The path was narrow and followed the higher part so that the brook's chattering noise was swiftly lost in the depths. Cicadas made their music here, bright lizards teased and darted, and small birds frolicked.

The sun was high and warm when I found the place where the boars ran. I sat on a boulder and devoured the bread and cheese, studying the trail as I ate. It told me nothing new. Only part of it was identifiable, where the animals emerged from the forest's undergrowth and swung around the very boulder where I sat to drink at the brook. Behind my boulder the land dropped sharply in a sheer-sided ravine, a gash in the gentler ground as if stabbed by an angry god.

I followed the trail towards the pines, but tracking was not one of my skills and it dissipated in the rough grass just a few strides beyond my boulder. Undeterred, I continued upwards to see what I could find in the woods, making little noise on the soft carpet of discarded foliage, but nonetheless enough to cause small birds to shrill their insults from the high branches. I grew fearful. This was not my domain; was I being watched? Would I be charged by the very animals that had aroused my interest? What other fearsome creatures stalked unwary prey in these darkened, untamed woods?

I returned to my rock.

And that's when I saw the girl.

SIX

There are many different ways of seeing. I had seen Leandra many times and thought her to be distant and aloof. But now I *saw* her.

She was standing on the very rock that I had considered mine, her back to me, arms outstretched as if in worship. Her long, black hair hung almost to her waist as she held her face to the skies, arching her slender back, her girlish hips tilted forward, and her agile legs held neatly together. A body in perfect balance.

Although the same age as me, she seemed at that moment to be a woman of strength and poise, an athlete who could run and throw the javelin, deserving of the praise of lesser mortals. She was motionless, save for the gentle movement of her hair in the slight breeze, her spirit drinking the power of the skies or the knowledge of the gods. I stood transfixed.

'Melqart.'

She spoke my name quietly. I said nothing because I could not find any words.

'Melqart.' Her voice was like music, not childish but womanly. 'I know you are there, just as every creature for leagues must have heard you. Have you lost your voice?'

I stammered a reply, hating myself for speaking without saying anything intelligible. She lowered her arms and turned, slowly. Her black eyes locked with mine, and my face reddened under her gaze. There was spirit in those eyes, joy and strength. She had a strong nose and a wide, smiling mouth that revealed white teeth framed by proud cheekbones and a firm, confident chin. The golden skin of her arms and legs was smooth, sculpting the contours of her young muscles. Energy seemed to flow boundlessly from every part of her.

She leaped effortlessly from the boulder and her long strides brought her to me. Her eyes were level with mine, and I fought to restore my composure, forcing myself not to look away. I found some words at last.

'What… Why are you here?' It sounded harshly interrogative; those laughing eyes were unsettling.

'Perhaps I should ask you the same?' Her voice was gentle and strangely warming. 'Anyway, I followed you here and watched you study these boar prints… Now, what have you got in mind, I wonder?'

I found some strength and smiled at her. 'I really don't know,' I confessed, 'though it will come to me. I think it would be wonderful to watch them pass, but even more wonderful to catch one for the butcher's slab.'

She laughed, rolling her eyes heavenward, and I laughed with her. My disjointed thoughts did seem ridiculous when I spoke them out loud.

'Do I understand you correctly? You want to catch and kill a boar? Oh, that's so easy — all you have to do is stick a spear in it, and you have your prize! Tell me, Melqart, where is your spear?'

'I can get one,' I said, trying to sound as if the whole plan had been carefully organised.

'And have you ever used one?' Before I could confess that no, I had never used one outside Dracus's training ground, she added, 'And have you ever seen a boar, even a young one, that has not been killed with the first thrust, how it snaps and savages at you with the strength of ten?'

'Have you?' I asked.

'Of course not,' she smiled. 'Neither of us knows the first thing about killing a boar, so should we forget the whole silly idea and go home to play with dolls and wooden toys instead? Or shall we say that two knowing nothing means twice the chance of success? Do you have courage, dear Melqart?'

I no longer wanted her to use my given name. 'Please call me Pito,' I replied, gently. 'My family calls me Agapito, but I am no longer a child, though I like the name. So please call me Pito, and we'll be friends and conspirators.'

She nodded, but before she could say my new name, I went on, 'And, actually, we need more than spears and courage. We need understanding.' I touched my temple as I spoke. 'We must plan this thing. Knowing how they run, how they fight, and how they die, we must make it happen swiftly with no opportunity for them to injure us.'

'Well, Pito —' she said my name with respect and made my heart beat faster — 'what a team we make. You have brains — no, much more than that, you have the sight, I think — and if I had one, I would offer you my sword!'

'I think you have great speed, strength and wits ... for a girl.' I winked, for I believed we both knew that she was fleeter of foot and, though I was the stronger, it was her ability to channel strength that would complement my ability to think and plan outside of the accepted boundaries.

She winked back, laughing.

We were so engrossed as we walked back to the village that at first we did not see the eagle. He was high, circling on a thermal of rising air, when Leandra first spotted him. He looked majestic, his wings barely moving as he rode the wind, surveying all and commanding the skies. We watched in reverent silence.

He circled ever lower, each minute adjustment of his wing tips bringing him closer. His white underbelly and kingly wing patterns became clearer. Neither of us moved, barely breathing. Then, with the subtlest tip of his body, he was gliding towards Titan's craggy ravines.

Leandra turned to me, her eyes and wide smile showing her amazement. To be visited by this exalted creature was rare indeed, and we had no doubt that we had been honoured.

'I have met him before,' I ventured, breaking the silence. 'He showed me the boar trail.' I recounted how the eagle had twice flown in front of us as Lizard and I returned from the mountain, and how I had stood before him and discovered the trail.

'So you think he was showing you the trail…?' There was no mockery in Leandra's eyes as she said this.

'Who knows? It's what I like to think.' I could feel my face colouring again.

'Oh, Pito, you're so sweet. Of course he was showing you, and why not? I think you have an affinity with nature, with the animals, though you seem to be a little greedy where the boars are concerned!'

I think I fell in love with Leandra when she put her arm in mine, wanting me to support her on the dirt path that climbed into Munda. My heart swelled: this I recognised as pride, wanting all to see us.

SEVEN

The days were warm, the sky clear and the breeze courteously light. We spent afternoons at the rock, sometimes studying the lie of the land and fine-tuning our plan, at other times just talking and laughing. Leandra's well-aimed pinecones, or occasionally a hard olive, brought mock battles and chases through the trees, reminding us that we were both loath to leave the joys of childhood.

On one occasion, Lizard came with us. Although he was as jovial and enthusiastic as ever, I found myself resenting his company, especially when Leandra laughed at his antics. I found new ways of excluding him.

Once, when Leandra had been silent for some minutes atop the massive rock — now our rock, not mine — as we lay on our backs looking up at the sky, we heard the boars moving past on their trail towards the mountain. We kept still, not daring to make a sound, so we did not see them but sensed that there were two, perhaps three. The younger one snuffled while another, which must have been an adult, made a deep grunting noise that seemed to be a warning that any unwelcome wolf or human should move away. Above, the eagle circled, watching over us.

Behind the boulder there was a small but deep ravine, caused by the cracking and rending of the land not uncommon in times of drought. Next to this we positioned a rock so large that it took all of our strength to heave it end upon end. Its resting place, on the edge of the ravine, was precarious; somehow we managed to ease it into a position where one more concerted shove would send it crashing perhaps five times the height of a man.

To this we attached the length of rope we had begged from Blas, an uncle of mine who had taken over Baku's old workshop. Because he was my uncle and doted on me — he had no family other than ours — Blas was delighted to let us rummage through his dark and dusty workshop under the pretence that we were tidying it. There we found wooden pegs and iron bonding spikes, waiting to tack together some ageing piece of furniture, as well as ancient farming tools and even older weaponry. Leandra selected a spear, which she oiled and burnished until it was fit for a seasoned cavalryman. I chose a hunting knife, which I sharpened dutifully after removing the rust and grime. Much of what we found was nothing more than junk, for which Blas would one day find a use, but it was the old rope netting that had once been used to hold ripe watermelons for the market that had given us our first foolish plot.

We put everything in place and practised all save the plunging rock, though I calculated the force and distance this weight would bring about. And then we waited, hidden from the boar trail by our rock, my feet resting on the smaller boulder we had placed at the ravine edge. On the second day, we saw the eagle again, but he was high, perhaps searching for rabbits or partridge in the scrubland. On the third day we felt foolish and agreed that we had better things to do; I hoped Leandra would not think me dull and tire of our friendship as quickly as it had formed. We both had duties to perform, our families were questioning our long absences, and we feared that Zebul or Dagan, or their scheming friends, would discover what we were about.

Then, late in the day, the eagle's cry pierced the still air. I heard the beating of wings, the thunder of hooves, the sudden, impossible acrobatics of the giant bird, the swirling dust, the squeal of alarm, the heavy grunt of a now stationary sow. I felt a sharp pain in my legs as I pushed the rock with all my might. It disappeared into the ravine, the rope taut and tearing at the thick branch over which it had been hooked. The ravine echoed with the outraged roar of the trapped beasts.

Leandra was quick to react, grasping her spear and leaping up onto our rock. I crawled on my hands and knees, coughing dust, and saw a retreating boar, evidently one of the young that had not yet developed the fighting spirit of an adult. Leandra called to me, her voice assured and calm, and I climbed onto the rock.

Hanging from the old olive tree was our net, now filled with two boars. They were a furious mass of black, writhing, roaring aggression, the ropes straining to hold them. Open-mouthed and rigid, I watched as Leandra leaped down, landed before the ugly prey, and thrust her spear into the throat of the sow, silencing her in an instant. She then withdrew the weapon to despatch the second, younger boar. She was like a seasoned warrior, knowing instinctively where to stab to snatch life in an instant.

She turned to me, the look in her eye triumphant. My legs buckled and I sat heavily. I was not a coward, but I did not have the instinct of a killer.

We embraced, the dark blood on her tunic and face already sticky in the afternoon heat. She sighed, and I thought she would cry, but then she whispered in my ear, 'Look there.'

I pulled away and saw that her gaze was fixed behind me. I turned to our rock, and I understood the sounds we had heard and the ally we had in our fanatical conspiracy.

Standing serene and majestic on the rock, where a moment before we had stood to observe our success, was the eagle.

We knelt before the Lord of the Skies. His regal head was crowned with a ridge of black and brown plumage, like a general's helmet. His eye did not leave us even with the sharp movements of his head.

This godlike creature had seen our plans and had ushered our prey into the ambush, startling them forward then halting them in the mouth of the net, allowing us to spring the trap. On our own, we could not have achieved anything. Therefore, a tithe was due to the king.

I stood, turned to the still swinging net where blood dripped to the ground, took my hunting knife and slashed through the straining rope near the base. The knife cut easily, and on the third stroke delivered its unholy birth. Leandra helped me to separate the two boars — they were far heavier than I had expected — and I set to jointing away a foreleg of the younger animal. This we laid near the base of the rock. The eagle watched but did not move.

'What now?' I asked, not taking my eyes off the eagle. 'I don't think we can carry these, do you?'

'Perhaps the younger, between us, on my spear.' Leandra, too, kept her awed gaze on our co-conspirator.

The children saw us first and swarmed around us like the flies at the boar's eyes and the wound at its throat. We drank in their clamour and answered pestering questions as we walked, the boar heavy on the bending spear, chafing our shoulders, but we felt no pain. By the time we entered the village through the west gate, there were at least fifty gawkers and cheerers, half of them children, among them Lizard and my sisters. And Zebul. And Dagan.

They may have been strong and tall, always holding the attention of Munda's young women, but at that moment I did not feel one pang of jealousy. I walked with the beautiful Leandra and the evidence was there for all to see that we were athletes and hunters in our own right; we had killed the boar and we had provided for a feast. And none of these onlookers knew yet that we had taken not one, but two of these great animals for the table. Tomorrow night our village would celebrate.

Zebul did not cheer. He tried to seem disinterested, but I saw in the way that he looked at me that he was not finished with his evil and that I had better watch my back. Fortunately, he was not close enough to provoke me again. Dagan, his elder brother, on the other hand, at least made a pretence of showing admiration, but I knew he yearned for it to be him and his brother bringing home the spoils.

We carried the boar in procession, Pidray and Tallay among the children skipping ahead to the main square where the boar would be cleaned and dressed, anointed with spices and herbs and made ready for the spit. My mother and father were there by now, as was Leandra's mother — who looked at me suspiciously for a moment — and we revealed to them and those nearest that this was far less than half of the feast, as a great boar lay dead and ready to be carried back to the village. Leandra explained where to find the prize, and a small party was sent to recover it. The eagle would be long gone.

My mother embraced me and then set about gently scolding me for my recklessness and long absence from home and my studies. But we both knew she was thrilled at my success and, I was sure, my association with Leandra. My father winked and embraced me far more strongly than ever before.

'Now go and clean yourself up,' he smiled. I looked down at my bloodied tunic. He ruffled my matted, dirty hair. 'How is it that your accomplice can retain such beauty while you look like you have just lost a drunken brawl?'

I laughed. He was right; Leandra looked wonderful as she modestly told her mother of our escapades.

But neither of us mentioned the eagle.

EIGHT

To the people of Munda, it was just another feast. To me, and to Leandra, it was the first Day of the Eagle — several times that night we raised our cups in unspoken, mutual respect, both of us still awed by what had happened.

Five open fires had been lit at dusk in the main square and our two boars were spit-roasted, the fat causing the hot embers to hiss and flare furiously. On separate fires were turned hares, rabbits, pheasant, chickens, ducks and two of the great geese from the flocks raised outside the village for this very purpose. Impromptu stalls were laden with dishes of burgol, eggs, onions and pimentos, aromatic herbs, nuts and spiced vegetables, all laced with the season's rich olive oil. Piquant fragrances mixed with the aromatic smoke that lay over the town, the laughter and chatter of elated souls sounding a celebration that must have been heard in nearby Lacibis. Our taverns enjoyed better business that night than they had during mid-summer or the winter saturnalia; our wines demanded to be quaffed, not sipped, and the ale would cause many a brawl if it did not take away a man's ability to throw a punch or aim a kick.

The gods had prepared well, for as luck would have it, entertainers from the coast port of Silniana were passing through on their way to Corduba in the north, and the wonderful sounds of pipes and drums filled the air, rising to crescendo after crescendo with the shrill voices of the swirling, hand-clapping women from across the sea. My father not only allowed me to drink the wine, he actively encouraged it, and though it was mixed with water I truly felt like a man. I don't know how many times he told me he was proud of me.

I was not too addled to notice Lucius. I hadn't expected to speak with him; if I had known he would seek me out, I would have been more circumspect. I had already spilled wine on my tunic and Leandra had mischievously smeared pork grease on my nose, so I was not at my finest when a gentle hand was laid on my shoulder and I turned to look into those lively brown eyes. His face was battle-worn, craggy and lined, but his eyes were young and alive. The lady Livia stood at his side, her skin pale and smooth, belying her age.

'All hail the hero,' Lucius said, just loudly enough to overcome the clamour. 'I understand we have you to thank for this impromptu feast.'

'Sir,' I stammered, 'it was mere luck…' My voice tailed off and I rebuked myself for being so feeble.

'Fluke or well-planned victory, the result is the same in my book, and you do well to be modest.' I looked at my feet, blushing, and he went on, 'I would like to talk more with you, perhaps in a few days when we have all overcome the effects of this fine wine.'

'Of course, sir.'

'I have been impressed with the maps you have made, and I am certainly impressed with this feast. I think you have a maturity beyond your years, and maybe many hidden talents. It seems you have much to contribute.'

Livia gave me a warm smile and then they were both gone, mingling happily with the crowds. Lucius was unafraid to put his arm around the lowliest old man, and at one stage I saw him in deep conversation with my father.

I tried in vain to stay close to Leandra, but she, my beautiful sprite, was here and there like a leaf blown in the wind, laughing and playing the fool with her friends. I was not alone; Pidray and Tallay saw to that, grasping my hands and pulling me from one childish adventure to another. Eventually, I broke free to take more wine and eat with some of the older villagers, a boy hunter among the tough, the bearded and the wise.

Soon my words became slurred, and I blushed when unable to speak simple Latin, a foreign tongue seemingly wringing itself from my mouth, yet strangely understood by all around me. No one mocked; perhaps I had found a strange new gift.

The madness of Bacchus was upon us.

I slipped away when the drink demanded to be passed. I found a quiet street and, with some difficulty, freed my clothing enough to allow relief.

At first, I thought the violent shove in my back, causing me to wet my feet in the long emptying of my bladder, was simply a friendly push, a little manly jockeying. But it wasn't a jest; it was too violent for that, though my addled brain was slow to recognise it. I steadied myself and turned, trying to focus.

Zebul's normally handsome face was ugly with rage, his mouth twisted in a cruel sneer, his eyes dazed and dangerous. Dagan, as usual more in control than his younger brother, stood at his shoulder, as if encouraging him on. Both were tall and strong, though I sensed that Zebul was loose-limbed from too much strong drink, and I was not afraid. He pushed me again, and my shoulder blade crunched painfully onto the wall that moments ago had been my latrine. His right arm crushed my windpipe and the bronze bracelets on his forearm tore savagely at my neck. Slowly, pain registered, but anger rather than shame welled within me.

'You worthless brat! You think you are so clever…' Now his sandaled foot was crushing mine, his knee pinning my thigh to the wall so I could not move or speak. 'Well, you're not. You're just a stupid baker's son, and I'm going to stick you where it hurts.' With his free left hand he drew his hunting knife and held the point to my eye.

Now I was afraid. I stopped my futile struggling. His rancid breath was hot and foul, the smell of his sweat mingling with stale wine. He sneered, enjoying the fear in my eyes.

'This is going to hurt, little boy,' he hissed. The sharp point of his blade drew blood at the corner of my eye, then parted the flesh down towards my cheek. I tried to cry out, but no sound came, so fierce was the pressure on my neck. I couldn't breathe, and I couldn't move. The pain was sharp, forcing its way through my fuddled stupor, the blood mingling with the cold sweat of fear. They both laughed, savouring their moment of cruelty.

The tears came. I was a child again, all the bravery of the hunter gone.

'See how he snivels, Dagan?' Zebul's words were contemptuous. 'He would piss himself if he hadn't just emptied his bladder.'

I wanted to fight, but my body was pinned and I could barely breathe.

'Take him outside the walls,' Dagan said. Zebul's eyes gleamed with cruel fire, his thin lips forming a crooked smile. Without a word he pushed me savagely away from the revellers in the direction of the west gate, and I stumbled meekly, a prisoner led away on the road to torture and death. There was no fight in me. My head was still spinning with unaccustomed terror, and I vomited a foul mess of red wine and undigested food to add to the stains on my tunic.

They pushed me even more viciously towards the gate. And then I heard her voice, the last voice I wanted to hear, not because of the state I was in, but because I feared for her.

'Leave him alone, you bastards!' Leandra cried as she ran full tilt into Dagan, her fists flailing, her lithe body the warrior again. Dagan simply caught her by the wrists and held her strongly as she kicked out at him. Zebul laughed. In one swift movement, Dagan swirled her around and, forcing her arm up between her shoulder blades until it must surely snap, he released the other wrist and grasped her by her long hair, snapping her head back to expose her slender neck. Leandra's eyes were wide with new fear; she could not move.

I groaned and at last found words. 'Let her be,' I croaked. 'Let us both go, and we'll say nothing about this.' I tasted the blood that now ran from my cheek wound into the corner of my mouth.

Zebul laughed at me. Dagan pushed Leandra, now struggling like a goose at the slaughter, so that she stumbled with a gasp. Zebul followed, his knife at my throat.

Dawn's soft light persuaded the mountains to wake. No birds sang, perhaps sensing the abhorrence of what was taking place. Through the mist of blood and tears I thought I saw our eagle, soaring high on his dawn hunt, but it may have been a crow. There was spittle on my lip and my throat was painfully bruised. Flies settled on the caking blood.

Dagan, still gripping Leandra by her hair and with her arm forced behind her back, pushed on towards the olive groves. I could see her futile struggles as Zebul roughly shoved me ahead. Where was my planning now? I could find no strength to resist, to fight, to escape from whatever evils these brothers had in mind for us.

Somewhere nearby a dog barked, answered far across the valley. A cock crowed, but on this day it was not the joyful sound of an awakening world.

Dagan chose a place where the brow of a low hill and the higher shoots of the olive trees obscured us from the village. The ground was soft and broken from the latest ploughing, and nearby the farmer's wooden spikes lay half submerged in the red earth like the bleached bones of a long-dead warrior. Dagan pointed to the leather straps that hung from the plough.

'Bind him.'

Zebul pushed me to the ground and reached for the harness, his foot pressing harshly between my shoulder blades. Gritty soil filled my mouth and the wound on my cheek. Then, kneeling on my back so that my ribs bruised and cracked, he forced my arms behind me and tied my wrists, mocking my cries of pain.

'Leave him!' Leandra screamed. Dagan slapped her viciously, silencing her, but though I could not see her, I sensed her spirit was strong enough for both of us.

Zebul threw the loose end of the makeshift rope over a low olive branch and pulled hard. My arms were forced upward, wrenching at my shoulder blades. I cried out in agony.

'Stand, cockroach, or you will lose your arms.' Zebul was enjoying himself, still laughing. Again he pulled, and I must have passed out, for when I opened my eyes again the pain was shooting through my back and neck. In my head was a persistent drum, each thunderous throb bringing waves of nausea. Blood, made thin and pale by sweat and tears, dripped freely on the ground.

I tried to raise my head, but it was too heavy for my twisted neck to lift. I heard the sounds of heavy breathing and Leandra's voice, not screaming but firm with defiance: 'No.

No, no, no, NO!' I overcame the pain and lifted my head, eyes stinging and misted with sweat, to see what these demons planned for her. Dagan still held her arms behind her back, still pulled her matted hair sharply back. Zebul gripped her jaw brutally, his face thrust close to her wild eyes. Somehow, though her face was being squeezed grotesquely, she spat at him, her spittle finding its target. With his free hand, Zebul backhanded her, his jewelled rings tearing the corner of her eye and snapping her head to the side. A deep red welt covered half her face as she turned her head to level her eyes not at Zebul, but at me.

How I loved her then; how I willed for me to suffer in her place. I held her gaze, sensing her courage.

'Don't look at him!' screamed Zebul. 'Look at me, your lover. The one you really want.'

Leandra continued to look into my eyes, slowly lifted her gaze upwards, then deliberately looked back to me.

Ignoring the pain, I rolled my head and forced it upwards, raising my line of sight. I saw what she had seen: the eagle was silently circling, coming closer with each wide loop, its fierce head angled to observe.

Slowly, I looked back to Leandra.

Dagan spoke. 'Take her, brother. She's yours to take. Enjoy her now.'

Zebul looked at his brother and grinned. Still holding her twisted face, he tore swiftly at her tunic, baring her shoulder. Leandra gasped for breath, yet still somehow held me in her sight, her eyes now wide with alarm. Again Zebul tore, baring her young breasts. Anger and revulsion welled within me, dizzying in its intensity. With the hand that had struck her, Zebul was fumbling with his braccae, freeing his phallus, and though I could not see this indecency, my rage was fanned hotter and Leandra still held me with her eyes.

Then my anger found voice, but it was not mine. A single cry came with a familiar rush of air, and retribution visited Zebul. Huge talons tore his head, neck and shoulder, a mass of grey and brown crowning the king of evil. His bloodied head was pulled savagely backwards, and his brother screamed with terror, scrambling away as Zebul's flesh was clawed to the bone.

Then the eagle was gone. And so was Dagan. I did not see him run as the last of my strength had drained while my fury lanced out, and my head hung low. The next thing I knew was Leandra's gentle caress as she freed my bonds. I collapsed as my arms were released, the freedom bringing fresh pains to my shoulders. A thousand needles stung my entire body as the blood returned. Weakly, I embraced Leandra and wept, neither of us aware of her nakedness.

And what of Zebul? When we broke our long embrace he was gone. Only the gods knew how he survived the talons and the slashing beak, but the thick blood on the dry earth bore testament to the scars he would wear for the rest of his life.

NINE

When we had covered Leandra as best we could and staunched the bleeding where Zebul had hit her, we moved painfully away from the scene of the brothers' and our eagle's violence. Supporting each other carefully, we walked away from Munda towards the slopes of Titan, neither of us ready for the probing and questioning of our families. We came across a small stream and stooped to wash away the blood.

We hadn't spoken since the eagle's ferocious visit. Words were unnecessary; we cared for each other in the tending of our wounds. My shoulders and neck ached remorselessly, my head spun and my vision was blurred. I knew I could not walk any further and slumped against Leandra by the brook, burying my head in her hair.

A cough brought us back into the world and we both turned, fearing the return of Dagan or the nightmare of a torn and bleeding Zebul. But it was neither. A man, not ten strides away, watched us with small black eyes and an inquisitive look on his leathery face. His eyes were quick and sharp, filled with knowledge of the woodland and the mountains. He was of indecipherable age, as old as the mountains but as young as the babbling brook. He was not muscular, but lean and wiry, dressed in a homespun tunic and leggings with sturdy sandals held around his ankles with twine.

He said nothing, just watched. Too weary to move, we watched back.

Then he beckoned, and with protesting muscles we followed meekly as he leapt to his feet, making off along the course of the stream.

Each leaden step sent jabbing pains along my spine. Leandra, as ever driven by her mysterious inner force, gave encouragement by gently squeezing my arm.

The man hopped and trotted ahead like a forest sprite, frequently stopping to wait for us. It seemed a long way, though it was not, and eventually we saw our guide's homestead of stone and earth walls. It was shaped like an outsized beehive and built into the steep side of a hillock. It had been cleverly designed to conceal the mouth of a cave where the summer sun could not penetrate. To one side of the beehive building lay neat rows of legumes, root vegetables and a mass of plants, some of which I recognised as the herbs my mother sold at market and my father used in his secret baking.

But it was the woman standing at the low door who commanded the scene. She was taller than her man, long-legged and slim. Her lustrous flame-red hair, flecked with grey, was tied at the side and fell long in front of her shoulder. She was blessed with high, finely chiselled cheekbones and the ruddy, weathered complexion of those who live alongside nature. Her strong body was clothed simply in a knee-length tunic, which was loosely clasped with a woven tie that accentuated her shape. Pleasing wrinkles around her eyes revealed the woman's true age. She, too, watched us with sparkling, inquisitive eyes. I had seen her before, in the village, but only at a distance.

'Come.' Her voice was gentle and low-pitched, with a magical tone that would charm a wild cat. She held out both arms and we went to her as she drew us inside her home.

She sent her man to heat water and gestured for us to sit on the low couch that was draped with surprisingly luxurious cloth, richly woven with deep reds and regal dark blues. We obeyed gladly.

'Lady, we…' I began, but she put a slender finger to my lips while her other hand gently stroked Leandra's hair.

'There will be time for talk later,' she said. 'It is clear you have endured some ordeal, otherwise you would not have been brought here. You are most welcome, and you will recover in mind and body swiftly, for you are young and your spirits will be restored. I perceive that your worst injuries are not those that cause bruises and bleeding.'

I felt Leandra relax with a sigh. The woman continued to stroke her hair, looking from her eyes to mine. Then she rose in one easy movement and went to pour us water from a pitcher nearby. It was fresh and reviving.

For the first time I noticed the calming aroma and saw its source — a small copper burner containing herb flowers and oils, heated by candles. I looked around and was surprised by the quality of the simple but well-crafted furnishings. There were more tapestries suspended from rustic wooden beams to serve as room dividers, separating the inner cave, which no doubt housed their sleeping quarter. The floor was almost completely covered by a flax-woven rug. A large winter fireplace was surrounded by heavy metal pots and plain pottery dishes, none in use as cooking and eating were best enjoyed outside in our temperate land.

This was no hovel but a home, and we were glad to have been brought to it.

I must have slept, and I think Leandra did too, for we woke to the sound of the woman calling, 'Is it ready for them?' and a gruff, affirmative reply. She returned to the room, and we were led out and along a paved path to a place where the rock was cleft. A large stone slab lay on the ground and above it a clay shoot widened at the mouth; a looped rope hung next to it. Pungent woodsmoke hung heavily in the still air.

'Come,' she said, taking Leandra by the hand. Then she turned to me. 'Go with my husband and rest. We'll call you soon.' Intrigued, but not enough to linger when commanded to do otherwise, I went with the man and we sat in silence, looking out over the valley that lay between us and Munda, and beyond to where the land was flatter and undulated to the distant hills that stood between our village and Lacibis. Our eagle circled in the distance, hovering watchfully over the road that led to that town.

We heard the women's low talk, then the sound of splashing water and a squeal of delight that was unmistakably Leandra's. It was the sound of restored joy, and I hoped the magic would work for me, too, for my body ached and my head still throbbed. After what seemed an age, Leandra and the woman reappeared and the transformation was astonishing: Leandra, wrapped in a sheet of white linen, was aglow and smiling, her wet hair combed back, her skin pink and flushed. Though still marked by Zebul's blow, all of the dirt had been washed from her. She was fresh and happy again.

'Your turn,' she laughed. 'I think you're going to like this.'

The man led me to the outdoor contraption and indicated that I should remove my clothes. When I hesitated, he began tugging at my torn tunic, so I swiftly did as I was bid. Surprisingly, I felt no shame as I stood there naked. He pointed to the rope and demonstrated a tugging movement, and when I did this a delightful surge of warm water sprayed downwards over my head and shoulders, instantly freshening and cleansing my tired, aching body. He handed me a pottery flagon and bade me pour it over my head, and the oils and herbs filled my nostrils with their healing aromas and refreshed my skin as I rubbed. Then he took a sea sponge and though I tried to protest, he rubbed hard on my back and shoulders, while I washed the filth and congealed blood from my face as gently as I could. The wound on my cheek stung at my touch, but it still felt good to wash away Zebul's malevolence. I luxuriated in this new experience and marvelled at this man's ingenuity in contriving such a beneficial contraption.

Too soon the water's flow ceased. I tugged on the rope in mild annoyance and the old man laughed, handing me a linen sheet like the one Leandra had worn. I wrapped it around my waist and shook my hair, sending drips of oiled water over the man, who evidently shared my delight.

We slept in the dappled shade of an almond tree, its generous pink blossom bursting with the promise of bounty to come, the sounds of singing birds providing the music to soothe away our hurts. When I awoke, the sun was dropping softly behind the mountain, casting its slopes into shadow and bringing the first chill of night. A fire blazed invitingly in a stone hearth near the entrance of our new home, and in a blackened pot hooked to a tripod over the fire there simmered a stew of meats, vegetables and herbs. The man and the woman sat cross-legged nearby, facing each other and holding hands, their eyes closed in apparent worship of their idyllic surroundings. They were humming gently while small birds busied themselves nearby, feeding their noisy young. Bees droned as they hurried to use the last of the day.

I watched Leandra's face until she slowly awoke. Dreamily, she looked into my eyes and smiled. Our first kiss was tender, our lips drawn together in the most natural way. Her mouth was soft and warm and we held each other close. Too soon, she gently pushed me away, but only far enough to speak.

'Pito.' Her eyes were soft and alive. 'Oh, Pito, that was so nice. This is so nice.'

I had no words so I just smiled at her, willing her to feel my love.

Then she frowned. 'We forget our manners. Come, we must thank these kind people and return home. Our parents will be beside themselves.'

I had not even thought of this. I had thought of nothing but Leandra since waking, and her common sense brought a surge of disappointment. Holding hands, we went to find our rescuers.

The woman spoke without opening her eyes. 'There's no need to go. Melqart, your mother knows you are with us, though she does not know what has happened. Your parents know you are safe, and they are happy to let you stay here for as long as you wish. They know of our herbcraft, and they consider it to be part of your education.'

At this, still looking at Leandra, I raised an eyebrow in query. She nodded almost imperceptibly, and I gave her shoulders a gentle squeeze.

We talked long into the night, after the woman had treated our cuts and bruises with a strong-smelling unguent that she told us was made by bees but stung surprisingly little. The cut on my face looked worse than it was, though the scar would never fade.

The man's name was Reva, which meant 'chieftain' in the old tongue, though the woman told us this with something of a chuckle. 'He has no men at his command, but he is revered by a legion of grasshoppers and an army of ants as a great general!'

Reva said nothing to defend his honour, watching us as his wife spoke. Her name was Nabia, meaning 'otherworldly', as fitting a name as she could possibly have.

Nabia explained that both she and Reva were Kemeletoi, a peaceful, hard-working race whose ancestors had migrated from the northern isles countless ages ago. They worshipped the stars by night and nature by day, and rarely formed settlements in large numbers, choosing individuality, yet always with a wide range of skills that served the common good. In their constant need for open spaces, the ancients had spread across the whole of the Hispanic peninsula, never choosing rulers, driven by the law of nature rather than the laws of man, and always avoiding conflict and war. This was why they and their kin were so rarely seen in the busy villages and towns nearby.

'When you have something of value, others will always try to steal it,' Nabia explained. 'We choose to give what we have freely, though we are not slow to enter into trade for the things that we need with people we trust.'

'So, is your gift the plants that we have seen growing here?' Leandra enquired.

'Yes, and more.' With a wide sweep of her hands, Nabia indicated the land around their home with its vegetable fields and fruit trees. 'We have five children, some of them with mates and their own families, and all of them contributing something unique to mankind. In this way, the lifeforce grows ever stronger. It is only when people live too close together that greed and jealousy breed evil. As you have both witnessed.'

She spoke with total conviction, while Reva said little. Their lives were simple yet clearly rewarding — Nabia with her plants and Reva with his engineering skills. Reva had built their home many years ago, or rather, as Nabia put it, started building it — he never seemed to be satisfied and would often rebuild a wall or a room.

At dawn the next day, after Nabia had fussed and tutted over our cuts and bruises, she took us both by the hand to her gardens, where she showed us many of her herbs. Some looked delicate, as if they could be removed in one mouthful by a munching mule, while others were sturdy and tall with their fragrant leaves and exotic berries.

Covering the whole of a bank beside the cave was a carpet of five-petalled yellow flowers supported by a mass of dark green foliage. Nabia knelt, and tenderly picked one of the brilliant flowers.

'Have you ever seen a sad goat?' We looked at her, confused. 'We call this goat weed, and it brings a sense of well-being and calm, lifting the mood as it has in Munda for many years since your mother came to me in a time of sadness.'

This surprised me, as I could not recall my mother ever appearing to be depressed in any way. But then, perhaps this tiny flower had a power that lasted.

'This goat weed was also in the ointment which I have applied to your cuts,' she continued, 'and the mothers of your town have long used it for all those scrapes that you boys get into. But in truth I know this goat weed will cure all manner of illnesses, especially those diseases caused by infection and spread by unclean water or the filth of less civilised people. Many have laughed at our belief, but not those whom your mother has helped.'

Leandra was sitting amid the tiny flowers on the bank, dreamily running the flat of her hand over the plants and humming quietly to herself. Nabia watched her for a moment, then added, 'Now come and see the king of my little people.'

Again, she led us by the hand some twenty paces to a thicket of small trees, their branches tangling with each other, their trunks exuding a sticky, yellow and red gum. The trees did not appear to be kingly in any way, and I remarked on this to Nabia.

'This is myrrh,' she said, and reached into the pouch concealed inside her tunic. She pulled out a necklace of hardened resin nuggets, deep reds, oranges and yellows, threaded onto a leather thong. Striking ochre feathers discarded by a Golden Oriole were tied into the necklace, which she handed solemnly to Leandra.

'Wear this and you will feel the preserving power of myrrh in times of hurt or stress,' she commanded. 'It will feed the reserves of strength in your heart and in your mind. It has power to cool the body and the blood, and will grant you joy when there should be none, strength when your limbs fail you and knowledge when those around you are ignorant.'

'Thank you,' Leandra smiled, reaching to take the gift. She tied it around her neck.

'And you, Melqart, myrrh is your gift too.' She reached into the same pouch, withdrawing a single flame-red stone of hardened gum, drilled through and made into a pendant with the same leather cord. She tied it about my neck and made her vow. 'This will give you long life and your strength will feed others. You will see when all around you is darkness. You will be a beacon in the night, your enemies will be blinded by your light, and those that love you will be guided safely to the haven of truth.'

TEN

Reva left with the dawn, about his business somewhere on the mountain slopes. We soon discovered what that business was as he returned with two younger men, taller than he, with the same dark eyes and confident, powerful strides.

Nabia greeted them happily, embracing the tallest then running her fingers through his thick, dark hair and down his cheeks. 'This is our eldest son,' she said.

'My name is Drenan.' His voice was resonant and tuneful. 'And this is my friend, Turon.' The two men bowed to us.

'Turon saw what happened,' Drenan continued. 'He was hidden and was about to defend you when the eagle came.'

I silently wondered why he had not chosen to untie me after the brothers had run. I thought I knew. 'Do you know what became of Zebul and Dagan?'

Turon spat on the ground, indicating his disgust. 'I could not follow two. The elder one returned to Munda, but I know not what became of the younger. He deserved to die alone, but I do not think his wounds were fatal. We have never before seen a great eagle come near or behave in this way. You are truly honoured by the gods.'

Then Reva spoke, the first full sentence we had heard from him, though the impact did not dawn on me for some moments.

'You have been accused of murder.'

The words hung in the air. No one spoke or moved. Then I looked at Leandra and Nabia, then back to Reva. Drenan studied his feet and Turon gazed out over the forest towards Munda.

'What? How…' I began.

'Turon returned to Munda and found this boy Dagan by the spring, washing his guilt away along with the night's filth.' Reva also spat, as if this was a ritual of his people when talking of evil. 'Turon watched and followed him from a distance. He returned to his house and soon afterwards an older, hastily dressed man came out and hurried towards the Roman master's villa. Later in the day word was spread in the streets that you were being sought, with the girl, and it is believed that you ambushed and killed the boy's younger brother.'

'But that's ridiculous,' Leandra protested. We were both incredulous.

Reva gestured for us to be calm, then continued his report. I reached for Leandra's hand as he spoke. 'Turon has a pure heart, but what use is a lone voice among strangers? He came back to the hills to find Drenan, and both returned to Munda to watch and listen.'

'And our parents? What of them?' I asked, flushing from the shame of being accused.

Drenan spoke. 'I have met with Hann, whom I know and respect. He knows this is not the truth, and we will bring him to you. Even now, he is calming your mother, who will in turn reassure Leandra's parents. But you must choose whether to flee or trust Roman justice.'

'I trust the justice of truth,' I blurted, speaking with more courage than I felt. 'They only have to see Zebul's wounds to know they were not caused by a knife or arrow. We must find him.'

'I doubt you will,' said Reva. 'I have heard that he was seen heading north.'

'Then you know he's not dead!' I cried with relief.

'Those who have told me are not people you will see in the town. They will not speak for you,' Reva replied solemnly.

'But I will,' put in Turon.

We all turned to look at him. Like Drenan, he had the honest look of people of the land.

'I may not be believed, for I am of the wild folk,' he added. 'But I am not afraid to speak the truth to a Roman or any other foreigner. I will stand with you, as will Drenan. We have spoken of this and agreed.'

'Then we will return with all haste,' I said.

Nabia spent more time than was necessary tending to my cut, and fussed endlessly over Leandra's hair, oiling and combing it. She also applied potions to her face that gave her a remarkable serenity, dark-eyed and noble like a warrior queen.

Reva and the two men had slipped away without farewells.

Though I itched to face my accuser, the warm, windless day calmed us and we talked of what we had heard.

'Did you consider running?' Leandra half turned to me with a questioning look.

'Of course not. Did you?'

'No.' She smiled at me. 'We are of Munda, and Munda is in us. She is our roots and branches, and no matter how far we travel from her, she will always draw us back.'

Later, as woodsmoke mingled with the heady smells of baking bread and Nabia's cooking, my parents came to our woodland refuge. Led by Turon and Drenan, they broke into a run when they saw us. My mother's embrace was crushing, her eyes wet with tears of happiness, while my father gripped my shoulders in a gesture of pride and support.

Both then turned to Nabia, and their love of this dignified woman was evident. I was surprised to see both my mother and father make a sign of the spirits, bowing to Nabia as they touched their foreheads then lips to the tips of their fingers, then gesturing to her with open hands. She returned the formality. I had not seen this ancient greeting before, being more used to coarser Roman ways.

Reva appeared seemingly from nowhere, and my parents gave the same greeting. He had watched over their journey from afar, in the way of his people.

I hoped it would always be so for my family, for Leandra, and for myself.

Munda seemed noisy and crowded in comparison with our remote haven in the mountain woods. People went about their business with gusto and children swarmed in the streets, yelling and whooping in the excitement of their games and chases. My father led us towards Leandra's home as Turon and Drenan followed, carrying the packages of herbs and roots that Nabia had offered for my mother's preparations.

As we entered the village, I lowered my head and my gaze, feeling the awesome weight of accusations against me and expecting Dagan to appear with haughty slander and callous words. But he was nowhere to be seen, and there were no angry glares as we made our way to Leandra's home.

Leandra's mother greeted us at her door. A rounded, ruddy-faced woman of about my own mother's age, she clasped her daughter to her bosom while calling for her husband. Leandra's father, a squat and muscular man with thick forearms that would suit a blacksmith, beamed at all of us and kissed Leandra, who was instantly a little girl again, skittish and shy.

He looked at my father. 'Hann, we have been summoned to the procurator's villa, and we are to be there before the sun goes down.'

'That doesn't give us much time,' my father replied. 'Our two families must hastily prepare, and we will walk together to face down this dreadful charge.'

'No.' My voice was firm and surprisingly deep. There was a silence while everyone looked at me in amazement, apart from Turon who wore a knowing expression. 'I do not mean to be disobedient, but I believe this is a matter I must deal with alone. I will speak for Leandra.'

'You will do no such thing.' Leandra was indignant, and I saw anger flash in her eyes. 'I am accused too, and we will face our accuser together, though I agree that we should not be crowded and distracted by our families.'

'Now, just wait, and consider…' Leandra's father began, but he was cut short by my father.

'The boy may be right,' he said, raising a hand to bring calm. 'Both are no longer children and together are capable of defending themselves. But one of us must go as a second to vouch for them.'

'We will go,' said Turon, who was standing behind us with Drenan. My father looked at him, then at me.

I nodded. It was agreed.

The late afternoon sun had lost its burning power as we walked the thousand paces to the villa, yet still a film of sweat dampened my brow and my back. The other three seemed unaffected and strode purposefully on; perhaps fear was the source of my discomfort. We said little.

Procurator Lucius's guards must have been expecting us, for we were not challenged and were ushered through with a nod. Tall cypress trees cast shadows on the perimeter walls as we passed through the huge gates and trod the flat-stoned approach. Drenan and Turon paused to take in the magnificence of the solid building, or perhaps it was suspicion and dislike for the Roman way of taming nature, but our purpose returned and we walked abreast to the massive wooden doors, open in expectation of our arrival. Two leggy mules were tethered nearby — our accusers awaited us within.

We passed through the doors and entered a cool, open courtyard. Its floor of smoothed stone was embraced by high walls, with open archways on two storeys and climbing plants that bore bright orange blooms. Clay pots of various shapes and sizes held exotic flowers rarely seen in Munda. In the centre of the courtyard was an ancient olive tree, its girth thick with history and its branches low and sturdy.

We were so captivated by the splendour of this shaded courtyard that at first we did not notice Dagan and his father. They stood together in the far corner, partly obscured by the olive tree, whispering their lies and plans to each other. There was nobody else in the courtyard. Both men stopped their discussion as we entered and turned with black stares. Dagan, his look thunderous and his fists clenched, took an aggressive step towards us before Neran caught him by his cloak and pulled him back. We stood, impassive. I glanced at Leandra, expecting to see fear or revulsion in her, but she returned Dagan's glare with proud, flashing eyes.

'Gentlemen, welcome to my home.'

The rich tone of Lucius Marcellus's confident voice came from above, and we all turned to see him in one of the higher archways, his hands placed casually on the balcony wall. There were two others with him. We heard the rhythmic click of their metal-studded sandals on the stairs as they made for the courtyard. This, it seemed, was to be our judgement hall.

Small birds scattered as the three Romans entered. Lucius wore a white toga, lavishly braided at the edges. His short, dark hair was flecked with grey, giving him a look of authority and wisdom. The others were young and dressed in off-duty soldiers' tunics with thick leather belts and wrist guards. Both had a gladius short sword at their hip, the scabbards laced with gold, their ivory and gold handles revealing their bearers to be of high standing.

Neran stepped towards Lucius — too hastily, I thought. Lucius held up his hand and the authority of Rome halted the self-important advocate in his tracks, forcing him to choke back his premature accusations.

'Before I hear this complaint,' Lucius said calmly, 'we are honoured to have with us the sons of the sole consul in Rome, Gnaeus Pompeius Magnus, scourge of Spartacus and Mithridates, conqueror of the eastern provinces, and now consolidator of peace in Rome.'

We were all awed. Neran seemed to shrivel and stepped back to his son's side. I looked at these two men, neither many years older than me, and saw the pride and might of Rome in their eyes. Pompey's sons, here in a distant outpost in Hispania that until recently few in Rome had heard of.

Lucius gestured forward the older of the two, a tall, muscular youth with cropped black hair, dark eyes and a large, hooked Roman nose. 'Gnaeus Pompeius, eldest son of the Great Pompey and Mucia Tertia.'

Gnaeus gave only the slightest hint of a stiff bow in acknowledgement.

'His younger brother, Sextus Pompeius.' Lucius ushered forward the other youth and it was immediately apparent that Sextus was the livelier, more intelligent of the two as he smiled, bowed then winked at Leandra. His movements were quick and alert, a boyish grin splitting his handsome features. This melted any tinge of jealousy in me, and I knew that here was a kindred spirit. His hair was lighter and longer than his brother's, though not unkempt, and his blue eyes revealed a hunger for adventure.

'We are honoured to meet you,' he said, his voice young and respectful, despite the mischief in his demeanour. Gnaeus said nothing but gave his younger brother a disdainful look.

Smiling, Lucius then gestured to our group of four. 'These are Melqart and Leandra, who have come here with their two supporters...' He waited to hear the names of the two he had not met.

'I am Drenan, son of Reva and Nabia, and this is Turon, my friend. We are Kemeletoi.'

Dagan let out a low hiss, as if Drenan and Turon were reptiles. Lucius turned and appeared to study him for some moments until Dagan blushed and looked down.

'This is Dagan and his father, Neran, who came to me yesterday with serious claims about the murder of his youngest son, Zebul. We will hear from them first, and Melqart will answer. Gnaeus and Sextus will assist me in my judgement.'

Neran bustled forward, Dagan a step behind. I was terrified, but I had trusted in the truth. Neran was a bully, and so were his sons. Outnumber a bully as we had done, face up to him with dignity and honour, and he will seek the easiest escape.

He started well, I had to admit, and while he spoke I silently prayed that my friends would remain impassive, especially Leandra, for the truth was not aided by panicked desperation. Though his story was riddled with venom — he evidently believed we had actually murdered his son — we remained impassive and not once did we challenge his lies.

His case was that we, with other unnamed youths, had conspired to lead Zebul out into the country away from the town, and there turned upon him, using the same technique to end his life as we had used to capture and kill two wild boars. For motive, he alleged jealousy of Zebul's stature in the community, his breeding — at this he puffed out his chest and raised his head proudly — and undoubted physical prowess. In Leandra, he said, glowering at her, was the rage of a young woman whose desires for his son had been repeatedly spurned.

I felt Leandra stiffen, but she held her tongue.

His evidence, when prompted by Lucius, hinged entirely on Dagan, who had searched for his younger brother and stumbled upon signs of a struggle, some recently used bindings and bloodstains on the ground.

'But no body?' Lucius asked.

No body, Neran confirmed, because in their bloodlust these murderous youths — he waved an arm in the direction of all four of us — had disposed of his body in some dark forest ritual and concealed their crime well.

'And no witnesses, no confessions?' Lucius now looked directly at me. Still I waited, saying nothing. Neran seemed to deflate, sensing that his case was weak. He had evidently believed Dagan's account and in his passion had neglected to answer these simple questions in his own mind before delivering his complaint. I saw the sons of Pompey steal a glance at each other, as if silently mocking the paucity of Neran's accusations.

But Neran was saved from his faltering embarrassment as Lucius stood and faced our group. 'And you,' he said, pointing directly at me, 'where is your alibi? Where were you so late at night, and why are your parents not here to defend you?' His voice was commanding and the strength drained from my legs.

'Well, I … we…' I was stammering. I was making myself and my friends appear guilty. I had not expected to be questioned until I had explained the truth of what had happened, and I was wrong-footed.

Leandra touched my hand, and I drew from her strength and calmed myself. I found my voice and managed to explain that yes, I had seen Zebul, but I had also seen Dagan. I recounted the tale with all of its vile details, finding strength in the concentrated attention that the three Romans — and our accusers — gave me. There was a moment of silence when I finished, the wound on my face throbbing with the exertion of giving testimony.

Lucius spoke again. 'So you say that only you and Leandra were involved, and that you were attacked and taken out of the town by two older boys, Zebul and Dagan? Yet you have no witnesses, either.'

'I am a witness.' Turon spoke quietly, then, looking at Lucius, added, 'I saw what Neran's sons did, and there was no murder.'

Dagan and his father stepped forward, both protesting loudly that we were all liars and that no one should listen to any of the wild savages who lived in caves and were incapable of contributing anything to a civilised society like ours.

'Silence!' Lucius restored order. 'I will hear this man speak.'

Turon was impressive, not as an orator, but as a man of truth and inner strength. When he had recounted what he saw, and explained his actions, I knew that should I survive this day I had found a true friend. I thought that Lucius, Gnaeus and Sextus were equally impressed as they listened in silence.

But Dagan and Neran were not.

They protested and blustered, claiming that no Roman society should recognise an unwashed Kemeletoi, that I was a liar, a murderer and a thief, and that Leandra was no more than a cheap whore. Somehow, we managed to remain calm throughout this outburst, as did the Romans.

When all was quiet again, with nobody responding to Neran and Dagan, everyone in that room knew what Lucius's decision would be.

But he never gave it. Father and son just walked out. They knew they had not been believed, and summoning the last scraps of their shattered dignity, they left. Lucius did nothing to stop them.

ELEVEN

There was a long, heavy silence after Neran and Dagan left the courtyard. Even the birds nesting in the eaves overhanging the upper galleries were still after their long day of feeding hungry chicks. Enough had been said; it was a time to restore peace.

I studied my feet. The other three stood still, watching and waiting. I wasn't sure whether to leave quietly or make some kind of final statement before disappearing from this unfamiliar Roman court. But I was saved from making this decision.

Lucius motioned Sextus and Gnaeus to sit — they had stood rigidly throughout the hearing as we had — and called for wine and sweetmeats. 'And bring four more chairs!' he bellowed to the unseen servants who had obviously been awaiting such orders in the halls adjoining the courtyard. Without waiting for our reaction, he summoned all four of us forward.

'Enough time has been wasted by those two,' he said gruffly. 'I hope it is the last we see of them, but somehow I doubt it. However, we have matters of far greater importance to discuss…'

'Sir, we should leave,' I stammered.

'Why?' Lucius seemed to be playing with us, and I wished the others would speak to save my embarrassment. When servants brought the chairs, we sat around a low, rustic table on which was placed a jug of wine, a larger pitcher of water, and trays of various breads, nuts and honeyed cakes. I recognised my father's handiwork.

Lucius poured wine and motioned for us to eat, but it was Sextus who spoke, ignoring the cup placed before him.

'We need your help,' he said, looking into my eyes, then gazing at each of the others before returning to me with an engaging smile.

I was dumbfounded, but before any of us could find the words to ask how on earth two inexperienced young people and two mysterious mountain men could offer the might of Rome any assistance, Sextus continued while Gnaeus examined his fingernails and Lucius sipped his wine.

'We need your help to raise an army.'

Of course this was laughable, but we didn't laugh. As it turned out, the help needed was nothing so grand as wearing armour and fighting wars. We were, indeed, a very insignificant part of the politics of Hispania, and not even noticeable in the greater scheme of things beyond the sea to our south or the mountains to the north.

But as Sextus spoke, with occasional interjections by Gnaeus and Lucius, we began to see how Hispania could again have a part to play as the world clawed its way towards civilisation.

The problem was that the Roman way of bringing civilisation was with the sword. This might be nothing new to the warlike tribes in Gaul and the wet, windswept isles beyond, but to us the thought of armies, war and slavery was abhorrent.

But it was inevitable.

Sextus told us how Gaius Julius Caesar had swept northwards and subdued the savage hordes, as he put it, uniting them and absorbing the best fighting tribes into his legions, even creating new ones. There had been setbacks, especially when Caesar had been distracted by ill-advised expeditions to the island of the Britons, allowing the tribes of northern Gaul to rally under a chieftain called Vercingetorix.

Sextus could barely disguise his admiration for this Vercingetorix, and I suspected that, deep down, he harboured a niggling dislike for Caesar, despite the general's undoubted triumphs.

Sextus reported how Caesar had continued to have the news of his victories published in Rome, including the defeat of Vercingetorix, who was now held captive, presumably to be paraded in Rome along with the vast spoils of Caesar's campaigns. I tried to imagine the splendour of Rome and the pride of this courageous barbarian, and what it must be like to fight hand-to-hand with these garishly painted warriors and be thrust into combat when so massively outnumbered, as Caesar was.

Sextus continued to talk. His lively demeanour made him a natural orator; he was urgent and energetic when describing a military campaign, and softer and more menacing when speaking of the politics of Rome. He could win hearts and minds, and no doubt even the obedience of old Tanasus's donkey.

His father, Pompey, had immersed himself in the restoration of Rome following years of decline brought on by the self-interest of the Senate and Caesar's unyielding demands for funds in Gaul. Only now, with some of the gold and fresh slaves being sent to Rome — and Pompey's decision to get the job done as a dictator, though Sextus did not use that word, with the approval of the Senate — was Rome once again safe from the petty thieves and thugs who had terrorised the city. That Rome was great again was clearly down to Pompey — at least that was the impression we got from Sextus, confirmed with nodding approval from Lucius and Gnaeus.

'But there's a problem.' Sextus paused. None of us said anything but waited expectantly. Lucius straightened his tunic, while Gnaeus was impassive.

'My father does not trust Caesar. They have worked together for Rome before, but now Caesar lives by the sword and knows nothing of living in civilised order. If he marches south, it will be with swords loosened in their scabbards and his famous cavalry in the vanguard. Any that oppose him will feel the blades of his Tenth Legion, and as that will include our father, Gnaeus and I have no doubts that eventually he will face us, too. We must be prepared to make our stand.'

Leandra, perceptive as ever, interrupted, 'But why should Caesar's greed for Roman fame lead him here? What has our innocent country to do with the politics of your senators and dictators?'

I feared for her then. What right has a young girl to debate in the court of the rich and powerful? But the Romans paid her respect.

Lucius smiled at her. 'When Caesar was here before,' he said, 'he was a good general and did not crush the people of Hispania, wanting only the gold and iron he could extract where his men mined, and he became rich and fearless. He will not forget Hispania.'

He paused, took a draught of wine, and added, 'But neither will Pompey. He was here before Caesar, and I was with him on his second campaign when we defeated Sertorius. But in that war, we came to realise the formidable strengths of Hispania's tribes, their fearless defence of their territory, and above all, their right to live in peace in this land. Pompey knows this.'

I had to interrupt. 'But wasn't Sertorius a Roman?' I had paid rapt attention in my history lessons with both my tutor and my father.

Lucius nodded. 'Indeed he was. He trained the northern and eastern tribes well in Roman ways, though he never forced them to pay homage to Rome. Only to themselves, their families and their land. Hispanics understand only this, as I believe do most conquered people.'

'Which is why our father has sent us,' put in Gnaeus. He hadn't said much, and his words were clipped, to the point. 'I may be a soldier, but I also see the wider picture. Hispania must always remain independent from Empire builders because she is an Empire in her own right. An Empire made up of peaceful, independent tribes. We will help her remain thus.'

I did not believe Gnaeus. He and his father would always be vultures, just like this Julius Caesar who had apparently become much more warlike since the day he had come to Munda as Governor of Hispania. I bit my lip and remained silent.

However, I trusted Sextus.

Whatever it was that this triumvirate of foreigners wanted, I was their man. I felt their passion for our land, the excitement of what might be. I glanced sideways at Leandra, and beyond her to Turon and Drenan. They, too, seemed captivated, though it was hard to read the face of any Kemeletoi. But what did these Romans want of us?

The moment was shattered by the sudden entry of one of the guards we had seen at the gate. He was breathless, and behind him were my father and Leandra's, concern for our welfare written on their faces.

Before the guard could speak, Lucius had risen and was walking purposefully towards my father with his arms outstretched. 'Hann,' he said and embraced him. I was amazed. Was this a conspiracy? Had they spoken about me before? Of course they had, I realised, at the feast just a few days earlier. I had forgotten.

My father whispered to Lucius while Leandra and her father embraced. Then Lucius turned to me, apologetically. 'I am sorry, Melqart, but I had forgotten how young you are, such have been your exploits! Go now, and return tomorrow with your friends, and we will resume our conversation.'

'But I am not tired,' I protested.

'Well, by the gods, we are,' replied Sextus, with a chuckle. 'What we have to discuss can wait through the night. Sleep well, and we'll talk tomorrow with refreshed minds. And keep away from the girl — now that she's met a real man, she is not for you.'

Leandra stuck her tongue out at him, and we left arm in arm, Turon and Drenan following.

When I arrived home, I was advised that Dagan and Neran had left Munda, with a few possessions strapped to their mules. I was not sorry to hear it. I told my parents all that had passed, and they agreed to let Turon and Drenan stay with us. They slept in my mother's herbarium, among the plants they knew best.

We did not return to the villa the next day. Turon, Drenan and I had agreed to meet Leandra in the square near the spring as soon after dawn as we were allowed, but when we arrived there was no sign of her.

We called at her house. Her mother opened the door just enough to peek at us, and we could tell from her face that we were not going to see our beloved sprite that day.

'She is unwell, and you would do well to leave her be, young Melqart. I suspect you are nothing but trouble.' But her look was not black with anger, and I refused to let my hopes subside.

We pleaded with her to let Leandra come with us, for we felt weaker without her. But the woman was adamant and shut the door on our entreaties. Slowly, we walked away. Perhaps Leandra would find a means of escape.

Sextus and Gnaeus were at the western gate, mounted on the finest stallions I had ever seen, and tethered nearby were four more horses.

'Where is the girl? Does she pine for me in her bed?' Sextus was every bit his arrogant self, even so early. 'And you, Melqart, you look as if that eagle friend of yours has attacked you in the night. My, if you were my enemy, I would already be pouring the cup of celebration!'

I didn't know where my courage came from when I retorted, 'It's only that stick up your arse that keeps you upright, Roman!' Truth be told, I had heard the same jest when listening outside Tanasus's brewery when they were "checking" the ale.

'Ho ho, little boar warrior, so brave.' And he leaped down from his horse in one easy movement. 'Kindly remove it for me.'

We were eye to eye. Gnaeus was laughing. I stepped back. Suddenly Drenan was there in my place, a hand taller than Sextus, his muscled arm reaching downwards, gently squeezing the Roman's testicles. The look on Sextus's face was a joy, and I wished Leandra had been there to see it.

'I've castrated bigger rabbits,' growled Drenan.

'And I've decapitated bigger village idiots,' replied Sextus, and suddenly I could see the whole adventure, whatever it might be, crumbling before my eyes.

But Drenan just laughed and let go. 'Maybe we'll castrate and decapitate someone else today,' he said. 'So Romans have no fear or sense, eh?'

'Whoever said a Roman had sense?' Sextus retorted, and clapped Drenan's shoulder. 'Now you have let my manhood loose, there is no stopping my immortality!'

We all laughed.

'Come,' he said, 'we have much to see and much to do. Strap these provisions onto the spare mount, and we'll ride. Turon, you will lead us south through the passes that lead towards the coast.'

I felt proud riding around the edge of Munda and regretted that there were so few to see us. We rode down the overgrown trails and rocky roads that led towards the sea. The sun fought with the early morning clouds that rolled down the mountainside, allowing us clear views of the wooded slopes and plunging valleys. Exotic birds called and more than once we heard the rumbling protest of startled boar. My eagle circled to the east.

Turon led us, his mount sure-footed and confident under his control. Gnaeus and Sextus rode as if they knew no fear, for often the path would seem to take us towards a ravine edge, then veer away to safer footing. It was breathtaking country, filled with the sounds of a thousand birds and insects, yet we saw no man or horse, save us.

We rode until the sun was high. When a flat clearing came into view, Sextus whistled to Turon to rein in, as the spot was perfect for resting and eating. As Drenan and Turon unstrapped the provisions, Gnaeus, Sextus and I looked to the south, where we could see over the treetops to the blue ocean. It was a sight I had seen only once before, and it called to me — flat, vast and mysterious.

Sextus nudged me. 'I think it does the same for you as it does for me.'

I turned to him quizzically.

'I live for that sea,' he confessed. 'It cannot be controlled and it has such power, yet I cannot leave it alone. Sometimes I think I should live out there, not on this rocky, dusty ground.'

'Is that where we are going?' I asked, feeling my excitement rising.

'Not today, but believe me, we will. Have you ever been to the far shores?'

'To Africa? Of course not. Have you?'

'Once only. It's a strange land, with a vast desert and people who are either your lifelong friends or your deadliest enemies. My father believes it is important territory, but then, so does Caesar, and so does Rome.'

'I have heard it is not far,' I replied. 'We have seen people from there in our village, and we always welcome them and trade with them. Their jewels are bright, and their silver is magnificent, but not as good as their singing and dancing.'

'Then we'll go there one day, and dance until the gods applaud. But first, let me show you what it is that we ask of you.'

As we ate the rough bread, hard cheese and onions, and drank from skins of water, Sextus pointed south.

'That sea is important to every nation where a Roman has set foot. It is trade, and it is safety to any people who can build ships. It is the route the great Hannibal took when he shook Rome to its foundations, and whoever controls that trade, controls wealth and nations.' Then he pointed north. 'That way is Hispania, a vast country of wealth and a people who don't even know that they live in heaven on earth.'

'That's a matter of opinion,' laughed Drenan. 'Most of us are perfectly aware that the gods were smiling when they made Hispania.'

Sextus ignored the invitation to digress. 'So, I have much to learn about your people, but I fear I will not be able to spend enough time among you to enrich my soul.' He smiled at Drenan, who smiled back. 'But we are here because my father has asked us to open a route from the sea to Corduba. This route is so important, the future of your land may depend on it.'

Somehow I doubted that was true, but we listened intently.

'Corduba is strategic. It is the main city of the region, and as such it garrisons its own legion. But to supply it, we need the sea route and roads overland. We must make these passes easier to ride, so that supplies and even armies can move easily and swiftly inland.' He turned to me with an intent look that bordered on appreciation. 'Your maps have already confirmed that this route passes Munda, which I think will be an important fort for trade and a mustering point for reinforcements — if we should ever have need of them.'

I still wondered where I, and my friends, might fit into this.

'If you look, there is a mountain peak close to the shore, there.' Sextus was indicating the mountain that seemingly rose from the sea itself. Then he pointed to another ridge, then a mountain peak behind us, in the direction from which we had ridden.

'As we develop this road, there will be danger upon danger, for in every land there are always bandits, raiders and greedy men. The passes must be watched. So, too, must the sea, for the threat of invasion will either come from the people in Africa or from the northern tribes. We must watch for peace, as watching brings forewarning.'

What I could not grasp was why anyone would want to invade a land they knew nothing about, like ours.

Sextus answered my unspoken question. 'You remember how last night I said we needed your help to build an army?'

We all nodded.

'Well, my father wants new legions, both here and further north in Corduba. Your map showed a valley behind your village, vast and hidden, where we can build barracks and train an army.'

Turon gasped. 'I know this valley,' he said. 'You would place an army there?'

'Yes, but with the permission and the involvement of your people. We seek men like you to work with our generals to train such an army.'

Turon shook his head sadly. But before he could speak, Sextus turned to me.

'And we need men like you to be the watchers.' He pointed to the nearest peak. 'Do you think you could form a system of signals, so that what happens on the sea can be seen and understood in Munda and Lacibis, and maybe even in Corduba? Swiftly, so our Hispanic armies can respond?'

'Hispanic armies?' queried Drenan. 'Not Roman?'

Sextus would not be diverted. 'Answer me, Melqart. You have knowledge, from what I've heard, and you know how this can be done. Communication is the key to our safety, and yours.'

I looked at the peaks, one by one, and I saw that it could be done.

'Call me Pito,' I said as I nodded. 'I'd like to do that. But not without Turon, Drenan … and Leandra.'

Sextus grinned and slapped me on the back.

'I think you'll make a great watcher, Pito. But keep your eyes on the job, not on the ladies, understand?'

PART TWO: THE WATCHERS

TWELVE

49 BC

I fingered the myrrh stone at my chest as we positioned the second of our huge, burnished bronzes on Concha, the mountain that overlooked the Great Sea and the sacred Pillar; the lofty rock that guarded the western approaches. Drenan grunted as he, with Turon and five other muscular mountain youths, heaved the weighty metal sheet into position. It had taken the military's metallurgists almost half a year to make the six concave reflectors that we needed, and with ropes, horses and carts the soldiers had hauled them and the massive timber frames to the four summits between the coast and Munda.

The idea had come to me in a flash. At first we used swift horses to carry messages, but the new road was not yet near completion and despite the agility of these beautiful animals, which we had bought in Silniana's market, we lost too many on the steeper climbs. Then we tried fire and smoke but could not find a way to create a message other than 'something is happening'. But then I saw the flash of sunlight on a shield across the hidden valley where the new legion was training, and I understood.

We lashed the bronze to the frame and sought the sun, angling its reflected beam towards the bronze we had placed opposite on the peak of Fat Mountain. Immediately our light flashed back to us, and we knew we had covered a quarter of the distance back to Munda in less time than it takes to saddle a horse. We cheered, and I was relieved, flushed with the success of my first engineering task. Now all that remained was to position the giant bronzes, one on Concha and one on Titan, and two on each of the two peaks between, then devise the language of long and short flashes to be able to send almost instant messages from our coastal observation.

I thanked the gods that they had given us a land where the sun shone bright almost every day and shown us the way to harness it.

I didn't see Sextus again for two years. It didn't feel like two years, as I threw myself wholeheartedly into my commission, which I enjoyed so much that time flew by. But I thought of Sextus often as I rode the track through the mountains or sat by the night fire on Concha.

He took Dracus with him to Rome, convincing Lucius that such a battle-hardened warrior was essential to toughen his father's personal guard. Gnaeus went too, but it was the younger Roman who held a special part of me, the part that promised adventure and camaraderie. He sent me letters with florid openings:

I, Sextus Pompeius Pius, General, Captain of the Seas, Flayer of Barbarians, Bringer of Truth and Liberty, to my brother across the Great Sea, to Melqart, Light of Munda, First Eunuch of Hispania and he who is adored by the Goddess and her Vestals, Greetings and Salutations.

I wondered if the scribe had been able to keep a straight face as he wrote. Sextus maintained his mischievous turn of phrase with every letter that arrived. They always bore the consular seal which, though not guaranteeing delivery by the sleek warships that came to the bustling ports on the coast, carried enough authority for most of them to reach me, and subsequently gave me something of a reputation as being important to the senate in far-off Rome. If the legate who solemnly handed me the scrolls had known of the nonsense that Sextus wrote, he might not have treated me with such stiff-backed respect. After all, I was a mere youth in those days and not used to military formality, so I said little and tried to appear grim and important when in his rooms. I think it worked.

However, his letters were not all nonsense and giggling fancy — Sextus wrote to me of life in Rome, which was not the cradle of civilisation that other writers had led us to believe. Far from it. Ruffians and extortionists had made the city's streets and public places dangerous at night, and his father was having his 'greatness' questioned as he sought to restore law and order.

Those with the means to hire bodyguards from among the many retired gladiators and discharged legionaries were safe only as long as they were not outnumbered by plebeian gangs, but Sextus was clever enough to outwit any such attack. The same could not be said of Gnaeus, wrote Sextus, who on several occasions had found himself cornered and had relied on brute force to escape.

Sextus was at his best when writing of military campaigns, and it was through these letters that I learned of Gaius Julius Caesar's astonishing success in annexing Gaul to the growing Empire. So complete was this war against the northern tribes that Pompey, who had pulled off the unexpected manoeuvre of having himself appointed sole consul two years earlier, now feared that Caesar would seek a return to Rome, no doubt to claim power of similar proportions.

As the letters appeared, sometimes as frequently as ten days apart, sometimes every few months, the burden of Caesar's threat to the Pompey faction became more and more apparent. Sextus was clearly grappling with his conscience as he tried to shrug off the weight of this threat: it was his father's burden, not his, but at what point should a young man share the trials of his parents? Ultimately, although the young Roman found the politics intriguing, he allowed the worry to fall from his shoulders like the silk gowns he slipped off his adoring lovers.

Much of this went over my head. After all, I was a simple village boy with a man's job that seemed to be the simplest thing in the world to fulfil. It allowed me to wander the mountains with my small band of volunteers mounted on superb horses from across the sea, paid for with Pompey's gold. If we were to thank anyone for bringing prosperity to our mountain village, it was Sextus, though his father's riches that arrived under armed guard would turn the eyes of the greedy upon us too, for where there is gold there is evil. But in my innocence, I embraced all that Rome sent to us — I dressed in fine linen and wore gold armbands to signify my importance. But I did not crop my hair in the military style, preferring it long and free in the mountain winds. I was not a soldier and declined to ever carry a cumbersome shield or wear mail and armour.

I was grateful for the life that Sextus had given me, enthralled by his letters and excited by each consignment that arrived by land or sea.

But then he sent Dracus back to Munda, and this time he had a bite to match his bark.

Dracus arrived on one of those rare days when black clouds threw their angry flashes around Titan and driving rain swept across our valley. Most sheltered, but I sat with Leandra near the north gate and luxuriated in the cleansing rain.

The squat and grisly old soldier rode a fearsome warhorse at the head of a cavalry column and was clearly not amused by the rivulets of water that ran down his thick beard, penetrating cloak, leather and undergarments alike.

I recognised him immediately, despite the helmet crammed over his thick, curly hair. But at first he didn't recognise me, perhaps because the rain had flattened my hair, or more likely because I was never one of his favourites.

'You there, I seek Lucius Marcellus.' His voice was still like thunder. His small eyes, piercing and knowing, looked straight at me, ignoring Leandra.

'Sir, I respectfully enquire in whose name you seek the procurator…' My voice sounded more like that of a squeaking mouse than a man of sixteen years entrusted with a Roman commission, but Dracus coolly appraised me and did not laugh. Then he leaned forward in his saddle.

'Young Melqart? The baker's son? Well, well, you've grown. I hope you've learned how to use a sword…'

'Dracus,' I said, annoyed that I was no longer an anonymous youth. 'You've come back home. And no, I'm still useless at fighting, but now that you're here we're all safe.'

He uttered what might have passed as a laugh. 'In answer to your question, I've been sent here by Sextus to help Lucius whip all you girls and children into shape. Where can I find him — here or at his villa?'

A child? Was that how he saw me? I opened my mouth to speak, but it was Leandra who stepped forward and again I found myself awed by her courage. 'You will find Lucius Marcellus if you follow the track around the new town walls and beyond to his fortress on the hill.' She indicated the way. 'But if you come in peace as we all hope, you should detach your riders to the barracks —' she indicated the opposite direction — 'and they will be safe from all of us girls and children, as you put it.'

Leandra could be so eloquent. Dracus looked at her with surprise, for he was not used to women of strength, and there was fleeting respect in those stormy eyes. 'Perhaps I would have such as you to train,' he said, 'if you were not such a distraction to my men.' Several of the mounted soldiers laughed but were quickly silenced by Dracus, who detached all but two of the riders to find the barracks. He wheeled his warhorse, sending diamond droplets flying from its black mane, and the three rode to the procurator's villa.

'Somehow I don't think Munda will ever be the same again,' Leandra said ruefully.

'No,' I agreed, 'it won't. It seems we are some kind of focal point for Pompey's ambitions. Come on, let's get ourselves dry and see if my father has managed to keep the rain out of his bakery. I'm starving.'

We ran, hand in hand, through the downpour to find that my father had indeed managed to overcome the elements. The enticing smell of new bread refused to be dampened in the storm.

As soon as the rain had passed, Leandra came with me as we rode with fresh supplies to each of the mountaintop signalling stations. A dozen replacement watchers, as we had become known, rode with us, including my childhood friend and fellow conspirator, Lizard, who had sought me out to volunteer. The job suited him perfectly.

Turon and Drenan were waiting for us on Titan. The land all around us was refreshed and green again. The small brooks tumbled down the mountainside to feed Munda's springs, while the olive groves stretched below us, celebrating in the sunshine after the rejuvenating torrents.

We took our time visiting each of the stations, enjoying the night fires and roasted rabbit, washed down with skins of our local wine. We took three days to reach the coast and Concha, a distance that could easily be covered in a day now that the road was nearing completion. We rehearsed the signals using the bronzes, and I was pleased to see how adept the watchers had become at flashing short messages across such a great distance. The metal reflectors swung easily in their wooden frames and the messages were becoming more sophisticated as we increased the vocabulary to include numbers and words like "ships", "pirates", "traders" and "soldiers".

No bandits or thieves troubled us; we were too many, and well-armed. No doubt once the road was completed there would be selective raids, but for now the ruffians and outcasts confined themselves to the area around Lacibis and the road north to Corduba. We did see the eagle, soaring high in the bright post-storm sky, seemingly tracking our route south. 'The watcher of the watchers,' Turon remarked. And as we climbed laboriously towards our camp beneath the summit of Concha, we saw him settle on the northern slopes.

We greeted the watchers, who had hardened visibly during their week on Concha. They were bearded, tousle-haired, brown-skinned, muscular and dirty — for it was a long climb back from the brook where we had filled skins and refreshed our sweating bodies, and these men made the trek daily. We drank wine together and discussed the events of the last few days. There had only been traders, including smaller ships from our own coastline carrying leather and silverware.

Nothing much worth reporting — until the pirates came.

THIRTEEN

There was nothing unusual about the small fleet sailing from the east but then, as we watched, the ships turned as one towards the coastal settlement beneath Concha. We could make out the double bank of oars that rose and fell as the square sail of the leading ship dropped. The other three ships that followed were slightly smaller, with one row of oars each, but they easily held pace with the larger ship.

'They don't look like traders,' I said, turning to Drenan, whose eye was as sharp as our mountain eagle's. 'What do you see?'

'They are soldiers, or raiders.' Drenan narrowed his eyes and moved forward two paces. 'See, they have shields mounted next to each rower, which means these ships are not powered by slaves, but each warrior commands his own oar.'

'What else?' I had seen the knot of men in the bow of the lead ship, and the sun flashed from their spearheads.

'Not military,' Drenan said urgently. 'They are armoured haphazardly, most not at all. I do not recognise their banner — I think it's a wolf's head with bared teeth. These are definitely raiders.'

'Agreed?' I asked Turon. He nodded.

I turned back to Drenan. 'How many?'

He counted the oars. 'One hundred and fifty fighters, maybe twenty or thirty relief rowers, plus commanders.' The small settlement to which they were headed had no chance. There was no garrison there, just widely spaced homesteads around a market square, and a single stone dock where traders would barter for our olive oil, almonds, cheeses and cured meats and exchange gold, silver and goods from other places to the east and south.

'Test signal!' I ordered. The watchers easily swung the bronze to take the correct angle of the sun and aim it at the station on Fat Mountain, or 'Fat' as it had become known. A flash was returned from Fat immediately; the watchers there would be readying themselves to relay our signal. A piece of parchment was taken from its greased leather holder, identical to those at each station on the other peaks, and the watchers we had come to replace eagerly positioned themselves around the massive bronze.

'Confirmation received!' shouted the tallest, who looked as wild as any Kemeletoi but had actually been hand-picked by me over a jug of Tanasus's better ale in Munda. From the moment of the test signal, he had not taken his eyes off the distant peak of Fat, watching for the confirmation flags.

'Ready to send!' I barked, proud of the note of importance in my voice. I stole a glance at Leandra, but she was with Drenan, observing the approaching ships. 'Drenan? Anything more?'

'They're attacking, Pito. Closing on the dock. People are fleeing the settlement — they're definitely pirates and they don't look like they want to discuss the weather.'

'Send "pirates, two hundred, Concha coast". Now.'

The tall watcher consulted the code written on the parchment and yelled a series of commands that were simply 'on' or 'off' but spaced to allow short and long flashes. The whole message took less than a hundred heartbeats to send.

'Awaiting confirmation!' he called. We all watched for the flags on Fat, and when the signal came a few seconds later, we returned to Drenan to see what would happen. The signal was sent, and if everything worked properly, the garrison at Munda would know about the raid almost before it happened.

The return signal indicated that a company was coming, but even if all were mounted it would be dawn the next day before they arrived.

As the lead ship drove onto the shingle, and the other three ships followed, shipping oars as they ground onto the settlement's shore, Drenan and Turon were all for dashing down the mountain to fight the raiders. I restrained them.

'Think about it,' I said calmly. 'We can't get there in time to make a blind bit of difference, but if we watch from here we can give valuable information to our men when they arrive.'

'If they arrive,' said Drenan, 'and the pirates will be long gone by then.'

'It will be too late, I know, but they will arrive. Trust me.'

The pirates leapt from their ships, yelling and brandishing longswords and spears, most not even bothering to detach their shields from their positions on the ships. They knew they would find only peaceful villagers with just a few armed men as a token guard for the oil stores. There would be plenteous supplies to steal, maybe some treasure to unearth, and women to rape.

A steady stream of desperate refugees ran inland, and a small band of men had hurriedly snatched up weapons to make a stand near the port. They were quickly cut down. The pirates were lean and fit, muscles honed from hours of rowing, and our men were brave in their futile stand.

We could not make out much detail, but screams drifted upwards as the killing and raping continued. Leandra buried her head in her hands and wept. Drenan, Turon and I lay side by side, mainly guessing at the butchery that must be taking place, watching grimly as evil visited our precious coast.

Some reached the relative security of the trees and scrubland at the base of Concha, perhaps seeking out hiding places known since childhood. Most did not escape the blades and malicious intent of the pirates. One woman had concealed herself and her baby where oleander and fig provided a dense cover of foliage, but the baby must have cried out, for a group of raiders suddenly descended on the hiding place and she broke cover, running for her life with long strides, her child clutched to her breast. She was easily tripped with the butt of a spear, the baby tumbling out of her grasp. Her terrible wail reached us over the din of the raid as her precious baby was speared, then held aloft. The wail subsided to an awful keening as four of the men approached her, unbuckling their breeches.

Thankfully, Leandra was not watching, her head still in her hands, her tears dampening the sparse soil of the mountain ledge.

I thought the four pirates were intending to take the woman back to the settlement for the others to take their turn, but she bit the arm of the one who dragged her and he yelled in pain before slashing angrily at her throat with his sword. She was brave and did not deserve this — nobody did. I wept then, too.

Night fell and the pirates did not leave. As we continued to keep watch from Concha, I dared to hope that they would stay until the Munda detachment arrived. I wanted revenge and I know that every one of the watchers felt the same. We did not eat and few slept — except Turon, who could sleep anywhere at any time. We lit a fire on the side of the mountain that was well concealed from the settlement, while the pirates gorged themselves on slaughtered livestock and broke open most of the casks of wine that had lined the stone dock, ready for shipment to some wealthy Roman colony. Their music was tuneless and their raping barbarous. I hoped they would all die in the morning.

Before dawn we led our horses down the winding track to the road. We left three fresh watchers for a turn of duty, and the relieved team stayed with us, choosing not to go to their homes to rest. All of us, a dozen in all, were silent, angry and bent on revenge.

We heard the riders approach as the morning sun spread its gentle rose-glow in the east. I ordered the watchers to take cover at the side of the road and stood, my night cloak wrapped firmly around me, concealing the longsword at my side. I thought I would never be a soldier, but the blood coursing at my temple told me differently that morning.

The column halted abruptly as their leader spotted me in the shadowy dawn light. He rode ahead and the great black warhorse stopped just an arm's length from where I stood, its hot breath steaming from flared nostrils. I was glad to be on the same side as that beast.

It was Dracus, fully armoured and even more menacing than the last time I had seen him, just a few days before. His men were ordered, silent and equally menacing, including the new recruits who rode with them. He's still a very demanding trainer, I thought.

'Melqart of the watchers?' His voice was still a deep growl, but now there was a hint of respect.

I bowed slightly but held his eyes, as I considered myself at least his equal in all things except fighting.

'Your system is remarkable,' he conceded, 'but surely by now the enemy has fled?'

'On the contrary, they remain, and I think they will have sore heads and weakened limbs when they open their debauched eyes and see the riders of Munda bearing down on them.'

'Lead us to the nearest place where you can show me their deployment, and my men can rest while we plan how best to deal with these pirates.'

There was a wooded glade that gave cover and a commanding view of the settlement, and I led Dracus there. His men made little noise; there were about a hundred riders, nothing like a proper cohort. Though there were fewer of them than the pirates, they looked well armed with spears and longswords and wore the lighter leather armour to allow easier movement on horseback. Some, like Dracus, carried small bronze shields with pointed iron bosses that served as an additional weapon. Their helmets were iron caps with leather neck covers, but Dracus wore a cavalry officer's helmet with silver inlay and an ostentatious red mane.

Dracus dismounted, as did his men, and beckoned his second-in-command forward. 'This is Marcus, who came with me.' We clasped wrist to wrist, and I saw a man younger than Dracus but nonetheless battle-hardened.

'I am Melqart of the watchers,' I said.

'You watch, we'll fight,' he replied curtly, and I thought I could get to like him.

I summoned Drenan, whose broad shoulders and dignified stance always commanded respect. Dracus and Marcus looked him up and down.

'You're wasted playing girls' games with smoke and mirrors,' said Dracus, then laughed. 'Fancy a scrap?'

Normally, not I nor Drenan nor any of the watchers would want to fight in an army, but I thought Dracus knew from our demeanour that today we would indeed wish to help rid our land of these marauders.

The early light danced on the dawn sea, too beautiful a backdrop for the scenes of devastation we could now see much more closely. I pointed out the four pirate ships, which were pulled onto the shingle with only their wooden tillers in the gentle breakers. The smaller ships would need ten men to launch, the larger one twice that number. A thin column of smoke rose from a dying fire around which five men lay asleep, the guards not expecting any opposition that day.

Only one of the settlement homesteads had been burned, and it was obvious that the raiders were inside the best houses, sleeping off their overindulgence. The bodies of murdered men, women and children lay scattered indiscriminately around, torsos savagely gashed and limbs at impossible angles. Thin dogs hungrily chewed at fingers and feet. The birds were not singing.

Dracus showed no emotion, but he said, 'We have avenging to do, and we will do it cleanly and swiftly. But I want the leader alive. Can you describe him to me?'

I looked at Drenan. I didn't think any of us, however good our eyesight, could offer a description given the distance from our station to the settlement.

'Taller than the rest and long-haired — dark or black, I think.' Drenan put his hand on his upper arm. 'And he had gold armbands, I don't know how many, on both arms.'

'Right,' Dracus said, 'this will be a pincer movement. Marcus will ride with half the men in a sweep approaching the enemy from the east. The raiders will raise the alarm and either stand and fight or make for their ships. I will lead the rest in silent formation using the cover of those trees and that riverbed to ride through the surf, arriving at the ships, with luck, as that alarm is raised. When they see they outnumber Marcus's riders four to one, they are likely to stand and fight, but remember that these pirates fight women and children. They are cowards.

And there should be enough confusion to prevent the guards from firing the ships before we arrive. Any questions?'

'None,' said Marcus.

'Er, yes,' I said weakly. 'We have good horses and we want to ride with you.'

'Out of the question,' replied Dracus. 'You have no training and you are not protected with armour.'

'Sir,' put in Marcus, 'will you not need to leave men to guard the ships after they have been secured, while you attack the pirates from the rear?'

Dracus harrumphed. 'I suppose you are right. Melqart, bring three watchers and ride with me. The rest can guard the road at its narrowest point in case any escape northwards.'

Orders were swiftly given, and Marcus peeled off with fifty men riding away from the camp to begin their sweep. I went to my horse, my heart thumping, and I realised that the mare was as nervous as I was, probably because of the proximity of Dracus's nasty war stallion. I whispered in her ear, and she calmed. I pointed to my chosen three — Drenan, Turon and Leandra, the latter only because she would have come anyway. Dracus did not notice that one of our party was a girl, because she had her hair pinned beneath a woven hood and carried a sword at her hip. Besides, he was only thinking about the battle ahead.

We moved off on foot, leading our horses behind as much cover as possible, with the four Watchers bringing up the rear. I heaved when we passed the body of the young mother, her mouth twisted in anguish and hatred, her long hair matted with dried blood, a feast for the swarming flies. Her dead baby lay nearby, still with the spear through its tiny body. Drenan made his sign of the spirits, and we all touched our sword hilts, each hoping that the metal would find the hearts of the monsters who did this.

No one stirred in the settlement — the wine had done its work.

At a signal from Dracus, we mounted in the riverbed, which despite the recent rains contained only small pools of stagnant water that helped feed the cane, which now gave us cover.

Suddenly, at a signal I did not see or hear as we were in the rear, we were riding. My mare surged forward, following the mounts of the soldiers in front. We wheeled through the mouth of the river and through the surf towards the ships. I could just make out the guards stumbling to their feet in shock and terror as the drumming, splashing hooves bore down on them, and in the distance I saw a cloud of dust as Marcus and his men rode down on the settlement.

Our column did not check as it rode over the pirate guards. They stood no chance and all died in one swift cutting arc of the leading longswords; the man Dracus despatched lost his head, which flew upwards, spinning blood into the air.

Then the column was past the ships and, increasing its battle charge, crashed into the pirates who had formed up to face Marcus's fifty. Many threw down their weapons, for although there were more of them, they were on foot and attacked from two sides by fully armed cavalry who did not have hangovers and over-full bellies. They were shown no mercy. The ground drank more blood that morning.

This all happened so swiftly that the watchers — we had pulled our mounts to a halt next to the ships — did not notice the activity in the larger vessel. I saw movement out of the corner of my eye, and turned to see a tall, lithe man of about twenty-five years, stripped to the waist and standing at the poop of the ship. His appearance was wild, a scar running from ear to shoulder, his unruly hair shifting gently in the morning breeze. His eyes were an astonishing blue, but rimmed with black from the night's exertions, his face covered in black stubble. At his feet lay the crumpled form of a woman from the village, her dress ripped, revealing bruised breasts. Hair covered her face, but I knew this would be horribly bruised, too.

The pirate captain was strapping his sword belt to his waist, his cold blue eyes ignoring us and taking in the scenes in the settlement. Then he looked at the dead guards and the dying embers of the fire on the beach. Finally, he looked at the four of us, mounted, but clearly not soldiers.

Sore head or not, he leapt from the poop deck and ran lightly over the rowers' seats to the bow, where he looked down at us. He picked up a pail and threw it onto the sandy shingle at my horse's feet.

'You!' He pointed at me. 'Scoop up those embers and bring them to me.'

'And if I do not?' The hatred in me kept my voice steady.

'Then I will kill three of you and force the fourth to do what I so courteously ask.' At this he looked at Leandra. 'It will be the pretty boy that lives long enough to do my bidding.'

I glanced towards the settlement to see if Dracus and Marcus had finished their work, but I could see no sign that they had seen the pirate on the ship, and no one was detaching from the skirmish to come to our aid. I looked at the other watchers and realised that my hesitation was giving the pirate more confidence.

It was Turon who replied, surprising me because he was the silent type who spoke only when he had something important to say. And this was important.

'Which one of us will you kill first, turd king of the seas?' His voice was liquid gold and mesmerising. My bowels churned, and the strength drained from me.

'You, by your own choice, as you have more courage than these bird-brained lizards,' the pirate retorted. And with that, he hurdled the ship's storm structure and landed neatly on the shingle. The horses, startled, all stepped back. Turon spun from his saddle and somehow landed with his sword drawn, facing the pirate. I immediately moved to dismount, as did Leandra, but Drenan stopped us. 'You must leave him to deal with his enemy alone,' he said, sternly. 'It is his way and the way of our people.'

We froze, and I looked back to Turon and the pirate leader. Had Turon ever fought with a sword before? I realised I did not know. I had assumed the Kemeletoi were a peaceful people.

It didn't look good. The pirate drew a curved sword from a jewelled scabbard, the blade flashing as he went through a few practice strokes, while Turon stood motionless, his eyes closed and his sword tip pointed to the ground. This served to confuse the pirate, who, suspecting a trick, seemed to slow down. He bent his knees and held his sword high, ready to attack or defend.

Still Turon stood as still as a statue, yet the air around him seemed to crackle with energy. Suddenly his eyes snapped open, and his fierce gaze locked with that of the pirate. The pirate seemed to suddenly realise that his opponent had an energy about him unlike anything he had encountered before. So he lunged at Turon, who barely moved as the curved blade knifed past his arm. The pirate stepped back, and with a blood-curdling scream leaped with his sword high, ready to bring it down in a lethal, slashing movement. It hissed through the air, but such was the force the pirate had put behind it that he was off-balance and tumbled forward in a blur of arms and legs.

The pirate landed behind Turon and gathered himself to begin his next attack. But then he gasped and fell to his knees. A thin red line magically appeared across his chest, from his left shoulder to his right hip. The pirate looked down, his blue eyes widening. He dropped his sword and touched the wound, looking at his hand, which was now streaked with his own blood. Part of his intestine peeped out from the lower end of the great gash, and he knew he was dead.

Turon kicked the curved sword away and crouched in front of his kneeling enemy. 'It probably hurts,' he said quietly to the motionless man. 'I wish you felt as much pain as you have caused my kinsmen.'

I dismounted, still feeling weak, but able to stand next to the crouching Turon. The others joined us.

'We must finish him,' I said, drawing my dagger.

Drenan put a hand on my shoulder, restraining me. 'No. That is for Turon to decide.'

Still looking into the pirate's fading eyes, Turon spoke. 'Leave us. We have things to discuss.'

The others looked at me and I nodded. We lifted Leandra onto the ship to help the woman who had been defiled by the pirate leader, then Drenan and I walked slowly towards the settlement, where the company was clearing bodies and stripping weapons, armour and valuables from the dead raiders.

High on Concha, an eagle cried.

FOURTEEN

Turon's gentle words only served to make the pirate's agony linger. As gulls fought boisterously over the slain nearby, Turon whispered to the pirate as the sun grew hotter, promising him a swift death if he would reveal where his base was, how many more ships and men there were, what they were doing in the area, and any other details he could think of. The questions continued for an age. He waved Dracus away when the swarthy soldier demanded to join in the fun, as he put it. Turon's calm authority seemed to confuse the hardened veteran.

Eventually, without taking his eyes off the pirate, Turon took his dagger and the light went from the pleading blue eyes. Dracus stepped forward, protesting, but Turon ignored him.

Marcus selected one of the better buildings in which we could shelter from the sun while we — Dracus, Marcus and the four watchers — discussed what Turon had discovered and decided what to do about the village. Of the villagers who returned from hiding, none seemed to hold any authority; the attack had destroyed a community and stolen its life force. The only villager present in our conference was the woman found on the pirate ship, for she would not leave Leandra's side. Her name was Cassia and I could see that, despite the bruises, she was an attractive young woman of about nineteen or twenty years, her long hair lighter than most from these parts, with a high brow and strong cheekbones and chin. She was washed and refreshed, and I could see that Leandra had worked miracles with her damaged mind as well as her wounded body.

Dracus bridled at the presence of two women at what he considered his debriefing, but he was ignored by everyone, leaving him no choice but to get on with the business of the day. Two of the soldiers who had been assigned to cooking duties brought hams, olives, figs, and some wine. There was evidently enough to refresh the entire detachment — a bounty that had attracted the pirates in the first place.

It took an unnecessarily long time for Dracus to congratulate himself on his genius by summarising the skirmish as a great military victory. I suspected this was Roman sarcasm, but his report for Lucius Marcellus would, he said, show how the attack on far larger numbers had been precise enough that the new cavalry had lost just two men while annihilating the enemy. Marcus would share in the honours, and perhaps Turon, but then Dracus frowned at the mountain man and warned him that he had, potentially, disobeyed a senior Roman officer — an offence that carried the severest of penalties.

I leapt to my feet. 'Sir, he is not under your command. He is under mine.'

With a dismissive wave, Dracus continued, 'I am in command here, but whether your man is a hero or villain depends entirely on what he tells us now.'

Turon, who sat impassively with his chin resting on the hilt of his sword, the point anchored in the hard mud floor, lifted his head and looked first at Dracus and then deliberately at me. He made his report, with typical economy of words. The enemy force was a hotchpotch of condemned men and runaway slaves who had formed a community at Tingi on the Mauretanian coast to the south, where it had grown rich at the expense of the new Roman trading settlements on the Hispanic coastline. For many days they had been raiding the coast east of Gades, hiding their plunder after each raid.

'Two days ago they dared to attack Silniana,' Turon reported, 'but they left empty-handed because the Roman garrison there is well ordered and appeared too strong.'

'And what of their leader?' asked Dracus, sharply. 'Who was he and are there more raiders for us to defend against?'

'He was Tarkus, who learned his seafaring ways as a youth in Syracuse, wherever that may be.'

'Sicilia,' Dracus replied curtly. 'Go on…'

Turon had extracted so much information that at times during his measured, deliberate monologue I suspected he had filled in some gaps from his own imagination. But the report seemed sound: Sicilia raised both traders and pirates, the latter initially to protect the former as a kind of navy, but in recent years they'd taken the opportunity to raid cargoes destined for Rome. All fabulous material for Dracus to report to his superiors, through the procurator at Munda and all the correct channels to Pompey the Great himself. It wouldn't be news in Rome, but it would give great credit to our small community that seemed to be of rising importance to Pompey.

Abruptly, Turon stopped speaking, his pause tugging me back from my political reveries.

'Is that all?' Dracus's face showed no emotion, and Turon said nothing. 'Well,' said Dracus, 'your powers of interrogation are excellent in all aspects save one. You should have asked the most important question of all as a matter of priority before executing your prisoner.' He looked around the makeshift council. 'Does anyone here have any suggestions as to what that question might be?'

It was Leandra who spoke, again startling Dracus with her sharp mind. 'If I know Romans and their desire for anything that glistens like gold, I suspect that you would dearly like to know where the treasure is hidden, from here all along the coast to far-off Gades. Am I right?'

Dracus reddened. I could tell he was wrestling with his anger; he was, after all, a misogynist for whom women were either servants or playthings. But he controlled himself and said, 'You are right, and Turon here appears to be one piece of vital information short of a reprieve for his insubordination.'

Turon smiled. 'You will find, if you search the pirate's ship, a chest filled with coins and Hispanic gold. The bottom of that chest has a hidden compartment, and in it there is a map showing the locations of each hoard. These were not rich pickings, though you will find arms, jewels and trinkets to tickle your fancy.'

'A hero you are, then,' said Dracus begrudgingly, and he despatched Marcus to organise a search of the four ships.

Dracus was decisive as a commander should be. He left Marcus in charge of rebuilding the village community and gave him all the pirate treasure we had so far to fund the creation of a bigger, busier trading port. He gave the settlement the four ships and charged Marcus with finding crews and galley slaves to operate them. And, most surprisingly of all, he made Leandra deputy and assistant in all things except the military, a move that clearly delighted her as she would have stayed anyway. 'That should keep you out of my hair,' Dracus laughed, and I felt the inevitable pang of jealousy as I saw Marcus smile, too. Cassia, who was looking better with each hour that passed, beamed a glorious smile that made her even more beautiful, and I thought what a handsome team the three made for the new community.

The settlement had been called Umbra, which meant shadow, and clearly referred to the shadow of Concha that rose above it. Leandra immediately announced that a new community needed a new name, something far sunnier than 'shadow'. Her first suggestion was adopted without fuss, Dracus and Marcus having better things to do. From that day, the embryonic trading port was known as Apollacta, which meant Apollo's shore.

Marcus ordered the burial of the dead and despatched his fifty in teams of ten to take turns at digging firepits. Others were sent to round up livestock that had largely stampeded in all directions with the coming of fire and sword, and Dracus surprised me by ordering the sacrifice of a goat, a pig and a hen — to which god I wasn't certain. The whole ceremony seemed pointless, as there had been enough death to appease even the nastiest little deity, and Dracus did not have an ounce of reverence or mysticism in his aggressive, barrel-chested body.

Then, with his forearms dripping in animal blood, he announced that his fifty would ride to Silniana and beyond to check on the raided communities there. Of course, his real aim was to find the hidden treasure troves. He would then come back to regroup the whole company and return via the eastern coastal route around the mountains to Lacibis and Munda. That gave Marcus and the rest of us time to begin the restoration of Apollacta — and learn how to sail a galley.

Dracus returned after three days, time enough for some of the men to become adept at rowing in unison and harnessing the wind and currents. By the supper fires, the talk was of the sea, but Marcus had to remind his men that this was merely a short diversion and their duties lay inland.

Dracus had no time for our maritime frolics and ordered the entire company to be ready to depart at dawn the next day. At dusk we built a large fire and after dark pulled embers aside for cooking. We dined on bass, bream and fruits that grew in abundance along the coast. Leandra sat beside me, locking her arm in mine and laying her head on my shoulder.

'Pito,' she began, her voice husky with tiredness, 'when you return to Munda, will you find my parents and tell them what has happened, and that I have remained here?'

'Of course,' I replied, trying to disguise the disappointment I felt.

'My place is here, with Cassia and Turon.'

'Turon? But he is vital to our operation in the mountains!'

'Oh, nonsense, Pito. You have many good men, and besides, Turon feels an affinity with this place after, you know…' She left the sentence hanging, but I knew what she meant.

'If that's what he wants, then I suppose it makes sense. You will need his help while Marcus is not here. And of course we can all meet whenever Drenan and I return to Concha.'

'Not only that —' Leandra turned her face to mine, the firelight reflecting in her eyes — 'but we can supply the nearer two signalling stations with food and water and look after the men when they are off-duty.'

'Hmmm. I'm not so sure about that — all those strong, handsome men being cared for by you and Cassia. They'll spend too much time in Apollacta.'

'Or we might linger on the mountain top, just to see what comes up…'

I punched her playfully on the arm, and she responded by embracing me. We held each other tight. Perhaps I knew then that although our paths would cross, we were not to be together. Our Roman overlords had taken away our childhood by giving us serious tasks that demanded all of our time, and we had willingly taken on our separate roles, each creating a brave new life for ourselves.

The exquisite joy of that night — we did not sleep until just before dawn, when we lay exhausted from our tender loving — heralded our impending separation. I loved Leandra the way a man can love only once. For both of us it was our first time, and for me it was the moment I became a man destined to know so much sorrow. Even as dawn cast its first silver fingers across the slate sea, Leandra was gone about her business in the new trading port of Apollacta, and I was to ride with Dracus.

After I left, I could still feel her fingers on my chest and her long hair on my belly. I could still smell her skin and hear her soft moans of joy.

I decided that I would not follow the god who gave only to take away again, if I ever found out which one was responsible.

FIFTEEN

The journey along the coast to Flavia Malacita was easiest on horseback. Dracus and Marcus led us along the shoreline and, where the beaches were shallowest, through the surf where the horses whinnied and splashed in the cooling water. We arrived at dusk, having smelled the fish for which the port was famed for some miles. As we rode into the town, we could see the rows of wooden drying racks lined with silvery fish of all descriptions and hundreds of crates into which salted fish were being stacked for winter supplies and transport to inland communities.

There were three Roman triremes moored in the port, dwarfing the smaller ramshackle fishing boats, their single masts and neatly furled sails demonstrating Roman order in a working port that was untidy and malodorous. Armed guards played dice on the dock nearest to the three warships, and on their decks men were stripped to the waist, scrubbing, cleaning and repairing woodwork. I wondered what naval or military commander had come to Malacita and why, and said as much to Drenan. He shrugged his shoulders; Roman politics and commerce did not concern him.

Our noses covered against the pungent smell, we were ordered to dismount near the port and there we sought refreshment in the cool taverns that edged the docks while Dracus and Marcus went to find the garrison commander. In too short a time we were summoned to remount and, emerging from the dingy candlelit gloom of the tavern, I came face to face with Sextus.

Two years had added small crow's feet around his blue eyes, and there were frown lines on his forehead, but it was the same boyish, charming Sextus who flung his arms around me and whooped like a child.

'Pito! You young devil, what are you doing here? If you're looking for a woman, let me warn you that they all smell of fish in this hellhole.' He stepped back and looked me up and down. 'Well, well, if I didn't know better I'd think you've been exercising yourself fairly regularly — in a horizontal sort of way!' We both laughed, and for a moment I thought he might have guessed what Leandra and I had been doing not many hours earlier.

'Sextus. How good to see you.' We were holding each other at arm's length now, our hands on each other's shoulders. 'Where are you heading? We have much to talk about.'

'I'm coming with you,' he smiled. 'Dracus here may be a bit of an oaf, but he's a good man and I need to inspect the new legion at Munda, as well as others in this part of Hispania. Much has happened in Rome, and I do not have long, so we can talk as we journey.'

With that, he whistled to a small group of servants who stood near the Roman ships, and they brought a fine high-stepping grey, a stallion that would have fetched a ridiculous price in any of the world's markets.

Drenan and I flanked Sextus as we rode inland through the town, which appeared even more squalid further away from the port. The smell of fish turned to the fetid odours of sewage and rotting carcasses. It gave me pride to think how clean and pleasant our small mountain town was, not too far inland from here.

Our excitement at meeting Sextus so unexpectedly was muted by his news. Caesar had crossed the Rubicon. I had never heard of this insignificant river that apparently marked the boundary of everything Roman, and Sextus had to explain to us the implications of Caesar returning with his legions and daring to cross this boundary marker without the full approval and summons of the senate.

But the senate was still in full support of Pompey the Great, who in turn was acting unilaterally as sole consul in a time of military and political crisis. Caesar's action in crossing the Rubicon with his Thirteenth Legion was a direct attack on Pompey, and thus against Rome.

'The saddest thing,' Sextus went on, 'is that my father left Rome.'

I was stunned. 'But why would such a great commander flee, especially as the people would surely look to him, not to a usurper?'

'As I said in my letters, Rome is not as it used to be, my father is no longer the man that he was, and no one is sure who supports him and who supports Caesar. The people are fickle.'

Sextus told how he had travelled south to the heel of Italia with his father and those in the Senate who were loyal, or scared. Caesar had not marched on Rome immediately, choosing instead to shadow Pompey's fleeing army while showing mercy to the towns and garrisons that had surrendered to him. Meanwhile, Pompey had shown some of his organisational skills, assembling the fleet at Brundisium to take the Senate and Pompey's legions on board. They set sail for Greece as Caesar looked on impotently from beyond the barricades around the port, which had held firm throughout a short siege. Then Caesar had entered Rome, declared himself Dictator, and named Marcus Antonius as tribune before leading the Thirteenth north.

'They are already in Hispania, I suspect.' Sextus spoke in a low voice now in order not to alarm Dracus's men. 'In the north, he seeks to subdue my father's legions while they have no leader worth his salt, but I doubt he will march south. We have taken great care to keep our activities here a secret from the Senate and, hopefully, from Caesar. As soon as he is finished, if he is victorious, Caesar will march back to Greece to engage my father. And there, Pompey the Great will put a stop to all this nonsense once and for all.'

When we were far enough outside the town to benefit from fresher air, the order was given to make camp near the river, which was returning the bright, babbling mountain streams to the nearby sea with a good enough flow to serve our small force. Sextus, Drenan and I picked a spot beneath some tall cypress trees that had shed a soft carpet of pine needles, and with the other returning watchers, we laid out our sleeping blankets and set about building a fire for cooking and to ward off the night-time chill.

Sextus and I talked late into the night, occasionally slapping at persistent mosquitoes, chewing on pickled garlic bulbs (my mother's remedy for keeping the night's biting insects at bay) and quaffing probably far too much wine. He was impressed with my tale of the signalling system and how it had enabled us to surprise the pirates when they were at their most vulnerable.

'We need to be able to communicate quickly with the legions at Gades and Corduba,' he said with a serious look on his face. 'Also across the sea to our allies in Africa, though I doubt it's possible.' He gazed into the flames, their reflection playing across his thoughtful face. After a moment, he added, 'The fire's going out.'

I looked at the tall flames crackling around the dry brushwood. 'Sextus, you're losing it.'

He glanced at me. 'No, not that fire, Pito. The one in my heart.'

'What do you mean?'

'I mean my father expects me to give everything in the forthcoming fight against Caesar. Gnaeus, too, though he will bloody his swords on Caesar's legions with his last breath. I just don't think my heart is in it.'

'Then don't fight. Stay here with us. We're safe here, more or less, and we can live in peace while building a community where everyone lives together in harmony.'

'Dreamer,' he accused.

'And, if that isn't enough, we can explore by sea and set up new trading routes.'

His eyes lit up at this. Sextus had told me how he loved the sea and had spent many happy years as a child in Sicilia sailing with traders and pirates alike. I told him more about the pirate leader that Turon had killed.

'In my day,' he sighed, 'pirates were respectable. They could sail in and out of the great harbour at Syracuse in peace as long as they continued to offer protection to the local captains. All raiding and thieving was far away from the island — it was an unwritten rule — and the pirates and traders who had suffered so much under the evil governor Verres formed friendships. Now, from what you say, all that nobility seems to have gone. No pirate ship in the time I was there would have killed and raped like these. You did well to destroy them.'

'Actually,' I confessed, 'I sat on my arse throughout the whole thing, hoping that I wouldn't have to draw my sword. I'm useless at fighting. Always have been. Not like Turon — now he was impressive!'

'Well then, starting tomorrow, we shall have sword practice, just you and me — maybe with Dracus too if he's in the mood, which I doubt. We'll have you twirling, slashing and stabbing in no time.'

The next day we circled behind the low mountain range that led to Lacibis and Munda beyond, making good time. Late in the day, Dracus pulled aside to study the higher ground to our left. Sextus and I halted our horses next to him.

'Look over there. What do you see?' Dracus pointed to foothills of the mountain. Above the treeline there was nothing but rocky outcrops and thin, wispy grasses.

'There —' Dracus pointed — 'look to the right of that ruined fortress, amid the trees.'

Sextus and I peered, then I thought I saw movement and watched the spot carefully. Suddenly, from behind a well-wooded outcrop, a line of about ten horsemen appeared, riding at a trot parallel to our column.

Without taking his eyes off the horsemen, Dracus growled, 'They are watching us.'

'I could lead a detachment to investigate,' volunteered Sextus.

'No. We leave them be ... for now. But I want the guards doubled at our camp tonight.'

Dracus quickened the pace and we noticed that the ten riders did too, raising a dust cloud as they eased their mounts into a canter. Then, as we approached the place Dracus had chosen for our camp, we came upon a small farmstead. Or rather, what was left of a farmstead.

Blackened roof beams, still smouldering, were held only precariously by the ancient walls, though in the centre the entire roof had collapsed as fire had ravaged everything inside.

But it was the scene outside that was most sickening. A dozen sheep lay haphazardly in their pen, tangled entrails strewn across the bloodied ground. Their hind quarters appeared to have been savaged by a pack of vicious dogs. Flies swarmed on the stinking, gory feast.

Outside the pen lay goats and the remains of two cows, butchered and quartered where they fell. And beyond them, hands wrenched behind them and tied to posts, were a man and a woman of indeterminable age and two children, a boy and a girl, probably no more than eleven or twelve. As I turned to vomit, the memory of my own ordeal at the hands of Dagan and Zebul flashed back to me. The same method had been used to torture and murder this family.

The men were silent, sickened. Even the hardened soldiers, who had seen more than their share of death and destruction, were moved. Many vomited as I had.

'Listen!' It was Drenan, ears as sharp as his sight. 'Over there.' He pointed to a shack some fifty paces beyond the farm, probably a latrine that would hold no interest for country bandits who did not care where they defecated. Drenan dismounted and set off towards it, and I followed. As we approached, I could hear a low whimpering — surely another child, this one alive. Gently, Drenan pushed open the door. The smell that wafted over us confirmed it was a latrine, and as our eyes became accustomed to the dark interior and we heard the sound of weeping over the incessant buzz of flies, we saw a boy huddled in the corner. He was terrified, holding his arms out in front as if to feebly ward us off, his eyes tightly shut to deny everything he had seen, and would yet see.

Drenan made reassuring sounds and reached to take the boy by his hands. He recoiled, his eyes still tightly shut, and his whimpering became a scream. Drenan spoke again, gently, and the child opened his eyes. His mouth still open, the scream went hoarse. Drenan took him in his arms. We knew what he had witnessed.

Drenan carried the child away from the column while I went to find water, food and other essentials to give him a calm night. We chose a spot that was quiet save for the tuneless cicadas, and he was compliant as we cleaned him with fresh water from the skins we had brought. His tears stopped, and he ate hungrily as Drenan won him over.

'What's your name?'

The child eyed him warily, and eventually whispered a word that sounded rude to me.

Drenan smiled, turned to me and said, 'It means "Pipsqueak" in the old tongue.' He turned back to the child. 'How old are you?'

Pipsqueak held up seven fingers, then thoughtfully added an eighth.

'Well, you're a big lad, aren't you? And brave. Tell me what happened.' And Pipsqueak did, describing the bad people who had burnt his home, killed his family and stolen the lambs and the few coins his father had hidden. He said more, but clearly didn't understand what they had done to his mother and sister. He cried again, silently this time.

Later, Drenan asked, 'Did you notice anything unusual about the bad men so we can catch them?'

'They were all very bad,' said Pipsqueak, 'but the worst of them all only had one eye. He had a black cloth tied around his head to cover his horrid eyehole, but I saw it when he took the cloth off afterwards. He was very ugly. The others called him One-Eye.'

SIXTEEN

The bandit horsemen were nowhere to be seen that night, nor when we broke camp soon after dawn the next day. They must have seen us finding the evidence of their evil raid and made themselves scarce.

We reached Munda at the sun's zenith, the riders peeling off to their barracks. Sextus went with them, while Drenan and I took Pipsqueak straight to my parents' house. The greeting was noisy and warm as we embraced, my mother smothering me with embarrassing kisses and clucking over little Pipsqueak. She called for Pidray and Tallay, my sisters, who were equally noisy and demonstrative even though they were now young women. My little brother, Elvir, was quieter, watching Pipsqueak from behind my father. Two years older than the unfortunate orphan, he regarded him coolly, though not unkindly.

Drenan, too, was welcomed and we all sat in the shady courtyard drinking fresh fruit juices mixed with water and herbs that made me surprisingly light-headed. It had the same effect on Drenan and my sisters, making our chatter raucous. My mother brought pastries stuffed with olives and nuts, and for the children honey-soaked cakes. My father's home-baked bread was more delicious than I remembered when scooped into a bowl of new olive oil then dipped into spices. It was good to be home.

Pipsqueak sat with Elvir. They did not talk but somehow they communicated, and soon they were off exploring the things that boys explore. My mother took the opportunity to discuss the newcomer — she had watched him closely and I could see that her soul wept for him. She was the kind of person who would take in strays and waifs, and I knew she discerned pain there that needed healing. But she knew what could and could not be healed by her herbal potions. Pipsqueak needed inner healing, and that was the domain of the Kemeletoi.

'He can be a friend to Elvir,' my mother said hopefully, still expecting she could offer the boy a home. 'He needs a new life, and…'

'You know what he needs, my love,' said my father. 'But Elvir can go with him. He needs a break from his studies.'

My mother clearly hadn't thought of that. 'Oh, but Elvir is so young, so impressionable…'

'And who better than Nabia and Reva to make an impression? It will do him good to spend time away from Munda. That part of his education cannot be taught in Latin.'

I supported my father's theory, recalling how swift and complete had been my own healing and that of Leandra at the feet of the serene couple in the foothills. 'I will take him tomorrow if Drenan will come with me, and if we find Nabia and Reva agreeable to the idea.'

'Oh, they will agree,' put in Drenan, 'as will I. It is time I had a little brother, and maybe I can teach him some bad Roman ways.' My mother thumped him playfully and he responded by kissing her sweetly on both cheeks. 'I jest, earth mother. None can replace the Kemeletoi way of life and laughter.'

The next day, my father announced that we were all going to see Nabia and Reva. It was to be a family day out, which meant that it was late morning before we left as nothing could tempt Pidray and Tallay away from our house until they were both convinced that they were wearing the right clothes and the kohl around their eyes was just perfect. We travelled on foot with gifts and food loaded onto The Flying Poppy, which was drawn by the old family mule.

Elvir had found his tongue and spent much of the trip telling Pipsqueak about the fabulous adventure he was embarking upon. Pipsqueak, understandably, was uncertain what to expect, but he was happier than we had seen him thus far.

We were welcomed in the normal Kemeletoi fashion with food and wine. Drenan embraced his parents, then each of the children were kissed by Nabia and Reva. Nabia took special care to show warmth and love to Pipsqueak, as if she already knew of his ordeal, and he gazed into her eyes as if seeing his own mother there.

The boys and my sisters went off to explore, while the rest of us sat in the shade of a huge fig tree to talk. The conversation was chiefly of Pipsqueak, and it was made clear that this was to be his home for as long as it felt like his home, which could mean until he was an adult if necessary.

I was determined to return to my duties as soon as the sun rose the next day. I needed to laugh again, but even that was denied me. Because on the fourth night after the joy of knowing Leandra's loving, the darkness closed in around me.

I dreamed of a huge black eagle flying, it seemed, from the north, not floating serenely on thermals like our eagle, but surging menacingly with each fearsome beat of its heavy wings. Its talons dripped with blood that fed the crimson storm in the sky behind it. It flew straight at me, growing larger until I could see my own cowering image reflected in its fiery eyes.

But the bloodied talons did not rip my flesh. The eagle flew through me as if I did not exist, instead seizing cattle and people, all terrified and screaming. The eagle circled and returned, and this time it had three heads, each with a slashing beak that scythed through buildings, exposing helpless, weeping peasants who were all crushed and mangled by those brutal claws. I awoke, sweating and gasping for breath as the talons lunged for my precious family.

I did not sleep for two nights.

'Which hedge did you sleep under?' asked Sextus when I reported to the barracks. He was not his usual jocular self, but then neither was I. Sombrely, he announced that he was returning to his galleys and thence to Greece to resume the war against Caesar. That country, he was certain, was where hostilities would come to a head, because Pompey Magnus was there with eleven legions.

But the news closer to home was more worrying to me and only served to darken my mood. My dream troubled me. We had encountered pirates and this attack on an innocent community — could this One-Eye character be Zebul? — but something far more fearful was coming our way. I knew it, as sure as night follows day.

Dracus had led a small squad of riders north to seek out and destroy the bandits who had so cruelly savaged Pipsqueak's family, returning with a prisoner after pursuing One-Eye northwards. The fugitives had all escaped bar one, whose horse had stumbled, throwing his rider and making him easy to capture. Dracus, it turned out, was skilled in torture — this did not surprise me in the least — and he had enjoyed exacting revenge as the man screamed and then whimpered his way to a painful death.

He took a long time to die, Sextus took delight in telling me, and hovering in that dreamworld between consciousness and oblivion, the man had revealed how One-Eye had been sending secret reports to Caesar, for which he was paid well in gold and Roman sesterces. He had ridden north to meet his new paymaster and had escaped Dracus's riders with ease because he knew the country like the back of his hand.

The fact that Caesar had come this far south so swiftly was worrying news for Dracus and Sextus. Travelling fast with six hundred cavalry and no foot soldiers, he had already set up an outpost near Corduba and must surely know what Sextus and Gnaeus had been up to in Munda. And Marcus Varro, the general in charge of the garrison at Gades, had already sued for peace and offered his two legions to Caesar.

'Now the game is afoot,' said Sextus. 'Caesar will leave Spain because if he doesn't, my father will establish Greece, Asia and Africa as his own and will then surely crush Caesar and return to Rome.' He said this with a wistful look, as if thinking it would make it so. 'I will leave full reports with Lucius and the commanders here, and when Caesar leaves, you and your people can return to your primitive ways. You won't see me again until I come with my galleys to take you fishing in Sicilia, where the tuna fight like demons and the women —'

'Enough,' I interrupted, managing a chuckle. 'Go to your father and take your wars to another land. Come back here when it's over, without your sword.'

Sextus was proved right, but only in part. Caesar disappeared from Hispania as quickly as he had arrived, and there was no civil war in our country. For four years we were the forgotten land and peacefully built our communities into a heaven on earth.

Until hell visited us like an avenging eagle.

PART THREE: VOYAGE TO SICILIA

SEVENTEEN

45 BC

Titus Labienus stretched his muscular frame as he entered the command tent outside the city of Corduba, undid his sword belt and called for wine. I thought it rather rude of him, but he was held in high regard by Gnaeus and Sextus because he knew Caesar so well.

The man's stiffness and painful movement, brought on by his years as Caesar's legate in the rain and chill of Gaul, had gone with our benevolent climate. He had defected to the Pompey camp after Caesar crossed the Rubicon and now he was here, ready to pledge his sword to any who opposed Caesar.

He collapsed into one of the chairs arranged around the relief map of Corduba, took a long draught of the wine that had been placed before him and belched.

'Gentlemen,' he said, his voice like mountain thunder, 'Caesar is here.'

Gnaeus sat bolt upright. 'But that means he has crossed into Hispania in just one month. Impossible.'

'You don't know the man. You think you do, but you don't.' Labienus paused and drank some more, a few drops of the blood-red wine dripping onto his beard. He wiped his mouth.

'And how many with him?' asked Sextus, who seemed the least afraid.

'My scouts report eight legions, and perhaps eight thousand cavalry. They have force marched and come almost to Corduba like a storm.'

'But we still outnumber them,' said Sextus, looking nonchalantly at his well-manicured fingernails. 'We can take him and end these years of misery.'

'We outnumbered him at Thapsus,' scowled Labienus, clearly still bitter about a previous military defeat. 'And at Pharsalus where it all began. Why should this be different?'

'Because we can choose the ground.' Gnaeus was defiant, more so than Sextus.

'I pray that you are right. And I suppose you choose Munda?'

'It is the best fortress in the whole of Hispania Ulterior, and that is where the rest of our legions are — or will be in a few days — ready and well-armed.'

'You are right to choose Munda.' Labienus looked fiercely around the table where the other generals sat. I was there as a representative of the watchers, though I would not dare to speak. 'But first you must offer resistance here, to halt his march and take his attention away from Gades and the ports on the coast. Make him stop here, concentrating on Corduba and this region, then tempt him to your own ground.'

'Harry him,' put in Sextus, his interest aroused, 'like a swarm of annoying wasps.'

'Indeed, but do not offer full battle. Hold the towns and if you withdraw, do so with apparent reluctance and lead him mile by mile towards the south.' I thought Labienus liked Sextus the best of all the commanders, despite his youth. Then he looked at Gnaeus again. 'Have you chosen your men well? Who are they, and how have you trained them?'

Gnaeus, as senior general, answered dismissively. 'You will find our men efficient and quite capable of defeating Caesar at long last.' He turned to his clerk, who sat behind him with several wax tablets containing all the information that his general might need. They whispered together for a few moments, the clerk referring to his notes, then Gnaeus turned back to Labienus. 'We have thirteen legions including yours, and six thousand cavalry commanded personally by Dracus, who trained the new Hispanic legion at Munda, which will also be placed under your command. These men are true warriors and will acquit themselves well.'

Labienus was thoughtful. 'We outnumber Caesar almost two to one, but his cavalry is celebrated and more numerous than ours. How crucial will this prove, I wonder?'

'If we lure him to Munda, we can negate his cavalry,' replied Gnaeus. 'Providing we bring him almost to the fortress and force him to cross the river, his cavalry will be unable to charge our lines.'

'And our horse?' Labienus raised an eyebrow.

'Equally useless in such terrain, except for bolstering the lines and passing signals at the height of battle,' replied Gnaeus. 'Therefore we must fight on our terms, looking down upon a smaller army if we choose our positions well and hold them. Tell me, Titus, will Caesar have his machines of mass destruction?'

'Yes, especially scorpios.'

'But the terrain we choose will be uneven, and in any case he will have to shoot these silverfish uphill…'

'If that is the case, they will be mostly ineffective.'

Gnaeus turned to Sextus with his haughty elder brother look. 'Then maybe this time we will end the usurper's fruitless campaign once and for all. Now all we have to do is lead Caesar by the nose all the way back to Munda.'

Sextus glanced at me. 'Any ideas, Pito?'

'Of course,' I replied, and remembering my lowly rank among these generals, I added, 'sir.'

But the truth was, I didn't have any ideas. I was hoping that if I thought long and hard enough, something would occur to me.

Sextus suggested that we retire to his private quarters. There he called for his attendants, among them two attractive dark-haired young women who were very adept at massage techniques and, on account of their varied abilities and striking looks, were treated with considerable respect and not a little jollity. Sextus knew how to enjoy the good things in life.

'You and I need to relax,' he said, and held his arms out wide as his attendants disrobed him. A fine-boned youth pulled at my belt, and I thought about protesting until I realised that Sextus was already completely naked. I allowed my clothes to be taken from me, only slightly embarrassed by the faint odour the humid air had given me, and clumsily lay face down on the couch that Sextus indicated to me. The male attendants left the two lissom young women to attend to our needs.

'The young lady whose navel is now level with your eyes is Nahalia, in case you were wondering,' Sextus murmured, as the other woman's long fingers began kneading his shoulders. Nahalia giggled as I raised my head to look into her lovely brown eyes, darkened with kohl. They sparkled with mischief. I smiled weakly at her and she bent to plant a warm, wet kiss on my lips. I tasted olive mixed with mint, and silently thanked the gods that I lay on that part of me that responded immediately and uncomfortably. She pushed my head down and went to work on my neck and shoulders, which she first laced with aromatic oil.

'And this is her sister Bashira,' continued Sextus, his words punctuated by stabs of pain and ecstasy. 'I rescued them from an evil Egyptian who treated them like slaves.'

At some stage I slept, but not before I had discovered, in a half dream, pleasures that hitherto had been both unimagined and unexpected. When I woke, the sun was casting its last liquid rays through the muslin tent folds and the young women had gone, leaving me and Sextus covered with crisp sheets. My body felt free and clean, every knot undone. My skin tingled with a sheen of almond and olive oils.

Sextus snored gently. I woke him when I fell over trying to put on my clothes, still in the feeble state induced by the ministrations of a Levantine angel. We dressed and he poured wine, preferring not to summon his attendants. Since we were alone, we talked.

Sextus was concerned. 'Our forces are too fragmented and spread out to be able to present Caesar with a united front,' he explained. 'Gnaeus charges off on his own missions, Labienus keeps himself to himself, and we are too far north to know what is happening at the garrisons of Munda and Malacita. We must be able to keep each part of our army informed of Caesar's movements and our plan to halt him.'

I hoped his words were not a criticism of the watchers. Our signalling system now worked between Lacibis and Munda with a vastly increased vocabulary of codes, as well as from there on to the coast, and in each direction new fast ships — liburnians — could reach Malacita in a few hours and the Pillars of Hercules in less than a day. However, we had lost the port of Gades and the last message from there had not been well received by Gnaeus.

I replied confidently. 'The problem lies only between Corduba and Lacibis, and that can only be overcome with fast horses and stabling stages along the way.'

'Agreed,' said Sextus. 'But it must work smoothly, and the staging posts must also be manned sufficiently to enable us to fight a rearguard action if needed when Caesar follows.'

Sextus promised me men and horses to organise the staging posts. We would need three between Corduba and Lacibis, and though he was reluctant to reduce the strength of his cavalry, he told me to take my pick of his horses and augment them with any of the fine animals that we could buy from the markets where superb beasts were sold by the African traders who always sniffed out the Roman need for fast, sure-footed animals. They would sell to Caesar or to a Pompeian, so it was best that every available horse was secured with our gold to deny the enemy before he arrived.

He also gave me Nahalia. But while he was explaining that she was strictly on loan as the sisters were inseparable, there was a commotion outside.

Gnaeus had returned from one of his excursions. New green grass was thrusting aside the dead brown legacy of a hot summer as Gnaeus and his men rode slowly and wearily into the Corduba military camp. The mounted cohort was dejected, with the men slumped in their saddles and the horses' heads hanging low with exhaustion. Four hundred had ridden out with anger and purpose, and half that number limped back.

Sextus lost no time in commanding that refreshments be brought to his tent and sent a slave scurrying into the town to find Labienus. Gnaeus slid from his horse, handing the reins to an attendant, then strode into the tent. I followed.

Gnaeus took a pitcher of cold, clean water from Bashira and poured it over his head without removing his leathers, shaking drops from his lank hair and leaving puddles to soak into the ornate carpet. Bashira frowned but knew better than to protest in front of the senior Pompeian brother.

'Now bring me wine,' Gnaeus barked to nobody in particular, 'and make sure my men are given food and ale.' Bashira bowed and backed out of the tent to obey.

Labienus came into the tent in obvious haste and greeted Gnaeus, who then dropped into one of the sturdy wooden chairs. Bashira returned with wine and rustic clay goblets. Not knowing what to do, I took these from her and poured, handing each man their draught.

'Well, brother,' said Sextus, 'I trust that the enemy suffered worse than you?'

Gnaeus gave a half chuckle. 'Of course, but we were outnumbered. Not an hour's ride from here we came across Caesar's scout group and surprised them, but they retreated in orderly fashion just out of range of our archers.'

'Let me guess,' put in Labienus, 'they led you right into a trap?'

'Hardly. But we did meet Caesar's cavalry on ground not of our choosing — at least some of them, protecting foragers who are commandeering land, farmsteads and livestock. We did not expect them this far south, but of the main army we have seen nothing.'

'So you offered them battle?' I was not certain whether Labienus said this with respect or disdain.

'Naturally. Wouldn't you?'

'Probably. Your father delayed too long. Perhaps you are headstrong where he was cautious.' Gnaeus grimaced at this provocation but was too weary to challenge the experienced campaigner.

'Our first charge divided the enemy cavalry, but they regrouped and hit us from two sides.' Gnaeus sighed and drank from his goblet. 'By sheer luck they cornered some of our men against a rock face while the rest of us took to higher ground to make our next charge easier. I'm ashamed to say these trapped men surrendered, I expect because they faced fellow Romans rather than barbarian warriors. It was a mistake they could only make once.'

'What do you mean?' Sextus was alarmed at this.

'I mean, brother, that they all died in that place. They were disarmed and forced to kneel. By the time my remaining men had turned to make a second attack, the captured men were being executed in threes.' Gnaeus paused and sighed again. 'From where we stood it appeared that one of the scouts was commanding the executions. Their heads were being hacked off, not many of them cleanly, either.'

Labienus looked concerned. 'Then either Caesar has become uncharacteristically cruel, or his men are out of control. Knowing Caesar as I do, I doubt that his men would behave in this way towards fellow Romans unless they had been ordered to spare none.'

'Can you describe this scout leader?' asked Sextus.

'Black cloak, tall, thin, with a patch over one eye.'

His words hit me like a hammer blow. It could only be Zebul, the one-eyed bandit. We knew he had been offering his services to Caesar's faction, but how had he risen to a position of authority so quickly? He must have promised much to be given this trust — perhaps his local knowledge combined with his scheming mind had appealed to the enemy.

While I puzzled over this, the others were talking.

'The men fought furiously after witnessing this cruelty,' Gnaeus was saying, 'and though we killed and wounded both men and horses, we were taking too many casualties, so I ordered the retreat.'

'Did Caesar's men not follow and try to rout you?' asked Labienus.

'No. As soon as we withdrew, so did they. I don't think they were looking to finish it.'

Labienus continued with his questions. 'Did you observe what Caesar's men did next?'

Gnaeus looked at him coldly. For a moment he struggled with his emotions, then went on, 'When I realised we were not being pursued, I sent two men to observe. Their report was exemplary. The enemy moved off back the way they had come, so we were able to return to bury our dead. They could have given chase, but that would have brought them closer to Corduba, and I do not think Caesar wants to engage with our legions until he has established himself with supplies and fresh men. In the meantime, he clearly wants to enrage us.'

At last Labienus smiled, easing the tension. 'You did well,' he said to Gnaeus, 'and I think you are right. It will be harder than I thought to bring him south.'□

EIGHTEEN

It was Caesar who started the cruelty, but Labienus and Gnaeus heightened matters like the tensioned ratchet of a ballista. Every sortie resulted in more executions, which soon turned into merciless tortures, each side seeking to outdo the other with hideous crucifixions and mutilations.

The watchers heard of these dreadful things with the daily reports that were to be passed to Dracus and Lucius at Munda, and beyond to the coastal legions. It all seemed so pointless to me, and if the penalty had not been death I would have taken Nahalia to Leandra at Apollacta and the three of us could have sailed away to a new life far away from this death and destruction.

My friends were loyal, always calm and confident in their duties, but I could tell they hated the intrusion of warfare in our idyllic mountains. With each week that passed, the blackness crept ever closer until it lay upon the whole region like a blanket of evil. It suppressed the songs of the birds, quietened the crickets, and even the citrus fruit seemed to rot on the trees. There was no sign of our eagle, or any eagle: they were as disgusted as the Kemeletoi mountain people, who melted away to the extremities of the more inhospitable mountains to the west.

It was the beginning of March when I was making one of my regular visits to Corduba that I came face to face with the great Caesar. I was with Sextus in his tent, discussing the movements of the various legions under the command of Gnaeus, and wondering whether the joy of our friendship and the spark of life would ever return. Even Nahalia and Bashira were restrained and unhappy.

A messenger entered and bowed. 'Sir,' he said to Sextus, 'the generals Gnaeus and Labienus request your attendance. They are at the north gate.'

'Tell them I will be there immediately,' Sextus replied, and then added, 'Tell them also that I bring Melqart of the watchers.' The messenger saluted, his fist thumping to his chest, and left.

I walked with Sextus to the gates — he would hurry for nobody — and we arrived to find horses being saddled for ten men. Labienus and Gnaeus were huddled in conversation, but as we arrived Labienus beckoned to us to join them. Both wore polished armour and carried their plumed helmets, but Sextus and I wore simple tunics with short swords at our sides.

'Look at the base of that hill over there,' he said, pointing. In open ground was a line of horsemen. They were stationary, waiting for something.

'How long have they been there?' asked Sextus, squinting in the direction of the enemy.

'Quite long enough,' replied Labienus. 'They seem to want to talk. We should follow standard procedure and ride halfway towards them.'

'We'll waste no time in finding out what Caesar has in mind,' said Gnaeus, who seemed unduly excited. 'Let's go!'

I hesitated while the others mounted, and Sextus, his grey skittishly pounding the dry earth, nodded to the one remaining horse. 'Pito, what are you waiting for?' he asked. 'This is your chance to look into the eyes of the enemy. Come on…'

I mounted and we rode at a gallop towards the strangers on the hillside. Gnaeus raised his arm and we stopped together in a cloud of dust. I noticed a small snake slithering to the safety of a nearby rock.

We, too, ordered our horses in line abreast to wait for a response, and almost immediately one horseman separated from the others and rode towards us, his black cloak billowing behind him, his spear held in his right hand pointed to the earth in a small gesture of respite. With a sharp tug at the reins he brought his horse to a standstill, the animal's nostrils flaring in anger and disgust, and with one good eye Zebul fixed his gaze on each of us in turn.

Before I realised what I was doing, I half drew my sword as if I could break a truce and best the evil One-Eye in hand-to-hand combat. Sextus reached across and gently laid a hand on my arm.

'You can kill him any time but now,' he muttered through clenched teeth, 'and maybe I will help you. But for now, we play this by the rules.' I let my sword drop back into its scabbard, not taking my eyes off the man who had tried to break me, had tried to rape Leandra, and had become so evil that he and his men could butcher Pipsqueak's family without a second thought. But here he was, no longer a youth, his torn flesh healed into ugly scars, made all the more hideous by his black clothing and snarling demeanour.

He spoke, his voice guttural, deeper than the voice of the youth who had trussed me like a sacrificial chicken six years ago. 'I see you, Melqart, and you are still a child in the presence of men.'

I nudged my horse forward two paces and surprised myself with my control. 'You only see me with one eye, Zebul the woman-beater, and next time you will lose that too.'

Sextus and Gnaeus laughed, Labienus said nothing, and Zebul looked at me with a familiar hatred.

'I would dearly love to settle the score now, little man, but I am here on a greater mission.' Turning to Gnaeus, he said, 'Gaius Julius Caesar invites you to end this war now.'

'Does he want to fight here and now?' spat Gnaeus. 'Or does the old man wish to surrender?'

'Why not ask him yourself?' Zebul held his spear aloft and waved it three times.

A moment later, Julius Caesar himself rode out at a gentle trot from the line of mysterious horsemen.

When Caesar had come to Munda all those years ago to appoint a procurator, he had seemed such a big man to me, but I was a child then. Now he seemed to have no more presence than any other man as he rode towards us, flanked by eight of the other horsemen. I observed the conqueror of Gaul and bane of Pompey the Great: bare-headed, he wore a breastplate of burnished silver inlaid with gold, a similar pattern on the greaves that clad his shins, and behind him fluttered his favoured purple cloak.

The most obvious thing about him was not his balding head or beaked nose, but an ugly rash that ran from his left ear and across half his face and neck, angry and inflamed from incessant scratching. I recognised the symptoms of the infectious ear mite and remembered the appropriate remedy that my mother would have immediately dug out of her apothecary.

His horse was the same as the others — small but well bred and in good condition, black as night — so the only things that set him apart from the other riders were his cloak and armour. He was not particularly muscular, but neither did the skin sag around his neck and upper arms as it tended to with men of his age. His back was straight and he seemed to control his horse with his thighs and knees rather than the reins.

All nine horses stopped together. I saw no signal and I had no idea how they did that. They were a stone's throw away from our line; none of us had moved or said anything as the Dictator approached. Then Caesar nudged his horse to a walk and came to within ten paces, alone.

He studied each of us in turn with hooded grey eyes. He looked weary as each of us returned his stare with no flicker of emotion. Then he leaned forward in the saddle and called, 'Am I to shout? Titus Labienus, I would talk with you.'

I saw a look of indignation cross Gnaeus's face, who then barked, 'I lead our Optimates, and I speak for the Republic!'

'And I don't speak to children about matters that concern men. Labienus, come forward and let us talk man to man.'

'Enough!' cried Labienus. He turned to Gnaeus and with a nod of his head indicated that they should advance together.

Caesar laughed then, a deep, forced chuckle as he half turned to look back at his men. I wondered whether Gnaeus would let his rage fly and try to kill Caesar, but I knew that even this hotheaded son of Pompey would not disgrace himself in this way. The two generals halted a javelin's length from Caesar, who looked intently at Labienus. For a long moment he seemed lost for words, facing the man who had once been his legate but had switched sides only because he had been overlooked for promotion.

'Oh Titus, Titus. You should have stayed.'

'Hello, Julius. Nasty rash you have there. Been shaving with a blunt knife?'

Caesar's hand went instinctively to his infected face, then he swatted away a fly. It promptly settled at the corner of his horse's eye. The mare twitched, annoyed.

'Trade insults all you like, Titus. The fact is that you were no use at Thapsus and you are losing here.'

Gnaeus could no longer keep silent. 'We haven't even begun, Caesar, and you know it.'

Caesar looked at him in silence, then turned back to Titus. 'As I was saying, you are losing here because your men defect to my Populares in their hundreds and the people detest the iron fist of this —' he gave Gnaeus a swift glance — 'this ignorant pup who does not yet know that if you want to rule, you must first win the hearts of the people.'

I sensed Sextus wince next to me. Caesar was right. Gnaeus seemed intent on using plunder and murder to add to his wealth with little regard for the feelings of proud and noble tribes.

'So what were you doing in Gaul?' Gnaeus sneered. 'Throwing jolly parties for Vercingetorix and his grateful tribes?'

Caesar was unmoved. 'When our armies meet, you are as likely to be killed by a Gallic or Germanic hand as by a Roman. You see, they have come with me because I brought them civilisation and a better way of life.' Then, before Gnaeus could reply, he turned back to Labienus. 'And you, Titus, you know that many times I have faced worse odds than you can offer in this pitiful corner of my domains, and each time I have won. Tell me, why should this be different?'

Labienus was unruffled, and replied brusquely, 'Because you are old, and like an old man you don't have the stomach for a fight anymore.'

I was surprised when Caesar smiled. 'You are quite right. My bones ache when I get out of bed and I find it impossible to get drunk anymore.' He looked contemplative for a moment and then, as if struck by a sudden thought, added, 'You can have the islands of the Britons. Leave your legions to me, take a ship, go past the Pillars of Hercules, turn right and you'll find your new home after a week sailing north.'

Even Gnaeus found that funny, but Labienus fumed. 'Enough of this. Your one-eyed slave said you wanted to end the war right now. What do you propose?'

'If we fight, thousands will die,' said Caesar. 'Think for a moment where your predecessors are, each of whom I have fought in turn. Where is Pompey the Great? Where is Scipio? Cato? And Juba who ran away with his entire army at Thapsus? What makes you so different, Titus Labienus — will you run, too? Or will you be disembowelled by a humble Gaul?'

Labienus stiffened so suddenly at this that his horse danced nervously and turned in a full circle while its rider brought it back under control. Then Labienus pointed at Caesar, his face thunderous. 'Bring your pitiful army to us, and we will show you how to end this war. You are nothing but a jumped-up soldier with ideas far above your station. You are not bigger than Rome, and if you are ready to pay the price for your crimes, your judgement day awaits you.'

Caesar continued to smile and slowly shook his head, but before he could reply, Gnaeus spoke.

'Coward.'

Suddenly Caesar's smile vanished, his eyes flashed and he edged his horse forward until it was almost touching his opponent's.

'Coward? You call me a coward? It is usually you and your shambolic legions that are running away, crying like girls.'

Labienus interjected. 'It is you that slaughtered them at Thapsus when they threw down their arms in their thousands,' he snarled. 'Some say you could not stop them because you lay writhing on the floor of your tent like a dying snake, but many more say you feasted in your tent while your countrymen were put to the sword. I, too, say you are a coward, and your knees knock together at the thought of facing us.'

Caesar did not flinch. 'I came here because I thought, mistakenly, that we could commune together like Romans,' he growled. 'But I see that you, Titus, have lost none of your charm and as for you, Gnaeus, run away like your father did before you feel the wrath of my sword.'

With that he galloped back towards the woods, his men following in single file. Zebul remained where his horse had stood, away from the conference but near enough to hear everything. He was smiling, though the scars on his face made it look more like a vicious grimace, then he pulled sharply on his reins and cantered after Caesar.

For a while, our line remained standing. Then Labienus looked at Gnaeus and said, 'So we fight him again.'

'One last time,' said Gnaeus.

NINETEEN

Summoned to Corduba's great hall by a sniffy centurion, I joined Gnaeus, Labienus and Sextus, who were huddled with around twenty armoured officers. On the table was a crude map drawn onto the wooden surface with charcoal. Gnaeus was stabbing his finger at it and yelling at a tribune twice his age. Nobody noticed me arrive, so I just watched the mayhem as Gnaeus and Labienus delivered orders and men went scurrying to obey. The army, scattered though it was between Corduba, Munda and the several sieges that Gnaeus had ordered, was being summoned and mobilised as a unit.

Sextus noticed me, for he was not embroiled in the importance of the moment like his brother. He sauntered over and put his arm around me.

'Where have you been, Pito?' he asked. 'They've been asking for you.' He nodded in the direction of his animated brother and the curt Labienus.

'Out and about,' I replied, 'wondering why hell is about to break loose in our quiet corner.'

'It will all be over soon, and we can get back to the important things in life.' Sextus was as easy and confident as ever. I wish I could have shared his optimism.

'So what's the plan?'

'Same as it always was.' Sextus sighed. 'Only I am to remain here with a single cohort while everyone else withdraws to Munda. That's still where we offer battle. Sorry, old friend.'

'And what is my role in this?'

'Simple. Send messages to the legions to gather at Munda. The town must have additional fortifications and traps laid by the time Caesar arrives, as he will, and each of your staging posts must prepare as many nasty little tricks as you can dream up.'

'Why are you staying? You can't hold Corduba with a single cohort.'

'Indeed not. But neither am I meant to. I have to make it look like we are making a stand here, just long enough to delay Caesar while our men sneak away south.'

It seemed to me that he was being offered as a sacrificial lamb, and that Gnaeus and Labienus were callously putting the junior member of their leadership in harm's way.

Reading my thoughts, Sextus said, 'Don't you worry about me and my men, Pito. I'll be out of here in good time before those nasty Populares —' he used the term given to Caesar's armies — 'come storming over the walls, and we'll catch up with you at the first staging post. Then we'll take a gentle stroll together back to Munda.'

'And then?'

'Bit of a scrap coming up, I suspect. It's just what those two need.' Again, he nodded in the direction of Gnaeus and Labienus. 'They're itching for a fight. Might do them good.' He paused, then added, 'Oh, I thought you might like to know that I've arranged for Nahalia and Bashira to ride with the baggage train when the army leaves here. They'll be with the other household slaves, so they'll be safe.'

'Perhaps they should seek out my family at Munda?' I suggested.

'Don't worry, they can look after themselves. They have a knack of avoiding trouble, and by the gods this looks like being a particularly messy spot of trouble.'

Sextus sensed the chord of fear in my gut whenever he mentioned the coming fight, but he seemed to think that warning me what to expect would save me from some unforeseen trauma.

'Look,' he went on, lowering his voice, 'I realise you have never seen warfare on this scale. It's the most degrading and loathsome thing a decent man can find himself caught up in. It turns human beings into animals and all around you is savagery, pure savagery…' Like me, he was trapped in a plight that followed him wherever he went like a swarm of locusts, consuming his spirit.

'Run, Sextus,' I whispered. 'Turn your back on it.'

His focus snapped back, and he smiled. 'Don't for one moment think it hasn't crossed my mind, Pito. But don't ever say that again — at least not in this sort of company. I'm ashamed of what Rome has brought to your home.' He glanced across the room to where Gnaeus was emphasising a point to a confused-looking scribe attempting to write down orders on a wax tablet. 'I'm not like him, am I? Not like them. Not like my father…'

I wanted to help him in his moment of need. I wanted to reach inside him and exorcise his Roman demons, to heal the wounds caused by this hungry war machine. I had always known that Sextus did not believe the Roman lie in his heart.

At that moment, Gnaeus called for me. My compliance with the curse of Rome was demanded.

I left Corduba before dawn with the army's advance scouts, about twenty men. Half of them had orders to remain with me at the first staging post, from which we would send reports of Caesar's movements before withdrawing at the last moment. Among these was my childhood friend, Lizard, as dependable a spy as any and one of my best men in our signalling network. Like me, few had slept that night — there seemed to be little point when we knew we had to pull down tents, sharpen weapons, oil armour, pack a few meagre necessities, and form up ready to move at dawn.

Sextus had not slept, either. He was there, already in full armour, saying his farewells to Nahalia and Bashira, no doubt warning them not to flaunt their obvious assets in front of the soldiers. He saw me watching them and strode to my side.

'See you in a few days,' he smiled, cuffing me on the back of my head. 'Look out for me.'

'I expect I'll hear you coming, belching and farting on all that fine wine you've got stashed here.'

'You jest,' he laughed. 'What Labienus hasn't drunk already, Gnaeus has moved into his personal wagon. What you'll hear is my stomach rumbling with hunger, so make sure you have some wild boar roasting and I'll follow my nose.' Then he added, 'Oh, I nearly forgot. The watchword we've just agreed is "piety". Hardly appropriate for any of us, I think!' And with that, he went to attend to his duties.

I led my men and our horses past the stores, where the camp was at its busiest. A tribune was checking sacks of grain, wooden crates filled with vegetables and fruit that were already rotting but deemed good enough for the cooking pots, and enclosures packed with scrawny goats too emaciated to muster more than the occasional protest. This army would have to live off the land that it crossed, denuding it of grain and livestock and leaving Caesar as little as possible. Despite orders to respect the local population, I had no doubt that there would be some who would fulfil other appetites, and I prayed that the communities dotted along our route would have the good sense to get out of the way.

We crossed Corduba's bridge, travelling light, and continued at a walk until the sun cast its first light on the road.

Grim, shadowy riders, we cantered south.

TWENTY

The lightning came during the third night after leaving Corduba. It terrified the horses, which screamed and dragged at their bridles, the vivid flashes illuminating eyes wide with fear. Each of our men tried to calm their own mounts, but the almost simultaneous crashes of thunder made their task impossible. For an hour we spoke gently to them, stroking and blowing into their nostrils, until eventually Jupiter's anger moved away and the torrential rain began.

The makeshift shelters of the staging post had been designed to keep the midday sun off the horses, not to withstand the downpours that can swamp the mountains, sometimes for an hour, sometimes for days on end. Our heads dropped, horses and men alike. We had nowhere to shelter, not even beneath the trees. A wall of water made the night blacker, the noise drowning all other sounds.

The horsemen were almost upon us before we realised the danger, alerted by a whinny loud enough to penetrate the drumming rain. Uncertain whether it was Sextus or the enemy approaching, we remained silent and prayed that the horses were too dispirited to respond to other animals in the vicinity. If it was Sextus, he would know he was near and call the watchword. But there was no shout, and I sensed these were not our men.

I reached out for the nearest of my men and tapped him on the shoulder — I wasn't surprised to discover it was Lizard — and speaking close to his ear, I told him to follow. We crept forward, slithering in cloying mud that blackened everything. We could not be seen. We groped our way to the base of a huge olive tree overlooking the track that led south and waited — the horsemen would have to pass this way if they did not know where the track branched to our concealed staging post, and that would likely make them the enemy. The rain relented slightly, allowing the faintest glow of moonlight, but we were well concealed.

We heard them approach, the horses' hooves splashing and squelching on the wet, muddy track. We could barely see them as they moved past and were unable to count how many there were, but we could just make out the leader, a shadowy figure crouched low on his horse as if searching the ground. I thought the rain must surely make this fruitless, but suddenly he halted. Neither of us breathed. He looked around, or rather he seemed to be sensing around him, as he would surely be unable to see anything. I, too, sensed him — could this dark figure be Zebul? Suddenly he pulled sharply on his horse's reins, causing its hind quarters to slide in the mire, then pushed back past his following men, summoning them as he went.

We lost sight of them immediately, and slowly it dawned on me why they had suddenly changed direction. I grabbed Lizard by the collar of his sodden jerkin and we tried in vain to climb back the way we had come. Then we heard a shout, followed by the clash of steel, yelling and cursing, and the cries of the dying and wounded. It was over too quickly. I feared the worst and we redoubled our efforts to climb slowly through the mud and soaked undergrowth. Then we heard the horsemen again, returning on the track where we had first peered at them in the dark, sensing their renewed purpose in moving ahead of the enemy army. My heart sank; surely my men were all dead.

They lay where they had fallen, their blood already washed into the black mud, deep gashes in their throats and chests. The horses had gone, along with most of my men's weapons. I dropped to my knees before the body of one of them and cradled his mutilated head. Lizard stood and peered into the gloom, open-mouthed.

I remained prone and let my tears mingle with the mud and gore, then felt Lizard's hands on my shoulders, pulling me upright. He shook me and yelled at me to pull myself together, and he was right. This was no time for self-pity. I had to think. But the rain hammered onto my face, rivulets ran down my back, and I couldn't expel the throbbing inside my head.

Lizard led me away, and we slumped beneath a tree just a few paces away. I tried to sleep, but the horrors of the night and the drumming rain kept me awake. Then, suddenly, I opened my eyes and saw blue sky, the sun low but warm on my face. Lizard snored.

I found a solitary horse foraging on the hillside. The mare must have been overlooked or slipped away in the confusion of the attack, a small miracle amid the madness and pain of that dreadful night.

I woke Lizard. He was the better horseman, so I told him to ride for the second staging post to warn them, avoiding the main track, though speed rather than stealth was our only ally. He mounted easily, and with a wave of his bony hand he was gone.

I used my sword to cut a prickly pear and sucked on the juicy flesh in a feeble attempt to revive my body and soul, then set off for the higher ground where, hopefully, I could better appraise what was going on around me. The morning was calm, belying the horrors of just a few hours ago. Timid mountain flowers meekly spread their colours beneath proud cypress trees, darting dragonflies danced in the damp air and overhead a dozen storks languidly beat their way towards their breeding grounds in the north. I saw a pair of eagles over a higher peak bathed in pale sunshine and, always guided by the lofty god, I chose that for my vantage point.

It was well chosen. Collapsing on the soft heather to catch my breath, I looked around to discover that I had a perfect view of two valleys leading south. The sun was overhead now, its warmth soothing my spirit. I knew that our Optimates army would be far to the south by now, so any movement could only be Caesar or Sextus. The eagles had moved off in the direction from which they would come.

I thought I heard the distant boom of last night's retreating thunder, a rumbling on the still air. Then it became louder, and I realised it was the sound of thousands of pounding feet, a far-off thump, thump, thump of an army marching in rhythm. Leaping up, I strained to see what must be Caesar's army concentrating on the main valley through which our army must have passed, but I could see nothing. I scanned the other valley, and then something caught my eye, the unmistakable flash of sun on armour. Peering below, I could make out a line of horsemen moving quickly, too few to be part of Caesar's army and the wrong side of the mountain range. I hoped it was Sextus.

Looking back to the parallel valley, I could now see the beginnings of a sea of men, moving forward in organised rows of at least fifty. They were too distant for me to see any detail, but they were undoubtedly the disciplined legions of Caesar. I could make out a knot of horsemen in the van, resplendent riders that probably included the conqueror of Gaul himself. I shuddered. Death and destruction were marching south towards my home.

I turned back to the other valley and could now make out about thirty horses pushing hard, hardly breaking stride as they followed a twisting track. Like a fool I waved my arms and shouted, but they were too distant and I was not positioned to break the skyline. If only I had the resources of the watchers on their mountain tops to reflect a signal that Sextus would recognise. Perhaps a fire? It would take too long, and everything was still damp from the rains.

Then a thought struck me. I drew my sword, immediately gratified that the oil I had rubbed on it before leaving Corduba had maintained its bright surface. It was a small area to reflect the sun, but I could try. I turned the blade this way and that, giving the light a wide area to attract the attention of the tiny column far below. At first nothing happened, but then one of the horsemen pulled his mount aside and, obviously calling to the leader, pointed up at the peak where I stood. I continued the sweeping reflection, confident now that I had attracted their attention. This was confirmed when a cloak was hastily tied to a spear shaft and waved. The spear was thrust into the ground to mark the spot where I could meet them, and the riders melted into the woods near the track to wait, hidden from the enemy's eyes.

I took another look at the army in the other valley. There were more ranks of soldiers, and more were coming from the hazy distance. The sound of a huge army on the move was louder now, trumpeted commands piercing the damp, heavy air — this was clearly Caesar's entire army. The pair of eagles circled directly above the leading horsemen.

I began to scramble down the mountainside.

'It looks like Melqart, but it stinks like a goat,' Sextus laughed as I approached. If I looked half as bad as I felt — weary, grimy and sweating — then perhaps Sextus spoke the truth. 'We smelled you before we saw your signal.'

I managed a weak smile. 'How did you know it was me up on the mountain?'

'Because nobody else could have dreamed up such a deranged method of signalling, and anyway you're always climbing mountains. It was a safe bet.'

'Did you know Caesar is just the other side?' I asked, pointing the spear I had pulled out of the soft ground. I noticed one of the eagles was still circling high beyond the peak where I had stood.

'Yes, actually I did,' said Sextus, a little cockily. 'Not for one moment did he believe Corduba was defended. He didn't bother entering the walls and camped nearby, drilling his men late into the night. It looked like all eight legions were there.'

'From what I've just seen, you're right. They are marching south.'

'Then the plan seems to be working. We'd better ride for Munda.'

I hesitated. 'But weren't you ordered to hold Corduba?'

'There's no point now that Caesar is on the move. As everyone keeps saying, this is the big moment. Whoever survives this battle will rule the world.' He offered his hand, inviting me to ride behind him as there were no spare mounts in his company.

'And another thing,' Sextus added, 'an order from a brother doesn't count. Besides, you need me to look after you while you do your crazy signalling!'

Munda looked resplendent as we rode the last miles along the wide valley approach, secure behind the sturdy walls and great wooden gates banded with iron that had been built with Roman engineering skills. Lucius had made the town an easily defended fortress. Behind the squat, grey walls, white houses were dotted with the garish red of cascading blooms and the deep blue that was the favoured colour for doors and window shutters. Munda was an innocent lamb upon Rome's ugly altar, unaware of the sharpened knife at its throat.

Sextus believed we were at least two days ahead of Caesar, precious time for planning his defeat. We had watched the eagle circle for a short time before it was too distant to see; I was convinced it was marking the head of the advancing army. If I was right, judging by the slower progress of the eagle, we did indeed have about two days. But no general would entertain such a ludicrous concept, so I kept this to myself.

The sun was sinking behind Titan, so I was given the night to see my family before reporting back for orders at dawn. I ran to embrace them all, wasting no time in eating, drinking and talking in hushed tones. I tried to berate my father for not leaving the town, and he told me I was probably right but any battle would be between Romans and take place outside our walls. He wanted me to stay in the house until the battle was over, but I reminded him that however friendly I was with Sextus, Gnaeus would have me executed as a deserter. Anyway, I had a handful of men whose skills were needed to observe and report the movements of legions, and I would probably spend the entire confrontation on a hill well out of harm's way.

I felt long-awaited sleep descending upon me, and for the first time in my life I was in my bed before Pidray, Tallay and even young Elvir. But I awoke suddenly in the darkest hour, the horrifying dream of the avenging eagle having returned to haunt me. I slept only fitfully after that.

At dawn I went to find Sextus. I saw a huddle of soldiers playing dice beneath the walls not far from what I took to be the command tent and guessed that would be the best place to search for him. As I approached I heard the groans of the soldiers from whom he had won a mound of sesterces, and he looked up grinning as I shook my head.

He swept up his winnings and, chuckling at his good fortune, nodded for me to step aside with him somewhere quieter. I looked at the command tent, with its grim guards and several horses tethered outside, but Sextus shook his head. 'No need to go there, Pito. They've already told me what they want from you.'

'Oh?' I was surprised, but relieved to avoid witnessing the rough manner of Labienus and Gnaeus again. 'Anything I should know about? Do they want me to make myself scarce, by any stroke of luck?'

'No. You're a crucial part of the Optimates war machine. But the best bit is that we're together, which either means that you've been promoted, or I've been demoted. All we've got to do is observe. We can take a flagon of wine and a loaf of bread and relax…'

'Come on, Sextus, be serious.' Though I dreaded this battle, I was eager to know my part in it.

He looked at me, still smiling. 'How would you like to be the one who tells these oafish generals exactly what to do with their equally oafish legions?'

With that, he put his arm around my shoulders and we went to plan a battle.

TWENTY-ONE

Sextus led me to a nearby hill overlooking the wide valley that lay in front of Munda and led for several miles north to Lacibis. It was well chosen, providing a sweeping view and crowned with enough trees and bushes to offer concealment from the enemy. It could be easily defended with a few men, as a craggy outcrop facing the valley would make a direct assault impossible, and the only way to walk to the summit was by using a winding goat track that we discovered behind the hill.

The view was impressive, and for a while we were silent as we caught our breath after the climb. Below us, hundreds of men were stripped to the waist, digging ditches and piling the earth for ramparts that would hinder any cavalry crossing the river in front of the town. I could see Gnaeus in a distinctive blue tunic and the ebullient Labienus, pointing out positions to their officers and sending men off to pace out the range for our archers. It was clear that Gnaeus intended to hold the slope between the river and the town where the valley narrowed, using the river and a winter swamp as a natural defence. The battleground was well chosen, and our vantage point was close enough to the engagement for the generals to observe my signals.

Opposite us were the new stone and mortar walls of Munda, the height of two men and the same in breadth. Solid and impenetrable, they wrapped the hillside town like the arms of a protective god. Through the huge wooden gates poured a steady stream of soldiers and servants with amphorae of water from the town's springs to refresh the sweating labourers.

I looked north, half expecting to see the first ranks of the enemy swarming across the flat valley towards us. But it was quiet and still, in contrast with the zealous activity below the walls.

Sextus followed my gaze and read my thoughts.

'It's unlikely that Caesar's men would have the time or the inclination to bother with this hill,' he said, 'unless, that is, we are spotted using it for directing our troops.'

'And if they do discover us?' After witnessing the horrors of the campaign so far, I was sure that Caesar would slaughter us without mercy.

'I will have fifty men, some guarding the track and the rest concealed in these woods.' Sextus looked around, as if confirming to himself that there was enough cover to hide his men. 'You and your watchers will be well protected.'

'That's all right then,' I replied doubtfully.

We searched around the edge of the summit and found a flat area partly screened by the rock face and a few thorny bushes that clung precariously to the steep hillside. Some broken pottery and faeces dried hard by the sun were telltale signs that we had stumbled upon a shepherd's secret resting place, which with its partially concealed outlook over the valley would serve our purpose well.

I looked at Sextus. 'There's just one small problem to resolve.' He raised an eyebrow, and I continued, 'We can't use the sun unless the battle takes place later in the day, and even if we could choose the time of Caesar's advance, it's completely impractical, as the generals will be otherwise engaged and there isn't time to teach them the codes.'

Sextus said nothing, gesturing for me to continue.

'We could try shouting,' I joked, 'but from what I gather, warfare is a pretty noisy occasion…'

'So that leaves…?' Sextus let the question hang in the air.

'Flags.'

'Of course. And you have those to hand, don't you?'

'Unfortunately, they're all on mountaintops between here and the coast,' I replied disconsolately.

'Good thing someone around here thinks ahead,' Sextus smiled. 'I sent for your men and their pretty flags. But I don't envy you teaching Labienus what the different colours and combinations mean. He may be a good soldier, but he's a little on the dull side.'

'I'll tell him you said that,' I laughed.

We heard the unmistakable rhythmic tramp of men on the march and went to watch Dracus lead two legions out of the hidden valley to prepare their positions before the walls of Munda.

The watchers returned from the staging posts at intervals during the day, riding hard in twos and threes. Turon was last in from the north, his face lined and drawn from the strains of looking after his men while being daring enough to observe the enemy as closely as possible. He had guessed that something had happened to our men at the first staging post, as messages from us had abruptly ceased.

'Did Lizard not report to you?' I asked him. 'I sent him to you after the first post was slaughtered.'

'No, we did not see him.' There was pain in his eyes. 'We knew nothing of the attack, but then one of my men observed you riding with Sextus. We were relieved to see you alive — though we feared for the others.'

I put a gentle hand on his shoulder. 'I am afraid there is worse to come, but for now tell me what else you have observed. The generals want to know everything.'

Turon quietly reported how Caesar's advance scouts, led by the murderous Zebul One-Eye, had scoured the hilly terrain looking for Optimates stragglers. Though he had not found any of the staging posts since the first, he had wiped out several innocent communities on the basis that they could be spies. None had been left alive, not even children.

The gloom deepened when Turon reported the arrival of King Bogud with an army of his Mauretanians, perhaps as many as fifteen thousand men, many of them mounted on swift horses transported across the sea from Africa's coast. These had a mix of Roman and Carthaginian blood, descended from the ancient Phoenician race — the same people as me and my family.

And now they were the enemy.

Leandra came from the south to bring sunshine to my oppressed spirit, accompanied by Cassia and guarded by Marcus and several cavalrymen. Drenan was with them too, together with the skeleton watcher teams that had manned the mountaintop signalling stations between Munda and the coast. They had brought as much equipment as they could carry, including the huge, coloured flags we had used for signalling when the sun was concealed by cloud.

Leandra looked more beautiful than ever, and Cassia too — a bronzed, regal pair. Marcus seemed unduly pleased to be their guardian. Seeing me, Leandra threw her arms around my neck and held me close while my heart thumped with joy, painfully crushing her studded leather breastplate to my chest. Both women were armed with well-crafted long knives at their belts, and sheathed on the flanks of their horses were ornate bows and a plentiful supply of deadly shafts. Six watchers were similarly armed. I doubted the women needed any protection from Marcus.

The question burst from my lips all too soon. 'Leandra, why are you here? There's going to be a battle, and —'

'If you tell me it's no place for women, I'll thump you, Pito!' she interrupted. 'I am only here to take my parents back to Apollacta, and any children that will follow us. Cassia and I have our community to defend, and we don't intend to do it by fighting like puffed-up bully boys!'

I led Leandra away from the others. 'Look,' I said, 'if you're taking your family away from here, I must ask a favour. I've tried to persuade my family to leave, but they don't seem to share my apprehension about what's going to happen here.'

She looked at me, the innocent cheerfulness suddenly gone. 'So why do you ask them to leave while you're staying to fight?'

I explained to her the orders that Sextus and I had been given to use the flags to signal Caesar's movements, and the fact that apart from this, we wouldn't be involved in any of the fighting.

Leandra frowned. 'I wouldn't depend on it. You had better take these fine bowmen —' she indicated the six watchers and Drenan — 'as your personal bodyguard. When I see you again, I don't expect to see a single scratch on you.'

Drenan smiled his agreement, pleased to have a good reason not to fight under Dracus on the front line.

I looked into Leandra's eyes. 'I promise I won't come within spitting distance of any of Caesar's Romans,' I laughed. 'But there is something else you can do for me. Find my brother Elvir and take him with you. He is young and headstrong, and I don't trust him not to get himself into trouble, but he will be an asset to you on your return journey.'

'Of course.' Leandra was thoughtful for a moment, then a timorous look crossed her face. 'Perhaps he is brave and strong enough to be our guardian on our journey back? After all, we need to replace Marcus, and we women are so scared of the nasty Romans and all those bandits…'

'Sometimes, Leandra, I think you understand the minds of men better than we do ourselves.'

'That's not hard,' she chuckled.

Later, as I waited outside Gnaeus's tent with Drenan and Turon, I watched young Elvir lead Leandra and Cassia and their small following out of the town gates. They had managed to find a sure-footed pony for Elvir, who rode as if he was the King of the West, dressed in a leather jerkin and one of my mother's dark cloaks. A sheathed short sword slapped at his thigh. He saw me and waved.

'Take care of those women!' I called to him.

'I will!' he shouted, his voice surprisingly masculine.

Both women waved, and Leandra patted her bow. They laughed and were gone, Elvir leading them at an easy canter. It suddenly dawned on me that he was exactly the same age as I had been when Leandra and I trapped the boars and encountered the malevolence of Zebul. Elvir would look after them well.

I was gazing after them when Sextus appeared at the entrance to the command tent, his summons pulling me out of my reverie.

'Time to talk to the high and mighty,' he said with an amused expression. 'The generals would like us to explain the flag signals.'

I felt as nervous as he looked self-assured.

'But first,' Sextus added, 'I'd better explain how they want this to work. I am to command the hill from which we will observe Caesar's advance, not only to defend it, but to make certain decisions about the movements of our legions as the need arises.'

'That's quite a responsibility,' I remarked.

'Not enough, in my opinion. Labienus will command our right with two legions and the cavalry, with Gnaeus holding the high ground before the walls in the centre, and Dracus commanding the left wing. Lucius Marcellus will be in command of the supply camp behind Dracus's legions. You can imagine my anger at not hearing my name being announced for any of these vital positions by my noble brother.'

'Perhaps he is looking out for you?' I suggested weakly. Thinking of my own concern for Elvir, I added, 'It's the way older brothers are...'

'The way he put it was that we needed the brightest brains in charge of overseeing signals. Until now, we have done this by using trumpets, but though it works for Caesar it went wrong for us at Thapsus. There was just too much noise and confusion.'

'So Gnaeus believes that this new method will work, even though it's untried,' I mused.

'It had better work. But everything hinges on having simple signals, and on the commanders memorising what they mean.'

'And on us staying alive...?'

'That's the least of my worries,' Sextus smiled. 'Come on. We've got a class to teach, and a battle to win.'

I held up a black flag and pointed at Labienus.

'Caesar,' he grumbled reluctantly.

I moved it to the left.

'Caesar engaging on the left.'

'Whose left?' Sextus interjected curtly, enjoying his seniority. 'Yours or Caesar's?'

Labienus scowled. 'Obviously Caesar's left, because that's the way the flag is pointing.' He looked as if he would like to be fighting Sextus, not Caesar, but he controlled his petulance.

'And if he raises it up and down?' asked Sextus, sweetly.

'Then it's an attack at the centre, and if he waves it to the right it's an attack in that direction…'

'All right, all right,' Sextus interrupted. 'Let's see if someone else is as clever as Labienus here. Dracus, what colour flag are you?'

'Green,' he replied triumphantly, 'my favourite colour, as it happens.'

'So if you see a green flag moving to your right, what do you do?' Sextus could be condescending without the offence being noticed by a warrior like Dracus.

With a sigh, Dracus said he would move the main force of his men to his right.

'Excellent,' declared Sextus. 'Now, who is represented by yellow?'

Labienus shifted in his seat and waved his fingers in an attempt not to look like a schoolboy.

'Red?'

Gnaeus coughed, then said, 'The least I expect is a cheer at my colour!' At last, the mood was lightened and the officers crowding behind the generals gave a mock cheer.

Sextus held up his hands for quiet. 'Now the complicated bit,' he said, seriously. 'Here's Melqart with the colour combinations…'

And I explained to them how to recognise the different signals for weaknesses in the enemy ranks, where they were exposed, the massing of troops for a concerted push, and if they were retreating.

As the sun yielded the last of its warmth to the cool mountain air, the men of our Optimates lit a thousand cooking fires. Spread out by legion and century beneath the town and across the valley, the day's labours ceased and everywhere exhausted men sat to eat, play dice, sharpen their weapons and pray. Sweet woodsmoke lay heavily over the camp, a white mantle tugged gently by the breeze towards the foothills.

Sextus had asked me to stay after our signalling demonstration, during which only the gravity of warfare had saved me from being ridiculed by hard-bitten officers, most of whom seemed to resent my inexperience. I tried to become invisible, and fortunately none of the commanders paid me any attention as they received the day's final reports on Caesar's movements.

So it was that I heard Labienus remind all of the officers that the plan remained to hold our line and force Caesar to come to us, and to tell every century, cohort and legion the same so that no hothead would grow impatient and break the unity of the army. The plan depended on patience, he emphasised, so that Caesar was forced to fight in the place of our choosing where Optimates outnumbered Caesar's Populares.

Late in the day, I heard the report of how Caesar had camped in the wide plain to the south of Lacibis, a place that in my childhood had always seemed so far away, but now in manhood was not distant enough. I knew that a man could ride between Lacibis and Munda in the time it took to burn two rings on an hour candle, but would an army take less time or more?

It didn't matter. Gaius Julius Caesar would be here tomorrow.

TWENTY-TWO

I must have slept, for it was dawn when Drenan shook me. He said nothing, just pointed northwards. I tried to focus and looked dully around me. Most of our small force was huddled in groups, sharing bread and olives, though a few still slept on the bare ground. I then looked down and saw that the army was in full battle order. I blinked. How had I not heard trumpets, the shout of orders, the clamour of arms being readied? The weariness of military life lay stiffly upon me.

Drenan nudged me and pointed again. I looked into the clear sky and saw an eagle circling, which I took to be the marker of the head of Caesar's forces, heralding the coming of an invader. I looked out over the valley and could see nothing.

'They come,' said Drenan. His eyes, flint-grey in the half-light, showed no enthusiasm for battle.

I tried to shake the sleep from my head and looked again. Nothing, but now I could hear the distant rumble of marching soldiers. Drenan picked up his bow and ran to position the watchers in the woodland near the hill's crest, waking prone bodies as he went. I looked around for Sextus but could not see him.

I drank from my waterskin and looked again. Yes, there was movement, which I sensed rather than saw — a dark mass moving inexorably towards us, the rich red earth of our valley trampled by the innumerable stomping feet of the invader.

Our legions sensed them too, and as I looked towards them a tension ran through the lines, like a ripple across a millpond, muscles tightening, backs straightened, spears gripped tightly, jaws set firm. Then there was a murmur: was it fear or courage? Probably both, stirring in the guts of seventy thousand men.

I was impressed. Thirteen legions stretched from the foot of our hill right across to the far side of our agreeable valley, dour armed men in ordered rows, shield and spear held ready. Before them were three horsemen, holding their mounts at bay; plumed helmets and bright armour marked out Gnaeus in the centre, Labienus nearest and Dracus in the far distance on the left wing. Labienus was loosening his sword as he stared intently towards the north. The veteran of a hundred battles, the grim survivor of cut and thrust, a loveless killer without a care for those he had butchered.

I followed his gaze and saw the rising sun casting its light into the valley, illuminating the advancing host. A hillock stood like an island in a misty sea of marching legions, upon it a lone horseman, tiny and insignificant in the distance but great in his arrogance and resolve to rule the world.

'Good morning, Melqart the Mighty.'

I hadn't noticed Sextus return. He wore the most flamboyant armour I had ever seen, a jewelled breastplate over a fine mail shirt with gold shoulder-pieces, a ridiculous bronze codpiece and ornate greaves strapped over shiny leather leggings. A longsword hung at his side and his customary curved dagger was strapped to his thigh.

'Are you going to a party or fighting a battle, General?' I looked at him askance.

'Very funny. Actually, I'm toying with the idea of having you charged with dereliction of duty.'

'What do you mean?' I looked for the usual spark of humour on his face.

'Is that, or is that not Gaius Julius Caesar over there looking somewhat aggressive? If I'm not mistaken, it's your job to signal his approach.'

I decided to play Sextus at his own game. 'Have your men rustle up some breakfast first. I'm starving.'

A smile cracked his face. 'And how would "sir" like his eggs today? We have some rather fine cured pork and preserved peacock tongues all the way from Rome, and as today is the Feast of Bacchus, maybe we should open one of my brother's vintage wines?'

My stomach turned at the thought. 'Maybe I'll wait until after this is over,' I said ruefully. Gathering my sword belt, I started for my position below the hillcrest where the signal flags were stored.

'Let's get started then,' Sextus replied cheerfully. 'Remember, my men will be here guarding the track to this position, so you just concentrate on flagging the orders I give. Just you and I, controlling the fate of the world together.'

'I just want the old world back,' I muttered, but I didn't think he heard me.

I picked up the black flag and signalled the approach of Caesar, but the generals weren't even looking.

Two trumpet blasts drifted on the still air towards us and promptly the enemy halted. In one liquid movement, Caesar's army began to fan out across the valley facing us, taking up well-rehearsed battle formations with no noise or fuss. Caesar was still a lone figure on the knoll, motionless and threatening, yet his army had responded with immaculate precision as if an extension of his mind. I doubted that our legions would be so in tune with Gnaeus.

Caesar's army, like ours, stretched across the valley, legion by legion in perfect order. Huge scutum shields interlocked in the front line, and burnished spear heads pointed like a host of accusing fingers at Munda and the Optimates' defenders before it. For the first time I regretted not wearing any armour.

From his vantage point, Caesar could look down a gentle slope that ran for about two miles across open ground to the brook that crossed our valley, and from there up a steeper incline to our legions. He had chosen his battleground: both commanders wanted the enemy to attack uphill, Caesar because he was outnumbered and Gnaeus because so many of his recruits were raw and untried.

I scanned the enemy lines, looking for something to signal, but there was no point because each army could see the other's massed ranks and neither was showing any inclination to move from their chosen spot. The weak morning sun was rising above Caesar's left wing where for now his cavalry stood, the silhouetted horsemen menacing in their perfect formation.

The line of enemy shields parted and a lone rider emerged, keeping his horse to a controlled walk. Behind was a solitary figure on foot. The horseman came at a walk down the slope, his mount swaggering with an easy gait, but the walker stumbled and fell. It was then that I realised he was tied up, a prisoner. As the rider jerked him to his feet, the unfortunate figure stumbled on. As they came nearer I could see that he was naked, his bare feet bloodied by the thorns and sharp rocks on the untilled ground.

I recognised the thin, wiry frame. It was Lizard, one of my best men, and I felt his shame.

They advanced down the slope towards our positions, Lizard stumbling frequently. At one stage his body was dragged over the merciless ground before he mustered enough strength and dignity to rise to his feet and half trot after the dark rider. As they approached, I could see the rider had a covering for a ruined eye, and behind me I heard Sextus curse the reappearance of Zebul One-Eye.

Drenan came and squatted beside us with one of his bowmen. 'The moment that nasty creep moves within bow shot, kill him,' he murmured to the archer, but we could all see that was unlikely.

Zebul stopped short of the brook, well out of range of the Optimates' bows. He dropped the rope and moved his horse behind Lizard, who stood, swaying, attempting to cover his shame with bound hands. He gazed over the vast ranks of our men and showed no fear, daring an advance to rescue his prisoner. None of our men moved a muscle, and Gnaeus, who was nearest, stared at Zebul from behind his golden helmet.

The sun gave Lizard no warmth and he was shivering as the sweat from his exertion cooled on his naked body, but still he held his head high, proud and defiant. The silence stretched out.

Zebul drew his sword and held it towards the Optimates' ranks, his outstretched arm moving slowly from one wing to the other. He then brought the blade back to point directly at Gnaeus.

'Are you all cowards?' His words were shouted in a strong, clear voice, audible to the commanders and the centre of our army, and echoed back from the walls behind them.

Still nobody moved. Zebul walked his horse around Lizard.

'Did you not hear me?' he called again. 'Come and save this man; he is no use to us.'

With that, he swept his sword across Lizard's back, opening a wound that sprayed drops of blood in an arc as the prisoner dropped to his knees. At last our army responded, a deep murmur of disgust and threat rising in the throats of angry men. Some took a step forward, but Gnaeus turned his horse to face his men and cried, 'Hold!' The ranks were stilled and held their line.

'Not even Gnaeus will be sucked into that,' Sextus whispered. 'It's just a display in the hope that we are undisciplined.'

'But that's my man suffering out there,' I stammered. Lizard was painfully trying to rise to his feet again. 'Surely someone can just ride out and kill Zebul?'

Lizard was gasping for breath, bright blood running down his back.

'All they want is some breaking of the ranks to encourage others to advance,' Sextus murmured. 'Caesar must be desperate for us to engage him on his terms, but this won't work. It's all futile.'

As if he had heard, Zebul spurred his horse in a wide sweep towards Labienus's wing, leaving Lizard kneeling weakly. Again, he pointed his sword at a Roman general.

'Where is the might of Titus Labienus?' he yelled. Now that he was nearer to our position, I could see the ugly scars on his face and neck, but he rode well and his horse was muscular and swift.

Again, no one in our right wing moved, and I thought how Labienus must have been struggling with the temptation to hurl insults and ride out to deal with this insignificant bumpkin. But if he did, his men would follow and our discipline would be lost.

'Cowards, all of you!' Zebul shouted, and rode at a gallop back towards Lizard and decapitated him with a single sweep of his sword. Lizard crumpled to the ground, and I buried my head in my hands.

Sextus put his arm around me. 'Let's hope we meet up with him later in the day, though I doubt we'll see that pile of dung in the front line.'

I could not speak.

Zebul cantered cockily back towards Caesar's lines. Nobody followed.

After that, the armies faced each other across the plain for what seemed an interminable time. The only movement was when a burial detachment was sent across the brook to retrieve Lizard's remains, the first dishonourable casualty of a day that surely must reap many more souls.

The sun was high when at last something happened. A trumpet sounded, and Caesar's entire army advanced down the slope, renewing the anticipation in our men who had begun to relax during the long wait.

I signalled the enemy's advance, more for something to do than through any sense of urgency, but then Caesar's cavalry wheeled away, hundreds of horsemen moving as one. Their hooves created an ominous thunder as they swept left and behind the main army to appear dramatically on Caesar's right. I flagged my first meaningful message — Caesar's renowned tenth Equestris was feared by all the enemies of Rome for its enviable organisation and unfailing ability to break a defensive line.

But Sextus was calm. 'Gnaeus knows this is just manoeuvring. There's no need to react yet.'

Another trumpet blast, and Caesar's army halted, still in perfect formation. I looked at Gnaeus and saw him turn his head towards Labienus, who gestured that the army should wait. But I could see Gnaeus was becoming impatient, and his horse seemed to sense the tension, its hoofs scuffing the ground.

The temptation to move was too much. Gnaeus dug his heels into his horse's flanks and rode towards Labienus. With his spare hand, he indicated that the officers of his centre legions should hold their positions. The two generals conferred.

Sextus took a long draught from his waterskin and, wiping the drops from his mouth, sighed. 'I'm afraid this waiting is all too much for Gnaeus. If I know my brother, he's telling Labienus we need to change the plans and attack Caesar before everyone drops off to sleep!'

'Do you want me to signal an advance?' I asked.

'Absolutely not. As long as Gnaeus holds his nerve, Caesar will crack before we do. It's always been his way, to attack hard and fast even when the odds are stacked against him.' He paused, then added, 'Perhaps we can give him something. Can you signal a partial advance?'

'Like moving a couple of legions around to make it look like we're on the move? Like Caesar did?'

'Let's give it a go.' Sextus looked down to where his brother was arguing with Labienus, their horses twitching and snapping testily at each other. He put two fingers between his lips and gave a shrill whistle, attracting the attention of both men instantly. It was hardly the way for a general to behave, but Sextus never had much regard for the rules and his method was far more effective than any flag-waving on my part.

'Signal a general advance,' he said confidently, 'but halt them halfway to the brook. It's vital we remain on this higher ground when the fighting starts.'

I thought he was clutching at straws, but I made the signals and Gnaeus rode back to his position while Labienus ordered his advance. Dracus, too, inched his legions forward, the thousands of boots kicking up dust and scattering a hundred small birds into the air to seek refuge in the surrounding hills.

Immediately, there was a response from the enemy. A group detached itself from the legions in the centre, dragging heavy, wheeled objects. Scorpios, I guessed, a good reason not to advance too far. The bolts they fired were lethal on level ground but were most effective when an enemy was charging — they were too clumsy to be positioned during any rapid advance by Caesar.

'Halt them now,' Sextus snapped. 'Let Caesar think we are scared of his machines.'

I signalled. Labienus and Gnaeus saw the message, but Dracus continued his advance almost to the brook.

Caesar saw his opportunity and took the bait.

His cavalry charged.

TWENTY-THREE

When the Optimates saw Caesar's Equestris sweeping towards them, and the enemy rank and file moving steadily down the slope, a roar went up. The challenge was deafening as swords were clashed on shields right along the lines, while Labienus's cavalry shifted and horses whinnied restlessly as they awaited orders to reposition.

Surprisingly, Sextus didn't ask me to signal our cavalry to support Dracus where the enemy cavalry was closing in on our left: not that Dracus would mind, as he had trained his men for four years to be ready for this moment. Besides, Caesar's cavalry would have to slow to take the brook and avoid the marsh that lay on our extreme left, preventing the enemy horsemen from circling behind our lines. The attack would be head-on, the deadly cavalry riding across a natural obstacle to meet a shield wall — from behind this would come a hailstorm of javelins and arrows.

Grateful for my detached position, I looked for weakness in the enemy advance and saw none. The first of the enemy cavalry were now at the brook, the horses gathering on powerful haunches to propel themselves across and up into the bristling spines of our ranks. I could make out Dracus's plumed helmet in the front line and I saw the first men to die as several javelins found their mark, punching through breastplates and piercing yielding horseflesh. With a terrible crash, the enemy cavalry hurled itself at the shields, hooves flailing and swords flashing down.

But the line held. Where a man fell, others stepped up to fill the gaps and link shields. Dracus fought like a demon, and even if I had sent him a signal he would not have seen it.

Then Caesar's foot soldiers reached the brook and crossed it, screaming abuse at the ranks in front of them. Gnaeus and Labienus had both ridden to the rear, as was the custom of Roman generals, leaving centurions to marshal their men and send the first volleys of javelins. Many of these men were inexperienced, and I saw several javelins arc into the air too early, only to fall ineffectively short.

Sextus thumped my shoulder. 'Signal Labienus to send his cavalry now, while there are so many in the brook.'

I could see that the moment was right; the first ranks of the enemy would have no momentum and be an easy target. I made the signal, and Labienus himself led half of his cavalry out through the narrow gap between our hill and his foot soldiers, sweeping down with murderous cries in their throats, their longswords slashing at panting men as they clambered out of the ditch. Men screamed and died. The bravest tried to hamstring horses as they surged past but were cut down by the deadly blades. Labienus led his cavalry across the front of his shield wall, intending to continue the charge along the centre's front line, but here the enemy had already crossed the brook and were being engaged by Gnaeus's men. Continuing would endanger Gnaeus's troops, so Labienus regrouped and returned at full gallop to repeat the deadly process in front of his own men as more of Caesar's troops climbed over the mangled bodies of their comrades.

'This is where we can win it, right here in front of us.' Sextus was breathing heavily, the excitement of the first exchanges flashing in his eyes. 'Signal Labienus to advance his legions and push them back.'

Thankfully, Labienus had pulled up after his second sweep and saw the signal. He nodded once and screamed orders to the centurions in his front ranks of foot soldiers. They smashed swords on shields in the rhythm of a fast walk and advanced to repel Caesar's bloodied left wing. Labienus and several of his cavalry officers dismounted and joined them, and with a loud grunt the solid Optimates line crashed into the fragmented Caesarean soldiers and forced them back. Little by little, Labienus's legions advanced and the heaving mass of men waiting to cross the stream found their way blocked by their own men, who were edging backwards under the onslaught of Labienus's raw recruits.

The fighting was fierce and my heart thumped in my throat. Sextus yelled at me over the screams and curses of dying men, the horrendous clashing of arms.

'Get a grip, Pito!' he shrieked into my ear. 'Make the signal!'

'What signal?' I realised I hadn't heard him for some minutes.

'Caesar's flag! Get Caesar's flag! He's joining the fight!' He pointed over to the far side of the battle, where Dracus's legions were locked in a heaving struggle with Caesar's tenth and the cavalry, many of them dismounted now and fighting hand to hand. I could see the rear ranks parting to allow a small group of horsemen to advance to the front line.

'It can't be,' I said in disbelief.

'I'm telling you it is Caesar, Pito. I've kept an eye on him since the early exchanges, and the man himself is joining the battle.'

I reached for the black flag and made the appropriate signals. I could see no response — I didn't even know where Labienus and Gnaeus were — so I made the signal again. Then I saw

Gnaeus as he crossed both his arms above his head to acknowledge my signal. Calling the officers of his reserve cohorts, he bellowed orders while gesticulating wildly in the direction of Caesar's approach. The Dictator was moving towards Dracus's position on the left. Gnaeus led his men behind his lines to join the fray and meet his nemesis.

I was watching Gnaeus leave the centre to attempt to fight Caesar in person when Sextus nudged me and pointed to one of the groups of reserves that Caesar had positioned behind his legions. An officer was pointing up at our hill, and around him were several soldiers watching us. By some stroke of luck they must have seen Gnaeus make his arm-waving signal to us and guessed that this was some kind of command centre.

Sextus and I both ducked behind a bush, but not before I had seen the black cloak of one of the men the officer was talking to.

Zebul One-Eye.

'Looks like it's our turn next,' Sextus said ruefully.

'If they come, it will take them some time to find the best point of attack.' I was trying to sound confident.

'And they don't know if this hill is defended. My bet is they'll send a small strike force.'

'You had better go and warn your men. They can't climb up this part, so I'll take care of any signalling while you organise your defences.'

Sextus thought about my suggestion for a while, then nodded. 'You know what to do. Keep looking for weaknesses and point them out to Labienus. I don't think you'll be able to get Gnaeus's attention for a while, though. I'll be back as soon as we know what's going on back there.'

'Take my bowmen; they could make all the difference in an ambush.'

'No, they're here to protect you.'

'Take them, Sextus. You can't give any more protection than stopping Caesar's men from capturing this hill. Go.'

Reluctantly, he did, calling the archers to him as he went.

I could hear nothing of Sextus or the men once they had left, because the noise of battle was so great. I concentrated on trying to watch the progress of each section, searching for signs of advance or retreat, but such was the confusion of slaughter that I could not see who was winning. Besides, all three of our generals were embroiled in the fighting and would not see any of my signals, and as far as I could tell, so too were most of Caesar's commanders. It was a struggle to the death, all mayhem and bloody disorder.

Nearest me, our right wing under Labienus was still apparently pushing back the Populares' left. Our centre, with its well-formed shield wall, seemed to be holding, but every so often one side would give ground and then advance with renewed effort. But now the heaviest fighting was at the far end of the front line, furthest away from me, where Caesar's seasoned Tenth led by the Dictator in person was slowly but surely pushing back our left wing up the slope towards our main supply camp.

I wondered if I should attempt to signal reinforcements to counter Caesar's progress, but then I realised these would have to come from Labienus's wing and might damage his chances of success. So I just watched, fascinated, horrified and deafened.

I therefore didn't see or hear the dark figure clambering up the last few feet of the rock face to my right. I glimpsed movement out of the corner of my eye and Zebul was there, calmly brushing grit and soil from his black leather jerkin. A lopsided grin spread across his thin lips as his one eye fixed me with a familiar evil intent.

I looked around for any sign of Sextus or our archers, then realised they must have been drawn into a diversion on the approaches on the other side of the hill. Zebul had gambled on this, and now it was just him and me.

'No friends to look after your precious skin this time?' Zebul stepped towards me, his heavy leather boots crunching on the loose stones. His black eye patch was held in place with braided thongs to which were attached black eagle feathers, giving him an even more sinister look. Strapped to his back was a longsword with a polished obsidian stone fixed to the leather-bound hilt. A curved dagger was thrust through his iron-studded belt.

He fingered one of the eagle feathers that hung from his head as he walked towards me. 'This used to belong to one of your friends,' he snarled, making no move to draw either of his weapons. I stood rooted to the ground as his lips twisted into a sneer. 'In fact, I only keep one feather from each eagle I kill, and as you can see I have four. Today I'm going to add a lock of your hair, which you won't notice me take because I'll have cut off your balls and stuffed them into your mouth.'

I unsheathed my sword. I could think of nothing else apart from running, but even though I was not a warrior, neither was I a coward.

Zebul reached behind his head and drew the longsword in an easy motion, the sharp iron blade rasping from its leather sheath. He cut the air with frightening hacks as he walked towards me. I held my sword in two hands, trying to calm my short breaths and my thumping heart.

The first blow came from over Zebul's head and was well enough signalled for me to block it, the crash of iron on iron sending a shudder through my arms and my shoulders. His next came from the side and I jumped back, then jumped again as the flashing blade swept in from the other side. It missed, but I stumbled on a rock and fell hard on my back. Pain lanced through my hips where I had fallen awkwardly, and Zebul was upon me, drawing his dagger and leaping through the air in one motion; then the blade was at my throat.

I expected to die, then, alone on a hill outside my precious hometown.

But I didn't die. Zebul stayed the blade and brought his face close to mine, his one eye alive with bloodlust, the scars on his neck pulsing, his breath rank with stale wine.

'You're going to do something very simple for me,' he growled. 'Take your clever flags and signal a retreat, starting with your left wing, then your right.'

So he had seen our flags. It dawned on me that my stupidity in sending the guard with Sextus could easily have cost us the battle, and the war.

I shook my head.

'Still a stupid little boy, aren't you?' Zebul moved the dagger from my throat and, grasping my hair, pulled me into a seated position. He held the dagger behind my back. 'Pain that you can't see coming is always the sharpest,' he scowled, probably remembering the eagle's attack not that far from here. I felt the prick of the knife's point between my shoulder blades but held my gaze firmly on his one good eye.

'You'll get nothing from me.' I meant it, too, the words coming from some deep resolve that I hadn't known existed.

I felt the sharp point again, but the pain was not unbearable.

'Which flag is for Labienus?' he asked quietly.

I shook my head.

Then I felt real pain. It was searingly hot, and the most excruciating thing was that I could not tell where the agony came from, where the metal had entered. I gasped.

'That's right, take a deep breath and talk to me.' Zebul's voice was strangely reassuring. 'Now then, Labienus's flag?'

Again, I shook my head.

This time I felt the blade inside me, the flesh parting, the scrape on a rib, and again the searing heat inside my lungs and flaming through my chest. I tried to cry out but blew bloody bubbles instead. My head felt as if it would burst.

Zebul held his face close to mine, watching my confusion as I wrestled with death, enjoying my anguish as my eyes flickered on the edge of consciousness. He let me go, and I remained seated, unable to move as waves of pain washed over me.

I watched blankly as he picked up several flags and dragged them to the edge of the overhang. I saw him pick one at random, yellow, Labienus's flag, and wave it over his head, then two others. Their meaning was beyond me as a numbness spread over me and I coughed blood and vomit.

Then my eyes closed and I felt nothing.

TWENTY-FOUR

I awoke when a dragonfly landed on my nose. It flew away, startled, when I opened my eyes and slowly focused on Nahalia's smiling brown face.

I started to speak, but she gently laid a finger on my lips to silence me.

'Your first question is no doubt "Where am I?", and your second "What happened?" But you must be patient.' Her voice was warm and soothing.

I moved my head and a searing pain stabbed between my shoulder blades, worsening when I sucked in air.

'Lie still. You must not move suddenly.'

Nahalia reached for a mortar in which a brown substance had been crushed with a pestle to form a paste. She took some and put it to my lips. 'Chew this slowly,' she said. 'It's willow bark mixed with goat weed. It'll ease the pain and make you feel better.'

I did as I was told and the fibrous potion numbed my mouth as I swallowed the bitter juice. I managed a smile as Nahalia stroked my hair.

'From what I've discovered, the goat weed will take effect quickly,' she said. Seeing the look in my eyes, she added, 'But don't go getting any ideas. You're under strict instructions to keep still.'

'From whom?' I managed, very softly.

'Your friend Turon, who brought you here. He carried you all the way from the mountains where you were found, five days ago.'

'Where … am … I?'

Again Nahalia hushed me. 'Apollacta, and that's a long way to carry a lump like you. It was Sextus who saved you first. He thought you were dead when he found you, all lifeless and bleeding, but he ordered some of his men to carry you into the hill tops away from the slaughter and there Turon looked after you.'

Awful memories came flooding back at the mention of the word "slaughter".

'Who won…?'

Nahalia frowned, and sadness came into her eyes. 'You must wait for the others, but oh, Pito, it was dreadful. We have heard stories that Caesar ordered his men to kill everyone, and they didn't stop until nightfall. The river turned red with blood. But that's all I know. Leandra says we are safe here for the time being because the invaders are occupied besieging Munda.'

That news troubled me, and she saw it. What of my family? What was going to happen to Munda? These were all innocent people who were not interested in who ruled Rome.

Reading my alarm, Nahalia went on quickly, 'I'm sure everyone inside the town is safe. The walls are strong, and soon Caesar's army will have to worry about other things far from here.'

I wasn't so sure. I thought of the strange bloodlust that had seemed to come over Caesar in his impatience to finish the war, the surge of venom that had spurred him right into the thick of the battle. I wished that Caesar, Gnaeus and the rest would take their rage across the sea to their beloved Rome.

I did not feel any better when Nahalia brought me a steaming bowl of broth and gave me some more willow bark to chew. She changed the kelp poultice on the wound in my back, the fishy smell only slightly distracting me from the sharp pain as she gingerly moved me. Then I slept, but it did not feel like sleep to my anxious mind. I dreamt that Zebul's blade pierced right through my body, protruding from my chest as my blood dripped from its rusty, serrated edge.

'He's awake.' It was Elvir's voice.

I opened one eye at the sound of my little brother and resisted the urge to leap from my bed and embrace him.

Pipsqueak followed him in, an impish grin crossing his young features. At twelve years old, he was still small but his face was longer, showing the onset of manhood. Behind him was Leandra, still strikingly beautiful but with telltale worry lines at her temple, then the willowy figure of Cassia, and with them Turon.

'How's the patient today, then?' I could tell Leandra was trying to sound cheerful. 'Want some more medicine?'

She pushed back the heavy curtain from the open window, allowing a fresh breeze and the gentle sound of the sea into the room. Elvir winked and stepped back, pulling Pipsqueak by the collar to stand guard with him at the door.

I managed to speak without the crushing pain in my back and chest. My first words were for Turon, whom I thanked for his courage and care after the battle. He brushed aside my gratitude with a careless wave of his hand. 'It's what you would have done for me,' he said.

I held his gaze for a moment and hoped he understood my sincerity. Then, in a hoarse whisper, I asked, 'Any news from Munda?'

'There have been many refugees, mainly wounded and dispirited soldiers,' said Leandra, 'but none have escaped since Caesar started his siege.' She trailed off when she saw my pain, and Turon, ever the realist, took up the tale.

'My people have watched from the hills and sent word that although Caesar's men repelled two sorties by the remaining legionaries, they have failed to storm the town. Caesar has left his legate in charge of the siege while he seeks to subdue Corduba and unite Hispania under his Populares banner. Those that remain inside the walls are safe for now. But for how long, we cannot tell.'

'What would draw off Caesar's men?' I asked, speaking slowly as I seemed to have no air in my lungs.

'A diversion, perhaps. Maybe false news fed to his spies. But our army is in disarray, and mostly dead as it happens. Caesar showed no mercy, and the dead cannot be counted. There is no news of Gnaeus. I know that Labienus and Dracus are definitely dead, and we await the return of Sextus.'

'Drenan?' I managed.

'With Sextus,' said Turon calmly. 'He and your men took you to safety, then rode north. But they told me to wait for them here at Apollacta. Sextus may need the ships if Caesar pursues him.'

Leandra interrupted. 'There have been many Roman ships passing offshore in recent days. I think Caesar may be expecting Gnaeus and Sextus to flee by sea, so we have hidden our vessels as far up the river as we can to hide them from anything but a landing party. And thankfully we are unnoticed so far.'

Nahalia entered with wine and fruit, as well as more medicine for me. I saw the look that passed between the two women who meant the most to me — after my mother and sisters, of course. It was not a jealous look, but it was obvious that Leandra knew that Nahalia was more than a nurse to me, and I more than a patient to her. She smiled.

'Look after him well,' Leandra said happily. 'I have a feeling we're going to need his sharp wits if Caesar comes nosing around here.'

Nahalia beamed and Leandra cleared the room, leaving me to the gentle ministrations of my Egyptian companion. Turon was last to leave, turning at the door to look intently at me.

'I expect you want to know what happened?'

I nodded. 'You mean how it was that we seemed to be winning by sheer force of numbers and then, for some reason, we lost?'

'Yes. We will talk of this later, when you are rested.' He paused, then after a moment's thought, added, 'There's one thing I'd like to know, and so would some of those who survived...'

Nahalia glared at Turon, who held up his hands in surrender and backed towards the door.

'No, wait. Go on,' I insisted, somewhat weakly.

'Did you signal Labienus to pull back and move to our left wing?'

'No, of course not.' I closed my eyes and the memory of Zebul waving the yellow flag came flooding back. 'But I think I know who did.'

Not even Nahalia's smooth, oiled hands on my temple could drive out the nausea in the pit of my stomach.

The next morning, Turon returned with the blessing of Nahalia, who warned him not to alarm me as the healing would take longer in my mind than inside my body. I thought he admired and respected her, maybe even feared her — if that was possible for a Kemeletoi.

Nahalia propped me up with an abundance of soft pillows and left after planting a tender kiss on my lips. Turon raised an eyebrow and, after checking that she did not linger outside the door, pulled a small bottle from the pouch at his belt.

'This is real medicine,' he said, winking as he uncorked the bottle. The fumes told me it was distilled from the rare fruits and herbs harvested by the mountain people. The fire in my throat made my head swim.

'Did you come here to drink and sing, or to talk soberly?' I spluttered, handing back his bottle.

Turon drank and did not choke as I had. 'I have come to talk,' he said with a smile, 'and Nahalia has insisted that you do no more than listen.'

'Turon,' I said after a deep breath that hurt a little, 'the last thing I remember is Caesar attacking strongly against our left wing and pressing towards the reserve camp and stores, while Labienus on our right wing was pushing back the enemy, step by step. The centre was holding. How could that position of strength have gone so terribly wrong?'

Turon paced the room, before turning to me with his thoughts in order. 'It is all a confusion to me, as it is to you, because I was with Sextus holding off the enemy detachment that had been sent to take our hill. It was some time before we realised that they were not pressing as hard and as desperately as they might, and it was Sextus who took me aside from the fray and told me he was going to check on you. I went with him. We ran to your position, where first we saw that there had been a dramatic switch in the battle, and the men nearest to us were fleeing before the enemy. Then we looked over the lip of the hill and saw you lying in your own blood, seemingly dead. There was no sign of those who did this to you.'

'It was Zebul alone, and I'm sorry to say I didn't put up much of a fight. He must have climbed the rock face to reach me.' I was ashamed.

'The fault was ours for leaving you,' Turon countered. 'Sextus did his best for you and we found men to carry you on a shield away from the worst of the action. But it was hard for us to tear our eyes away from the scenes we were witnessing. We saw friends fall. We watched as thousands died, running away. We did not know why they had turned, and after Sextus realised that the fight was lost he commanded me to find out what I could and to meet him here — in how many days' time, I do not know.'

'I remember seeing Zebul with the flags, but then I must have passed out. Did you find out what happened after that?' I asked.

'Yes and no. When the fighting stopped, though the slaughter and wailing did not, I disguised myself as best I could with an old ragged cloak and went among the survivors. Then when too many suspicions were aroused, I took to the hills, where I knew my folk would have been watching for the outcome. I have pieced together as much as I can, but it will be for another to write it down, because I am sickened by the whole sorry mess.'

I motioned for him to sit on the edge of my bed, and he began his tale.

He told me the battle was wild and furious, and looked set to last for days if Caesar did not buckle under the sheer weight of numbers opposing him, and the misfortune of having to fight uphill. Suddenly, Labienus and his closest legionaries disengaged and pulled back to where they could remount. The fighting there seemed to stop, but not for long. Labienus's legions seemed confused for a moment, and then they saw the general riding hard away from the battle, then crossing behind our lines towards the left wing where Dracus was just about holding on under Caesar's onslaught. All of his cavalry followed; some say he was retreating, others that he was reinforcing Dracus.

That was where the battle was lost, he said. Suddenly, as if the thought struck every soldier on our right wing at the very same time, our men backed off. The enemy saw the opportunity and surged forward, and our men turned and ran. Man after man was cut down from behind, and soon the rearmost ranks could see or sense the retreat and they, too, turned and ran.

This unexpected success gave heart to the enemy. They redoubled their effort and soon the centre, and then our left, was demoralised and in retreat. But again, it was hard to retreat in an orderly fashion when the panic set in, and soon our entire army was running uphill towards the town, seeking the safety of its walls. Thousands of them died on the slope. Caesar's men were grim and full of hatred. They hacked at heads, legs and torsos as they chased. Some men, on reaching the walls, realised they could not reach the gates because the press was so great, so they threw down their arms but were slaughtered where they stood. No quarter was given.

The killing went on for hours. Caesar himself stood in the field, his arms, chest and legs red with the blood of his enemies. He yelled at his troops to press on, even when there was nothing more to be gained. When they had no more to kill, they began making great heaps of the dead, not even bothering to set aside the wounded, driven on by Caesar and his officers. They brought the captured eagle standards, thirteen of them in all, to Caesar, who sent them one at a time to be posted in the ground wherever an officer was found slain. There was a great shout when Labienus was found, another for Dracus, and saddest of all, one for Lucius Marcellus, who was so greatly loved in Munda for his fairness and gentleness of spirit.

Those soldiers and officers who reached the safety of Munda slammed shut the great gates before the enemy could secure it, and the walls were manned by the remnants of our Optimates. There they stood, exhausted and bleeding, defeated yet defiant, as the enemy shouted their scorn.

'The silence behind the walls of Munda is the only epitaph that will remain for the people of the hills,' Turon finished sadly. 'It is a town in mourning for the thousands of dead, among them so many Hispanic youths who deserved better than to die because one man wants to rule in Rome. For six days — or is it seven? — carrion-eaters have picked clean the bones. Only Labienus has been allowed the dignity of a funeral pyre, perhaps because he was once Caesar's man. The rest lie naked and bloody, and many of them headless, for Caesar has even mounted his ghastly trophies on spears to taunt the men of Munda. And those that remain in the town fear for their lives if Caesar is able to bring his siege engines to bear on those faithful walls.'

I lay with my eyes closed and imagined the horror, the noise of slaughter, the stink of decaying bodies abandoned in mangled heaps. I sensed the pain of my people, the evil blackness weighing heavily upon Munda. And what of my parents, and my sisters? Oh, how foolish not to have forced them to leave…

It was an age before I realised that Turon had left the room.

TWENTY-FIVE

As soon as I could leave my bed, I spent long hours alone by the shore, watching the vast sea ripple and change colour with the angry clouds that rolled in from the west. Behind me Concha towered above Apollacta, sometimes crowned with mist, but more often clear and proud like a regal sentinel. Somewhere near the summit was the first of our signal relays, lying unused for lack of men at the very time when information was needed most. I had no energy to spur me into restoring it.

I sent Elvir north in search of our parents and sisters. Turon went with him: I insisted on this as I had seen the mountain man's ability with a sword. Elvir took his bow, but both declined my suggestion that an armed guard go with them as they rightly pointed out that a few could hide from Caesar's patrols far better than a noisy group of armed riders. Pipsqueak rode too, proud and determined on his pony, a sword and a bow making him a man before his time. The trio seemed inadequate, but Turon insisted on a small number. Where once I had commanded twenty or thirty, now I had only children and Turon.

That same afternoon, Nahalia came to continue her healing of my mind. She sat on the crunching shingle next to me while waves lapped at our feet. She tossed a pebble lazily into the sapphire waters, then laid her head on my shoulder.

'Feeling better?'

'Only when I look out there, not when I look back towards Munda.'

'Maybe that's where you — we — should go.' She pointed towards the open sea. Nahalia could lift my mood just by sitting next to me. 'Let's make a start right now,' she giggled, and in one swift movement she pulled her tunic over her head, black locks bouncing free over her shoulders. She wore no underclothes, her slim hips framing a freckled belly above a modest shadow of curls. She reached for my tunic, pulling it upwards. 'Come on, last one in is a lazy slouch.'

'But what about my back?' I protested, lamely.

'The sea will do it good,' she laughed as she pulled my tunic free. I, too, wore nothing underneath. She ran into the chilly sea, a nymph with not one inhibition, and I followed gingerly, enjoying the salty caress on my tired and aching body, Neptune's tonic restoring sensations long forgotten.

Laughing, Nahalia was already swimming strongly into the gentle swell, and she turned to splash silvery drops at my head as I eased my body tentatively into the current.

She swam to me and put her arms around my neck as my toes found the soft sand below. A serious, intense look came into her eyes, the kohl running comically on her cheeks, but she didn't care about that. My arousal was a rebellion I could not overcome.

She wrapped her smooth legs around my waist and lowered herself onto me with a deliberate ease. The sea sparkled its appreciation back in a million pinpricks of silvery light on the wave crests. She moved deliberately, slowly, each wave lifting us both gently then lowering us to where my tentative footholds slipped in the sand. Nahalia whimpered while I held my breath, then suddenly exhaled in explosive release as she clutched me tighter still.

But then my exhilaration fought with guilt and lost. My hopes for my family faded as I submitted to the withering weight of self-reproach.

Munda fell while I frolicked in the sea.

It did not take Zebul One-Eye long to gain the ear of Caesar's legate and make him promise all manner of wealth and opportunity to end this unwanted siege. The secret gate, where the rubbish and town waste was poured, was the only unguarded way into Munda, and Zebul himself led a cohort into the streets and vented his venom on the innocent.

I know this because Elvir arrived too late to enter the town, and while Turon went to his own in the hills, my brother and Pipsqueak were sent south to bring the terrible news.

I berated him unfairly. 'Why did you not bring our family with you?' I ranted, and the child in him tried unsuccessfully to blink back the tears.

'Because every entrance was guarded and each had a watchword,' he replied, defending himself admirably. 'And don't think I didn't try.'

I held him close and whispered, 'What news of the townsfolk and our family?'

'Slaves, all of them,' he sobbed, fully releasing his sorrow now. 'They are needed by the enemy. Those with money or possessions have been stripped of everything and chained with the lowliest citizens. Except those who bend iron or make bricks.' The despair in his voice pierced my heart. 'I fear our family is lost, no doubt chained and led away to Gades to be shipped to some wealthy Roman's house across the sea. If they survive the galleys.'

I embraced him. He was all I had left. We wept together and I tried to find words of comfort, but none came.

Despite Nahalia's protests, I decided to return to Munda to attempt to find out what had befallen my family.

The decision was made easier for my nurse to accept when Drenan rode in from the east, announcing firmly that he, too, was returning to Munda to check on the welfare of his family and his people. Leandra, now fully accepted as leader in Apollacta, ordered the fires lit for a feast of fresh fish, served with artichokes and sweet onions from her lush gardens and fruit from the orchards.

Between eager mouthfuls, Drenan told us that Gnaeus had attempted to escape by sea, but Caesar's ships commanded by the able Gaius Didius had trapped his single vessel, forcing him to flee on foot. Gnaeus had been injured in his haste and had holed up in some mountain caves that could be easily defended with a handful of men. But Gnaeus was not a man to hide and cower and had foolishly decided to fight his way out of a corner, underestimating the numbers of Didius's men who lay in wait. Consequently, the eldest son of Pompey had been cut down and beheaded, yet another macabre trophy for the vengeful Caesar.

Sextus, said Drenan, had wasted no time in commandeering a ship and a crew, paid for with his jewelled armour and the coin he carried with him. Putting a brave face on such an ignominious defeat, he sailed for Sicilia. Before leaving, he had prevailed upon Drenan to find me at Apollacta and request that I join him in Syracuse as soon as events permitted me to do so. 'I am no longer in a position to issue orders to anyone, least of all my friend Pito,' Sextus had said.

I put this to the back of my mind, as there were more pressing matters. Drenan agreed that we should ride together, and the moment Elvir heard of this decision, he oiled his bow, groomed his horse and prepared provisions for the road. When challenged, he steadfastly refused to listen to any voice raised in opposition to his joining the expedition. Besides, it made sense as he had recently ridden the road to Munda and knew about its dangers and secret hiding places. But we only persuaded Pipsqueak to stay behind by insisting that Leandra and Cassia needed a warrior to guard them against unwanted visitors. And that was how Pipsqueak came to be gainfully employed as a man of means, beginning as a child with hopelessly oversized armour and later becoming a wise and loyal protector of the all-woman senate of Apollacta.

The journey was slow because every stride of my horse sent sharp pains shooting through my chest. My breathing was still shallow and laboured, but Drenan and Elvir were patient. We left the road at the first signs of anyone approaching from the opposite direction, but soon abandoned this policy as most were sorry refugees who had somehow managed to give Caesar's men the slip. Some were soldiers, dour men with no light in their eyes. None were the slightest bit interested in any more fighting. On one occasion we met a group of around fifteen, a mixture of our own men and deserters from Caesar's army. The scenes they had witnessed had purged them of fighting and killing, and in a subdued way they all seemed to have forged a bond. That night we shared with them the game Elvir had hunted, spit-roasted over a discreet fire in a clearing on the mountainside.

Some wounded, all dispirited, they were not talkative men, but one of them found his tongue after sampling the strong honey spirit we carried with us. He was, it transpired, the only one among them not from the lower ranks of either army, and his duties in Caesar's Fifth Alaudae legion had included acting as a field surgeon. Indeed, he looked different to the others, with a dignified, disinterested air and a deep voice that indicated a more cultured background than would normally be expected among his rank and file. He confirmed that he was not a Roman, but a Greek who had travelled to Rome to seek employment, hence his enrolment in the military. He told us his name was Paeon, after a lesser god of healing, though we suspected this was a new name he had given himself to maintain his anonymity.

After the battle, Paeon had been sent to tend Caesar himself. He had put crude stitches in a leg wound to staunch the flow of imperatorial blood but had been clumsy and suffered a backhand blow to the side of his head as a result. Dazed, he had wandered from the bloody field and the further he had wandered unchallenged, the more he had realised that this was the ideal opportunity to walk away from the army. He chuckled as he told us how he had removed a copper pendant bearing his name and tied it around the neck of a dead soldier, just in case his centurion was looking for him in the aftermath of the battle, which he considered unlikely. They had not enjoyed a close relationship.

I thought how useful a man like this would be to the villagers on the coast — though clearly not yet a great doctor, he had the intelligence and presence of mind to become one. And his story about how he had stitched the great Caesar on the field of battle would enliven the tavern gossip. I broached the subject, and this met with more enthusiasm than we had seen from any of the soldiers so far, so the next day we sent them south with instructions to report to Leandra as new citizens of

Apollacta, there to use their talents and knowledge in building, farming, chandlery, fishing and, in Paeon's case, as a doctor. They swore with honest, pleading eyes that their intentions were good, and we believed them.

The stench of death hung in the air a full half day before we reached Munda. We wrapped our cloaks around our faces in a vain attempt to shut out the stink and rode the final miles at a trot. We came upon the first smouldering remains as we rounded the pass that lay to the south of Munda. Great rings of blackened earth, like huge evil eyes staring up at the heavens, were dotted with the scorched remains of human limbs. Hunched figures in black raked fetid remains into the hottest parts where flames still flickered, while others hauled stiff bodies on creaking carts to new fires laid further away from the town. To the west a great ditch had been dug, its purpose betrayed by the lifeless limbs of men and horses reaching skyward in the pointless pleadings of the dead.

While we watched in grim silence, a line of roped prisoners emerged, guarded by thickset soldiers armed with spears. They were bowed, defeated. The line was halted with a shout near the ditch and three men were detached from the other unfortunates. Each was forced to face the gruesome grave and we turned our faces away, knowing what was coming. When we looked again, the three were no longer there, and the line of prisoners was shuffling unsteadily towards a makeshift wooden enclosure where the latest slaves for insatiable Rome were penned.

Without a word, we rode carefully to the gate, picking our way between the fires of the dead. Strangely, we were not challenged. Instead, dull eyes were averted; even soldiers seemed incapable of mustering the energy to check who was riding into a dying, defeated fort. We rode through the streets where once children had frolicked and traders had called out their bargains of the day, past Tanasus's crumbling brewery, to the main square where only the chuckling spring water bore testimony to a life that had been and was no more. There we dismounted and led our horses to my family home. I pushed the door open.

Three faces stared disbelievingly at me, wine goblets stilled at their lips. Their appearance betrayed veteran soldiers, confirmed by the sword belts that hung on the hooks that had been used by my mother for her cooking pots, for which each now reached. But Drenan was swift with his sword, and I not far behind him, and Elvir already had an arrow nocked. The three men froze, weighing up their options.

'And who by Jupiter's testicles do you think you are, shoving your way into our home with not so much as a please or a beg-your-pardon?' This was the elder of the soldiers, but all three appeared eager to defend their stolen lodgings.

It was Elvir who responded, surprising me with his courage. 'The first one to move gets this arrow in his guts; the next two get the blades of these men here.'

'All right son, all right,' sighed the leader, his hands held up in submission. None of us moved.

'Where are the people who lived here?' I demanded coldly.

'Gone, long ago.' The leader seemed to find new courage. 'This is our home now, so back off quietly or there'll be hell to pay.'

I pointed my sword directly at his eyes. 'And where did they go?'

The man answered my question without taking his eyes from my blade. 'To Rome, by way of the port at Gades. They belong to Caesar now, and this house belongs to us.'

I remained as calm as I could, though my heart thumped painfully. 'How long ago?'

'Three, four days. They'll be on a galley by now.'

'How many of them?' I hissed.

This alarmed the Roman, as he did not know my relation to the family he and his associates had evicted and sent away to a life of misery. He was even more cautious now. 'Four. An old couple and two … uh…' If he said anything that implied they had been touched, I'd put out his eye. He hesitated, watching me. 'Two daughters, I would guess, very well-to-do young ladies.'

One of his friends sniggered, and that was when Elvir loosed his arrow. The laugh was cut off abruptly, and the Roman thug looked down at the shaft protruding from his chest.

For a moment everyone was still, and nobody spoke. Then the wounded man slumped forward onto the table, his head sending wine spewing through the air, and the other two lunged for their swords. They didn't reach them. Drenan's sword plunged cleanly through the armpit of his man, deep enough to have severed his windpipe as it jerked upwards, and my blade entered the leader's brain from a point just below his skull at the nape of his neck. Blood spurted from the wound and no sound came from his wide-open mouth.

Drenan and Elvir turned to run, but I stood rooted to the floor.

'Wait,' I commanded. 'I have to check that there's no message for us.'

'But where would you look? It's a large house,' said Drenan, keen to escape.

'I know,' said Elvir, calmly. I was becoming more impressed with his confidence with every turn of events. 'Follow me.' He walked quickly into the herb garden and pushed over the small statue, beneath which we had all left notes and messages about our whereabouts. There, on the stone base, was a folded piece of parchment. Elvir glanced at the writing and handed it to me. We ran for the horses.

Nobody challenged us as we rode through the town and out through the gates. The pain in my chest was savage and insistent, but it did not compare with the pain in my heart.

Rome had taken my family.

TWENTY-SIX

The note was written in my father's hand and addressed to me.

We do not know whether we will see you again. If you are reading this message, you will already know of the terror that Rome has brought to Munda, but be assured that we are all alive, though Pidray is sick. Your mother and your sisters have a resilience of which you can be proud, as I am, and all of us refuse to believe that you are dead. Find Elvir and tell him of our deepest love for you both, and assure him that while we live, and beyond, you will both always feel our presence in spirit.

Our lives have been spared, though many have been executed on the whim of Roman officers and the hate of Zebul, who has returned here with an unchecked malice, the like of which I had hoped never to see in one of our own. Be aware, son, that the Pompeian soldiers who remain here have sworn their allegiance to Caesar — at least that is what their lips have said, and who can blame them when the choice was given at the point of a sword? For our lives we thank the centurion to whom we gave sustenance, and who sent word to Tribune Saxa that we should be treated well. This is fortuitous, as this tribune is of our race, but I am told that the best we can hope for is that as slaves in a far-off land we will not be separated. Forgive my haste. Kiss Elvir for me and for your mother.

I read the letter so many times that it began to fall apart at the folds, so I bought a leather trapper's pouch from a seller of charms and trinkets in the market at Gades. I tucked the letter inside, and next to it I placed my myrrh stone and the coins that had been my pay before Caesar destroyed my life. This I tied around my neck, beneath my tunic.

I formed no fond memories of the time I spent in Gades, which had corrupted better men than me. But we had to go there, because that was where my family was taken. I wished I had not taken Elvir but, like me, he had killed without hesitation and, with the discharged souls of our victims, innocence had taken flight.

The city mesmerised both me and my brother, but for Drenan and Turon, who had enthusiastically agreed to accompany us on our journey, Gades was anathema. Its bustling markets, filthy streets, raucous taverns and ignorant people infected them with a malaise that they could not shrug off until they returned to open country. The people had not been affected by the war, except that the harbour had been busier of late with the arrival of warships and the heavy, lumbering transports that brought horses and weapons, though I doubted anyone knew or cared for which army these had been intended. Most of these great ships had returned to Rome and the major cities of the Great Sea, laden with despondent slaves and the spoils of war.

Taking Elvir with me, I began my search for signs that our family had passed this way — we had no doubt that they had left Hispania's shores. We found some of the slave prisons, great wooden cages that must have recently housed many more unfortunates than we encountered there. Vacant, resigned eyes stared back at us as we called for our parents and sisters, and several times we were moved roughly on by guards who were pleased to have something more to do than endure the stench of sweat, urine and fly-infested faeces.

The port was like nothing we had ever seen before. Elvir gaped at the colourful market stalls lining the streets nearest the moorings, where merchants mingled with housewives looking for bargains, whether rare jewellery or sacks of grain.

One dark-skinned trader, his ears pierced with gold and his robe decorated with myriad seashells, was taking obscene amounts of coin for the beautiful caged birds displayed all around him. A small ape, not dissimilar to those in drawings my tutor had shown me years ago, sat impatiently on his shoulder.

We explored further to where two Roman galleys were moored side by side, held motionless by heavy ropes bleached white by the sun. The smell of rotting fish was overpowering here, the trademark of an overworked city-port, though we could see no catch being unloaded or stored nearby. A small group of officers and merchant traders huddled around a makeshift table, an abacus and wax tablets their accounting tools. We watched them haggling and arguing for a while, suspecting that the cargo under discussion might be more slaves to feed the Empire's voracious appetite for free labour.

It was Elvir who stepped forward, and I let him go, admiring his boldness. He tugged at the hemp tunic of the man nearest, like an innocent youth hoping for a treat or a beggar expecting a small coin. Watching him, it was hard to imagine he had loosed an arrow through the chest of a Roman soldier not seven days earlier.

The flabby, heavy-jowled man swatted at Elvir's hand without breaking his concentration on the urgent matters under discussion.

'Please, sir,' Elvir persisted.

The fat man glanced behind him and saw a beggar. 'Piss off.'

'Sir, I'm looking for my mother, my father and my sisters.' He began to cry and I was impressed.

'Then go home. That's the obvious place to find them.' Fat Man turned back to the debate.

'But sir, I think they have gone away in one of those big ships. Their names are...'

Fat Man was angry now and rounded on Elvir. 'Look, son, we have shipped thousands of people out of here in the last weeks, and not one of them has a name. Do you hear me, rat boy? They're just numbers, so if they've sailed out of here you won't ever see them again. Now bugger off and leave us alone.'

The other men were finding this more entertaining than their dispute and watched in amused silence. Elvir somehow managed a quivering lip to add to his fake tears, although perhaps these were now genuine, so frightening was Fat Man in his tirade. I decided to step in.

'Sirs, I am the boy's brother, and all we want to know is...'

'Just piss off, both of you!' Fat Man shouted. 'Can't you see we're busy?'

I looked at the other men, my eyes wide in appeal. One of them seemed to have a kinder face than Fat Man, and I concentrated my silent plea on him. It worked.

'We only deal in numbers here. It's just a cargo to us,' he said. 'But if you two really want to keep asking hopeless questions, you need to find Appius Pavo. He's the only one who knows what's going on around here.'

'Thank you, sir,' I replied, then added, 'Where can we find him?'

Turning back to the others, the man waved his arm dismissively. 'You won't get near him while the sun's up, but you can be sure to find him over there, later.' He indicated a squalid-looking tavern in a shaded corner of the harbour. 'He'll be in the House of Varro.'

Despite his protests, I left Elvir with Turon and Drenan at our lodgings while I went to look for information in the dubious

House of Varro.

I stood in the doorway as my eyes adjusted to the dark. The tavern was busy, not yet rowdy as I had imagined it would be, with several knots of hardened men fuelling their weary minds and bodies from bulbous pitchers, huddled in whispered conversation that would, I guessed, rise to raucous ribaldry as the night sweetened the sour wine. The host was easily identifiable from the grubby apron that tried unsuccessfully to cover an abundant belly, and the two jugs he held in his massive fists.

I was surprised to see two women standing near a door at the rear of the room, talking and laughing together, one dark-haired with a mysterious appearance, the other with blonde curls framing a painted face. Both were generously formed and dressed to draw attention. The blonde noticed me in the doorway and nudged her companion, who peered through the gloom and gave me an unmistakable wink. The other beckoned with a smile and a waved summons. *Somewhere to start*, I thought, and made my way carefully between precarious tables, carelessly outstretched legs and gesticulating arms.

'You're new here,' said the dark-haired woman.

'Yes,' I confirmed, hoping I did not appear too eager. 'I'm looking for someone.'

The blonde laid a hand on my arm. 'Would that someone be one of us, or both?'

I blushed but was saved from further embarrassment by the host, who was returning to the cellar for more wine.

'It's customary to buy a drink before sampling other delights,' he said tetchily.

'Oh, to be sure, but I'm here to speak to Appius Pavo, and I don't know what he looks like.' I looked hopefully into the host's piggy eyes.

'Over there.' He nodded towards a stocky man seated alone in a corner, leaning back heavily on the greasy wall. He was only slightly better dressed than the other patrons in the tavern, but an unkempt beard and long, tangled hair betrayed an older man who did not look after himself.

'Thanks,' I said, selecting two bronze coins from my money pouch. 'Can you bring us a jug of wine?'

He turned towards the cellar door, but I called him back. 'I forget my manners. When you bring the wine, please refresh the cups of these delightful ladies.'

Both giggled. 'How charming,' laughed the blonde.

'Be sure to come back later to finish what you're starting,' said her companion, pouting suggestively.

'I look forward to it,' I replied, and bowing a farewell, I turned towards the man who might know what had happened to my family.

Appius Pavo was not an easy man to talk to. He was tired and clearly not enthusiastic about his job, which seemed to be some kind of port clerk, or his wife, who apparently spent all of his meagre wages on clothes and jewellery. He could not even muster the energy to thank me for the wine that I had bought and seemed totally disinterested in my questions about cargo records. Until I pulled out a gold coin.

'What kind of cargo was it that you're interested in?' he asked, sitting upright now, his eyes fixed on the coin that I had placed on the table in front of me.

'Slaves. My family was taken in error, my parents and my two sisters.'

'That's tricky.' He scratched the bald patch on the top of his head. 'Where did they come from, these people?'

'Munda, after the battle.'

'Ah yes, we've had a lot of slaves from there. Caesar will be turning in a tidy profit from that lot, and no mistake.'

'What kind of records do you keep?'

'No names, just numbers.' He paused, remembering that he had to give me something if he was to keep the gold coin. 'But each shipment is assigned to the senior officer who despatched them from the place where they were taken. Do you know who that might have been?'

A glimmer of hope. I fingered the pouch that held my father's letter. 'The only name I have is Saxa. A tribune, I think.'

'Ah! Decidius Saxa. A fine man — hard to believe he's one of us. A fully-fledged Roman now, he is.'

'If you mean he's Hispanic, I know this already.' I put my finger on the coin as if to slide it back to my pouch.

Pavo put his hand on mine and smiled. 'Well, yes, he's from these parts originally, but no longer. He's a wealthy man and generous to those who help him.'

'You mean you've met him? Is he here?'

Pavo took his hand away and leaned back, smugly. 'He was. I handled his accounts personally and signed off his shipments just a few days ago.'

'Shipments of what? And to where?'

'Oh, slaves, more than enough for his expanding households, and plenty of the spoils of war. He's found favour with Caesar, you see.'

'Evidently. Do you remember any of the slaves, specifically?'

'That depends.' He eyed the coin. I slid it across to his side of the table. 'But I'm afraid they all look and smell the same to me.'

Undaunted, I described my parents and sisters in detail, hoping they would have seemed all the more distinctive if they had been kept together, as might have been the case if they had found the favour hinted at in my father's message. At my words, the look in Pavo's eye shifted just enough for me to realise my persistence had paid off, and I knew he would not be spinning me a false tale just to keep the gold coin.

'Yes,' he admitted, 'I saw this family. One of the girls was sick.' I had omitted this detail, so now it was confirmed.

I leaned forward. 'Where have they gone? Do your records show this?'

'Oh yes, indeed. They've gone to the same place as most of the ships that have left here in recent days. To Rome. But who knows where they go from there?'

'Don't your records indicate their onward passage?'

'No. But Saxa sailed with his plunder, which I expect will find its way to his new estates. As for slaves, they are more likely to be sold on arrival in Rome.'

Pavo had told me as much as he could, I thought, or at least as much as a gold coin was worth. I thanked him and stood to take my leave.

'One more thing,' he said, pocketing the coin. 'Word around here is that Saxa has been given estates in Italia, as befits a candidate for high office who enjoys the favour of Caesar. If he keeps them for his personal household, they will be well treated.'

I thanked him again and left him with the rest of the wine.

The painted ladies were too engrossed with a rowdy group of new arrivals to notice my going.

'What do you mean *you're* going to Rome?' Elvir demanded when I told him what had happened. 'You mean *we're* going to Rome!'

'Elvir, you are too young to make this journey.'

'But not too young to put an arrow through that Roman before you or Drenan moved!'

'You are smart and quick, but you are still too young…'

Elvir saw only an elder bully-brother with his mind set and turned to appeal to Turon and Drenan, who had watched as we argued.

'I think you'd probably end up saving his life and returning a great hero,' said Drenan with a gentle smile, and Elvir relaxed a little with the discovery of an ally. 'And I think we should all be going with Pito to save him from his own clumsiness and stupidity.' Drenan put his hands on Elvir's shoulders and looked into his eyes. 'But there are occasions when we must wait for the right time. Turon and I have need of you here.'

Elvir stared at the ally he had won and lost in the blink of an eye. 'What do you mean, you need me?'

Turon answered for Drenan. 'You may think that we are here to look after you and help you learn the ways of wisdom. A few days ago, that would have been true. But now we are three men of Munda, and each of us has need of the other two. Separate us now and we are incomplete. Drenan and I know we must stay in Hispania, and we want you to stay with us.'

Elvir remained silent, pondering this.

'We must entrust Pito to the gods,' continued Turon. 'He loves you, and he needs your understanding now.'

Elvir nodded. 'For a moment I thought you were going to tell me that you needed me to teach you how to fight,' he laughed. 'Which you do, of course.' He turned back to me and threw his arms around my neck. 'You'd better come back soon, with Mother and Father and our sisters…'

I tried to sound confident as I held him close. 'Just as soon as I can. Now, help me find a ship that will take me across the sea.'

TWENTY-SEVEN

Castor and *Pollux* were bound in brotherhood, their moorings allowing only the gentlest of motion. The soft moaning of timber harmonised with the distant cry of reckless gulls. A procession of slaves carried sacks of grain, amphorae of oil and sides of cured carcasses onto the nearest of the triremes, *Pollux*, under the watchful eyes of a burly centurion and six of his officers. Barefoot crew studiously bound split oars and daubed garish red paint on the rails and outriggers.

Beyond, a smaller, faster liburnian was making for port, her single rows of oars rising and falling in perfect time, thrusting her resolutely towards Gades' harbour with a silver spray splashing playfully at her bows. I watched, fascinated, as she rounded the defiant breakwater and, slowing in the port's calm, shipped oars to glide in an effortless arc towards *Castor*'s welcoming side. Ropes were flung to the larger ship and the liburnian was moored, nestling tight beside *Castor* like a junior sibling. Her crew busied themselves stowing oars and ropes while her officers hurdled the guardrails and clambered aboard the larger ship, greeted by uniformed optios from the two triremes.

Elvir and I watched, trying to identify the right officer to approach. The objective was simple: I would join as a crew member at the highest rank possible while Elvir would lend credibility as my personal assistant — he had stubbornly refused to take on the guise of a slave — and I would bluff my way onto this expedition.

The officer checking the cargo at the wide loading gangway seemed the obvious target. Bareheaded and wearing no armour apart from the silver inlaid leather belt and short sword that confirmed his rank, he was tall and muscled, with well-groomed dark hair that indicated he had enjoyed time ashore for the civilised necessities denied to seafarers for days on end. We waited until there was a break in the line of burdened slaves and approached him.

'Sir!' I called firmly but politely. He turned and inspected us quizzically as we stepped towards him, Elvir a respectful pace behind me. 'I beg your pardon, but I seek the enlisting officer. Would you be so kind as to direct me to him?'

'That depends on who you are and what you can offer.' His voice was deep, imposing. 'Oarsmen in these ships must be soldiers first, and tough, but neither of you look like you've done anything more strenuous than cling to your mother's skirts.'

Elvir bridled, but I replied quickly to keep the officer's attention on me.

'Sir, I have greater skills than paddling a boat, and my young assistant here does not seek employment on your fine ships.'

'I see. Good with a mop and bucket, are we?' he chuckled.

'About the enlisting officer, sir?'

Just then, a group of officers appeared at the top of the gangplank, laughing and chatting, looking forward to some time ashore.

'Stand aside,' ordered the gangway officer. 'Make way for the commander.'

We obeyed, and I looked at the young officer who led the other men down the gangway. He, too, was tall and had the haughty look of Roman nobility, dressed in a fine linen tunic embroidered with green and gold laurels. His mousy hair was fashionably unkempt, his striking countenance dominated by a dignified straight nose that appeared to force his eyes upward into an almost conceited expression. He walked with a powerful gait, at ease with his fellow officers. But the thing that struck me most about the fleet commander was that he was so young, barely older than me, perhaps no more than twenty-two years.

'What have we here, Quintus? Entertainment for the crew on our last night?' His voice matched his noble bearing, resonant and amiable.

Quintus laughed. 'No, sir, though we could ask them to give us a tune or a dance. The older one seeks a position with us, but he's a bit picky. Doesn't want to rough his hands up with an oar. I was just about to send him on his way.'

My hopes fell.

But the commander was not in a hurry, and he looked me up and down. 'Well, if you don't do oars, just what do you do?'

'General repairs, carpentry, accounting, whatever you have need of,' I replied a little too cockily.

The commander ignored the impudence. 'Can you cook? The lad on trial here has run home to his mother rather than face my opinion of the slop he served up last night.'

'Yes, sir, I can.'

'Then you're hired. You'll serve on my ship, *Castor*, and you'll keep a record of the ship's stores, serve the officers three hearty meals a day, keep the crew in good spirits with rations, and work on deck when you're not chopping and slicing. I'll decide what to pay you when we reach Rome.'

I beamed and bowed my head in acceptance.

'You can get started right away. I'll return after the sun has gone down, and we want to be impressed.' He looked at his fellow officers, then back to me. 'We dine on *Castor* tonight, nine of us, and we'll be extremely hungry.' The others laughed, and he began to move towards the town, then turned back.

'How remiss of me. What's your name, lad?'

'Melqart,' I said with a smile. I liked him already.

'And I'm Marcus Vipsanius Agrippa, appointed duovir navalis by Gaius Julius Caesar. But you can call me Sir, at least to my face.'

And with that, he led his men to the crowded streets of Gades to do battle with their thirst.

The wind shifted and, to the relief of the rowers who had strained all morning, Agrippa gave the order to go under sail. The horn sounded and the mainsails of each ship dropped obediently, flapping in protest until angled and tied, each now billowing like the pompous cheeks of Notus bringing his summer storms. The lighter liburnian, *Fides*, was first to ship oars, immediately surging like a frisky colt while the larger *Castor* and *Pollux* heaved themselves in pursuit, groaning timbers protesting at the wind's song in their rigging.

Gripping the deck rail as I tried to find the sea's rhythm, I looked across to *Castor*'s helmsman and saw the same wonder there as he watched the pennant dance wildly in the breeze to best judge the trireme's most favourable bearing. Hispania's rugged coast was still close, the faint sound of the cicada chorus borne delicately on the wind. We had left Gades with the dawn, the liburnian's flute whistle piping her oarsmen to lead the heavier ships with their tiered banks of oars, the energetic crews well fed on bread and cheese from my kitchen.

The wind teased my hair, just as I had ruffled Elvir's last night. Today, he would have left Gades to seek out Leandra, Cassia and Nahalia to tell them of my departure, and give them my promise to return to Apollacta one day when the gods permitted it. His mature resolve had collapsed when we parted, his tears warm on my neck as he swore to obey Turon and Drenan in everything. In return, he demanded a pledge that I would not come back without our family. Perhaps even now he watched from a hilltop as our three ships thrust their bow beaks into each swelling wave and drew the mighty Pillars of Hercules ever closer.

'By far the best way to travel, don't you think?' Agrippa's voice cut short my thoughts. I turned and tried to stand to attention but failed comically as the ship shuddered through a hostile wave.

'Sir,' I managed, clinging again to the rail.

'At ease, son,' he granted, leaning easily on the salty timber next to me. 'This your first time at sea?'

'No, sir,' I replied, recalling my first attempts at navigation in the calm seas off Apollacta. 'But this is my first time under Roman command.'

'Well, are you duly impressed?'

'Of course, sir. We're making swift progress to Rome.'

Agrippa smiled. 'It will be some weeks before we reach Italia. First we head for Utica for salt and spices, and perhaps a few days' rest on dry land.'

'Utica? But that's in Africa,' I said with alarm.

He noticed my despondency. 'So, you're in a hurry to reach Rome, are you? What about your commitment to the fleet? It seems like you intend to jump ship, and I might have other plans for a cook such as you.' His look was one of mock indignation. 'That was a fine feast you served up last night, and I'm not sure the imperial navy will want to let you go.'

'Sir, I … I…'

'You're stammering, lad.'

'Well, it's just that I had hoped to seek employment among the nobility of Rome,' I lied. 'I didn't realise…'

Agrippa slapped me on the back. 'Don't worry. I'm just teasing. I, too, have a bigger destiny than this command. Perhaps I'll take you with me to Illyria.'

'Sir…?'

Agrippa looked vaguely into the flecked grey waves as they surged powerfully along the ship's flank. 'We each have our own journey,' he said slowly. 'Mine is to study under Greek tutors the ancient ways of government and law and apply it to the brave new world that Caesar has forged.'

I bit my lip, not wanting to reveal my recent support of Caesar's enemies, and my bitterness over the fact that my own people had been the innocent victims.

Agrippa was still talking. 'But it is the sea that draws me, and that is where my ambition lies. Do you know what I mean?'

'Yes, sir, I do. When I came to your ship, I felt as though I was taking a step towards my destiny.'

'You're not running, then? I thought perhaps you were escaping from something.'

'On the contrary, I am seeking…' I let the object of my search hang in the air, just waving my arm towards the open sea. 'But I will return here someday.'

'A traveller, then, or an adventurer, but not a cook? Speaking of which, you've got a hungry crew and officers to feed. Hope you can do as well as you did last night. Better get on with it.'

'Yes, sir.' I felt as though I was slowly finding my balance as I staggered on the treacherous deck towards my meagre kitchen.

We sailed with fair winds and rowed when there were none, past the great rock that guarded Hispania's southern coast, where lithe dolphins performed their playful games in the bow's wash, and across the straits to hug Africa's hazy northern shore. We saw no other ships, the two triremes staying close like old friends while the impertinent *Fides* flitted and scurried, finding hidden coves to lie in wait for her lumbering companions. Here, her crew netted hundreds of darting silvery fish to supplement the supplies for all three vessels. At dusk each day we lay off sandy beaches, the ships held by stern anchors and the bows roped to the sturdy olive trees that grew at random in the fertile soil near river estuaries. On several occasions, children in precarious small craft sought coins and trinkets by ferrying officers to their small settlements ashore. When no such favours were available, men and officers alike plunged overboard to make camp and hunt game for the night fires.

On the ninth evening we dared not go ashore. All day a small band of horsemen had followed our progress, watching our steady crawl along Mauretania's coastline. The sun caught the curved swords that dangled threateningly at the side of each black-robed rider. Although we outnumbered them, Agrippa announced that the risk would be too great, as he suspected they were scouts for a far greater number of nomadic warriors whose home was the desert, and whose trade was in blood. He ordered the fleet away from the shore before the sun went down, and with the last light of day the three ships were roped together in fortuitously calm seas, drifting in the light offshore wind throughout the moonless night.

There was no sight of land when the dawn light danced in silver celebration on the placid sea, and we ate in silent appreciation of the ocean's vastness. Agrippa ordered a southerly course, the oars dipping and rising in unison to break the flat calm into swirling eddies.

At midday we sighted the first ship since leaving Gades, and Agrippa changed course for the squat shape on the distant horizon. *Fides* broke away and made for the lone vessel, which had also changed course, no doubt fearing pirates, but she was no match for the nimble liburnian and soon we came up to a huge, cumbersome quinquereme that looked like a leftover from the Punic wars, her captain already in shouted conversation with his counterpart on *Fides*, an energetic young officer named Fabius.

As soon as we were close enough, Fabius reported to Agrippa on *Castor* that the vessel was an old Carthaginian trader bound for Utica with a cargo of silver and furs from the northern lands, as well as metal tools and slaves for the expansion of the city. Agrippa, standing on the stern platform with one arm wrapped lazily around the pennant staff, announced to the trader and to our other ships that we would escort the Carthaginian into Utica. I suspected this was more to cover up his own lack of experience in these waters than out of a desire to protect the trader.

Our progress was more leisurely now, matching the pace of the larger ship. Like our triremes, she had three rows of oars but her extra girth allowed more rowers to each oar as well as considerable space for her cargo. A deep sounding drumbeat came from the bowels, giving the oars a slower rhythm than on our triremes, where bawdy songs sung by the rowers themselves gave the timing. At times the huge trader wallowed even in the calm seas, sending a lateral wash that rocked the smaller ships, so Agrippa allowed our guarding fleet to move astern to less disturbed waters.

We reached Utica with the evening's setting sun and lay at anchor outside the port that night, watching the ancient city come to life. The sound of drums and pipes drifted over the black waters, punctuated with shrill wailing and alien songs, chafing weary minds and denying sleep. I wasn't sure it would be safe to go ashore in this land.

TWENTY-EIGHT

The night was hot, the day hotter still. Long before dawn I sought in vain any cooling breeze that might relieve the oppressive weight of the desert's furnace rolling in from the south, and watched the new day paint the waking city with brilliant light.

Utica's port is in the mouth of the Bagradas river, sluggish and brown from the fertile soil washed down from the farmlands behind the city. *Castor* nudged affectionately to the stone quay where the city's quaestor waited with his attendants, fat on the taxes that Utica afforded and pompous in his purple robes of office. Agrippa leapt ashore before the ropes had been secured and greeted the quaestor jovially, pretending not to notice the official's sniffy response. *Pollux* and *Fides* were docking nearby, the crew's laughter proclaiming their forthcoming shore leave.

We were ordered to remain on board while Agrippa deliberated with the quaestor, who seemed preoccupied with his accounts, frequently ordering his clerks to write on the wax tablets they carried. Agrippa, by contrast, had no scrolls or orders, just his infectious spirit and calm authority. Eventually, Agrippa called the captains of *Pollux* and *Fides* to him on the quayside and spoke quietly with them, then strolled breezily to *Castor* to take up his favoured vantage point in the stern. The other captains went to their own ships to address their crews.

'Gentlemen,' Agrippa said, seeming to put no effort into his golden voice, 'we have made good time thus far in our journey, and for that I praise you all.' There was a murmured response in appreciation. 'We have been welcomed here by the good quaestor, who has opened his city to us —' this time there were cheers — 'but he asks only that we pay a fair price for our needs and, er, desires and enjoy this city's kind hospitality with honour and fair play.'

The men looked at one another suspiciously.

'I took that to mean that we should enjoy ourselves to the full, like the good Romans we are.' Now the crew cheered with enthusiasm. 'But try not to drink the city dry of its ale and wine!'

'By Jupiter, not us!' one of the oarsmen shouted. 'We hardly broke a sweat at these oars, and we are not yet thirsty.' All of the rowers burst into laughter at the oarsman's sarcasm.

Agrippa laughed with his men and added, more solemnly, 'But with all good news, there is also some bad...' The laughter petered out. 'I know you will be distraught at this, but it is with a heavy heart that I must inform you that your run ashore will be deprived of its greatest source of joy and pleasure. I will not accompany you.'

There were cries of 'Shame!' and a few mock profanities.

'And neither will your Captain of the Cups, Fabius of the good ship *Fides*,' Agrippa went on when the jocular insults had run their course. 'Which means, of course, Marius Lentulus, captain of *Pollux*, is appointed *duovir navalis* in my absence with all authority to exact full chastisement for any — and I mean any — misdemeanour whatsoever. You know the rules, so stick to them.'

Agrippa then revealed he had been charged by Caesar to bring back an appraisal of the territory around Utica, the yield of its industry and its farmlands, to boost Rome's coffers.

'I will take with me Fabius, as I have already told you, and ten men.' Agrippa began to name them, and I found myself wondering when we could actually set foot on the quayside and enjoy the city's rich culture. '…Gallio Velius Marsallas, Cassipor of Gaul … and Melqart of Hispania.'

The man next to me thumped me on the back. 'Lucky you,' he whispered. 'You're off on a great adventure, where the rivers sparkle with gold and jewels!'

The crews of all three ships disembarked rowdily, leaving two guards on each vessel. The ten "volunteers" waited on the quayside, most showing disappointment at missing out on the fun of exploring the city. I could not deny the excitement I felt at the prospect of discovering what sights and sounds the hinterland held for us. The other men wore light armour and carried short swords and daggers, but no shields. I had my short sword but no armour, and I felt superfluous next to these tall and clearly experienced soldiers.

'Right then, lads,' said Agrippa as Fabius approached. 'The quaestor has arranged some fine local mounts for us and we'll be travelling light. Now, form up. The stables are over there.'

Not knowing what "form up" might mean, I ambled at the rear of the group. Agrippa led us along the quay towards a large arched building that served as the most impressive stables I had ever seen, home for even more impressive horses. These were swift desert horses, their manes plaited intricately, their long, well-groomed tails proud and frisky, most of them greys with alert ears and eager eyes. They sensed action, tugging sharply at their harnesses, stamping and snorting to attract attention.

Squatting nearby were their grooms, deep in discussion with a tall man whose black haik was wrapped tautly around a muscular torso. He wore leather armbands studded with polished bronze, and the jewelled hilt of his beautifully crafted dagger protruded from his knotted rope belt. His head was swathed in black cloth, edged with tiny silver disks, and his boots were soft goatskin, indicating independence and wealth. Sitting obediently at his side was a shorthaired hunting dog, long-nosed and long-legged for speed, its healthy coat covering lean muscle and a well-defined ribcage.

The man looked up as we approached and for a moment I was taken aback by his mysterious dark eyes.

I studied the warrior as Agrippa greeted him and saw a man comfortable in this world and confident of the next. He clasped Agrippa's hands in his.

'I am Ziri,' he said in a compelling, assured voice. 'And I am Amazigh, a free man who is ruled by no one. Who is it who seeks Ziri's guidance and protection?'

Agrippa surprised me with his reply. 'None but your servant from across the seas,' he replied, bowing slightly. 'My master in Rome seeks trade with this city and its lands, but I know little of the terrain and the customs of your people, so we have asked the quaestor to recommend a guide. He is afraid of you, I think, which makes me believe you are the right choice.'

Ziri chuckled. 'The quaestor does not understand our ways. His only concern is for taxes and personal wealth, which I fear is the way of Rome.'

'There are exceptions to the rule.' Agrippa was wise not to attempt to defend Rome.

'And you are one such exception?' Both men were enjoying the encounter, the deal having been struck at the first moment of meeting.

'You will find that out for yourself,' replied Agrippa. 'What will you require in recompense for three days of your valuable time?'

'Only that you swear to me an oath, here where we stand on the shores of the sea that separates our lands.'

'And that oath might be…?' Agrippa did not seem surprised that he was not being asked for Roman coin.

'That when your master or his generals come here, they will honour my people with the respect that is due to an ancient and noble race and will not take slaves or raid the lands where my Imazighen live. This respect your master has shown to our neighbours to the east, the land that you call Aegyptus.'

Agrippa broke into a smile. 'If I'm not mistaken, my master was inspired by the Great Queen of that land…?'

Ziri looked over the men in Agrippa's command, his gaze settling on me for an uncomfortable moment. 'If it is the delights of a woman you seek, you will find this and more in these lands.'

'No,' said Agrippa, still smiling. 'These men are not worthy of your humblest womenfolk.' A murmur of protest from my colleagues was silenced by Agrippa's upraised arm. 'We have work to do, and if you agree to be our guide, I will personally bear your stipulations to Caesar himself and seek a treaty on your behalf.'

'Then choose your mounts, but remember that these are fine horses, and the stable master will require silver as well as a purse against their safe return.'

Agrippa called Fabius forward to pay the stable master, a small, hunched man who looked as if he would drive a hard bargain. Then he bowed to Ziri.

'I think that your horses will be a priority when our new trade agreements begin,' he said. 'We are now in your hands, and glad of it.'

Ziri led us south along the coastline, where the land was low enough to allow a vast network of salt pans to be fed with seawater, burned in the sun to fields of glistening white. Fabius noted the extent of this valuable resource — the leather bags laid across the rump of his horse were crammed with expensive scrolls and various writing tools, and frequently he dropped behind as he was unable to ride and write at the same time.

Grateful for the white headscarves that protected us from the merciless sun, we rode inland across a patchwork of smallholdings fed with sluggish brown water from crude ditches. Where the ditches were at their most effective, fed from the snaking Bagradas river, wheat, vegetables and citrus fruit were growing in abundance. At the earliest encounter with the farming community, Agrippa ordered me to arrange for fresh supplies to be made ready for our return, and I found two sturdy carts for which I paid less than expected thanks to Ziri's skill as a negotiator. These were to be laden with fruit, preserved olives, dates and aromatic flat bread, and Ziri made all kinds of fearsome threats to a wizened old farmer who spoke for the community, telling him to have the carts prepared for our return in three days. The old man grovelled and bowed, swearing obedience on the life of his mother, at the same time holding out a calloused hand for coins. I gave him half of the agreed amount, promising him the rest and more if he fulfilled his part of the bargain. His leathery face cracked into a toothless grin, and he hobbled off to tell his family that unexpected prosperity had come their way.

We sheltered from the overwhelming heat of the afternoon beneath a cover of palm fronds precariously built onto the one remaining wall of an ancient farm lodge, partly held in place by a large fig tree that provided an abundance of the soft, ripe fruit. We filled our waterskins from the murky depths of a nearby well, guarded by a child goatherd whose small drove foraged in the rocky ground, their nagging chatter blending with the chimes of their bell collars.

Ziri was watching me as he sucked the crimson flesh from a plump fig, seated with his back against the tree, his hunting dog panting in the oppressive heat. I sat next to him and took the proffered fig, flicking away an angry wasp that competed for the sweet prize. I introduced myself and we sat in silence for a while, then talked about the customs of his people, about Hispania and the story of my journey to Africa. At the mention of Caesar, I lowered my voice, not wishing to attract attention to my part in the war, though strangely these horrific events no longer seemed to concern Agrippa or the sailors.

The dog chewed blissfully on discarded fig skins, and I cupped my hands for Ziri to pour water so the thirsty animal could lap gratefully. I asked what his name was, and Ziri told me that in his language and mine, it was simply "dog". We laughed together.

I stroked Dog until he slept in my lap, telling Ziri about the strange encounters with the eagles of our mountains. This clearly intrigued Ziri, who pointed to the distant mountain peaks that divided the coastal lowlands from the harsh desert beyond.

'There are many such creatures there,' he said solemnly, 'and they are all my friends. They guard our people, and we revere them as gods.'

'How close have you been to them?' I asked.

'I speak with them often, and I have flown with them.'

'That's impossible,' I interrupted dismissively.

'Then you know nothing of the higher nature, but you are young and bound to the earth like an immoveable rock.'

I opened my mouth to argue, but Agrippa's command to mount up was an untimely intrusion.

We travelled higher into the foothills, where the cultivated land was stepped to catch the meagre rainfall. It was the dry season, but the olive trees were thrusting silver-green branches heavenwards and I could tell the oil harvest would be plentiful in the coming winter. Fabius duly noted this.

I rode with Ziri that evening at the head of the column, travelling south towards the mountain range then west to skirt the more rugged, inhospitable terrain. He spoke of the ways of his people, who seemed to own everything and nothing at the same time, moving in caravans across frontiers and even through the Great Desert without fear or threat; a people whose women and children were made tough and self-dependent in a barren wilderness.

As the sun lost its fervour, lingering on the western horizon, Ziri called to Agrippa that he would ride ahead to our overnight position. He beckoned me to follow. We rode to the next ridge, Dog following at an easy lope, and from there saw in a green valley below, the vast black tents of wandering people spread at the junction of two brooks that formed the source of the Bagradas. Horses were corralled around a large lagoon dug from the hard ground and fed by one of the brooks. Camels lay in groups, long legs folded beneath their strange bodies, each gently chewing. Children played at being warriors under the watchful eyes of the brightly dressed women who washed clothing in the fresh, clear highland streams.

'Remember how I have told you of covenant?' Ziri asked without taking his eyes off the nomad camp.

'You mean, if I come in peace and beg your protection, you are honour-bound to provide it? Yes.'

'Do you have a gift?'

I didn't like where this was going. My hand went to my throat, my fingers curling around my myrrh stone, but I did not reply.

'Is that of great importance to you?' Ziri asked.

'It is. It was given to me by a woman who has great healing powers, though it has no value in itself. Why do you ask this?'

'Because you are going to ride alone into that camp and learn the noble ways of men. Only by taking this step can you begin to understand the higher nature that lies beyond.'

'But what if they kill me?'

'Then you will understand far quicker than you expected!' At last Ziri turned and looked at me. 'But they won't kill you, not if you ride purposefully straight to the large tent in the middle of the camp, and do not stop or turn your gaze from it, no matter who challenges you.'

'Ziri, why can't you come with me?'

'Because I have to return to your men and lead them here. Because you are hungry for knowledge. Because when you ride down there, you will learn something important. And because you are the cook for your sorry band of Romans, and you should find the kitchens to finally understand what good food is really like. Now go!'

Still clutching the stone at my neck, I urged my horse forward, small rocks and loose earth tumbling down the slope as I descended. I reached the plain and squeezed the mare into a canter, sending up dust as a clear signal that I approached. From the corner of my eye I sensed rather than saw two horsemen approach from behind and to one side. They rode hard to cross in front of me with their curved swords drawn, black headgear streaming behind them. I did not waver from my course, nor take my eyes from the camp. The horsemen formed up on either side and I went to learn the secrets of covenant.

TWENTY-NINE

The small children were intimidating. Like malicious horseflies, at least twenty were running barefoot alongside my mare, yelling what I could only assume was abuse and flinging small stones that stung where they hit exposed flesh. More ran towards me from the camp, attracted by the commotion. The two horsemen reined in, fearful of harming the growing mass of boisterous children. I was forced to do the same.

Dismounting, I led my terrified horse on. A child kicked me on the leg and another hit my thigh with a stick, but the two riders just watched, bemused. Now the camp's women joined in the tirade of abuse. They were dark-skinned and fine-boned, dressed in magnificently patterned clothes with an abundance of gold bracelets, but had shrill voices that belied their rich apparel.

I wished I had refused Ziri's order. This was a mad world far removed from the peace of the open sea.

I neared the large main tent. Arrayed in a line across the wide, carpeted entrance were the youth of this community, each as tall as me and dressed head to foot in the same black cloth that Ziri wore, and each holding a two-handed curved blade. Their black eyes stared in unblinking challenge.

Do not stop, no matter who challenges you, Ziri had said. My heart thumping, I strode forward, fixing my gaze on the eyes of the centremost youth. The children and women fell silent. I saw a look of confusion cross the youth's face and I lengthened my stride, forcing on him the choice of physically barring my way or stepping aside. He chose the latter, and as I passed I handed him the leading rein of my horse. He had no choice but to take one hand from his sword and grasp it. I stepped past him and suddenly I was in a different world, a world that halted me where an armed youth could not.

Outside I had trodden on dust and stone, but now I intruded like a filthy beggar on a luxurious crimson and gold carpet, delicately woven with images of birds and animals. Huge soft cushions were arranged around two beaten copper bowls, each the size of a cartwheel, filled with shimmering, clear water. Suspended over each was a brazier issuing aromatic smoke, sweet as sage. Billowing lace hung in delicate folds, concealing the dark inner rooms of this magnificent temple. There was nobody there.

Outside, the only sound was my mount's nervous snorting and in the distance the irreverent bleating of goats. My heartbeat pulsed in my ears.

I was turning to leave when the old man spoke.

'Who darkens the door of Ankhtar, King of the Desert and Lord of the Mountains?' This came from deep inside the tent.

A woman's hand, heavy with jewelled rings, pulled aside the curtain. I could make out a voluptuous figure obscured by the drifting lace. A honeyed voice spoke in a language I did not understand, and the King of the Desert grunted in reply.

When the woman pulled the curtain back I saw only her eyes, dark and regal. She looked me up and down, and her gaze alighted on my sword and then my feet.

She frowned and I understood. I unbuckled my sword belt and laid it to one side, then stooped to unfasten my sandals. I stood barefoot and unarmed, my tunic loosened and creased, my feet black between the toes from dust and sweat.

The woman beckoned me into the semi-dark of the inner tent, not taking her eyes from mine, and the King of the Desert stepped forward.

I did not know why I did it. Sometimes a man is compelled by forces beyond himself, especially a youth like me who could not know how to behave in a strange land with its unexpected customs. But the moment I saw the man's bearing and the wisdom in one so old and grey, I found myself on my knees with my hands grasping his ankles. Even the old man seemed surprised by my obeisance.

'Lord,' I said in a small, wavering voice, 'I seek your protection and your guidance.'

Mastering his shock, the King of the Desert was silent for a moment. Then he said, solemnly, 'Protection from whom?'

'My enemies,' I replied. 'And the children of your people who berate me.'

I sounded pathetic and wanted to stand, but I remained at his feet. He laughed and lifted me gently by the shoulders, his hands surprisingly strong and firm.

'And my guidance?'

'Yes.' I was more confident now I was standing. 'It is said that your people know the secrets of fine food, and the health it gives. I seek these secrets.'

'And I was of a mind to hand you to the torturers and have you executed for your impudence. Now you tell me you want to learn to cook!' I saw his eyes smile as he looked to the woman. 'What should I do with him, Lady of the Night Sky?'

The woman stepped forward, all grace and elegance, modestly wrapping her colourful robe around her shoulders, her eyes averted from mine. 'Surely, my lord, he has invoked the most ancient tradition of our race?' I could have sworn that she winked at him.

'But he is a barbarian, a Roman, is he not?'

'Lord,' I interrupted, 'I am a traveller from across the sea, but I am not a Roman.'

'But you bring Romans here. Only a few, I grant you, but you are armed, so how can I know this is not a trick?' I realised then that our approach must have been watched.

'But we come in peace,' I protested, now fearing for my life.

'If I grant you protection, will you also swear to protect me from my enemies?'

I could find no other answer than 'yes', not hesitating to think about what that might mean.

'So what's yours is mine and what's mine is yours?' He must have noticed my look of astonishment and continued swiftly, 'This covenant between us should be sealed with a gift on your part.'

He moved away to allow me time to think, his back to me. Hesitantly, I reached towards my neck and grasped the myrrh stone.

The woman smiled and nodded. I untied the thongs and held it out to him.

'To me, this looks like amber, which we have in abundance here. What is it to you?'

'It is a precious gift that carries a promise of health and long life.'

'Then I accept your gift and with it the health and long life that it carries.' He studied the stone for a moment. 'And in return you shall have my protection.'

The King of the Desert turned towards his inner tent, but the woman coughed delicately to catch his attention. He looked at her, kindly and inquisitively.

'My lord forgets that he should also impart a gift,' she smiled.

'Oh yes, of course.' He held out the myrrh stone. 'I think you have greater need of this, as I have already enjoyed a long life and good health. Take it. It is my gift to you.'

As I tied the thongs around my neck, the old man added, 'It has great power. I have felt it. But it lacks the power to make you clean.'

He clapped his hands and called for servants to wash the dust from my body, especially my feet.

Agrippa was taken aback to find me washed, shaved and dressed in a rich woollen robe that reached to my ankles, full of vibrant colours and embroidered with fine silver braid. I was even more shocked when the King of the Desert greeted his son, Ziri. I discovered that both had known all along of my coming to the nomad's camp and the treatment I should receive.

Agrippa's men seemed intimidated by the clamour around them, unsettled by the riotous children and keening women, until Fabius ordered them to stable their horses and wash themselves in the larger brook. Agrippa went with the old man and his elegant woman into the cool dark of the tent, presumably to learn more of the region's economy.

The King of the Desert had already handed me over to his royal cooks, all elderly women, and ordered them to treat me like a son and withhold nothing as they prepared the Great Feast for their guests. Treating me like a son meant they clucked over me, stroking my hair and touching me in places they should not. I couldn't understand anything they said but I got the impression that once their work was finished I would have other duties to perform. I grew used to having my cheeks pinched, and guessed from the lusty laughter that their chatter was not about cooking.

With the last of the light, the women prepared huge dishes of steaming ground wheat, each decorated differently with raisins, dates, olives and nuts. Three young goats, salted and basted with honey, were being slowly spit-roasted, the juices collected and mixed with aromatic herbs before being poured into clay pitchers. Sweet dishes were set aside — sticky confections laced with honey, cakes made with anise to aid digestion, dates, figs and fruits simmered in cinnamon and cloves.

I went with my giggling new friends to place the feast before the King of the Desert and his royal household, obediently seating myself on a luxurious cushion next to the old man when he gestured to me.

Ziri was all smiles and flourishing ritual, introducing his many brothers and sisters, and his mother, the gracious Lady of the Night Sky. It was hard to discern which, if any, of the old man's household were slaves, as all seemed to be equals, but later I observed the King of the Desert with two of the younger women who were clearly not his daughters. Ziri's mother appeared not to notice.

Outside the pipes wailed, then drums and timbrels picked up the rhythm. Agrippa and Fabius, seated opposite me, seemed relaxed as they tore strips of meat with their knives and used their fingers to scoop the fragrant grain into their mouths, copying their hosts. The atmosphere was light and infectious, made all the more so by the hot anise drink that was passed to me, the fiery spirit annulling the fatty meat juices that dribbled down my chin.

When we could eat no more, Ziri took a lyre and began a haunting song in his own tongue, his voice surprisingly pure, rising to long high notes and falling almost to a whisper, laden with emotion and enthralling Roman and Amazigh alike. When he had finished, an appreciative silence was eventually broken by Agrippa, who politely asked Ziri to explain the song. It was, said Ziri, a song about the mountains and the desert as seen by the Great Eagle as he watches over us.

Ziri joined me outside the tent, where I was taking the still night air. The music and dancing had ebbed, and now a hazy sense of wellbeing lay over the camp. The half-moon and brilliant stars bestowed a cold, blue light that contrasted with the pulsing embers of the camp's fires. Some slept beside the dying fires, while others stumbled to their tents.

'What have you learned today?' Ziri asked.

I thought for a moment, looking up at the stars. 'That you are full of surprises. That civilisation does not mean great temples and streets of stone. That your people are warm and generous and like to dance and laugh. And I think I have heard the song of eagles.'

Ziri said nothing; we shared the gentle euphoria of the night.

'It's easy to make a covenant in this peaceful land,' I added. 'I think I have enjoyed the best of the bargain, and I do not know how to repay you and your father.'

Ziri turned to me, the moon illuminating a serious look on his face. 'This land is not as peaceful as you think, Melqart. We are taught to fight almost before we can walk, to defend our tribe against many enemies. But tonight is for feasting, the love of a woman, and sleeping.'

'I've enjoyed the first, and my body tells me it is time for the third. I will sleep with the horses.'

'I understand; I too prefer to sleep under the stars. Before you sleep, watch, and count those that fall to the earth. You will see many tonight.'

THIRTY

It was still dark when Fabius woke me, putting his fingers to his lips in a gesture that could only mean "stay silent". The horses nearby were restless.

'The camp is in danger,' he whispered. 'Ziri's men believe an attack is imminent.'

'Attack? Who...?' I was still disoriented, but then I remembered where I was and found it hard to believe that anyone would want to raid these peaceful people.

'It doesn't matter who, or why. If these people are in danger, then we will help them. Bring your sword and stay quiet.'

I followed Fabius towards the central tent, buckling my sword belt as we went. All around me in the moon's weak light I could see men being roused to move swiftly and silently to the camp's perimeter. Others were bringing up horses from the corral, stroking their necks and murmuring to them to keep them quiet.

Agrippa was waiting with the old man when we reached his tent. The others from our group arrived in twos and threes, crouching in the tent's antechamber.

'As far as we can tell,' said Agrippa crisply, 'there is a small force of raiders to the east. How many, we do not know. My lord Ankhtar here thinks they may be slavers from Aegyptus. They probably think they have surprise on their side, as they creep closer without noise, but they will attack as soon as there is light.'

I looked at my colleagues and understood why they had been picked. Each one was unafraid and ready to fight.

'We have no shields,' Agrippa was saying, 'but we have our swords. Ankhtar's men will mount as soon as the attack begins, and Ziri will lead them fast and straight towards the enemy's throat. We will fight on foot, forming a line between the camp and the enemy as soon as we know for sure where they will attack.'

One of the Romans, a swarthy man with eyes red from lack of sleep, spoke for the others. 'If they are all horsemen, and we have only short swords and daggers, how will we stop them?'

Agrippa smiled and pointed to a pile of spears, each about twice the length of a man. 'We are given these, but the King of the Desert asks that you kill cleanly and do not break them. When we find our position you will have little time, so do your best to make the shaft steadfast in the earth, use your foot if you have to, and let the horses ride onto your spear. When the riders fall, despatch them. Understood?'

The men nodded.

Agrippa looked at me. 'Melqart, you are to stay close to Ankhtar. He has bowmen with him, but all of the swordsmen have gone with Ziri. You are his man now; defend him with your life.'

I nodded, and Agrippa wasted no time in handing a spear to each man and leading them into the gloom.

I looked at the King of the Desert and saw pride and fire in his eyes.

Ankhtar quietly commanded his four bowmen to lie down, feigning sleep to add to the impression that the tribe was unprepared. He had led us to a place near the edge of the camp, and I guessed that Agrippa was a stone's throw further out, no doubt affecting unreadiness as well. Each archer had a black-feathered arrow nocked and several spares nearby. As I lay beside them, sword in hand beneath my body, I hoped it would be enough.

The sun cast its first golden rays onto the hills behind us. The palm of my hand sweated as I clutched the sword's hilt tightly, my heart pounding. The ache in my back returned, reminding me of the agonies of warfare.

The enemy came, riding swiftly from behind a low hill, directly out of the rising sun. There was no war cry, just the thunder of hooves on the ground. I stole a glance and could make out Agrippa's men lying still near a small ridge — they had guessed the point of attack well, but the raiders were perilously close. There were probably a hundred of them, black-clothed riders leaning forward in the saddle, blades held horizontally forward as they charged.

Suddenly the King of the Desert was on his feet with his great curved sword unsheathed, his meagre band of bowmen kneeling beside him, bows taut, heads cocked to sight along their shafts. At the same time, Agrippa's men rose as one and dug their spear shafts into the base of the ridge, allowing no time for the riders to veer away. It was ten men against a hundred horsemen.

The first horses in the van crashed onto the spears, squealing and floundering as they pitched their riders forward. The Romans drew their swords in one movement and dodged the following horsemen, many of the surprised animals losing their footing as they hit the ridge then careered into their fallen comrades in a tangle of horses, men and dust. The riders in the rear of the charge saw the mayhem and swerved left and right to avoid catastrophe. But when they saw the Romans killing the fallen, a great cry of outrage filled the air. Surely they would return to butcher the Romans in revenge.

But then the first of our arrows hit home, our small group of kneeling men having been ignored in the first charge. Two men dropped from their horses, black feathers protruding from chest and neck, then three more as the second volley flew.

Ziri timed his attack to perfection, leading his own horsemen who had mounted at the first indication of attack. They swept out from behind the black tents and rode hard at the enemy, yelling and waving their curved swords high over their heads. The raiders saw this and made directly for Ziri's force. They clashed in a mass of whirling blades and severed limbs, horses screaming and men dying as dust rose in great shrouds. Still nobody attacked our position, but our archers could not loose more arrows while Ziri's men fought hand to hand. Perhaps I wouldn't have to fight after all.

But Ziri was outnumbered, and bit by bit he fell back under the raining blows of the enemy. The Romans had finished their foul work and, gathering fallen weapons as they ran, they went to support our beleaguered tribesmen. This spurred Ankhtar, who seemed to be growing in stature with each ebb and flow of the battle. With a cry, he sprinted like a demented gazelle towards the writhing dust cloud and I ran with him, struggling to keep up with the inspired old man. The archers followed, arrows nocked.

From the camp, the children came, showing no fear, and to my surprise, some of the women came too. All were armed with farm tools of one kind or another, each lethal with their reach and jagged edges. The enemy was now outnumbered and attacked on three sides. My lungs bursting, I caught up with the King of the Desert in time to slice my sword downwards on the turbaned head of an enemy swordsman who had lined up Ankhtar's approach. I saw the white of his skull before blood and gore welled up, and parried a blow from the horseman who followed behind my victim, my right arm numbed from the heavy blow. There was a sickening thud, and the familiar black feathers protruded from the warrior's chest, his eyes wide in surprise as he slid from his saddle.

I looked for Ankhtar and realised he had slashed and hewn a path into the heaving enemy, some distance away. I scampered to his side, wary of the flashing blades all around me as I spat dust and grit from my mouth. I tasted blood, as I had bitten my tongue in the furore.

The raider who rode hard at the King of the Desert must have recognised him as the head of the tribe. He was lithe, not over-muscled but fluid in his horsemanship, and his sword was raised to strike. I threw myself in front of Ankhtar just as an arrow buried itself in the horse's neck, deflecting the animal from its deadly charge and saving my life.

The flat of the curved sword caught my head and everything went black.

I came to with the sounds of battle ringing in my ears. I tried to get to my feet, but my legs were like dead weights. I still gripped my sword and tried to raise it to defend against the next attack, but I could not. I was ready to die.

Then I heard a soft voice calling and realised that the shrill battle cry came from the women, and the drumming was my own heart pumping with desperation. I heard Agrippa's voice in my ear.

'Easy, lad,' he said reassuringly. 'No need to fight me.'

'The king…' I stammered. 'Where…'

'He's safe, though he will need his nurses for a few days, I fear.'

'The enemy?' I asked, recalling the confusion of battle.

'Mostly dead, though some have fled. We beat them soundly.' His arms and shoulders were dark with blood, but he seemed energised.

'And Ziri, our men?' I felt blood trickle from the corner of my mouth, and I spoke thickly, unable to form the words properly.

'We have all lost friends today. But they have lost more. Lie still. You are wounded.'

I let my head flop back to the hard ground and watched the clouds swirl in a sickening circle before closing my eyes. 'How many dead?' I asked when the nausea eased.

'Fabius and one other of our men. Probably thirty of the tribesmen, some children too.' I opened my eyes and looked into his. I saw a great sadness there.

'I liked Fabius. He was a good man.'

'Indeed. He was my friend. He fought well and took many of those bastards with him.'

'What now?' I asked, trying to recall what Agrippa's plan had been for the day.

'Well,' he said with a smile, 'it would be rude to leave now, don't you think? Let's get you back on your feet first.'

We stayed with Ziri's people for two days while we buried fallen comrades, the women keening as much over Fabius as over their own dead. We were one family now.

We helped the tribe move camp to put as much distance between them and the scorched remains of the enemy dead as we could, before finding a new site where there was water from mountain brooks. Ziri's niece dressed the wound on my head and made me drink the strong anise spirit to numb the lacerations on my tongue and speed healing.

The King of the Desert recovered more quickly than I did, bringing me more anise and words of gratitude for saving his life. Of course I denied this, saying that I did what any man would do in a fight.

'You have kept your part of the bargain,' he said, helping me to my feet. He took me to see the last of the prisoners die in agony.

'Why do you do this?' I asked, appalled at the torture the man had suffered.

'So that we know who our enemies are,' he replied openly. 'The first one told us everything, but we tortured them all nonetheless.'

'So who were they?' I wanted to understand why this attack should have come so suddenly.

'Slave traders from Aegyptus, as we thought. You have helped save us from untold horrors in the land of the Nilus.'

'You and I have both suffered from this evil,' I confided, and told him about my family who were now, most probably, in Rome. 'But do not tell Agrippa of this,' I added hastily.

'Of course not. We are blood brothers now. What's yours is mine, remember? Including secrets.'

On the second night we celebrated our victory, but I could not dance.

THIRTY-ONE

Our parting was sorrowful. The King of the Desert held me like a son and gave me permission to leave his service. 'We have feasted together and we have fought like lions. I would like to show you my kingdom, but that must be left for another time. Go with your god.'

He gave me matching armbands of finely worked silver, one depicting an eagle in flight, the other a lion. 'Wear the eagle on your left,' he said, working the clasp shut so that it held tight on my forearm between my wrist and elbow. 'It will give you foresight. The lion, on your sword arm, will give you strength.'

I fingered the intricate designs, awestruck. 'But I have nothing to give you,' I said despondently. 'And what I gave you before, you returned to me.'

The old man laughed. 'When you have lived as long and as happily as I, you will understand that there is no better gift than a good friend, and certainly none better than one who is prepared to offer his life for you. Now, go and do the same for my son.'

I looked across to where Ziri and Agrippa lingered with the remainder of our group, mounted and waiting patiently. The horse that Fabius had ridden was laden with supplies and gifts from the women of the tribe. I embraced the King of the Desert and bowed to his gracious wife.

This time, the children were quiet and respectful as we rode out of the camp, the women's soft keening heartfelt. Even the hardened soldiers among us were moved, waving their last farewells to the women they had befriended.

Agrippa's inland task was only half fulfilled, but he had made a new ally for Rome.

We collected the supply carts within sight of Utica, as arranged with the farmer who had kept his part of the bargain, and we lingered briefly at the city's market to choose the freshest meat and fish, though most was malodorous and covered with flies. The journey's dust and sweat were washed away in Utica's baths.

'We're already a day late,' announced Agrippa as he counted out the exorbitant fee, 'so what harm can there be in a little extra time for some self-indulgence?'

The triremes were not as we had left them. As our column slowly approached, we could make out huge wooden contraptions attached to the foremasts of *Castor* and *Pollux*, hoisted upright and secured with ropes. The crew of *Pollux* were testing the manoeuvrability of the massive gangplank, the length of at least six men, by swinging it on its hinge and letting it drop onto bales of straw positioned on the quay. A long iron spike, embedded into the topmost part of the gangway, crashed ferociously into the straw like the beak of a giant bird.

'What in God's name is that?' exclaimed Ziri.

'We call it a corvus,' Agrippa replied, leaning forward in his saddle to watch the display. 'Once that spike hits the deck of an enemy ship, it won't let go and our men can jog along the bridge to board them.'

One of the men nearest Agrippa spoke up. 'Sir, we hardly saw any ships on our way here. Are we expecting trouble or something?'

'As a matter of fact, yes. The quaestor warned us when we arrived that there has been an increase in pirate activity in the waters near Sicilia, and that's the way we're heading next. If they come anywhere near us, we'll drop our nasty spikes on their decks and go across to have a quiet chat with their captain.'

'Surely they wouldn't dare attack a fully armed Roman galley?' the soldier added.

'Maybe not, but we're also escorting those traders.' Agrippa pointed to two large quinqueremes moored on the opposite side of the harbour. 'They'll slow us down, and they're very tempting prey for a pirate. But there'll be a bonus for everyone when we reach Ostia.'

Whether it was the prospect of another fight or Agrippa's mention of a bonus, the men were smiling. Ziri took his leave of us, with extravagant embraces and assurances that we would meet again, whether on the desert road or in the balmy palaces of Utica or Alexandria. And he reminded Agrippa of his promise to procure an alliance between the Imazighen of North Africa and the Senate in Rome.

We met the swell on the second day out of Utica, the triremes rolling alarmingly as the weight of the corvus on each foredeck emphasised the pitch of the larger ships. We were slower, too, as the smaller foresails had been removed to allow the boarding devices to be fitted.

Many of the oarsmen ignored my midday offering of ham, cheese, bread and figs as the waves rolled at an angle from behind, now occasionally foaming white as the wind strengthened from the southeast. I carried the pails of unwanted food back to my kitchen, lurching with the unpredictable motion, slipping on vomit and careening into cursing men. Fruit bounced across the groaning floor of my storeroom like lice scurrying to escape sunlight.

The sea grew mountainous, each wave now towering above the struggling, heaving *Castor*. It was difficult to make out the other vessels as the foaming breakers rolled in from astern.

Worst of all, Agrippa failed in his plan to reach Syracuse before nightfall. The single sail had long been dragged from its spar as demonic gusts hurled their fury. Each man cowered, desperately seeking respite from piercing rain and spray that cut viciously through inadequate clothing. The ominous grey became a terrifying black.

I crawled on deck, preferring wind and rain to the chaos of my kitchen. I made out Agrippa and the helmsman straining together on the rudder beam, but it was clear they could not control the ship.

No one saw the wave that was Neptune's fury. Brave *Castor* shuddered at the shock of it and heeled alarmingly so that the furious seas boiled around us, dragging screaming men overboard. The main mast snapped with a loud crack that could be heard over the storm's roaring as the ship yawed aimlessly into the trough that had followed the giant wave, her bows plunging downwards as if she would continue straight to the depths. For an age it seemed *Castor* was doomed, but then she rallied, and with water cascading from her decks, she met the next ridge with every ounce of her courage.

But she could not right herself. The corvus was swinging wildly over the side, its weight causing *Castor* to list dangerously, and again the black waters surged across the deck. Agrippa was shouting to the men nearest him to find an axe to cut it free before it took us all to the depths, pointing and gesticulating as demoralised men stared blankly at him.

Suddenly I realised what we needed to do. I dragged myself towards Agrippa as the next wave smashed over *Castor*. I pulled myself close and got his attention by tugging on his sodden jerkin.

'Sir,' I yelled, 'when we cut the corvus free, we must keep a rope attached to it.'

'What?' he shouted. 'What did you say?'

I repeated my suggestion.

'Why? That thing is going to sink us!'

'Sir, it could save us.' My voice was hoarse with effort. 'If we keep it roped, it will help to hold our position, bows into the waves.'

A look of understanding came over his face. 'You mean, like a kind of floating anchor?'

'Yes, sir. I think it's our only chance.'

'Go do it, then.'

Again I crawled across the deck, slipping and sliding with every savage attack. One of the men had found an axe and was hacking at the base of the foremast on which the corvus swung, his aim made erratic by the storm's fury. I grabbed his arm, and when he turned to me I yelled, 'Wait!' and pointed to the two ropes that held the corvus upright.

'As soon as you cut through,' I bawled in his ear, 'help me to secure those ropes in the bow.' He looked nonplussed, so I yelled, 'It's an order from Agrippa!'

He swung the axe as *Castor*'s crew got ready for the next towering wave. He struck a lucky blow and the mast sheered, toppling the corvus into the churning sea, crushing the forward railing as it fell. Immediately, *Castor* shuddered free as if in relief of a great burden and righted herself. I slithered to one rope while the axeman made for the other. I fumbled at the knot; my fingers were chilled into disobedience, but eventually it came free and the weight of the corvus almost tore my arms out of their sockets, dragging me clean across the deck, where I collided painfully with the severed mast stump. I pushed my feet against it and coiled the rope once around the stub, holding the corvus where it dragged powerfully in the water. The axeman saw his chance and tied the slack of his rope to the bow column.

'Leave enough free to add more rope!' I shouted above the storm's din. 'We may need to lengthen the drift.' Then I uncoiled my rope and secured it at the same place in the bow.

The corvus ropes held firm, the drag pulling *Castor*'s bows around to line up the next wave, which she rode like a champion, crashing into the following trough as the sea anchor held her in position.

I clapped the axeman on the back as best I could in a prone position, and he grinned back at me. More men came with sturdy ropes, which we tied to the slack before freeing the lengthened lines to allow a greater tow. *Castor* bucked and wallowed, but the storm could not claim us.

The warmth of the sun on my face awoke me. My clothes were soaked, but the storm had abated. All around me men lay sleeping, placid in exhausted repose like the sea was now.

Agrippa was pacing the deck, searching the horizon for *Pollux*, *Fides* and the traders. There was no sign of them, but a grey smudge of land could be seen to our south, if it was morning, to our north if it was afternoon. I was disoriented, but it felt like morning, so I decided the land was in the south.

Agrippa saw me struggle to my feet and ordered food for all. As I turned, he called, 'And well done, Melqart. Your quick thinking saved us.'

'Thank you, sir,' I acknowledged, and went below to salvage what I could from the shambles of my kitchen.

The crew ate in reflective silence, grateful for a reprieve from death. Agrippa went from man to man to share breakfast and offer words of encouragement, then addressed the ship's company from his stern platform.

'You may now all call yourselves sailors of the highest order,' he began, drawing an appreciative murmur. He considered we had been driven many miles further north than anyone could have expected, and while confessing to complete ignorance of our exact position, he confidently declared the land on the horizon to be the northern coast of Sicilia.

'But we are vulnerable without sail,' he continued, 'and therefore we must resort to the oars. I will ask no more of the crew than that we progress gently towards Sicilia and there seek a port for repairs and, who knows, we may find our lost colleagues. For now, we will seek renewed strength in those flagons that Ziri's people gave us for the journey, but I warn you not to overdo it, else you will find yourselves seeing strange visions. It is strong stuff, as tested by me personally.'

This time, the crew cheered.

We cut free the corvus that floated clumsily nearby, its iron spike weighing the contraption down so that it was half submerged, and with fewer than the usual numbers at oar, we made slow progress towards land.

Yet again, my ship was not bound for Rome.

There was nothing we could do but obey the terse commands shouted by the captain of a fast, black-sailed ship that intercepted us later in the day. *Castor* was low in the water and not in the mood for fighting, and nor was her crew.

Agrippa was polite, identifying *Castor* only as a ship of Rome wrecked in the night's storm, wisely not revealing that four other ships of the same fleet could be in the vicinity. Then he fired a salvo of questions.

'What is that land?'

'Sicilia.'

'The nearest port?'

'Panormus.'

'To whom is your allegiance?'

'To Sicilia.'

'Not to Rome?'

'Indeed not!'

'Are you a pirate?'

'Are you?'

'Then I take it you are a pirate.'

'Think what you will.'

And so the questions continued until the Sicilian captain tired of it and offered a towrope to assist *Castor* into Panormus. Agrippa declined and ordered the resting oarsmen to make up a full complement. He began a sprightly song to give a steady pace, as befitted a Roman vessel.

Castor docked in the very land that I knew was now home to Sextus, his island of adventure nestling somewhere near the southern coast of Italia. Barefoot, unkempt youths caught *Castor*'s mooring ropes and carelessly looped them around splintered pilings, at which Agrippa leaped ashore to tie the lines himself. The Sicilian escort came alongside and her captain made to board *Castor*, but hesitated when he was suddenly faced with the drawn swords of the Romans nearest him.

Agrippa laughed and ordered his men to stand down. 'Captain, you are welcome aboard my ship if you come in peace.'

The Sicilian was flustered.

'And state your business,' Agrippa added. 'Well?'

The Sicilian stepped back, warily eyeing the soldiers who had demonstrated such an instinctive will to defend their ship.

'Though it is my right to inspect this ship as a prize won at sea, I will demur on this occasion and refer you to the port authorities.'

'Listen, pirate, my ship is nobody's prize, and if you or anyone else from your "authority" comes anywhere near it, you'll feel the "authority" of our swords in your guts. Understand?'

It was obvious that the Sicilian didn't know what to do. So he backed off. 'All right, have it your way, but sooner or later you'll have to cough up some serious port fees.'

'Oh, we'll pay, don't worry about that. Just like we'll pay for repairs to our ship. Now, tell me who's in charge around here.'

There was no need for the Sicilian captain to respond. What appeared to be a century of soldiers, each disparately dressed, marched onto the quayside. Though they were strangely dressed for soldiers, their weapons were uniform; each carried a long throwing javelin, a short sword for close combat, and a light circular shield.

At their head was a magnificent figure riding a high-stepping white stallion. He wore full ceremonial armour, his silver breastplate contrasting with his black cloak, which lay regally across one shoulder and under the other. His head was covered by a silver helmet that left only his mouth and chin exposed, the ornate eye slits slanted downwards towards a golden nosepiece to give him a menacing air. The helmet was lavishly plumed with black feathers.

Slightly behind him and to one side rode a small man dressed in a plain brown summer tunic and leather sandals cross-tied to the knee. Both the rider and his plump horse were dwarfed by the imposing white stallion and its knight.

Arrayed like he was, the man had to be wealthy, perhaps even a local king. The column halted when the man raised one hand. The men at arms were not disciplined like Romans and shambled to a halt with poor timing. Agrippa, still standing on the quay dressed in the same clothes he had been wearing during the night's rigours, seemed duly impressed by the magnificence of the leader, if not with his men. He put one foot on the bollard that secured *Castor*'s stern, placed an elbow on his knee and rested his chin on his hand. In this pensive pose, he waited to be addressed.

After a short pause, the small man on the plump horse spoke. 'I am Alexandros, Magister of Panormus by popular decree.'

Agrippa was quick to reply. 'A lofty name and a lofty title,' he said, his chin still in his hand. 'Allow me to introduce myself. I am Marcus Vipsanius Agrippa, citizen of Rome.'

At the mention of his name, I thought I detected a sudden interest on the part of the silver knight. But the small man continued.

'Are you the master of this ship?'

'Indeed I am.'

'And what is your business in our waters?'

Agrippa took his foot off the bollard and stood erect, emanating authority even in his ruined clothes. 'I am not interested in your waters, only the waters of Rome, which are —' he looked out to sea and back again — 'all around you. Now, tell me what your business is and why you need so many men to support you.'

Alexandros flushed red with rage. 'You have trespassed here, and you and your men are under arrest. Your ship will be impounded pending the payment of five thousand denarii.' The horse sensed his master's aggravation and tossed its head in alarm, its sideways shuffle forcing Alexandros to cling comically to the pommel. He seemed not to notice the movement in *Castor* as a hundred sailors loosened their swords, and the motley men of Panormus bristled for a fight.

But the silver knight saw the threat and acted quickly. 'Hold,' he called, nudging his stallion forward a few paces and raising a mailed fist. Agrippa did not move, nor did he stand his men down.

The knight looked down at him and smiled. Unbuckling his silver helmet, he revealed a shock of golden hair. His piercing blue eyes looked straight at Agrippa.

'I am Azhar, commander of the armies of Sicilia.' His singsong voice reminded me of Sextus, all mischief and adventure, proud and confident in his shining apparel. 'And you, noble Agrippa, are greeted as an equal and friend, provided that you come in peace.'

'That depends on whether you intend to rob us or welcome us,' replied Agrippa, a hint of challenge in his voice.

'Unlike my clerk here, I can see that you have been through a terrible ordeal.' He ignored the small man's huffing and puffing at his dismissive words. 'You and your men will be treated well, offered food and wine and dry clothing from Alexandros's personal stores.' Alexandros looked as if he was about to protest, then thought better of it when Azhar glared at him. It was obvious who was truly in command.

'For that I thank you,' said Agrippa politely. 'But what of our ship? We need to repair the masts and inspect the hull on dry land. And —' he cleared his throat for effect — 'I hardly think that five thousand is a fair price. What do you say?'

'I say this: what is money but an evil over which men fight? We have all the coin we need and more. The price is two thousand, but when your ship is repaired we will hold a great games contest, your crew against an equal number of our young men. The winner will take the whole sum. Do you have this amount as surety?'

Agrippa smiled. 'I accept your challenge.'

THIRTY-TWO

If we were prisoners, it did not feel like it. We were given quarters in a large chandlery, kept cool by virtue of its thick stone walls and solid timber roof. We used it only for sleeping, as Agrippa had set us to work on repairing *Castor*, first hauling her through the shallows where the fishermen kept their small craft and, using rollers cut from tall eucalyptus trees, over the gradual rise of a sandy ridge to level ground. There the ship was propped with sturdy timber and warped planking was removed, every joint inspected, each loose dowel replaced. Pitch was used to caulk and then cover the bared wood. New masts were fashioned and oiled, then hoisted into place. Replacement rigging was prepared with the eager help of the town's women who flirted and giggled as they expertly spliced ropes and sewed seams on the new sails. Savaged but undefeated by the storm's malice, *Castor*'s graceful features were gradually restored.

Agrippa spent as much time as he could working with us, stripped to the waist, his shoulders and arms thick with muscle formed during his years of training with javelin, gladius and the heavy Roman shield. He had been groomed for Caesar's army from an early age. But he also spent long afternoons with Azhar, no doubt exchanging information about their respective homelands, trade possibilities, and the civil war that had drained Rome of men and resources for five years.

One night he returned to our dormitory a little drunk on Azhar's wine. He seemed eager to talk as I served him the remains of a spiced mutton stew that had left the men contented in their exhaustion. Filling my own cup as well as his, we sat together by the dying embers of my cooking fire.

Sicilia was, he rambled, a bastard country where Greek, Arab, Levantine and Roman blood had been mixed to the point where no one knew or cared where they came from.

'Stir that lot in a pot,' he said, 'and they don't know whether they want to fight like Arabs, trade like Phoenicians or think like Greeks. Take this fellow Azhar. He has an Arabian name but he looks like a demon from the north. I tell you, he isn't human. He has no roots. Mad as a marauding Gaul, too. He just pitches up on this island, climbs to the top of Aetna while it's belching fire and ash, surveys all he can see and decides to call it home. Next thing you know, he's rampaging around like he owns the place. Which he doesn't, by the way, because if you've got no roots it's every man for himself. Tells me he's just pulling a few threads together for young Pompey...'

'Pompey?' I interrupted. 'Pompey as in Sextus?'

He looked at me with wine-crazed eyes. 'The very same. Why do you ask?'

'Oh, no reason,' I hedged. 'We heard that the Pompey brothers had been defeated by Caesar...'

'Oh sure, I was there, remember?'

I tried to look vague, but I wanted to tease more information from him about Sextus. 'He came here, then?'

'Oh yes, and I suppose Julius Bloody Caesar would expect me to hunt him down like a dog. But oh no, not me. He can do it himself. I saw enough killing in Hispania, and if this young pup Sextus has the cheek to carve out a little kingdom for himself, then I say good for him. Let Caesar finish what he started.'

Agrippa drained his cup and promptly fell asleep.

I wiped a crust of bread around the last juices in the cooking pot and wondered if I would see Sextus before *Castor* sailed for Ostia and Rome.

I suppose I made the suggestion because I had spent my rest times watching the local fishermen in their single-sail small boats.

Agrippa had announced there would be five disciplines in the games to decide if we left Sicilia poorer to the tune of two thousand denarii, the odd number ensuring that there would be a winner. The games would be organised along the lines of the ancient Olympiad in honour of Sicilia's rich Greek influences, and the Panormians had nominated javelin and a foot race as their chosen events, generously allowing our crew as visitors to suggest three more.

The first suggestion, from the rear of the semi-circle where our crew sat, caused uproar. The joker who shouted 'Fututio' was roundly cheered and slapped on the back, and it took Agrippa some time to restore order.

'How about wrestling?' It was the deep, gruff voice of an oarsman known only as Bear, as much for his dark body hair as for his wide neck, muscled arms and thighs as thick as oaks.

'That'll do for one,' said Agrippa. 'Obviously, Bear, you're expected to win. Any more suggestions?'

'Archery?' a small voice chimed in. It belonged to a youth who had succeeded in picking off one of the great silver-blue fish that fed near the surface of our ocean.

'Another one we should win. Better get some practice in, lad.' Agrippa seemed confident. 'Any more ideas?'

'Sailing?' I suggested.

'Don't be daft!' someone shouted from the back. 'Since when have Greek games ever included sailing?'

But Agrippa saw the point. 'Well, it's what we're good at, so why not?'

There was some murmuring, but nobody else objected.

'Right then, in the absence of any further suggestions, we'll go for wrestling, archery and sailing, and may the best team win, as long as it's Roman!'

I was a little daunted when Agrippa appointed himself as my crew member and, insisting on as much practice as possible before the games began, commandeered one of the fishing boats that swung lazily at anchor in the harbour's shallows. A dozen gnarled old fishermen jeered from the shore, among them the boat's owner. He hawked and spat, giving us the evil eye. Nearby, a handful of *Castor*'s crew shouted encouragement.

We had so little time to prepare — the games were scheduled for the next day.

Agrippa held the boat steady while I unfurled the sail, a considerably smaller version of *Castor*'s square rig. While it flapped in the gentle breeze, I positioned the single sculling oar that would double as our rudder. I climbed in and sat on the edge of an open-topped box-like construction in the centre of the vessel and was alarmed to see it begin to fill with water.

Agrippa saw my agitation. 'Crazy Sicilians, they've put holes in the bottom to sink us.'

I noticed the water did not seep through the edges of the box where it was joined to the bottom of the boat with a thick coating of pitch. I motioned to Agrippa to climb aboard and watched the water level rise as he positioned himself next to the oar. The water stopped rising a hand's width from the top of the box, and it dawned on me what it was for.

'That's where they put the fish to keep them fresh,' I said excitedly. 'Ingenious.'

I pulled on the ropes to swivel the boom and caught the wind. The fishermen laughed and clapped as we crabbed sideways, with barely any forward motion. Agrippa steered the small boat so that the wind was directly behind us, and gradually we picked up speed.

'Not exactly fast, is she?' muttered Agrippa. 'Let's try taking her closer to the wind.'

He steered the boat in a gentle turn and I shortened sail. Heeling gently, she stubbornly refused forward motion.

'Try pushing the oar deeper,' I suggested. We needed something beneath us to stop the sideways drift.

The boat made a valiant attempt to move forward with the wind on her beam as Agrippa struggled to hold the oar blade deep. But it wasn't a big improvement. We would have to scull the boat back to shore.

I studied the box on which I sat, the water slopping near the top but easily contained. The water would rise no higher than the level of the sea itself, no matter how big the hole was. So why not…

We sailed to the mouth of the harbour and then came about, Agrippa sculling feverishly back the way we'd come. While he worked, I explained to him my new theory that if we found a way to put a vertical wing below us, it would stop the sideways drag and give us more speed.

His eyes lit up. 'You're thinking of hacking a slit in the bottom of the boat, aren't you? And putting this wing of yours through it.'

I nodded slowly.

'Right then, let's find a spot near to where the boys are working on *Castor* and we'll see what we can cook up to make this tub perform like a dolphin.'

We beached as far away from the bemused fishermen as we could and summoned six of the men to carry the boat over the sand ridge. I showed them what I wanted, and impressed on them the need to hurry before the fishermen or anyone from Panormus became inquisitive. At a sharp word from Agrippa, the incredulous craftsmen went to work.

Whether the adapted fishing boat had a name before, we didn't know, but now she was called *Seagull* after the wing that could be lowered through a slot in her belly as soon as we had cleared the shallows. I lowered the fashioned wood blade and eased the boom around while Agrippa steered *Seagull* at an angle to the wind. The little boat leaped joyfully forward, a generous wave foaming at her bow.

'Not too far out,' laughed Agrippa, the breeze tugging at his unruly hair. 'If this doesn't work, I'll have to paddle us back again.'

But it did work. At one stage I trimmed the sail to such an extent that we seemed to be sailing almost directly into the wind, a feat that every sailor knew was impossible. We beached, the wing withdrawn to be hidden from prying eyes, and we were immediately surrounded by our fellow crewmen, who slapped our backs in congratulation. Given the abilities of Bear the wrestler and our youthful archer, not to mention several fleet-of-foot runners and useful javelin throwers, surely we couldn't fail to win the right to sail out of Panormus toll-free.

One of the legacies of centuries of Roman influence was that Panormus boasted a fine amphitheatre, not more than a short walk from the port. Within it was packed our hundred and what appeared to be the whole of the town's population, as Alexandros had declared the day a holiday, or perhaps he had been ordered to. Since the games fell on Saturn's Day, there would be ample time for recovery from sore heads on the ensuing Day of the Sun.

I walked with the other Roman competitors into the amphitheatre to be instantly struck by the noise of three thousand excited citizens, and the colour of the occasion. A troupe of impish young women was leaping and dancing around the perimeter of the sandy arena, encouraged by pipers and drummers, who maintained a lively rhythm for the frenzied performers. Sections of the crowd rose to their feet, cheering and throwing flowers as they passed. Behind them, masked youths cavorted and twisted, dressed as demons or gods, some engaging in mock battles while others screamed nonsensical abuse at the nearest spectators, who wasted no time in shouting back. The loudest were the women and children.

A tempting aroma of roasted meat mingled with the spicy perfumes of the wealthier women and the sour odour from the latrines that had been dug that morning behind the rising tiers. Several drunks weaved and staggered in the centre of the arena, hampered in their comical attempts at wrestling by the wineskins they clutched. Whenever one of these unfortunates fell over, the crowd cheered.

Bear nudged me. 'Where's Agrippa?' he growled. We could see the Panormus team making their way to the centre of the arena, cheerfully accepting the proffered wineskins.

'I expect he'll turn up. He's probably bribing the judges.'

But Bear wasn't listening. He was studying our opposition, in particular a lofty youth, at least a head taller than Bear but despite his height not in the least uncoordinated. Bronzed and oiled, he walked confidently, like an athlete. This would be the perfect match: Bear's brute strength and greater experience pitted against a quicker and no doubt fit young opponent.

Such was the aura around this giant that those near him were a blur. So it was a strange moment when the face of the man behind him slowly came into focus. I almost jumped with shock when I realised who he was. He had always claimed this was his island, where his father had owned estates that heaved with ripened wheat at harvest time, where he had implored me to come as soon as I was able, where I had now arrived only by accident. The man was none other than Sextus Pompey.

Sextus's arm was draped lazily around Azhar's shoulders. They were two shining generals, dressed in fine summer tunics that, though informal, gave them the appearance of Sun Kings, confident and jovial. It would not surprise me if Sextus had already won the hearts of everyone in Sicilia.

'Come on then, lads.' It was Agrippa, who had joined us unnoticed. 'Time to show this lot what we're made of, but remember this is just a bit of fun. Fair play all round and greet their team as if you really like them!'

As we made our way to the centre of the arena to join our opponents, Sextus and Azhar looked towards us, as did the Panormus squad. When Sextus's eyes met mine, his jaw dropped and a look of surprise crossed his face.

'Melqart?' he mouthed. 'Pito?'

I smiled and nodded. A strange feeling of frustration washed over me, as if Sextus had somehow summoned me here against my will and would now attempt to divert me from my mission to find my family. I felt the pull of his claim on my life, like a plough that obediently follows the ox wherever it goes.

We embraced, his energy coursing through me like Apollo's radiance.

'What took you so long?' he whispered in my ear.

I broke free and moved back enough to allow me to look into his eyes. 'I've been trying to steer clear of troublemakers like you.' This induced a familiar grin. 'But your sort is everywhere. Can't seem to avoid them. So I'd better go with the flow…'

'Excuse me…' Agrippa jolted me back to reality.

I began to introduce Sextus, but Agrippa interrupted me sternly. 'I know full well who he is, but I want to know why you are in league with a fugitive of Rome…'

Shocked, I studied his face and could not determine whether he was serious. I looked to Sextus and saw that he was not threatened by Agrippa's outburst.

'I … we…' I began, disconcerted and a little embarrassed as our team looked on.

'Not now,' said Agrippa. 'We've got these games to win. But I want a full explanation as soon as they're over.'

THIRTY-THREE

The crowd's banter as we paraded around the amphitheatre was mostly amusing, except when it was tinged with anti-Roman venom, the missiles overripe fruit, yesterday's hardened bread and unripe olives that stung like bees. We waved and laughed with the spectators, who in the main directed their provocations at Bear, an obvious target as he loped powerfully in our midst and scowled at frightened children.

The Panormian team was hailed and saluted with acclamations fit for the gods, no doubt giving each of them supernatural strength and skill. It all went over Bear's head as he concentrated on building a reputation as Hercules and Polyphemus rolled into one very ugly fighting machine, flexing his muscles and grunting like a foraging pig.

I noticed that Sextus paraded with the Panormians. Turning to Agrippa, who walked nearby, I asked if he knew which were our sailing opponents. He didn't look at me, choosing instead to continue waving to the crowd, but there was no animosity in his voice.

'Fancies himself, does that one,' he said, loud enough to be heard over the background din. He was talking about Sextus. 'Reckons he's the best sailor since Odysseus, and he laughed when he heard I was taking part in one of his fishing smacks.'

'You've met him, then?'

'Yes, he arrived last night.' Now he looked at me, and still there was no anger. 'You did not know?'

I shook my head.

'He's quite a character. Seems to have got over his issues with Caesar. Didn't even consider me an enemy.'

'He's not like his father. Or his brother, Gnaeus.'

'I know what you mean. More of an adventurer, a survivor. He couldn't resist the opportunity to sail against us, single-handed. He even went out and bought himself a boat for at least twice its value.'

Trumpets interrupted our conversation to announce the start of the games.

The arrows thudded into the post at the amphitheatre's entrance; none of the four contestants could miss from ten paces.

'Back ten paces!' Alexandros bellowed at the archers, puffed up in his role as chief judge. The four men retreated to a new line and nocked their arrows.

The slight Roman youth, Niger, who had learned to use a bow almost before he could walk, loosed first, successfully. An older Panormian found the post with ease, his arrow almost touching Niger's as it quivered. Our second archer missed, the cheers of the partisan crowd drowning out the groans of our few supporters. The second Panormian archer embedded his arrow to more whooping delight.

'Back ten more,' demanded Alexandros, drawing a new line in the sand with his sword.

This time, only Niger and the Panormian old-timer found the post, and retreated twice to new marks in the sand, their arrows side by side each time. The final mark was so close to the crowd behind them that the spectators in the front row could almost reach out and touch them. It would have to be decided here. Both shot arrows into the post, Niger remaining calm as the entire crowd screamed and whistled to try to put him off.

There was a break while both archers retrieved their arrows, talking together like friends as they strode to the post, united in their sport.

Perhaps it was the gull that flapped close to the post as the Panormian shot that put him off. The gull now lay dead, the arrow protruding from its chest, leaving Niger the simple task of hitting the post. Our men celebrated like lunatics and the partisan Panormus crowd was silenced.

Six young boys led the javelin teams onto the sand — these children were to act as runners to collect the spears after they had landed and return them to the throwers. Three of our men and three local competitors followed them, each carrying his own weapon, favoured for its balance and craftsmanship. I noticed that the Panormian javelins were slightly longer than ours and each had a length of cord dangling from the grip.

Alexandros drew the line in the sand in front of the most vociferous section of the crowd, allowing little space for a run up. One of our throwers began to remonstrate with him, showing the little man how he needed at least ten paces to give him momentum. The Panormians watched, bemused, knowing from experience that Alexandros would get his way.

Even with so little room, the first Roman attempt was impressive, the javelin piercing the soft sand not far from the archer's post that had been left in the ground. The first Panormian stepped forward, slipping a loop of cord over his wrist. He arched his back and his right arm swept powerfully upwards.

It took us a while to work out what had enabled his javelin to arc at least twenty paces further than the Roman pilum. It soared high and straight, sent spinning through the air by the cord that had unravelled and now hung twitching from the wrist of the thrower. While the crowd danced and cheered, we looked at each other in amazement, the reality slowly dawning. The Panormian technique was vastly superior to ours, and the spin put on the javelin gave it extra distance.

We lost the javelin throwing by three to nothing, as the nearest spectators delighted in reminding us.

But we reminded them that the wrestling came next, pointing with enthusiasm at Bear, who was already making his way to the centre of the arena. There Alexandros scraped a circle, its radius perhaps twice the length of a javelin, measured with a rope spiked in the centre of the wrestling area. The rules were simple: the winner would be the one to dump the other outside the circle while remaining inside it. Alexandros explained this to the men, standing nervously between the tall Panormian and Bear.

The match began. Both men circled and feinted, the tall youth light on his feet, Bear more deliberate in his movements. Catcalls and shouts of 'Get on with it!' brought the first encounter, both men sensing the moment to clash chest to chest, each trying desperately to lock arms around the other to control the movement. But the younger man's body was so oiled that Bear's thick arms slipped and slithered, while his opponent managed to lock his fingers around the squat man's torso. With a loud grunt, the Panormian put all his effort into pulling Bear sideways, but the Roman was as immoveable as a half-buried boulder. He tried pushing, then pulling, with little success. Bear laughed, and the crowd jeered.

The sweating wrestlers parted, chests heaving with the exertion, looking for a new angle of attack. Again they grappled, but this time, as Bear leaned his bulk forward to meet the challenge, the Panormian stopped and in one swift movement leaned back, taking Bear's weight on his chest. The pair crashed to the ground and the Panormian heaved upwards with his knees to aid Bear's forward momentum. The bulky Roman upended, his huge legs cartwheeling ungracefully, and he landed on his back with a shuddering crash that sent sand and dust flying into the air, his feet inches from the boundary circle.

But he didn't let go of his opponent. With astonishing strength, even with the air blasted from his lungs in the fall, Bear continued the rolling motion and with the straining muscles of his mighty shoulders, neck and forearms, flipped the startled Panormian clean out of the circle.

The astonished crowd rose as one, putting aside its bias to cheer Bear's brute strength and unexpected agility. The hulking Roman heaved himself to his feet and walked the entire perimeter, soaking up the lavish applause, the animosity of earlier insults forgotten.

His opponent shook his head in disbelief and jogged to Bear's side to enjoy the acclamation with him.

Castor's crew could shoot with great accuracy and produce a wrestling champion, but we failed to produce a single runner to match the fleet-of-foot youth of Panormus. Each of five races was lost, the wild local teenagers gyrating in gleeful victory for the adoring girls in the ranks of spectators.

Therefore, the responsibility of securing the two thousand denarii rested squarely on Agrippa and myself.

Heralds were despatched around the arena to announce that the final event would start from the inner harbour and could be viewed from the quayside and the low hill not far from the amphitheatre. Soon the musicians and dancers had reassembled and were making their clamorous way towards the harbour, children skipping excitedly around them, the growing number of inebriated citizens weaving at the rear of the procession.

Both boats were lying in the shallows, sails flapping loose, bows bumping on the yielding shingle as the frisky breakers toyed with them. Beyond the breakwater a Sicilian trader had been anchored to mark the turning point, her pennants whipping in the unpredictable wind.

An oarsman brought the wooden wing, wrapped in a woollen bundle to disguise it as additional clothing for warmth. I placed the bundle near the mast and turned to look at Agrippa. He seemed more confident than I felt.

Sextus arrived, barefoot and dressed in leggings with a jerkin strapped tightly at the waist. He strode to his boat with a sanguine air about him, smiling at Agrippa and me. Alexandros and the heralds tried to move the encroaching townsfolk back to allow us more room.

'For Panormus and Sicilia,' he said, still smiling.

'For Rome,' replied Agrippa.

'And Hispania,' I added.

'Never heard of it,' laughed Sextus. 'May the best boat win.'

Alexandros cut in with a wordy polemic about the rules, which amounted to no more than an instruction to sail around the anchored trader and back again.

'Get on with it, man,' grunted Sextus.

Alexandros raised a red cloth, then let it drop. The crowd burst into vociferous encouragement as the three of us made our way to our boats, which we pushed afloat and climbed on board.

I unwrapped the wing and thrust it into its slot in the base of *Seagull*. However, it was not necessary as the southeasterly breeze came from behind to allow both boats to run with the wind, sails squared to fill lustily with the obliging gusts. Sextus had chosen well. His craft was smaller than *Seagull*, and livelier through the water as she pulled ahead, her bows angled directly for the end of the breaker wall. On this course, both boats could reach the trader in a straight line before beginning the arduous zigzag return course, and Sextus would reach the marking vessel first.

I called to Agrippa and pointed to the west, away from the end of the harbour promontory and seemingly away from the trader. He understood and nodded. I counted us down and Agrippa pushed on the steering oar while I hauled the sail tighter, at the last minute remembering to shift my body weight to *Seagull*'s windward side. Freed from the wallowing motion of a tail wind, *Seagull* bit into the choppier seas and surged forward, throwing stinging spray into our faces. I looked across and thought I could make out a confused expression on Sextus's face, but then he turned to the task in hand and continued on his course for the trader.

Agrippa's calmness gradually turned to concern as we raced across the Bay of Panormus away from the harbour, seeming to get no nearer to the trader way off to our left, while all the time Sextus was closing in on the anchored marker. I ignored Agrippa's raised eyebrow, which questioned my right to take such a huge risk with his money. We had to win this race.

In the distance, Sextus appeared to be right up against the trader, a speck against the larger ship. I nodded to Agrippa and, my heart thumping with the exhilaration, counted him down again. We went about, seemed to stop and flounder as I hauled on the sail ropes, then gradually picked up speed again, heeling away from the shore and bounding like an antelope for the marker. We came up to her at speed, laying a silvery wake behind us, and I thanked the gods when I saw that Sextus was not as close as he had appeared from a distance. We passed in front of him, and again I saw the look of amazement on his face. By contrast, his boat seemed almost stationary.

Manoeuvring around the trader was not so easy. As we passed in her lee, where the wind was suddenly snatched from our sail, we almost lost control as *Seagull* rocked in the direction of our weight, dipping us cruelly into the inky waters. The trader's skeleton crew laughed and hurled insults. Then we were away again, rounding the quinquereme's stern, catching the wind and flying towards the breakwater wall. Agrippa howled at the taut sail and punched the air with delight. My arms were aching and quivering as I clutched the ropes, my feet pressed hard against the watertight box that housed the sea wing.

Sextus was rounding the trader and beginning what would amount to a series of lumbering tacks to follow a zigzag course to the finish, which we would reach with time to spare. We would be well into the celebrations long before he ran his bows onto the shingle.

One more turn. Agrippa and I laughed as we counted and went about for the last time. But the wooden keel sheared with the stress as *Seagull* capsized. Terrified, I let go of the ropes too late and the sail was forced down, past the point of no return, fluttering impotently as it touched the waves and began to submerge, pitching both of us into the warm sea. I clung to the mast, kicking furiously, and saw Agrippa spitting salty water, cursing and gasping for breath.

'Quick, we have to right her!' I called to him.

'Any ideas how?' he asked when he had caught his breath.

'Swim under or around, and pull?' It was all I could think of.

We tried repeatedly, but the sail held an enormous deadweight of water, and the mast would not break clear of the seas that held *Seagull* in hopeless submission. Sextus sailed slowly by, whistling, pretending not to have seen us. Exhausted, we could only stare after him as his impudent boat made for the shore and ranks of cheering Panormians.

We held onto *Seagull*'s floundering flanks, riding the swell with our heads laid on the clinker hull, exhausted and dispirited.

Azhar and the victorious competitors accepted the laurels to the wild cheers of the townsfolk, whose numbers had been swelled throughout the evening as the musicians played on, their notes becoming more discordant with every draught of the local wine. Arguably the loudest cheer was reserved for Bear, who continued with his trademark scowl as the leaves were placed on his mass of dark curls. Later, while youths threw more branches onto the beach fire, he was seen with children on his knee or climbing around his bulging neck, singing in a surprisingly tuneful voice a song from his homeland about a duck and a wolf, still scowling between each garbled stanza. The crew of *Castor* joined in as they picked up the tune and chorus.

I was concentrating so hard on singing about a duck that foxed a wolf that I almost missed the discreet signal from Sextus summoning Agrippa and Azhar to a spot away from the fire's flickering light. I stopped singing and watched, turning back to the entertainment when they looked in my direction. There was some kind of negotiation going on, and I itched to know what it was.

Agrippa saw me watching and beckoned.

I tossed away the chicken bone I had been gnawing and, stooping to pick up the wineskin I had nursed since our rescue some hours earlier, joined the three leaders. I handed the skin to Agrippa, who expertly sent a gush of dark wine into his open mouth and passed it on to Sextus.

'It seems you are more valuable than I could have imagined when you begged passage on *Castor*,' he said with a grin.

'I don't know what you mean,' I protested, though I had guessed.

'Two thousand denarii. I didn't know I was carrying such an important person. Not even Caesar himself could demand a ransom like that.'

'I still don't know what you mean!'

Sextus helped Agrippa out. 'I … we are prepared to cancel the debt your captain owes if he will let you stay in Sicilia. We've heard you know how to cook —' he winked at me — 'and we need talents like yours here.'

'But I have business in Rome.' As I said it, I realised that my reasons for travelling through the Middle Sea were futile when compared with the price that Agrippa would no longer have to pay. 'All right, I will stay, but you, Sextus, know I am not bound by this.'

'Not by the price,' he smiled, 'but by our friendship.'

Sextus clasped Agrippa wrist to wrist, and Agrippa nodded acknowledgement of the deal to Azhar. Then Sextus looked at me.

'I want you to teach me how to make a fishing boat sail impossible angles against the wind.'

THIRTY-FOUR

Castor's trumpeter sounded a cheerful salute, the ship holding her course northwards as our two Sicilian liburnians shortened sail and peeled away to the east. I stood with Sextus on his command deck and watched the Roman ship under full sail, jaunty and vivacious in her renovation, bearing comrades like Agrippa and Bear away to new adventures in Caesar's hard-won empire.

There would be ample time to talk of the future, Sextus had said on the eve of our departure, as our leisurely journey to Syracuse would take three, perhaps four days. And what was the hurry? If I went with Agrippa and made my way to Rome, where would I begin my search for my family? And if I found them, how would I liberate them?

'I suppose that you think you can just walk into a Roman household and reason with some high-ranking patrician who would just happen to be so generous that he would gladly part with his valuable slaves?' Sextus asked sarcastically. 'It won't work. You have to have a plan.'

And so our two ships hugged the coast and made for Syracuse, on the other side of the island. By the time we put into Agathyrnum to shelter on the first night, Sextus had convinced me that I should spend the coming winter with him, gathering as much Roman coin and other valuables as possible in order to at least be able to attempt to buy my family back, if I ever found them. In the meantime, Sextus would send his spies to Rome, armed with all the information I could give them, to track them down before reporting back.

What he said made sense. I had embarked on this journey without thinking it through. The new strategy gave me fresh hope.

On the second day of our journey we sailed with fair winds past the Pelorum promontory and turned south through the narrow straits that led to the bustling port of Messana. Here, graceless traders squeezed between Sicilia and the Italian mainland, more ships of different shapes and sizes than I had seen since leaving Gades, gingerly nosing towards the insatiable markets of Rome and Gaul.

Sextus watched them with narrowed eyes. 'What do you see?' he asked.

'More ships than I thought existed,' I replied.

'Each of those will be paying our toll before long.' He watched the nearest, a clumsy penteconter making slow progress across the choppy waters, its rows of dipping oars depleted to make more room for a mountain of yellowing ivory tusks stacked forward of the main mast. I understood his reasoning; we were watching a ship with a lucrative cargo saving probably a precious week by using the straits.

'In Utica there was talk of pirates in these waters,' I said, 'so I wouldn't be surprised if these merchant captains needed some protection, too.'

Sextus laughed. 'You read my mind, Pito. We already have the makings of a good fleet. Our ships are fast and we will crew them with the best fighting men, soldiers of the sea. I'll show you when we get to Syracuse.'

'And the pirates? Who are they?'

'Remember those men that you and Dracus fought on the beach beneath the mountain?'

I nodded, recalling the rape and murder, and the speed of Turon's sword as he despatched the pirate leader.

'There are many such pirates; there always have been.' Sextus paused, a look of pain crossing his face. 'There was a time when my father was charged with ridding the seas of such people, and I believe he succeeded, but while Rome has been distracted with its civil wars, they have returned. Many of them live here and recruit their crews from among the Sicilians to raid innocent communities and capture the ships that carry their wares to and from Rome.'

He watched as the helmsman leaned on the rudder's beam to alter our course towards Messana.

'But one by one we will hunt them down,' he continued. There was a resolute note to his voice. 'Some are scum, and do not deserve to live. Others are just desperate, good men at heart and willing to serve a greater purpose. The day will soon come when we have a fleet to match anything that Rome can offer, commanded by these wild, adventurous men.'

'So you still want to fight Caesar?' I asked, incredulous.

'No, Pito, indeed not. That is not the reason why we are building this fleet. What we want here is independence, the right to live in peace and profit from the seas. We are fishermen and farmers, but Sicilian seas teem with much more than fish. Yes, every merchant who seeks passage should pay a toll, and perhaps a fee for our protection. If they do not, there are plenty of raiders who can remind them of the wisdom of our suggestion!'

I understood. Sextus was ever the opportunist. I shook my head in disbelief and he chuckled.

'So,' I said, 'let me get this straight. You are not a pirate, you are a businessman. But you won't hesitate to act like a pirate if your customers don't open their purses.'

'That would be about right,' he smiled.

The gold and blue pennants of Sextus streamed from the masts of both Sicilian liburnians as they surged through the calm waters of Messana's sickle-shaped natural harbour, guarded by the huge pharos tower at its entrance. It was dusk, and the first of the night's flames were showing weakly at its pinnacle.

Only when I saw the guard of honour on the quayside, summoned by the sight of the regal pennants as the ships had approached, did I begin to realise the status that Sextus had acquired in the brief time that he had called Sicilia his home. A hundred men, ceremonial breastplates shining as if kept in a constant state of readiness, snapped to attention as the ships moored. Their deep blue cloaks were worn in the same fashion that I had seen Azhar wear his when I first set foot on the island, over one shoulder and under the other, and each carried the curved swords of the tribal warriors from across the sea. Indeed, in colour, style and weaponry, the local military seemed to be proclaiming a marked difference from the legions of their cousins in Italia.

Sextus was hailed with a shout the moment his foot touched the newly mortared stonework. He smiled and saluted the prefect and his centurion, then beckoned me to walk with him as he inspected the soldiers. Some of them were known to him by name, and appreciative of a quip or a murmured comment.

He dismissed the guard.

Later, wrapped in the potent perfume of the baths, we reclined in the cavernous hall of the prefect's lavish villa while his wife, a round, generously bosomed woman who jangled and chimed with gold, fussed and chirped at the servants serving perhaps thirty of Sextus's friends in the city. The feast was a tantalising array of roasted game and the same spicy dishes with which Ziri's tribe had made allies of our appreciative stomachs. The prefect urged me to try the cooling cucumbers and onions covered with olive oil and chilled goat curds, mint and parsley laced with citron and more oil, and a dry yellow paste encrusted with tiny pine nuts — these were the real treasures brought to Sicilia by the wandering Levantines from eastern cities like Tyre, Damascus and Alexandria. He patted his quivering midriff and belched.

Sextus tore his eyes from a serving girl and asked me the question I had been expecting. Before he even said the names of Nahalia and Bashira, I knew he was thinking of them each time the servant girl averted her eyes from his persistent flirtations.

'Where are they?' he asked.

I remembered that I was supposed to bring them with me to Sicilia, but I had already explained the haste with which I had left Hispania. 'As far as I know, they are still in Apollacta with Leandra and Cassia,' I told him. 'They are in safe hands.'

'I hope you are right. But they would be safer here, and we would be all the more comfortable with them to look after us, don't you think?'

He winked and I agreed.

I left him explaining to the prefect exactly where Apollacta was and arranging for a ship to be despatched to bring our two companions to Sicilia. That night I slept soundly on the soft mattress that had been assigned to me, the lemon balm brazier by the door driving away all winged irritations.

The last leg of our journey to Syracuse could have been covered in less than half a day, but the sea was strangely calm. Sextus ordered a reverential pace using only four oars, gently dipped every ten heartbeats. We crept silently beneath the barren slopes of Aetna, worthless intruders under the lofty sentinel of the gods, awed by the hissing white breath of

Enceladus. No gulls cried, and no fish played in the lifeless weed that parted timorously for our bows.

We did not wake the Gigante or his guarding Cyclops, and as the sun passed its zenith, Sextus ordered the oarsmen on both ships to resume, their timing piped by a longhaired youth whose reed flute gave eerie praise to Neptune for our safe passage in these sacred seas.

The rugged hills of Heraea were framed by dusk's fire as we surged into the great harbour at Syracuse, the two liburnians competing with each other for the best anchorage nearest the city, Aetna's weighty mood now lifted. Syracuse claimed me, like she did all seafarers who sailed into her arms, for her beauty lay in her simplicity, her strength in hewn stone, her heritage watched over by the Spirits of Pantalica who rose from the City of the Dead at Athena's whim.

And it was to Athena's great temple that Sextus led me the next morning, our feet treading the worn stones laid by the ancients. We passed craggy diviners and animated sellers of trinkets and marble statuettes whose wares insulted the ornate mosaics and towering columns, and made our way to where the noble goddess stood, warrior and woman, teacher and protector.

We looked up at her. To me, she appeared like a pale version of Leandra, sinewy limbs veiled by femininity, bewitching sensuality lurking behind a sapient countenance. To an awed Sextus, she was no less than divinity, the embodiment of everything that he worshipped. I wondered why we stood here, silent and submissive.

I was relieved when he spoke.

'Have you ever heard of Archimedes?'

'Of course.' I searched my memory, wishing I had paid more attention to my tutor, for whom The Great Archimedes, as he always called him, was the ultimate hero of learning.

'He was born here, and he died here.' Sextus was still looking up at Athena. 'She was his inspiration. He probably stood on this very spot.'

'Didn't Archimedes invent a machine for tipping ships over in a battle?' That part had appealed to my sense of adventure and my fascination with mechanical contraptions.

'He did.' Now Sextus turned to me. 'He also claimed to be able to set a ship on fire without going anywhere near it. Sounds a bit fanciful to me, but that's where you come in.'

'What do you mean?'

'Let me show you. Come with me.'

We left the temple and walked the busy streets towards the river. In the distance, a pall of dust lay over the massive stone quarry where thousands of slaves were prizing out and shaping great stones for the city's expansion. We paused to buy honeyed almonds from a street seller who recognised Sextus and tried to decline the proffered coin, eventually receiving two, which was no doubt his original objective.

As we walked, Sextus explained that he was planning to take personal charge of Sicilia's growing navy while appointing Azhar, the shining knight of Panormus, as commander of the land forces. Meanwhile, he was forming a civilian government to look after the needs of the common folk who scraped a living from the land, and who deserved more as the island grew in prosperity.

It all seemed very imaginative, noble even. But he seemed to be including me in his plans, so I voiced my concern. And that was when he made a proposition that I couldn't refuse —

when Sextus wanted something, he always made sure that he was giving something in return.

'I'll be blunt,' he said. 'What I need from you is some creative thinking.' He saw I was about to object and added, hurriedly, 'But I realise I only have you for a few months, perhaps until the winter passes. While you are here, I will send my best men to the mainland in the guise of merchants and businessmen to discover the whereabouts of your family, as I have already promised.'

He saw my appreciative smile.

'In return,' he continued, 'all I ask is that you be your resourceful self. I will show you where Archimedes lived, and I hope to arrange lodgings with the old man who lives there now — he's totally deranged but quite harmless — so you can ascertain what papers and scrolls might remain. These may inspire you to continue the work you started when you created a signalling system using nothing but copper and sunlight.'

'It all sounds very reasonable, and your help in finding my family is appreciated,' I replied. 'But somehow I doubt that I can match the brilliance of Archimedes.'

'Pito, I'll be happy if you achieve nothing! Just having you here is reward enough. Ah, here's the house.'

We had rounded a corner and the paved street led to a villa whose gates had rotted, the gardens inside overgrown. We pushed our way through exotic foliage and vicious thistles to a main door, which Sextus pushed open to reveal a courtyard that had also succumbed to the invasion of numerous plants.

'Corban?' he shouted. 'Are you there, old man?'

There was a scuffing noise and a bent old man in a grubby, full-length smock appeared in a doorway opposite the main entrance. His long, grey beard was stained with egg and his bald head was scratched and bruised as if he had repeatedly walked into the low branches that had invaded his home. He peered at us and grunted, then shuffled towards us.

'Sextus, my boy,' he exclaimed. 'If it isn't the people's prince. You look more like your father with every passing day.'

'I hope not,' said Sextus, embracing the old man.

'And who's this? Not another fugitive from Rome that you want me to hide?'

Sextus laughed. 'No. In fact, he's not from Rome at all. Melqart here has come all the way from Hispania. He'd like to stay here for a while. Will you have him?'

'Gladly, gladly,' said Corban, peering at me. 'Hispania, eh? You probably don't understand a word I'm saying, do you?'

It was my turn to laugh. 'Yes, sir, I understand you perfectly.'

He clapped me on the shoulder with a twisted, freckly hand. 'Well then, you can tell me all about yourself and Hispania. I want to know everything. And I shall tell you all about Sicilia, where the women are as beautiful as the wine is strong.'

'I'll leave you to it, then,' said Sextus. Turning to leave as the old man shepherded me towards what I assumed would be my living quarters, he added, 'I'll send over some servants to tidy this place up, and some fresh supplies…'

The old man merely waved a dismissive hand in his direction. 'Now then,' he said, his arm still around my shoulders, 'have you ever heard of Archimedes…?'

THIRTY-FIVE

The autumn rains gave Corban's crazy garden even more energy to fight back against my pruning and hacking, but by Saturnalia I had it under control. The old man was of no use whatsoever as a gardener. In fact, he sowed chaos and untidiness everywhere, but his unexpected yet brilliant observations about my mechanical sketches were helpful. It transpired that he was a descendant of Archimedes and, given the way he took my drawings seriously, I could easily believe that.

The garden was my escape when my mind fogged and calculations were beyond me. I was grateful for some assistance when Nahalia returned with Bashira on one of Leandra's traders. Her care for all of my appetites gave me renewed vigour, both in the garden and by way of mental creativity.

I cleared a small area behind a decrepit wall where we often lay at night, wrapped in furs, gazing at the brilliant stars until the chill drove us to my small room to give each other warmth. We were free to live and love. And on those nights I could easily put aside my mission to rescue my family, but with the coming of each dawn I renewed my purpose and reminded Sextus of his promise. He would just shrug his shoulders and assure me that the matter was in hand.

My concerns for the welfare of my family apart, this was a rewarding time. War and killing were far away, the surges of creativity in my work left me dizzy with expectation, and Nahalia was a sensual lover, bringing joy to each day. Even the pains in my back nagged less.

It was the calm that comes before the storm. For below the Great Mountain, Vulcan awoke to stoke his furnaces.

A pair of eagles flew south, not circling on the hunt, but fleeing. Behind them a vast flock of smaller birds blackened the sky, ten thousand tiny wings rending the heavy air. Dogs barked everywhere, while the terrified screams of stabled horses announced the dread demons below.

Alone in the garden, I sank to my knees, nauseous and sweating as if gripped by sudden fever. The tremor silenced the world, if only for the briefest moment, as the blacksmith god stirred from his slumber.

Aetna growled and spat a plume of black and yellow smoke high into the air, and the ground shook as Vulcan fanned his fires. I lay flat on the tilled ground that boiled and heaved, a deafening roar pulsating through me as the world convulsed.

As suddenly as it came, all was still.

I lay prone, my mouth filled with gritty soil, my fingers curling into the soft ground. Slowly, I lifted my head, focusing on trembling leaves then looking over to where dust settled on a pile of rubble that had been a corner of Corban's house. Beyond, a pall of hideous smoke lay over Aetna.

But Vulcan was not finished. With a great crack of his hammer, he thrashed his forge and fiery tongues surged upwards; again and again he hammered while frenzied Titans hurled their rocks in confusion and anger and the great Cyclops bellowed its anguish. Huge fissures streaked the yielding slopes of the mountain, pouring forth crimson torrents as the mountain surrendered to the spite of the gods.

I tried to call out to Nahalia, but I could only croak pitifully. Hauling my reluctant body to my knees, I fought off another wave of nausea and crawled towards the house. A door was swinging from twisted hinges, behind it a swirling blackness and the sound of protesting beams. I pulled myself inside and my eyes adjusted to the gloom. Eventually I found my voice and called for Nahalia — a gentle sob told me she was alive. I found her hiding under our bed, unhurt apart from the same sickness that had overcome me. I held her close, whispering irrelevancies that meant the world to her, then helped her from the house.

We found Corban, or at least a protruding arm, crushed under the awful weight of collapsed masonry, still clutching a dead mouse that he had been removing from the house when Vulcan awoke. We tried to recover his broken body, but the stones were too heavy for us in our weakened condition.

We knelt beside his untidy tomb and Nahalia prayed in a tongue I did not understand, but we shared a common grief for the old man and there, in our fear and his peace, we wept.

Aetna continued to vent its foul-smelling sulphurous breath for seven days, blocking the sun and raining ash and grime. Surprisingly, Athena's temple stood proud amid the chaos of the city, her columns untouched by the petty fury of the minor gods beneath the earth. Fractious seas had swamped several smaller ships in the Great Harbour, and later we learned that at least two galleys outside the breakwater had been consumed by an immense wave and swept away south, never to be seen again.

Two entire settlements that nestled near the living mountain, Inessa and Hybla Gereatis, had been lost to fire and ash, and much of the port of Catana was reduced to rubble. Nahalia and I joined the rescue teams that were sent north by Sextus, returning exhausted and dispirited a week later. Even when

Aetna's grumbling ceased, the sun refused to shine and a land of warmth and joy died under a blanket of ash and ice.

Sicilia's rebirth was slow and painful, but inevitable. Her people had an indomitable spirit that never flinched, even under the weight of senatorial taxes and the corruption of its quaestors. In Sextus, they saw the future, and hope was dawning like the morning sun that was now fitfully returning. Of course, their faith needed the bolster of ritual sacrifice, and the island's stock of bulls, goats, sheep and hens was reduced dramatically in the days that followed the eruption. Sextus felt the same as I did about this pointless slaughter, but, accepting that it made the common people feel better, he indulged them for the sake of appearances.

The religious subculture came into its own — priests and priestesses, street prophets and self-proclaimed oracles found rich pickings among nobility and peasants alike. The mountain's fire and thunder were, of course, the voice and breath of Jupiter, or the stirring of Neptune, or the fearsome warnings of Mars: it meant the end of the world, the beginning of a new era, or an impending invasion by terrible armies. Strange proclamations gave birth to even stranger religions, to the point where the otherworldly fever became farcical and rather entertaining.

Two days of rain washed away the ash and the sun returned to warm the land.

Nahalia and I rebuilt Corban's house with the help of slaves loaned to us by Sextus. He was in the habit of forgetting to reclaim his property and these men, all of them well-versed in building techniques, earned their freedom by helping to create a beautiful home with a peaceful, shaded courtyard and the most talked-about gardens in Syracuse.

The old man had left no will, and as I was the sitting tenant and nobody came to claim the house, it became mine. I was the new Archimedes; I felt the approval of the man as I sat and worked among his citrus trees.

Peace was, for now, restored. Vulcan had finished with his forge beneath the mountain.

THIRTY-SIX

The trumpets sounded in the narrow streets of Syracuse, shredding the dawn like the screeching of a hundred harridans. I had been watching a rebellious streak of dark hair that lay across Nahalia's cheek when the alarm went up, killing my arousal instantly.

She slept through the clamour, peaceful and spent.

I dressed quickly, reached through the window to grasp a pomegranate, crept from the bedroom and ran through the garden.

At the brow of the hill I stopped, breathless, and looked out beyond the town and the harbour. I counted five ships heeling in the strong wind, two smaller vessels breaking for the safety of the port, and three powerful galleys bearing down on them, their bellicose beaks surging through the fitful seas like iron fists. Deck-mounted scorpios pitched badly aimed darts, while smoke billowed from the readied fire onagers. The two fugitives fought for the fastest line, sails tight to the wind as Sextus had taught them, oars dipping and straining, their gold and blue pennants of Sicilia dancing in the morning breeze. But from where I stood watching they seemed slow, so slow, unable to wrest themselves free from their dogged hunters.

The trumpets fell silent, the city now alerted to the danger but strangely still calm apart from the heaving activity in the harbour below, an ant nest rudely disturbed by an intrusive twig. Men dashed from the squat barracks, hastily tying sword belts or dragging vital equipment as they made for the ships that slept at their quayside births. One liburnian had already slipped her ropes and was nudging her bows away from the

312

land, muscular crewmen pushing their oars into the cloying mud to heave her reluctantly towards deeper water.

Mounted in her bows were two menacing sea spears, their ropes coiled from iron-tipped point to flat base, men already arming the tensioned firing lever. Beyond the inner harbour, six more sea spear launchers were staked to the low sea defence wall where Sextus and I had trained his sailors in their use, the thick wooden shafts pointing out to sea.

My sea spear. Sicilia's secret weapon.

Archimedes would have been proud of the creativity that had emerged from his dusty, ramshackle laboratory after so many winter days and nights.

It was the Sicilians themselves who had first alerted me to the principles that led to the invention. In my mind's eye, I replayed the arcing javelins as they outdistanced our own spears every time in the games at Panormus. Theirs were identical to our javelins, weighted and balanced to give distance and power as they dipped to pierce the hard ground or, in the case of battle, impale an armoured foot soldier or cause havoc among charging cavalry.

The only difference was in the launching technique. The cords had been looped around the wrists of the Sicilians and left dangling after each effortless throw. At first I was convinced this gave extra leverage and therefore distance, but if that were the purpose of the cords, they would surely remain attached to the javelins after they had been launched. There couldn't be enough purchase if the cords were not tied to the weapon.

The only other effect the cords had was to spin the javelin as it was launched into the air. And it was easy to prove that a spinning spear travelled further and truer than one that was not spinning.

I showed my findings to Sextus, who said dismissively, 'Tell me something new.'

So I did, a few days later.

The first sea spear was as thick as a pig's body and behaved like one. We cut the shafts from the Fraxinus forests between Acrae and Netum to the west, shaped and polished them, then mounted the first specimen in the bows of an old trireme on a runner smothered with animal fat. Around the thick spear was wound a strong rope, notched at the blunt end to allow the rope to loosen once unwound, and coiled tightly around the shaft to where it tapered to a point. To the free end we tied a heavy boulder that took four men to carry and several pulleys to load onto the bow of the trireme. A ballista lever, also made from the springy but strong Fraxinus wood, was mounted in the bowels of the ship, positioned to give the spear its forward thrust.

It was all about timing. I wished Sextus had not insisted on seeing the first trial of a sea spear for himself. He stood suspiciously in the bows, raising an eyebrow when the boulder gave the old ship an ominous list as we were rowed to the centre of the harbour. I gave the signal for the boulder to be released over the side into deep water at exactly the same time as the ballista was fired. The sea spear rolled sideways, hardly spinning, and fell with a whimpering splash into the calm sea while the ballista arm splintered the bow planking an arm's length from a startled Sextus.

We did not celebrate that night.

I spent a week putting the finishing touches to my second attempt by the spluttering light of an oil lamp. While the people of Syracuse celebrated Saturnalia, dressed in their colourful finery and silly hats, feasting until they were sick, I locked myself away from Nahalia.

This time I chose a broadside launching system. Using the same battered trireme, her bow still mangled from my first attempt, we sailed to the middle of the harbour. The sea spear was mounted at the widest part of the ship, again on a greased runner, but this time the spin and the forward motion were provided by a twisted hemp rope that crossed the deck and returned to a point directly below the pegged sea spear via a lubricated pulley. My theory, practised on a scale model at the old man's house, was that the rope could be tensioned to the required degree using a swivel made of iron rings at the point where it was attached to the bottom of the ship.

As we moved gently into the Great Harbour, Sextus pointed out that this new arrangement meant that we would have fewer rowers.

'But more fire power,' I said hopefully.

I ordered the rope to be twisted several more turns. The ship creaked and groaned as the tension strained the ageing timbers. I felt the ship could cope with a few more turns, but not wanting to risk another disaster I ordered the release. Using a large mallet, a sailor struck the iron peg cleanly from its housing, and the Melqart Sea Spear shot forwards, turning rather than spinning, and catapulted gracefully into the sea where it curved disobediently in a gentle circle before slowing, then wallowing like a dead fish.

There was silence, then someone sniggered. I sat down heavily and put my head in my hands.

It was Sextus who rescued me. 'Much better than last time,' he said cheerily. 'At least you launched it. Great entertainment for an enemy ship, though. Might take their minds off fighting us.'

There was still no celebration, but Sextus invited me to his lavish villa where we talked long into the night about ways of adapting the sea spear and the ships that would carry them. We looked at the negatives, especially his fixation with maintaining full banks of rowers, and then discussed ways of launching the weapon from the bows. 'That way, we can aim the spears and even follow up by ramming with the beak, which is, after all, what it was designed to do.' He was even getting excited about the project.

Our third trial took place as the first of the warm breezes hinted at the promise of spring. This time the spear was mounted in the bows on the same runner, but part of the bow railing had been cut away to allow a lower and shallower trajectory into the water. A pulley was mounted just above the waterline, creating a problem that would have to be addressed for rougher seas — how to make it watertight — but I assured Sextus I knew how to do this. The rope was again coiled tightly around the sea spear, now iron-tipped for more destructive power, and ran through the pulley and along the entire length of the ship to the ballista lever. When released, this would spring from the floor of the ship to an upright position to thud against a newly strengthened beam across the stern. The composite lever took two men to winch it into position but, I calculated, it stored enough energy to both thrust and spin the sea spear straight and true.

The big advantage, if this system worked, was that it could be reloaded at sea.

This time there was a crowd of spectators on the harbour walls, intrigued by our strange experiments and no doubt looking forward to some unusual entertainment.

I gave the signal and heard the retaining peg smashed aside below the decks. The spear spun and surged forward in the same moment, and there was a deafening "thwack" as the lever hit the new beam in the stern. The Melqart Sea Spear Version Three sped straight and true, thrusting like an arrow through the surface water for about three lengths of a trireme before slowing to drift in the gentle current.

This time the crew cheered loudly and Sextus punched the air, then threw his arms around me.

'Not bad for a Hispanic peasant,' he laughed.

That was why the liburnian with two mounted sea spears was first to leave its moorings to challenge the enemy ships that chased our vessels as they rowed for the Sicilian shoreline, and that was why I ran as fast as I could to the harbour wall where the six training spears were arrayed like accusing fingers, pointing out to sea.

Gasping for breath as I approached the barracks, I called out to a centurion I recognised, ordering him to find as many men as possible who had worked on the sea spear trials and bring them to the harbour wall. Our liburnian was now on its way to meet the enemy and was passing the breakwater into open sea as I reached the battery of spears.

I cupped my hands to my mouth. 'Who commands?' I called.

'Guess who?' came the reply across the short stretch of still water.

'Sextus,' I yelled, 'try to lure the enemy ships close to these spears. If they come within range, I can loose them from here.'

'Sounds like a good plan,' he called back as his ship turned into the choppier seas beyond the breakwater. 'Between us we'll sink all three before breakfast!'

A dozen men ran along the causeway to where I now stood, panting and sweating. I recognised two of them from previous exercises in the harbour and told them to show the others how the sea spears could be armed. They set to work immediately.

Sextus steered parallel to the land then changed course to approach the exposed sides of the enemy ships, his twin sea spears pointing directly at their long banks of oarsmen. I could make out voices raised in encouragement to the exhausted crews of the two fugitive liburnians and hoped Sextus would buy them time with his first attack. Some of the scorpio bolts were striking home now and I cringed at the bloody mayhem they must be causing. A great fireball looped into the sky and landed close to one of the Sicilian ships, hissing and boiling as it struck the water.

The chasing Roman galleys must have thought the approaching smaller ship was intending to ram one of them, and all three changed course simultaneously as the trumpet sounded its commands, now sailing at an angle to the attacking liburnian as it closed on them. A hail of arrows was loosed on the dwarfed attacker, but she seemed to lurch on with renewed vigour, gritty and bold in the face of the enemy.

Surely Sextus was close enough now. I began to worry that something was wrong with the firing mechanism.

Then there was a telltale splash as the spear met the sea, and another a moment later. I found myself counting down the time each would take to reach their target, though somehow I knew that the first missile had missed. But then the second galley in the line gave a distinct shudder. Most of the oars on that side suddenly stopped dipping, some tangling with those that were still in motion, and the Roman began to list, slowing and veering as her helmsman tried desperately to adjust. A great cheer went up from the crew on Sextus's ship.

Leaving the crippled galley to its own catastrophe, the remaining two triremes closed in on the impudent aggressor.

Their original prey was left to continue its course for Syracuse harbour. We had stung Rome's finest ships.

But the Sicilian liburnian wasn't finished yet. Only Sextus would refuse to run from the bigger craft, both equipped with fearsome scorpios and probably a hundred fully armed soldiers. Sextus sailed directly between them, braving a hail of arrows but none of the scorpio bolts or the fireballs, as the cumbersome machinery could not be easily turned on the cramped decks. Rather than waste energy on fighting back, the nimble Sicilian was a low, surging target as she danced between the larger ships, her crew mocking their opponents as she passed.

Outraged, the enemy pursued Sextus on a course that would, hopefully, pass my line of waiting sea spears.

Sextus steered his liburnian close to the Great Harbour entrance but then took a northerly course, staying as close to the breakwater as he dared, as if trying to make his escape in the shallower waters further up the coast. He allowed the two Roman triremes to close up enough to believe they could catch him. As the smaller ship passed our position, it was obvious that the oarsmen were rowing well within themselves, while Sextus leaned casually against the poop deck railing. I could see his smile as he passed. The two other Sicilians had reached the relative safety of port, their crews slumped over their oars, all strength sapped, too weary to take their ships to the quay.

The Roman ships approached our position, the tiers of oars making strange groaning sounds in their rowlocks that mingled with the intense grunting of the oarsmen in the bowels of the two vessels. The third was floundering, still listing and drifting away to the south.

I readied the men, their spears numbered one to six, each with a man poised over his lever release peg. All they had to do was pull out the pin from the iron ring swivels on my command. The first of the two huge galleys drew level, but I remained silent: I wanted both ships in the path of our sea spears.

In the bow of the first ship an officer was watching Sextus flee, his crimson cloak billowing in the wind, his fists clenching and unclenching in frustration. Suddenly he looked ashore and saw our battery of sea spears, then turned and barked an order to the helmsman: he had already witnessed the effect of our deadly weapon.

Both ships began to turn away from us. I gave the signal for the three spears nearest their approach to launch: 'Six, five and four, release.' The three missiles splashed into the sea as both ships turned agonisingly away, their helmsmen leaning powerfully on the rudder beams.

Only one spear hit, but of all the places to damage a ship, it was perfect. The rudder of the leading ship splintered as the iron tip crashed into it. The force flung the helmsman overboard, a shrill scream accompanying his frenzied clutching at air. The oarsmen did not break their rhythm and the great ship continued its reckless course out to sea, its companion following, putting as much water between themselves and the awesome Sicilian defences as they could.

Another cheer arose from the triumphant crew of Sextus's liburnian. But it was drowned by our own delirious celebrations.

A large crowd thronged on the quay where the two emancipated ships and Sextus's vessel were docking. My sea spear team jogged to the inner harbour to join them, determined to share in the glory, while several Sicilian craft were heading out of the harbour to capture and plunder the floundering galley that was drifting away south.

To get a better view of the Prince of Sicilia stepping ashore, I stood on a large wooden box of fish that had been landed at dawn, ignoring the pungent smell, my feet slipping on slime and scales.

Sextus pushed through the crowd to greet the captains of the liberated ships, no doubt eager to ascertain why three Roman vessels had chased them down so urgently. From my vantage point, I could see him talking to a tall youth of about his own age, perhaps a little younger, who had the same cropped blond hair and striking looks, his tunic creased and sweat-stained from the exertions of several days at sea in demanding conditions. He was speaking urgently to Sextus, who shook his head in apparent disbelief. As they talked, those nearest stopped their cheering and strained to hear, then turned to those behind them to pass on some item of news. Whatever they had heard was so intriguing that cheers turned to shock, and celebrations became the excited whispers of gossip.

The name I could hear repeatedly as the news spread was "Caesar". Jumping down from my platform, I pushed towards Sextus, slowing only to eavesdrop as the news was passed along. That Caesar was dead came as no surprise, but as I pieced together the snatches of excited conversation, I realised that this was no ordinary death.

Caesar had been assassinated by his own people.

My first thought was of the irony of it all — how a man who had thrown himself at the swords of countless tribal armies had survived only to die brutally at the hands of the very people he called "civilised". I suppressed the urge to laugh, ashamed of my callousness, and shouldered my way towards

Sextus, who was still in conversation with the new arrival. I caught his eye and he turned to me, smiling. Behind him, the crews and passengers of the two liburnians were disembarking, dishevelled and exhausted, some with vomit staining their clothing, others unsteady and in need of support.

Sextus pointed to a knot of people in the stern of the nearest ship, waiting their turn to come ashore, then in a moment of dizzying confusion I understood his smile.

My family had returned to me.

THIRTY-SEVEN

It was a frozen moment that stretched into eternity. I did not see anyone else apart from my parents and my sisters, and it was a while before they saw me. The cry caught in my throat and my head swam.

My father looked frail, his tangled hair whitened by whatever ordeals Rome had cast upon him, but his back was straight, unbowed by slavery. His arms held my sisters tightly, their startled faces streaked with tears, and beside him stood my angel mother, all serenity and dignity.

I found my voice, now shouting and waving, and then they saw me, their confusion becoming joy in an instant. Sextus barked orders and the gangplank's press was cleared for them. Then we were embracing, tears flowing freely, questions begun but not completed, laughing, sobbing, thanking deities and the fates.

My father's face was scored with lines that had not been there before, but his spirit was strong. He hushed Tallay's wild exclamations, and that was when I noticed that Pidray was quiet, almost sullen. My mother just smiled at me; she had aged, too. She touched the myrrh stone at my neck, drawing on its power.

I turned to Sextus for an explanation, but he held up his hand.

'Where do we begin?' He shrugged his shoulders. 'So many questions to ask and each one will take a day to answer.'

My father spoke then, indicating the powerful youth standing beside Sextus. 'We are here thanks in no small part to this man,

Durio. He brought us here at great risk to his own life.' He looked at Durio and added, 'We are in your debt.'

Durio bowed slightly in acknowledgement.

Sextus put a hand on the young man's shoulder. 'Durio isn't his real name, but it's as good as any. He's my half-brother, as it happens, and has been my eyes and ears on the streets of Rome this past year, continuing the struggle on behalf of the Republic.'

'And it would seem that the Republic has struck a telling blow with the death of Caesar,' I put in.

'Indeed,' said Sextus gravely, 'and I think you'll find my brother had a part to play in that, too. Hence the close attentions of those Roman galleys.'

Still Durio said nothing. He just smiled, knowingly.

Sextus gave us rooms in his villa on the edge of the city where Bashira, now his housekeeper, kept an army of servants on their toes to provide us with everything we might need, and more besides. My mother frowned at the rich food put before us, but enjoyed it nonetheless, then she and my sisters luxuriated in the hot baths and a limitless supply of rare oils and exotic hair treatments. My father took to wearing a colourful toga, not to mimic the patricians of Rome, but because it was comfortable. He would not have looked out of place in the senate.

The gardens were sublime in the spring sunshine. Small birds teased a pair of black cats that stalked lizards among the crimson blooms, while diligent bees farmed the lavenders that nestled beneath pine canopies. Tallay was preoccupied with the cats, which in turn patted the tiny silver bells that decorated the ends of her waist ties. Pidray daydreamed in a shaded corner, watching a small tortoise seek out the greenest foliage.

We talked for two days. Sometimes my sisters were there, interrupting, innocently spiralling the conversation away from the important issues, but mostly they entertained themselves or were spirited away by Bashira to explore the noisy, colourful markets or help her organise the day's sustenance.

My parents told me that the journey from Munda to Gades was tough for slaves, even those who had some promise of favour from their new Roman masters. The terrain along the southern coast of Hispania was mountainous and the ground stony. Sometimes the women were permitted to ride in bone-jarring wagons, but most of these were either damaged beyond repair or abandoned where the passes were unsuitable, so that a dispirited band of prisoners arrived to swell the numbers held in Gades' slave pens. Pidray's health deteriorated on this part of the journey and she became pale and sullen, the light in her eyes fading with each day. All huddled together for warmth during the cold nights, but Pidray shivered incessantly with fever.

She became worse on the subsequent voyage, during which the family were penned below decks amid degrading filth and vomit. There was a daily gathering on deck in small groups to be washed down by the crew with seawater hauled aboard in pails. My father refused to say more about that hellish journey.

Tribune Saxa met his shipment at the port of Ostia. At last the gods smiled on my family, as they were not separated but sold by private treaty to Gaius Cilnius Maecenas, a wealthy young socialite who seemed to my parents to be cordial and sincere. Maecenas questioned them at length about their knowledge of herbs, suggesting several times on their journey to his estates in Tibur that they help him to compile a literary work on the use of herbs in medicine.

On their arrival in Tibur, Maecenas put my parents to work in his kitchens, where my father naturally took control of the bakery and my mother employed all her wisdom in gathering herbs for the cooks and providing them with lists of spices to buy at the market. The villa was frequently filled with dashing young poets, historians and philosophers, all of whom hoped Maecenas was their ticket to fulfilling their dreams of fame and fortune. All were lavish in their praise for the dishes that emerged from the kitchens.

My sisters were given more onerous tasks about the house, Tallay frequently getting into trouble for her effrontery while Pidray became yet more withdrawn and morose. My mother was quiet while my father spoke of their daughters. They did not need to tell me of the lascivious nature of Roman "nobility", or their degenerate preferences. Whatever had happened to Pidray, who was always more striking to look at than her sister, was left unsaid — as if by not talking about it, it could be undone.

An older, wiser Maecenas would have easily recognised one of the young poets in his court as an impostor, so bad was his verse. It wasn't long, said my father, before this new poet wandered presumptuously into the kitchens and at an opportune moment whispered that he had been sent to seek out my family with a view to their liberation, refusing to enlighten my father as to who was his paymaster. It gave my parents hope, although they did not tell Tallay and Pidray for fear of wagging tongues.

For long months they heard nothing from their anonymous poet-spy, though occasionally they saw him in animated debate with other young writers, sometimes taking turns to read their work to murmurs of approval or raucous laughter at the more scandalous references to Rome's public figures, including

Caesar. It seemed Caesar was not as popular as I had imagined Pompey's conqueror would be, especially when he was appointed Dictator for Life by a cowed senate.

My father involuntarily lowered his voice when he talked of the shift in mood that seemed to grip the Maecenas household as the winter nights were at their longest. He had been summoned to build the fires throughout the villa and was obediently going about his business in his usual unfussy manner when he overheard talk of a plot against the Dictator.

It was at this time that my family first encountered Durio. Though they did not know it at the time, he was secretary to Gaius Cassius Longinus and was, as they now understood, seeking allies for a secret movement called the Liberatores, a loose organisation that favoured the old ways of the Republic. My father did not think Durio found much favour among Maecenas's followers, but then with hindsight that had not been the only purpose of his visits to Tibur. The poet-spy was his man.

Of course, my family was merely an afterthought in Durio's plotting, but if successful the assassination of Caesar would throw the whole of Rome and the nobility of Italia into confusion, creating an opportunity to fulfil the wishes of Sextus in his Sicilian stronghold and rescue a family of slaves that for some reason held considerable importance for him.

Bashira brought a silver tray laden with fruits and listened while I told my family of my adventures in Utica, of Ziri and the King of the Desert, and the fierce battle with the slavers from Aegyptus. I embellished my part in the fighting, and they marvelled when I showed them my silver armbands. Tallay and Pidray were awestruck; Bashira said such a gift was fit only for a hero like Herakles.

Over dinner that night, I recounted the story of the storm that had brought me to Sicilia, and the games at Panormus. Later, after my family had retired, I questioned Sextus about his part in the plot against Caesar.

'It was nothing to do with me,' he said, and I believed him. 'I sent word to Durio to get your family out if it was possible, though when he succeeded and at the same time brought word of Caesar's death, I started to believe the gods were smiling on us again.'

I held my cup out to him. 'It was a noble thing you did for me. For us.'

We drank to freedom.

The next morning, my parents described the dramatic events that had rocked Rome in recent days. One of the young literary hopefuls had ridden to the estate at Tibur to announce breathlessly to Maecenas that Caesar was dead.

This indeed caused the pandemonium that Durio had anticipated. Orders were barked, slaves and servants ran hither and thither, and the Maecenas household prepared to move to Rome to ensure that the correct allies were chosen in what must surely be a new order.

The way my father told it, on reaching Rome my family just kept going. But he was taking a shortcut in the telling, delicately corrected by my mother.

The reality was that Durio had arranged for two Sicilian ships to be ready at Ostia on the day of the funeral, five days after Caesar was murdered. He sent the poet-spy to bring word of this to my father, assuring him that four slaves would not be missed until long after the lament, heartfelt or otherwise, was over.

Maecenas had found Rome surprisingly calm, said my father, but that all changed on the day of the funeral, when Marcus Antonius held aloft the bloody clothes that Caesar had worn on the Ides of March. The mob turned on the conspirators, who until then had somehow placated the people with their assurances that the city would benefit from Caesar's vast wealth. Though Longinus had foreseen the troubles that were to take place in the city that day and made himself scarce, Durio was identified as a conspirator and narrowly escaped with his life.

He made for Ostia and the ships that waited there, pursued by a detachment from Caesar's personal guard who may have believed that Durio was helping Longinus to escape, and were determined to taste the blood of revenge.

Recalling the wild emotions of what must have been a terrifying day, my mother told how they had reached the port just in time to board the ship that would bring them to Sicilia and safety. Their relief as they cast off was short-lived. The two liburnians sailed south, flying no colours for fear that whichever pennant they displayed, they might encounter an opposing force.

But the pursuing Romans had used the name of Caesar and plenty of persuasive gold to secure three fully crewed galleys, and found the Sicilian vessels by chance off Tarracina, where the Appian Way met the sea.

At first the faster liburnians had put distance between themselves and their hunters, but the Romans managed to keep in touch. Throughout a windless night, Durio's ships were rowed south by the stars, but in the morning the enemy could still be seen, more determined than ever to catch them.

My father told me how the ship in which my family sailed sprang a leak, with some of the rowers forced to ship their oars and bail out the water that sloshed at their feet. The other Sicilian slowed protectively with them, allowing the hounding Romans to close the gap. It had been uncertain whether they would make it to Sicilia and the safety of Sextus's fleet.

But they did reach Syracuse, and led the three triremes onto the waiting sea spears, bringing with them my lost-and-found family, and news of the death of Caesar.

PART FOUR: COVENANT OF THE SEVEN

THIRTY-EIGHT

40 BC

Sextus longed to see Hispania again, but the draw of politics lay heavily upon him. Somehow he persuaded me and my family to stay in Sicilia longer than we had wanted, pressing upon me duties of engineering and upon my family the sweet repose of luxury to mend wounded spirits. There was always a reason, given with a warm smile, why we should not be boarding a ship bound for Hispania.

A political love affair with Marcus Antonius, a powerful figure in a Rome, had been short-lived. But the new power in Rome was nothing compared with the astonishing influx of fugitive slaves from mainland Italia. This ready-made army of people, desperate to escape the rigours of Roman rule and carve out a name and a place for themselves in Sicilia, was all the motivation Sextus needed. Almost every day small ships arrived in Messana, Catana and Syracuse, low in the water with the weight of slave families, or galleys rowed joyfully by mutinous crews, their harsh overlords having been tossed overboard, or if they were lucky, bound and gagged to be paraded in the streets by Sicilian rebels.

Sextus was drunk on the success of his precious island. And so were his half-brother, Durio, and Azhar, commander-in-chief of Sicilia's land forces. This preoccupation with the birth of a powerful new nation-state filled his thinking and his time, weakening his resolve to keep us in Sicilia. Eventually, he tired and let us go with a typically Sextus-like comment.

'What are you and your family doing here? Isn't it time you all went home instead of sucking my generosity dry? Go on, be off, and be sure to have a house and servant girls ready for me when I visit!'

Sextus presented me with precious gifts as we bade farewell on the worn quay at Syracuse. Next to our ship was a chest filled with silver coins minted in his fourth year as self-proclaimed praetor, though prince or king would have been more fitting. Beside this was an even larger chest of Roman jewels and gold raided from ships that had refused to pay the tax levied for safe passage through the Straits of Messana. Best of all, Nahalia stood next to this overwhelming treasure dressed in a flimsy silk gown.

'The price you must pay for Nahalia is your pledge that you will return,' Sextus smiled, 'and bring more of your science to help make Sicilia ruler of the seas.'

'Gladly,' I said, then pointed to my family, who waited patiently for us to finish our dramatic antics. 'You gave back to me those who are more precious than all the riches of Rome. One day I will return, not out of loyalty, but friendship alone.'

'There's one more thing you need to know before you return,' said Sextus, leading me aside with an arm draped around my shoulders. He handed me a rolled and sealed parchment.

'What's this? A letter you want delivering to some lovelorn girl in Hispania?'

Sextus laughed. 'Better than that.' He lowered his voice. 'Have you ever wondered what happened to all the gold and silver coin that was to have been paid to our armies after the battle of Munda?'

I was intrigued — it must amount to a massive fortune. 'Surely Caesar's men found it?'

'No, it was well hidden. My brother Gnaeus may not have been the brightest of generals, but he took the precaution of concealing the army's payroll the night before the battle. It was in the early hours when everyone either watched for the enemy or slept. This scroll will show you where.'

'But it belongs to you, as the only surviving general,' I said. 'I suppose you want me to return it to you here?'

'No. I have everything I need and more. Nothing would please me more than for you to find it and use it to repay just a little of the debt we Pompeians owe to your town.'

'Can I open it?'

He nodded. 'It's yours to do with as you please.'

I worked my thumb under the seal and broke it. The script was clumsy, clearly written in a hurry, or perhaps by a nervous hand.

'It says here, "at the source of life, behind the cleansing veil". What on earth could that mean?'

'You'll work it out.' Sextus smiled and added, 'It's closer to home than you think.'

'I'll do my best,' I said, and thanked him. 'I'll make sure everyone who has suffered is recompensed … if I find the treasure.'

I pocketed the scroll then helped my mother and father aboard the ship, which along with the crew of thirty veteran soldiers and sixty rowers, all paid in advance, was yet further evidence of Sextus's generosity. We left Syracuse to a cacophony of whistles and cheers rising from the quayside.

As soon as we cleared the breakwater, I stepped close to the captain and asked him to make for Utica.

Ziri pushed me into the harbour at Utica, indignant that I should ask him to take a chest of Sicilian coin to his father who had riches enough, thank you very much. Far from running around on my behalf like an errand boy, he told me he was damn well going to accompany me on an adventure to Hispania. My sisters screamed and cackled with delight at my discomfort as I spat out muddy water and paddled in a most ungainly way for the quayside. He signalled two of his formidable companions, both of whom had the right side of their faces and one shoulder intricately decorated with the dark ink that marked a great warrior, to carry the chest back on board, and he stepped lightly onto the ship after them.

'Lead on, fish face,' he said as I trod damply back on deck. 'Show me this land across the seas that needs the help of Ziri to understand what civilisation really is.'

I looked at the Prince of the Desert, his curved sword with its jewelled pommel barely concealed by his menacing black robes, and to his companions, who were similarly armed, and I was grateful to have such men on my return to Hispania. I shook my head in mock despair and introduced Ziri to my parents. Pidray and Tallay gawped and giggled like children, until my father's sharp words warned them to act modestly.

'I hope your friends are better behaved than you,' I said to Ziri. 'An introduction would be good.'

Ziri beckoned forward the elder of the two, lean and strong. He was the same height as me, with a wily look in his eyes, his age betrayed only by flecks of grey in his close-cropped hair. 'This is Ayyur, the moon, who can see at night when he hunts the lion.' The pattern that adorned the side of his face was indeed crescent shaped, like a half-moon.

He summoned the other, a younger man who was more muscled than his companion. 'And this is Izem, the lion, who cannot be stalked by anyone, not even Ayyur,' said Ziri proudly. 'We could not ask for finer warriors to look after your family in the heathen wilds of your country.'

I laughed, then realised that perhaps Ziri did not jest.

Ziri looked at my family, and Nahalia who stood with them. 'And this is your family?'

I introduced them. 'My father, Hann, and my mother Adela. These are my sisters, Tallay and Pidray. I also have a younger brother, Elvir, whom we will see when we arrive in Hispania.'

The three warriors bowed graciously to them, Ziri's teeth flashing white as he smiled. 'But Melqart, you have forgotten one, this eastern beauty with fire in her eyes. Is she your slave? Or were you hoping to conceal such a charming creature from one who is a better man than you?'

Nahalia spoke for herself. 'I am no slave,' she said confidently, though she lowered her eyes in the custom of her people. 'I am his woman and...'

'We should sail immediately.' I interrupted her because I knew in an instant that she was going to say that I was in fact her slave. They all looked at me.

'Why?' asked Ziri. 'There's plenty of time to feast and enjoy the city's pleasures, is there not?'

'No, there is not time,' my father put in, firmly. 'We have been away from home for five years and we are eager to return.'

Ziri shrugged. 'You are already well provisioned, then?'

'Indeed,' I said, and nodded to the captain. 'We can be in Flavia Malacita within six days, given fair winds, perhaps even Apollacta where my brother lives.'

'Never heard of either place,' said Ziri, dismissively. 'But then it wouldn't be such an adventure if I had, would it?'

The gods wanted us home, giving us an easterly wind for almost our entire voyage, never too strong to cause any discomfort. I argued playfully with Ziri about which god was behind the fair weather, and I taught him how to catch fish.

We used the long lines that were favoured by Sicilian fishermen, with bone hooks to which peacock feathers had been tied. These danced in our silvery wake to lure the great tuna, three of which we landed. They thrashed wildly on the decks before being clubbed by Ayyur and Izem. That night we baked our catch on our sandpit fires where we anchored close to Mauretania's coast.

The captain chose to turn northwards at exactly the right place and time. We sailed by the stars for one night, and at dawn we could make out the lofty, rugged mountains of Hispania's southernmost coast. We came up to Malacita, but there was time to make Apollacta before nightfall.

The well-drilled men who lined the shore were not to know that we offered no threat. Twenty archers formed up, kneeling on the beach, their arrows stabbed into the sand ready for rapid volleys. Behind them, armed soldiers bore light shields and Roman short swords. More archers lined the entrance to a new harbour where several trading vessels were moored, with them an imposing commander who watched our approach for signs of hostility.

I ran to the bows as the captain slowed our speed, waving and shouting that we came in peace. There was no reaction from the commander, grim and defiant beneath a plumed helmet, sword in hand, the resolute protector of a clearly thriving community. I cupped my hands and called across the shortening stretch of calm water.

'I am Melqart of Munda, returning home with my family.'

The commander stiffened, and for a moment I feared that Apollacta had fallen into unfriendly hands, but then with one easy movement the helmet was removed to release long braids of black hair.

Leandra.

'Pito?' she called back. 'Is that really you?'

I was lost for words, rooted in the prow as my childhood friend stood tall and proud, the ship agonisingly slow to reach the harbour. One of the bowmen ran to stand beside Leandra, a head taller than she, putting his fingers to his mouth to issue a shrill whistle. Then the archers on the harbour wall and the men on the beach were cheering and running to welcome the ship as she nosed into the port.

I leaped ashore before the mooring ropes had been secured and held Leandra in a crushing embrace, interrupted only by my demanding, inquisitive sisters and the attentions of the tall bowman at Leandra's side. He beamed at me as if I knew him.

'Pipsqueak…?' I gasped as recognition hit.

His smile broadened. 'That was my name, but now I am Sekis.'

Leandra explained, her fingers tracing the bulging muscle of the youth's sword arm. 'He outgrew his name and has proved himself to be a tower of strength again and again. Sekis means "strong" in the old tongue.' His features were certainly strong; the timid, frightened look had been replaced with confidence, a broad brow, a strong chin and a shock of dark hair. He was not what women would call "beautiful", but I could easily understand they would find him irresistible.

Leandra looked me up and down. 'Sekis isn't the only one who has changed. You seem … well, older and wiser.'

'And you are more beautiful than ever,' I replied truthfully. 'As far as soldiers go, at any rate.'

My mother was helped ashore as soon as our ship had been moored. She greeted Leandra warmly, but there was something of greater importance on her mind as she searched the faces on the quay.

'What about Elvir? Where is he?'

Leandra smiled at her. 'Your son is well, but he is not here. He leads the guard that watches the pass on the Munda road.' She indicated the track that led inland between the mountains. 'Turon is with him, and a dozen of our best men.'

'You said he leads a guard? Are you expecting trouble?' I asked.

Leandra sighed. 'We have to protect our people. This is no longer a peaceful land.'

That explained the rapid deployment of archers as we had approached. Indeed, beyond the neat buildings of a thriving community there was a defensive rampart overlooking the approach from the mountains — Apollacta was prepared for attack from land or sea. Ziri and his men were already studying the lie of the land and the design of the defences, no doubt unimpressed by the way Hispanics and Romans put their faith in solid buildings of stone and wood.

'There are many things that have changed these last five years,' Leandra continued. 'And most of them you are not going to like.'

THIRTY-NINE

We were tired after our long journey, but we sat under the bright stars and feasted on shellfish and sweet roasted lamb while Leandra and Cassia took it in turns to tell us how Caesar's violent legacy had stained a peaceful land with greed and confusion. The best lands had been given to loyal Roman generals to whom cruelty was second nature, but in many cases Caesar had rewarded local Hispanics who had helped him in his campaign against the Republicans.

Among this new breed of overlords was none other than my enemy, Zebul One-Eye.

Leandra explained that he had been given Munda as a reward for his part in the battle. The town was desolate, its people addled and vacant, the reek of death lingering as thousands of bodies were burned on mountainous pyres or left to rot where they lay. The lucky ones had crept out of Munda in the first dreadful days after the siege, but then Zebul had ordered the gates closed when he realised that he was losing valuable labour. All who remained, including women, children, the old and the infirm, were given burial and burning tasks that drained their souls. When that was completed, they were forced to labour on the restoration of the walls and buildings, as well as constructing a lavish new palace for Zebul and his arrogant family.

All trade was brought under the new procurator's control; all profits were Zebul's, extracted by brutal tax collectors armed with whips and clubs. These ruthless men became fat and rich as the downtrodden townsfolk became ever poorer. My Munda, once so happy and healthy, was dark and sick. Within a year, Zebul had begun to form a small army of his own that initially busied itself with the search for the lost treasure intended to pay the Optimates army. Rumours abounded of the hidden wealth, but the search for what became known as "Pompey's Gold" proved fruitless, so Zebul's men turned to raiding the soft mountain villages, their greed and lust spreading ever further afield. The nearby town of Lacibis was the only exception, for there Zebul's elder brother Dagan held high office. They formed an evil alliance to swell the numbers of fighting men and labourers who were no more than slaves in their eyes.

It wasn't long before Zebul's scouts discovered Apollacta. One-Eye himself had led a squadron of armed riders into the now thriving coastal community and demanded to speak to its leader. Hastily but inadequately, Turon and Elvir accompanied Leandra and Cassia to a meeting with Zebul's men on the edge of the bustling port, with most of the townsfolk crowding behind them in a heartening demonstration of support. Recognising Turon and Leandra, Zebul had bristled with anger before controlling himself, no doubt realising that he had stumbled upon an opportunity to avenge the indignity of his departure from Munda a decade ago.

But he was outnumbered and was not so foolish as to reveal his intentions there and then. He made a pretence of discussing trade agreements, which Leandra courteously declined, whereupon Zebul showed his true colours, spat hatefully and led his men at a gallop back the way they had come.

The first attack on Apollacta came in the spring, and though expected, it was almost the undoing of Leandra and Cassia's new settlement. Zebul's riders had broken through Elvir's inexperienced archers with few casualties and swept towards the port, looking for a swift and murderous victory, with

Leandra's head as their biggest prize. But they had not foreseen the fury and skill of Turon and his freshly formed century of swordsmen. They fought like demons in the streets, unhorsing many of the riders by savagely disembowelling their mounts, causing confusion and panic among the attackers. Zebul had underestimated not only Leandra as a leader, but the determination of her people to defend their homes and their families. The warrior goddess herself had fought at Turon's side, and together they struck terror into the hearts of Zebul's ruffians.

Following this rebuffed attack, Apollacta's defences had been carefully built and Turon not only trained hard with his century, fashioning them into a well-disciplined cavalry outfit, but also restored the signalling bronzes on the mountain summits between Apollacta and Munda, manning them with a new team of watchers to provide early warning of impending attacks. Elvir took it upon himself to organise patrols that would work in three-day shifts to observe Zebul's movements.

That was where Elvir was now, said Leandra.

And she doubted that my parents would recognise their youngest son.

The transformation of Elvir from a child into a warrior of nineteen was as much a surprise as that of Pipsqueak into Sekis. Word had reached him that we were in Apollacta and he had ridden ahead, leaping from his blowing, sweat-streaked horse before it had shambled to an exhausted halt, to sprint through the archway leading to the courtyard of Leandra's villa. He swept our mother off her feet, twirling her around until she begged him to stop, then embraced our sisters, our father and finally me.

'What took you so long?' he asked when he had caught his breath. 'If you had taken me, I'd have got you all back years ago…' Not as tall as Sekis, he was powerfully built but moved with a certain grace, light on his feet and expressive with his hands. His bronzed face was animated, full of humour and fortitude.

'Let's just say we had business to attend to,' I said.

My sisters were uncertain whether they could still get away with teasing him and instead admired his long, dark hair, oiled and braided with beads in the same style as Leandra's, and his ebony eyelashes, long for a man's.

Turon joined us, our friendship and trust still strong. He was Turon the mysterious mountain man, and he was Turon the centurion, commander of men. He still shunned ornate Roman armour, preferring the lighter leather protection of a horseman, and he carried two swords on his back, their pommels each balanced with rare onyx stones.

'If you'll excuse us,' said Leandra, interrupting the reunions, 'Elvir and Turon have a report to give.' After a moment, she added, 'You come too, Pito. I think you'll be interested to hear what our old friend Zebul has been up to.'

By the time we had gathered on Leandra's shaded terrace, Sekis and Ziri had joined us, Ziri bemused by the oddity of Apollacta's woman chieftain. She held his gaze as a leader should, and he gave her his respect with an almost imperceptible nod. Cassia sat with Leandra but remained silent, observing the newcomers and listening carefully to Elvir's report. Cheerful, intelligent youths ensured that each cup was kept full with the region's fruity wine.

It was on that balmy terrace, calmed by the music of the sea as it toyed with the whispering shingle, that The Seven gave their pledge. We would have been eight or nine, but both Leandra and Cassia declined to leave their beloved Apollacta.

The pledge we gave was firstly to liberate Munda — Ziri did not hesitate to offer his great curved sword, and those of Ayyur and Izem, even though he knew nothing of the mountain town. Secondly, we pledged allegiance and honour to Leandra, who was unquestionably the most noble and caring leader a community could wish to have. And thirdly, we pledged to recover "Pompey's Gold" and use it to bring light where Caesar and Zebul had brought only darkness.

I held the myrrh stone in my hand while I outlined these objectives and asked each in turn to speak their mind.

'We are few, but I think our strength lies in stealth,' said Turon.

Elvir agreed. 'Each of us has different skills. I bring my bow, Ziri and his brothers their swordsmanship, and you, Pito, bring insight and judgement.'

'You don't see me as a warrior, then?' I replied, and everyone laughed. It was not hurtful, for though I had honed my skills under great teachers from Dracus to Sextus, and lately Ziri, it was planning and perception that The Seven needed, someone who understood that warfare was a last resort in any mission to bring truth and light to Hispania.

Leandra looked at Sekis, smiling. 'And you,' she said to the little boy who was now the tallest among us, 'you are strangely silent. What is on your mind?'

His devotion to his warrior goddess was evident. 'I have served you these last five years and rarely left your side,' Sekis said slowly. 'I feel something mystical pulling at me to go with these men, but who will guard you and Cassia?'

'You know the answer to that,' replied Leandra, her voice betraying the love she felt for this young man. 'Apollacta is knit together with fidelity, and the people will look after us as we look after them. There's no need to doubt that.' She paused, then added, 'You and I both know, as do Turon and Melqart, what Zebul One-Eye did to your family, but I do not see hatred in your heart.'

Tears came to Sekis's eyes. I put a hand on his shoulder, the horror of that day flooding back to me. I remembered how we had found poor Pipsqueak alone and terrified while his family lay mutilated and murdered by Zebul's depraved butchers.

'Yes, I confess I feel loathing for this man,' said Sekis, his voice trembling. 'I think I will live with the pain for the rest of my life. But here, with you —' he looked at Leandra with dewy eyes — 'I have found something far better than hatred, and I swear on my family's graves that it is this that drives me, not mindless revenge.'

I did not doubt him for one moment, but I understood Leandra's need to bring this into the open. She and I both knew that our success would lie in working together as a team without the threat of anyone's hidden agenda.

In the respectful silence that followed, we were bonded. Eventually, I broke the spell.

'It is not just Sekis that has every right to feel hatred towards Zebul.' I looked at Leandra, knowing that she recalled the savagery of his attack outside Munda when the eagle had struck him. 'But his evil has reached into the place of our birth, where he rapes and kills our people, and steals their spirit. Our spirit.'

Ziri had been silent throughout this evocative discussion. Now he stood and looked at each of us in turn, his eyes fiery and intense. Ayyur and Izem rose with him.

'Melqart came to our people many seasons ago,' he said. 'He came as a youth and left a man. He became a man not because he fought our enemies with great courage, but because he learned the secrets of covenant. Each of us here has different words for it, but it is the same thing wherever you are, in a strange land or at the hearth of your own family. It means that a man gives his life into the hands of another, as Melqart gave himself into the protection of my father. Only my father can break that covenant. If we make this covenant to each other, nobody can break it unless we all break it at the same time. Therein lies our strength, each sworn to protect and serve the others until death.' He paused, the moment grave, then asked, 'What do you say?'

We all stood solemnly, seven men and two women. I took the myrrh stone from around my neck and held it out to the centre of the circle where we stood.

'This was given to me by a wise woman.' I looked at each of the others as I spoke, my words almost a whisper. 'She said it was a symbol of protection, and while I wore it others would share in its light.'

Leandra touched the necklace of bright beads around her neck. 'I remember this well,' she said reverently, 'how Nabia gave us these gifts for our healing and safekeeping.' She lifted her necklace over her head and placed it with the heavier myrrh stone, and then closed her hand over mine. One by one, the others put their hands over ours in a meaningful, unvoiced vow.

And then came the sound that I had not heard for so many years: the piercing cry of an eagle.

FORTY

The morning sun threw its marbled light onto the slopes of Concha where the distant eagle circled, guardian of the skies and emissary of the gods. The world was still, expectant.

I wheeled my mount, an experienced, reliable mare chosen for me by Leandra, leaving Turon to lead the rest of our group away from Apollacta. My family stood with Leandra and Cassia, watching us. I waved my farewell. They shouted encouragement and sent us on our way with the blessings of all the gods my sisters could think of.

The road was showing signs of disrepair, just one of the things that would need our attention if trade between the coastal ports and the inland towns was to resume. High above us on the mountainside the watchers were descending to make their report; we waited for them in a clearing where an old stone lodge housed their supplies of food, firewood and spare clothing.

They seemed too young to bear such responsibility, the three youths laughing and joking together as they burst into the clearing. Or was I getting old? They had nothing out of the ordinary to report — no troop movements meant that the road would be clear at least as far as Munda — except that there had been no signals for two days. They insisted there was nothing unusual about this.

Over fresh bread and the invigorating fruit we had brought from Apollacta, we outlined our plans and went over the various signals should we have need of reinforcements. After confirming that the mountaintop signalling system was still unknown to Zebul, we asked them to send word to the other three stations that we were on our way and would time our journey to arrive at Munda the next morning.

We wound through the pass beneath Titan, the beleaguered town of Munda hidden on the other side, and made camp. The air grew cold as the sun hid itself behind the mountain, but we allowed ourselves no fire as darkness fell, keeping our voices low as we went over our plans one last time.

Ziri and his men were sitting quietly in the dawn stillness when I awoke, watching the eagles hunt. I sat beside him and sensed his awe at the freshness and beauty of the Hispanic terrain.

'Where has Turon gone?' Ziri asked without preamble.

'Why do you ask? Do you not trust him?'

'He thought I slept when he slinked out of the camp. Why the secrecy?'

I sighed. 'What you have to remember,' I explained, 'is that these are his mountains, just as the desert is your desert, and your father's. Turon has many brothers who are hidden in these parts, watching us though we cannot see them. It pleases me that he seeks his own people, for we may yet need them.'

'I can't wait to meet a people whose roots are in the land, as mine are in the desert across the sea.' Ziri seemed content with my absolute trust of Turon and his Kemeletoi, who no doubt saw Zebul as the harbinger of evil and oppression. The mountain people cherished the old order, before the coming of Caesar, when peace ruled and trade was bountiful. We did not know how they might be able to help, but allies who knew the area as well as their own hands were friends worth having.

I woke Sekis and Elvir and they sat upright, blinking in the brightness of the morning sun. I told them to clear the site and ready the horses for our short journey to Munda, making sure they concealed the remaining silver that we had brought with us. They could take their time as we would not depart until we were sure Zebul and his men were unaware of our coming; in the meantime, I would seek out the watchers on Titan's summit.

Deciding to make the climb on foot, I cut a staff of cypress wood, filled a skin from the brook where we had camped, and set off for the signalling station.

The watchers on the summit of Titan were always at the greatest risk of discovery, especially as there were a number of people in Munda who had known about them before Caesar had changed the town's fortunes for the worse. Leandra had ensured that the station was manned by her own people from Apollacta, who spied on troop movements. They never visited Munda and always took precautions to remain unseen.

At first I was concerned by the lack of response to my calls, but I assumed the watchers on the summit were keeping silent and hidden, mistrustful of any visitor so close to Munda. Then I began to observe clues that all might not be well — flattened areas of grass, a carelessly misplaced arrow shaft, an odd sandal…

Then I found the first body.

The ground around the youth was dark with the dried blood shed from stab wounds in his chest and back. One eye had been gouged, leaving a dark, obscene cavern as the classic evidence of barbaric torture. I searched his clothing and found nothing to give me any further clues.

My heart thumping, I crept stealthily towards the summit and the place in its lee on the southern side where the great bronze was concealed. At least, it should have been if the site had not been moved. There was an eerie silence, no birds singing, no shrill cacophony of crickets, not even a breeze to rustle the hardy thistles.

On my hands and knees I reached the summit, weighed down by a crushing dread, and parted the thick grass to look down on the watchers' camp. The mangled bodies of two youths lay face down, a third tied to a stump, his hair stiff with blood, his head hanging down as if in despair. One fingerless hand was roped to a rock, bloodied and covered with feasting flies. The reflecting bronze had been torn from its posts and hung precariously on the edge of a precipice.

I looked away, feeling waves of nausea. Then, slowly, I looked back again, barely able to believe what I had seen.

Not ten paces away from the tortured youth, an eagle was perched on a boulder. It was as still as the rock on which it stood. There was no wind to disturb its magnificent feathers, no sound to distract the eye that watched me. Transfixed by its regal gaze, I could not move.

But I had to see if the youths were dead. Slowly, I willed my weakened limbs to raise me up, all the time watching the eagle. Still the lord of the skies did not move. I edged towards the first of the prone youths; there was evidence that he had crawled some distance before his life force had departed. The other's skull was crushed by a rock that lay near him, strands of his dark hair and fragments of bone fused to it by thick blood.

Cautiously, still holding the eagle's watchful gaze, I edged towards the third youth where he slumped against the splintered post. I put my head to his chest and felt rather then heard the faintest heartbeat, a spirit refusing to depart. Dampening the edge of my tunic with my waterskin, I dabbed his cracked, parched lips. He moaned. I loosed his violated hand from the ropes that bound his wrist, and his eyes flickered open. He tried to speak.

'Shh…' I held his head in my arms. My tears flowed for him. He was so near death. I dripped cool water over his anguished face.

The eagle watched.

'They…' the youth whispered, then closed his eyes. He tried to swallow water but could not.

'Stay still. I'll bring help.' I was lying — who could help this spent child?

'Wait,' he managed, his voice hoarse with pain. 'Stay … with … me.'

I held him, trying to send my own life force into him, but I did not know how.

'The … enemy did … this.'

'Did they have the codes?' I hated myself for asking him this most obvious question, but I could not let this youth die in vain.

'No … the secrets … were not given.'

'Tell me what happened.'

The youth closed his eyes and I thought he was gone, but then he drew a shallow breath. 'They saw the signal…' He coughed, then continued, 'It came yesterday… I think it was yesterday … when they had … attacked us.'

I tried to imagine the scene — Zebul's men confused by the flashing signals, then realising what was going on. Surely Zebul had tried to find out more.

I wiped his face again. 'Go on.'

'The one-eyed one…' He sobbed, looking at his bloody hand.

'I know, I know. He wanted you to tell him what it meant.'

'Yes…'

'And?'

He was still looking at his hand. He did not need to say anything. Was it when the first or the last finger was cruelly sliced away that he had told them that we were coming to Munda, pitifully undermanned?

I understood. I would have done the same, probably earlier.

'You have done well, and you will be rewarded when we return you to your family.'

He managed a smile. Then he died, his eyes glazing as he looked into mine.

It was then that the eagle moved, one eye still watching me.

Are you the same creature who showed me the boar trail, the same who saved Leandra, the same who took Zebul's eye?

He blinked once, then threw back his lordly head and let out a piercing cry that rent the stillness. The eagle's head swivelled, and its other eye was fixed on me.

I wanted to run away. But I could not, for my friends were in the valley below, in Munda, and in the surrounding mountains seeking the return of all that we held dear. I looked at the eagle, my angel of death, and my limbs were weak. Then I looked to the south, where the other signal stations of the watchers must surely be under threat.

Rising to my knees, I scrabbled in the dirt around me until I found a flat stone, and withdrew my dagger. Slowly and carefully, I scratched a warning onto the stone: *Watchers compromised. Hide.*

I looked up at the eagle and commanded him, holding his gaze. Then I lay in the dust, my face averted. At last there was wind, and I felt the eagle's great talons take the stone from my outstretched palm.

And he was gone.

FORTY-ONE

Zebul did not pursue the other watchers for, as I suspected, he now knew of our coming and was cautious. Perhaps too cautious.

I stumbled down the mountainside, hoping our camp had not been found. I was relieved to hear Elvir's voice.

'What in the name of Jupiter has happened to you?'

The look on his face told me I must appear the way I felt. Sekis came running from the brook where he had been filling waterskins and stopped in his tracks.

'Those bastards have slaughtered everyone up there,' I explained, sorrowfully.

Sekis spat. 'Then let us take our revenge.'

I saw the impetuosity of youth in his eyes, retribution smouldering as he strapped on his sword belt and gathered up his bow and quiver. Ziri, Ayyur and Izem walked calmly over to see what the fuss was about.

'Wait, Sekis. We must think about this. If we are expected now, we are too few to fight. We have lost the element of surprise. We have to turn back.'

He was about to argue when there was movement near the brook where the cane grew thickest. Sekis and Elvir both had an arrow ready in the blink of an eye.

But it was Turon who emerged, and with him a thin, wiry old man who I instantly recognised. It was Reva, the wise creature of the mountain woods who with his woman, Nabia, had given succour to me and Leandra after the assault by Zebul and his brother.

Turon strode into the camp, Reva hopping behind him, his ancient face lit up with a wide grin. Ziri looked at me in confusion as I bowed deeply to Reva, who in the manner of his people was modestly dressed and unarmed. But there was no smile on Turon's face as he beckoned us to gather round.

We squatted. Reva's quick eyes darted towards the Imazighen, taking in the strangely patterned faces of Ayyur and Izem and their menacing curved swords. Then he stared at Sekis for a long moment before the broad smile returned, revealing strong, white teeth — unusual in one so ancient.

Sekis nodded, his face lighting up at the arrival of the man who had done so much to bring healing to the anguished child he had once been.

'This is Reva,' Turon announced to all of us, but especially to the Imazighen, who still looked bemused, 'who has helped us before and will help us again.' Then he looked at me, solemnly. 'He has told me that our people know what happened on the mountain, or at least they guessed it, and we share in your sorrow and pain.'

'It is appreciated,' I said for lack of anything more meaningful. 'We are discovered and so we must return.'

Reva shook his head slowly. He was never one for words, so Turon spoke again. 'I'm afraid events are moving quickly. Reva tells me there is an evil in Munda greater than anything since Caesar put Zebul in command there, and now the one-eyed demon seeks retribution.'

'I don't understand,' I blurted, interrupting him. 'Retribution against whom, and for what? Surely he has bled the town dry already...'

'Retribution against us,' Turon said slowly, 'against Apollacta, maybe even you if his spies have told him of your return. You see, he is enraged that for so long we have operated the watchers right under his nose, and he suspects that it is your ingenuity that is behind it all.'

'But how do you know this? Isn't Munda closed off to your people, and certainly to anyone from Apollacta?'

Turon looked at Reva with admiration in his eyes. 'What we know is down to this man, and his son Drenan. Who suspects an old man, who walks with a stick and a hunched back when he isn't hopping like a frog around our mountains? Reva has spent much of his time playing the bumbling old madman in the streets of Munda in recent years, trusted by the poor and downcast, giving hope to all who have faith that one day Zebul One-Eye will be overthrown. You would be surprised how many there are who believe this and refuse to allow their spirits to be broken.'

'And Drenan?' I asked. 'What's his part in this? He is known to Zebul and could not risk entering Munda.'

'Reva meets his son on the ancient holy nights when the guards at the gate gladly let a wailing old priest out of the town to make his sacrifices. In turn, Drenan keeps our people informed of the atrocities that Zebul's ruffians mete out to your people.'

He paused, putting a hand on my shoulder as if steadying me for more bad news.

'And now he begins an even greater crime.' Turon's voice had dropped almost to a whisper. 'Reva tells me that since Zebul returned from Titan yesterday, his men have been placing stakes on the ground outside the main gates, each one roped and ready to erect into the hole dug next to it. Reva was confused as to what this might mean until he saw the first stake put to use.'

I looked at Turon, horrified. 'I think I know what you are going to tell me.'

He nodded, his eyes filling. 'It is the Roman form of execution, reserved for their worst criminals. They call it crucifixion.'

Sekis and Elvir were silent, confused, but Ziri spoke. 'I, too, have heard of this barbaric thing that they do. These Romans are a cruel race. So is this one-eyed monster a Roman?'

'No, he is — was — one of us, born and brought up here,' I said. 'But his heart is black, and when Caesar came he saw his opportunity with what he hoped would be a new order in Hispania. Perhaps he was right. Perhaps our time has gone, and his has come.'

That angered Turon. 'If you believe that,' he said firmly, 'then all Reva and Drenan have done is for nought. You would just give up and go back to Sicilia with your tail between your legs?'

'Not me,' said Sekis, running his finger along his taut bowstring. 'I've got unfinished business here.'

'Me too,' said Elvir.

Ziri looked at me, while his two warriors waited for their master to command them. 'And you, Melqart, what will you do now? We are sworn to you, and you to each of us. Will you break our covenant?'

'I was just testing you all,' I grinned, though I knew deep inside that I had almost lost heart. 'We must put an end to this evil right now.'

All military campaigns, whether the collision of massed armies or small, secret missions like ours, depended first on intelligence, secondly on planning and thirdly on purposeful command. So I had to pull myself together, fast.

I questioned Reva about the strength of Zebul's garrison at Munda. There were probably a hundred soldiers, not well trained but used to dominating through fear and brutality, and around twenty horsemen who were his elite, acting as Zebul's personal guards as well as a rapid strike force when the need arose. There were also bowmen, though Reva could not attest to their ability as he had not seen them in action.

The ruffian soldiers were mostly engaged in organising a mass crucifixion of Munda's citizens, clearly designed to draw our small party into the open to challenge them, where we would be outnumbered. Reva also reported that Dagan had arrived in Munda the previous day with a further thirty armed horsemen and, after conferring with his brother, had ridden east into the hidden valley. I thought this suspicious, as it must have been after the tortured watcher had revealed our coming. I realised how easy it would be for Dagan to lead his men along one of the many dried stream beds to cut off our retreat.

So we had no option but to proceed to Munda, where we would be expected and outnumbered. I voiced my decision, and my fears, and was gladdened by the eager response of my men. There was no doubting their courage and self-belief.

Reva stood to leave. 'You will not be outnumbered,' he said in his musical, high pitched voice, 'if I can reach our people in time. And you will find more fighting spirit in Munda than you are expecting.' With that he hopped away, lithe and sure-footed.

I took the myrrh stone from around my neck and held it out. Each man placed a hand on mine, and we repeated our promise to each other.

Our progress was painfully slow, but we suspected an ambush and rode in single file, using hand signals to maintain our stealth, listening for any sound of the enemy.

A pair of eagles circled ahead, as if watching the road before us. I led, keeping an eye on the lazy sweeps of the huge birds for any sudden change in direction. Elvir followed me, his bow readied, guarding our left flank. Then came Ziri, Ayyur and Izem, grim and equally watchful, then Sekis, also with his bow readied, searching the undergrowth on our right. Bringing up the rear was Turon, one of his longswords unsheathed and held across the pommel of his saddle.

One of the eagles tightened its circle and slowed, losing height until I could see its wing feathers flutter. I held up an arm, fist curled, and the column stopped. I beckoned Elvir and Sekis, then pointed to the slowing eagle, indicating that they should dismount and move ahead on foot.

Suddenly, the eagle dropped, wings folded, talons outstretched. There was a cry as it hit the top of an olive tree, but the cry was not the eagle's. Elvir took aim and, as the eagle rose, he loosed at a target I could not see. Another cry, and a body fell through the dusty foliage to land on the hard ground. The other eagle came lower at another tree near the first, and I saw an arrow fly past its majestic wing before it, too, hit its target. Sekis had taken out the exposed ambusher with an arrow through his chest.

An arrow hissed past my ear, and then the air was thick with them. I heard a cry that sounded like Izem or Ayyur and screamed an order to make for the denser undergrowth away from the road, there to seek cover. Sekis and Elvir were crouched behind a large boulder, loosing shaft after shaft, mostly finding their mark. The attack was lessening in its intensity as Turon crept close.

'We must not let them get away,' he panted, 'then we will own the element of surprise instead.'

'Is anyone hurt?' I was looking for the others, sure at least one enemy arrow had struck home.

'Izem has a shaft in his thigh,' he replied. 'The others are untouched.'

Sekis and Elvir were on their feet now, running forward unchallenged, bows readied for further resistance.

'Come on, then.' We ran for our horses, mounted, and rode after our two young archers. We passed seven or eight bodies before rounding a bend in the road and saw that four enemy archers had turned to face their pursuers, swords drawn. Elvir and Sekis were running fearlessly at them. The enemy clearly relished the odds, but then they saw two horsemen with longswords bearing down on them. They ran, but not very far. We overtook our relieved colleagues and Zebul lost another four men — one was trampled, Turon killed two with one easy arc of his sword, and the other took my blade at the base of his neck, the blood spraying over my leather jerkin and the flank of my horse.

We rode ahead a short distance to make sure none had escaped back to Munda, then returned to the others. Sekis and Elvir were arguing over how many each had killed with their deadly aim. Ziri and Ayyur bent over Izem's injured leg, bandaging it with strips from their black cloaks. Beside them was a bloody shaft.

They helped Izem to his feet while I watched; he didn't even wince when he put his weight on his wounded leg. He spoke rapidly to Ziri in his own tongue, which the Amazigh prince immediately translated.

'Izem says he is ashamed that he has taken a wound without so much as aiming a blow at the enemy. He pleads with you to engage these shrivelled worms as soon as possible so he can acquit himself with honour.'

'But what about his injury?' I asked, impressed at the man's fortitude.

'Oh, there's no need to worry about that,' replied Ziri with a chuckle. 'Izem with one leg is worth ten of your enemy with two.'

We rode hard for Munda, confident that there was unlikely to be another ambush. Knowing of Zebul's unparalleled arrogance, we assumed that he would not be expecting our arrival unharmed, small in number though we were. We swept beyond Titan's foothills, emerging from the woodland within sight of the town. We then reined in our horses to stand in line before my beloved home.

Low clouds had swept in from the west, shrouding the familiar countryside, darkening the stout walls of Munda and giving the houses beyond a gloomy appearance. Zebul's new palace stood on the central hill, its lines stark and angry, dominating the untidy streets, a monument to greed and conceit.

The great gates that had denied Caesar were open. Before them was a pathetic group of townsfolk, herded by hooded ruffians armed with spears and clubs. A line of twenty stakes stood upright before the walls, watched by the weeping community, more than half of them bearing a writhing body, hands aloft, legs twisted at impossible angles. More soldiers stood on the walls, laughing and jeering.

The soldiers and their unfortunate captives were watching, as were we in our horror and disgust, a mass crucifixion.

FORTY-TWO

There was no plan in my mind as we advanced, our horses walking in line abreast. The only thing that mattered was that this killing must be stopped, and if we were the reason that my people were being slaughtered, then we had to face up to Zebul without delay, outnumbered or not.

Such was the intensity of Zebul's macabre work that none of his men spotted us until we were but a hundred paces from the grisly scenes of execution. One of his soldiers pointed towards us with a shout, then all of his men turned. It was easy to pick out Zebul, even from this distance — he was the only man wearing full Roman armour, his black eye patch held in place by a thong decorated with eagle feathers. He strode towards us while his brutes stood and stared. Many of the forlorn, condemned townsfolk turned to look too, but what hope could seven horsemen bring them when they were guarded by at least ten times that number?

I signalled The Seven to halt, and Zebul stood before his shameful killing ground, staring at us with his one evil eye.

'Declare yourselves!' he shouted.

I remained silent.

Now that the hammering of nails through flesh had stopped, I could hear the pitiful moaning of dying innocents where they hung, bruised and bleeding.

'Did you not hear me? Declare yourselves!'

None of us averted our avenging stare. I knew then that despite the odds, we would find a way to overcome the sickness that had gripped my town these past five years.

Fired by this revelation, I was about to address my old enemy when I realised I no longer had his attention.

A large group had emerged silently from the treeline behind us and now stood overlooking the valley where we faced Zebul and his band of thugs. Reva's Kemeletoi were each as quietly indignant as we. There were no war cries, no battle horns, and no spears being beaten on shields — just an awesome, heavy stillness.

The weight of justice lay upon Zebul, too, who stared open-mouthed at the mysterious mountain men, some with long spears cut hastily in the woods from which they had materialised, some with hunting bows across their shoulders. Without taking his eyes off the ranks that had now gathered to oppose him, Zebul barked an order to snap his men into line. They formed up behind him, leaving the condemned to mill around, confused by their apparent reprieve. Several women ran to the stakes where, weeping, they tried to free loved ones from their agonised death throes. From the open gates, Zebul's twenty horsemen rode out, hastily armed with spears and short swords, one of the riders yielding his mount to Munda's usurper.

I turned to Ziri. 'I estimate about a hundred men on foot, and twenty horse.'

'If the old man is to be believed,' murmured Ziri, 'that's his entire force.'

'Oh, you can trust Reva's numbers,' put in Turon, 'so we're equally matched in numbers, although Zebul has more cavalry.'

'How well can your people fight?' I asked Turon, hopefully.

'Like demons, if pushed to it, which believe me they are. Besides, I think you'll find Drenan is with them.'

I scanned the line of mountain men and sure enough, one of them stood taller than the rest, straight-backed and proud. *That must be Drenan*, I thought, glad that my old friend and fellow watcher was there, no doubt with his trusty sword.

'They don't appear to have any proper weapons, though.'

'True, but what they lack in iron and bronze, they more than make up for in spirit and courage.'

I wheeled my mare to face my riders and saw grim determination in their eyes.

'Then let's lead them,' I said, and we moved to join Reva's men.

We rode along the line of Kemeletoi mountain men, greeting them warmly, and indeed Drenan was among them. Our eyes locked briefly: proper greetings would have to wait.

'We have the higher ground, so we must make them come to us.' The authoritative tone in my voice surprised me.

Reva nodded agreement, showing no fear. It was apparent that he did not need to relay any orders to his men, who stood silently, ready to give their lives to rid this land of Zebul's sickness.

'When they charge, have your men with the longest spears root them in the ground and point them at the horses, not the men. Your bowmen can shoot the riders from behind the spears.'

Reva nodded again. These Kemeletoi were a peaceful people, but not afraid to defend themselves when it mattered most.

Zebul was leading his cavalry and his foot soldiers in a ragged line up the slope towards us. The old wound in my back throbbed dully, a reminder of our last meeting; twice I had encountered his enmity, and twice I had suffered indignity at his hand. *This time, Zebul One-Eye, you will pay for your crimes*, I thought fiercely.

'Pito! Look there.' It was Elvir who called, stationed on the left of our inadequate cavalry line.

He was pointing to the very place where we had first emerged before the town. I narrowed my eyes to see a small band of riders on the road we had travelled, perhaps thirty horsemen at a trot.

Drenan ran forward. His eyesight had always been the sharpest among the watchers.

'Who?' I asked him. 'They don't look like Leandra's people.'

'That's Dagan,' he said coldly. 'We tracked them this morning, trying to circle behind you, so we laid a false trail. We had hoped to delay him longer.'

Zebul was approaching from our front, and now Dagan's men of Lacibis were on our left flank. *He who divides his enemy has the upper hand.* I didn't know why that thought came into my mind, but with a sinking feeling I realised that the odds had changed again and we would have to split our forces to face this new threat.

I turned back to Drenan and Reva. 'We will ride to meet Dagan. Hold firm here and we will return as soon as we have dealt with them.'

Father and son showed no fear. It was Drenan who spoke for them.

'If you can, lead them close to the woods. There are more bowmen there, and they will even the numbers.'

I smiled my thanks and led The Seven to meet Dagan's thirty warriors.

I did not see the first engagements between Zebul's men and Reva's Kemeletoi, nor did I see the people of Munda seize their opportunity to stream out of the gates and vent their anger on One-Eye's ruffians.

We rode at a trot towards Dagan's light cavalry and then, when they saw us approaching and turned to meet us, we feigned timidity and fled towards the treeline. Dagan followed, his men yelling obscenities that abruptly stopped when a volley of black-feathered shafts took a dozen of them clean from their saddles. Dagan's horse buckled and crashed to the ground, pitching him in a rolling heap on the dry, stony ground.

I ordered The Seven to dismount and form a semi-circle of five, placing Sekis and Elvir with their bows behind us. The terrain where we stood was rocky and difficult for a full-blooded mounted attack, and the enemy riders were still in confusion, their horses frightened and skittish. Dagan stood, his arms and legs grazed from the fall but otherwise unharmed, and tried in vain to catch the reins of a riderless horse. Another man fell to a Kemeletoi arrow, but it was apparent that most of the concealed archers had withdrawn to safety. Still outnumbered two to one, impossible odds if our enemy could charge as a unit, the three Imazighen, Turon and I drew our swords and readied ourselves for the fight.

Dagan saw the futility of continuing on horseback and ordered his remaining men to dismount. They approached tentatively, giving us time to look the enemy in the eye. They were mainly youths, hopefully inexperienced; only Dagan appeared to have the confidence that filled those who had killed before.

Too late, Dagan saw the two archers that stood behind the five armed men he faced. Four more of his men died in the moments he needed to decide that his only option was to rush at us before more arrows massacred his dwindling force. It was Dagan's sword that whined as it sliced down towards me, but I parried the blow with my own weapon, ignoring the jarring pain that clattered through my arms and neck, and heaved Dagan sideways. He stumbled onward, as if he would break through our line. But with a grunt, he stopped suddenly, the reddened, dripping end of Izem's curved sword protruding upwards between his shoulder blades.

Izem was fast, and was heaving his blade from Dagan's lifeless body, but already another man was at the gap, sword raised to finish the warrior who had killed his leader. I swung my longsword and felt it slice through leather and flesh to grind against bone, warm sprays of blood sprinkling my face and arms. I then crashed the hilt into the next man's jaw as he came at me.

Gasping for breath, I looked for the next attacker but there was none. Three youths were running down the hill, stumbling in their terror. Dazed, I looked around. At first I thought the blood must mean my men had suffered fatal wounds, but all were standing, Ziri even flashing a wide smile at me. There were three bodies at his feet, more beside Ayyur and Turon, and three lying between me and Izem, one still writhing in his own blood and vomit.

'Better recover our arrows, then,' said Elvir, lightly. 'We're running a bit short.'

'Yes, yes … off you go.' I didn't know what else to say.

Then Turon shook me and pointed.

And I remembered that we were only a small part of the battle that raged in our war-torn valley.

It took a few moments to take in what was happening. The Kemeletoi line was holding against a concerted attack by Zebul's foot soldiers, but they had not needed to repel a cavalry assault. The twenty enemy horse had instead been led by Zebul himself to cut off the threat emanating from within

Munda, and I could barely imagine the terror his first charge had struck into the hearts of the defenceless townsfolk. Many of them lay crumpled before the gates, probably trampled rather than struck by conventional weapons.

But the spirit of Munda was not that easily crushed. As I looked, more were scurrying to the open valley carrying pitchforks, axes, broom handles — anything they could lay their hands on — clearly intent on ending Zebul's tyranny. One old man was riding a donkey, thrashing its rump and screaming encouragement to the swarming masses, brandishing what appeared to be a spiked club. *That must be Tanasus the brewer*, I thought, recognising the weapon as his favourite grain-masher.

Zebul, though, was wheeling his small cavalry outfit for another attack that would leave more innocents dead, at little risk to his own men.

'Find horses, quick!' I shouted, only then realising that my men were already doing this. Our own were grazing not far away, so used to the noise of battle they had not cantered away like Dagan's mounts. As I hauled myself back into the saddle, I outlined what I felt would be the best course of action.

'First we sweep across the rear of the main enemy assault on Reva's people. If we can turn them to face us, Reva and Drenan can press home an advantage.' Then I pointed to the scenes outside Munda's gates. 'Our main effort must be there. We have to stop this massacre.'

For the first time, our Imazighen screamed their terrifying war cry and led The Seven straight towards the rear of Zebul's men where they fought the hard-pressed mountain people. Many of the enemy turned and watched in fear as we rode them down, the great curved blades flashing again and again, followed by the scourge of Turon's blade and the thundering of trampling horses that left mangled bodies in our wake.

Only one pass was needed. Reva and Drenan urged their men on, and we knew the job would be finished swiftly.

Without breaking stride we rode down the hill, each of us taking up Ziri's war cry in the hope of halting Zebul's bloodthirsty advance on the innocent. But our efforts had the reverse effect. While we no doubt gave hope to our tyrannised people, Zebul was not prepared to give up his slaughter, and manoeuvred his horsemen so that hundreds of terrified townsfolk now shielded him from our attack. Savage blows rained upon unprotected heads, screams and shouts adding to the horror. But the people of Munda had been oppressed for too long, and this was their only chance to strike for freedom.

We reined in, looking at each other in confusion. We could try to ride behind him, but there was nothing to stop the enemy horse repositioning so that innocent people were always preventing our attack.

I looked to Turon for inspiration, and he shrugged.

'We've got to do something,' I said, a feeling of helplessness weakening me. 'We can't just watch while our people die.'

I saw a blur out of the corner of my eye, and then another.

'What in hell's name is that?'

Then I saw and understood.

The eagles had come in our darkest hour.

I marvelled that they didn't injure themselves, hurtling like rocks from an onager, smashing into the surprised cavalrymen, and striking terror into their mounts, which reared and screamed. I counted at least five silent killers from the air.

Those who were unhorsed were immediately clubbed mercilessly by the mob. Those that did not fall were easy prey for eager hands pulling at them while they looked around in confusion and fear.

Then the great birds were gone. We watched as they beat their great wings to rise majestically towards their distant mountain homes.

I looked for their victims, but could make out only one left standing, still resplendent in his Roman armour, sweeping his sword in a wide arc to keep the hostile horde at bay. They inched towards him, crude weapons at the ready, but his long blade was an effective deterrent.

I looked behind me to see that the mountain men had won the day and were despatching the last of Zebul's ruffians, then signalled the advance on the sole survivor of a tyrannical regime. The townsfolk saw us coming and eased back, their clubs and axes twitching, unbloodied. Zebul looked around in confusion, then saw me as I dismounted.

'You!' It was said with undiminished hatred, tinged with madness.

'Yes, it's me, and I am going to kill you.' I drew my sword.

Zebul laughed, as if what I was suggesting was the most improbable thing he had ever heard.

Someone placed a hand on my shoulder. I turned and looked up into the face of Sekis, who wore a calm expression. I studied his eyes and understood. I nodded my approval, seeing an assurance in this youth that came only to those who overcame their pain and suffering with hope and love.

He looked past me to where Zebul stood, his burnished armour bright, his one eye darting menacingly between us.

'You might not remember me,' said Sekis quietly, 'but I had a family once. We were farmers, on the plain near Lacibis, and I had an older brother and sister. We were very happy there.'

'What in the name of the gods has this got to do with me?' Zebul spat.

'I'll tell you, and then I will kill you.' Sekis stared hard at Zebul until the tyrant averted his eyes. 'Look at me!' he shouted, and Zebul did, startled, and perhaps he knew then that he was about to lose his life.

'You probably don't remember burning our farm, raping my mother and torturing my family one by one, do you?'

Zebul looked at Sekis blankly.

'Is it coming back to you, or was it all in a day's work for murdering scum like you? You probably had no idea that a terrified little child was hidden there, watching you go about your depraved, evil business. And for what? We had nothing of value. So you killed them all.'

Sekis looked away, his eyes wet with tears. Then he handed his bow to Elvir and drew his sword. It was smeared red but had not finished its day's work.

The two men began their fight to the death. As Zebul shifted and feinted, and his blade swept down in shattering blows, every one of us feared for Sekis's life.

It was Zebul's handicap, inflicted by the eagle so many years ago, that proved his undoing. Time and again, Zebul's deft blows had sent Sekis spinning or staggering to his right, so that each subsequent move was swift and almost deadly. But as Zebul weakened, it became apparent that the younger man had the reserve to adjust his balance more nimbly. Sekis was straining to manoeuvre himself into Zebul's blind spot, but the older man's blows repeatedly forced him back, sending sparks and chunks of weakened iron into the air like lightning. Sekis had to break the pattern. There was a gasp from the watching townsfolk when Sekis stumbled, so convincing was his ruse to allow One-Eye his chance to finish it. But Zebul's death lunge was parried strongly by Sekis, who found surprising strength to move swiftly left and, though off balance, thrust his blade downwards between Zebul's neck and his collar bone.

The thrust was not deep, but it was fatal, and Zebul knew it.

He walked a few paces towards me, and for a moment I thought he wanted to resume his argument with me, too. He stood before me and hatred crossed his sweating face. My hand went to my sword, but then his eyes began to glaze over.

His knees gave way and he crumpled to the ground.

EPILOGUE: POMPEY'S GOLD

My father broke open a hot loaf and my mouth watered. His first batch of bread baked in his own kitchens for five wretched years drew a gratified sigh, and a tear formed in his eye. He handed a piece to my mother, who took the ageing hand that offered it in both of hers with a warm, loving smile. Then she accepted the steaming crust, and my father broke another piece for me. Outside, I heard Nahalia shriek as Elvir chased her, while Tallay and Pidray giggled like children.

Together, we dipped our bread in the bowl of salted olive oil and savoured the fresh promise of life. For a moment, I let my mind drift back to the moment when, in this very room, I had killed for the first time, recalling the blurred swiftness with which the three Romans had died for their crime against my family, but I pushed away the unwanted nightmare and beamed at my parents.

'Thank you,' said my mother. 'You brought us home safely.'

I blushed, thinking of the kindness and support that so many had given. Sextus, in faraway Sicilia, Turon and Drenan, Agrippa, Ziri's people, and Corban, the amusing old Sicilian whose house I now owned. Elvir, a man before his time, Leandra and Cassia, stately leaders of a prosperous trading port, and Sekis, once a lost little child and now a warrior of irreproachable integrity. Lizard, whose vibrant life had been snatched in its prime.

And Nahalia — beautiful, mysterious and devoted.

'Will you marry her?' My mother had been reading my mind.

I frowned, and I thought I saw a flicker of disappointment on her serene face.

'You are not staying, are you?' My father's voice was steady, respectful.

I sighed. 'No.'

'Munda needs leadership, and the people want you. I think they are right.'

'Father...' I searched for the right words. 'I want to stay here with my family, but something inside me is pulling me away. I don't know what it is...'

'You want to travel, to see the world.'

'Yes, but it's more than that. I want to learn, to understand. When I was at Utica I realised that this world is bigger than Rome thinks it is. Caesar thought he was a god, and he came here in all his self-importance and trampled on his enemies. Within a year, his own people killed him. Now the Romans are fighting among themselves again. And for what? Land? Power? It's all so pointless.'

When I had stopped gesturing, my mother put her hand on mine.

'Son, it terrifies me that you want to venture out into such a world. Surely you can find peace and harmony here with us, in Munda?'

My mother's words, as ever, illuminated my path, and I understood. I did not want to go into the Roman world, I wanted to go beyond it. And yes, I sought peace and harmony, which of course I would find with my family in our reborn mountain community. But only to a degree. I knew my father understood this, and in time, so would my mother.

'I'm in no rush,' I reassured them, reaching for more of the marvellous bread. 'The food's not bad, and I have missed the comfort of my own bed.'

My mother chuckled and my father winked at me.

A few days later, Munda elected Turon as its leader. The townsfolk and a good number of the Kemeletoi mountain people gathered in the town square and unanimously decided that they did not want a procurator, a magistrate, or any Roman official to rule them. They wanted one of their own, assisted by a council of men and women with specific skills to ensure Munda was protected while it built a flourishing trade. They wanted a warrior-priest.

My name was put forward and I promptly and courteously declined. I then nominated Leandra, who also declined as she was already committed to the people of Apollacta. She immediately nominated Turon, who looked so astonished that I thought he would turn and run, but the crowd had tired of our procrastination and he was cheered long and loud. Garlands of flowers were placed around his neck by excited children, and he was paraded on the shoulders of two stout youths through the streets of Munda. The celebrations lasted most of the night, thanks in no small part to the ale that Tanasus had brewed in secret during the last months of Zebul's oppressive rule.

At first Turon struggled with his high position, but he was the right man for the job as proved by his handling of the vast wealth that had fallen to Munda — enough Roman coin to pay thirteen legions, hidden by Gnaeus in the caves behind the waterfall where the underground streams tumbled into a rocky ravine. Pompey's Gold. He commissioned the stonemasons of Malacita to create a marble monument to bear testimony to those who had been murdered by Zebul, and although no amount could compensate for their loss, he ordered large sums to be paid to each grieving family. He set agreed fees to be paid to all craftsmen and builders, who eagerly went about the restoration and improvement of the town, and the treasury paid for new roads to neighbouring communities, especially the one that wound down between the mountains to Apollacta, our most important trading partner.

Next he addressed the need to conceal Munda from the unwanted attentions of Roman rule. He asked Leandra and I to lead a delegation to inform the new governor of Hispania Ulterior at Corduba that the procurator of Munda had passed away peacefully in his sleep and that the town was now governed by a loyal council of citizens. But the governor, preoccupied as he was with the greater importance of events in Rome, impatiently waved us away.

Munda, it seemed, no longer held any importance for the Romans, which was just the way we wanted it.

We took time on our return journey to explore the rivers and valleys of Baetica, discovering many smaller communities that lived in peace, hidden by the rugged mountains and wild forests. Each thrived on the exchange of knowledge and skills, none the least bit interested in the wider world of Roman politics. Sometimes we accepted their hospitality, feasting long into the night with music and dancing, and at other times we lay under the stars and breathed in the cool, pure air of the mountains, listening to the night sounds and allowing paradise to wash away the painful memories of a time when fear had gripped our land.

As we approached Munda on the new road from Lacibis, we passed the hill where Caesar himself had surveyed the Pompeian army of Gnaeus arrayed before him. We rode our horses to its summit and looked across to our town. The gates were open, the fields were being tilled, and happy voices drifted from the olive groves where whole families tapped the precious fruit from the laden branches with their canes.

Smoke from their prunings curled towards Titan, where an eagle floated on the still morning air.

HISTORICAL NOTES

Where was Munda?

There is a town called Monda in the mountains about 15km from Marbella. It nestles between several hills and mountains, and before it, running more or less north, is a wide valley. It is here that many people believe Caesar fought the Pompey brothers. However, some historians believe the actual site was near a place called Osuna, around 80km further northwest. Nobody can be sure of the actual site, but I have found much evidence of Roman occupation at Monda. I also happen to feel a strong affinity with the place, and everyone I asked in my halting Spanish whether it was true that there was a great battle here looked at me askance, as if I was mad to suggest otherwise. Rightly or wrongly, this little town is the place I have chosen for this decisive battle. If I am proved wrong, forgive me.

Lucius Marcellus

My procurator, inducted in Munda by Julius Caesar when he was governor of Hispania in 60 BC, is entirely fictional. At the time, powerful Romans needed sound men to manage their extensive private and public domains. Caesar could not employ a quaestor, for example, because quaestors would have to be selected from among those who were, or had been, senators. Caesar needed a local manager. Therefore, he was likely to have made procurators responsible for local laws and taxation in the provinces, even before he technically had the power to do so. So far from Rome and far from prying eyes, he was building a power base. But he was not to know then that one day his appointed procurator would show loyalty to the general he had served under, Pompey the Great. Later, under Augustus and Claudius for example, procurators held a far more powerful rank, wielding the authority of the Emperor himself.

Gnaeus and Sextus Pompey

During the writing of this book, I found myself not liking Gnaeus very much but admiring the audacity and sense of adventure that emerged in Sextus. History tells us that within days of the Battle of Munda, Gnaeus was hunted down and beheaded. Sextus escaped and became an influential pirate based in Sicily. He even had a contract with Mark Antony for a while. However, things turned bad again for Sextus, and according to history, the naval general Agrippa defeated him. While on the run, he was discovered and executed in Miletus in Asia Minor (modern Turkey) in 35 BC.

Apollacta

This settlement on the coast nearest Munda is entirely fictional. At least the name is. It means "Apollo's Shore", that is, coast of the sun god, perhaps the first ever reference to the Costa del Sol. In my mind, Apollacta is more or less the site of modern-day Marbella.

Discussion and credits

I do not profess to be a historian, and I know there are many people who know far more than I about the periods in which my novels are set. Please forgive any inaccuracies. I am indebted to my wife and family for their help and support, and the authors whose works of historical fiction I admire: Bernard Cornwell, Douglas Jackson, Conn Iggulden, Robert Harris, Simon Turney, Carlos Ruiz Zafón, Mary Renault, Mary Teresa Ronalds, James A. Michener et al. To you all, and many more, thank you.

A NOTE TO THE READER

Dear Reader,

Thank you for reading *Libertas*. Reviews by knowledgeable readers are an essential part of a modern author's success, so if you enjoyed this novel I would be grateful if you could spare the short time required to post a review on **Amazon** and **Goodreads**. You can also connect with me on <u>my website</u> and <u>sign up to my newsletter on Substack</u>.

Alistair Forrest

<u>alistairforrest.com</u>

Sapere Books is an exciting new publisher of brilliant fiction and popular history.

To find out more about our latest releases and our monthly bargain books visit our website: **saperebooks.com**

www.ingramcontent.com/pod-product-compliance
Lightning Source LLC
Chambersburg PA
CBHW071246250626
47163CB00002B/344